This Tide Waits

Carl T. Cone

OntheMove Publications

Dedicated to Diana, David, Aaron and Todd Cone. Also to Earlene Thompson Cone and Cornelius Taft Cone.

Contents

Prologue

For you I know I'd even try to turn the tide.
JOHNNY CASH

*Life is a tide; float on it. Go down with it and go up
with it, but be detached. Then it is not difficult.*
PREM RAWAT

*And te tide and te time pat tu iboren
were, schal beon iblescet.*
ST. MARHER

Time and tide wait for no man.
GEOFFREY CHAUCER

THIS TIDE WAITS

Chapter One

P ity the wretched soul never satisfied, for his is the saddest lot in the wretched human condition. Inability to be satisfied, whether from lust, greed, covetousness—that's misery, pure and simple. Doss Neesh vowed throughout his life to content himself with the basics—or at least try. "A person has a million bucks, now wants two, then ten," he often complained. "Why not hundreds of millions? That would command extreme respect—even envy. Then, there's the billion dollar mark. How about a roof over everyone's head and edible food?" "Something most people don't have —a roof or food. Most folks will never see five hundred dollars in one place and time," Doss's eldest son, David, could recite those rants by rote—even add to them —"satisfaction-starved ingrates with overabundance to the point of surfeit—never happy."

That's not to say Doss didn't harbor ambitious goals. He aspired highly. Probably too many. As a dedicated student of law, he had loved doctrines and theories of jurisprudence, and pursued teaching them. He had been a lawyer in private practice and a prosecutor. By 2018, the man had taught for thirty years. He was a pilot, a singer, and a writer. He had studied French and Spanish and was fairly fluent in both languages. He grew tea—*Camellia Sinensis.* The same plant that produces beautiful flowers, especially in the southern

United States, is the one from which tea comes. He loved to repair vintage fountain pens—Parkers, Shaeffer's, Waterman's. Doss was also a photographer-and he took all his avocations seriously.

On this very trip to the Florida Keys, his aspiration was to capture on film an astonishing oceanic creature and win a prize. Doss had a long-standing contest with Aaron, his middle son to place first in *The Fin*, a scuba diving magazine. The payout of $20,000 went to the most memorable, unique, beautiful underwater image, and the publisher awarded it once each year, in its January issue. Doss was "aging, but not old," he would tell friends. In his mind, he still had at least a few years before *Das Nicht*—German for nothing—ended it all. After ten years of trying, the prize had eluded him, and he had to beat Aaron—and that would be challenging given his middle son's prowess as a photographer. The two were competitive that way.

Doss sat on the edge of the dock at Key Largo casually tearing off bits of sliced turkey his wife Daisy had packed for him and the boys. His mind was still focused on Belle Glade, his hometown 130 miles to the north. He and two of his three sons had stopped in that sugarcane-growing hamlet the day before. The village nestled on the shores of Lake Okeechobee, a massive body of water which more resembled an ocean than a lake, was surrounded by countless stalks of sugar cane. Long spear leaves waved with gentle breezes. Wet sweet aromas of lakeshore grasses still played delicately in his nostrils. In the sheltered community where practically everyone knew everyone else, Doss had been cradled and nurtured for the first twenty-two years of his life. He later moved to Georgia, but returned to Belle Glade often. While walking the grounds of his former elementary school yesterday, he felt nostalgic mists form around eyelids. Tears had formed 50 years earlier, almost at that same spot by the *Golden Rams* statue. A favorite uncle had died the morning before school started. Even then, his cousin, a girl who noticed too much, had noticed his eyes. "You've been crying," was her comment.

A barracuda was suspended two feet beneath the clear, turquoise water near the dock. The toothy silver creature with dark splotches, hovered, watching tiny snapper hatchlings feeding off the morsels the man tossed. Doss had almost trashed the uneaten meat, but was happy he had changed his mind. A concretion of tiny critters bolted to the hunks near the dock piling darkened with creosote. "Perhaps the only feast they will enjoy—before they in turn are feasted upon," he thought. "Only two or three out of thousands will live to maturity." It reminded him of spermatozoa swimming toward an egg, desperate to fertilize or perish— only the first one wins—or loses—all part of life's lottery.

Doss had a weakness for sentient creatures, and especially those in need. Just a quirk. Each life, whether that of a minnow, fly, flea, or ant, was as meaningful as his own—or, could it be that his existence was as insignificant as theirs?

In a lazy sort of mind-resting daydream, he pondered a skiing trip six months earlier to Colorado, and a vivid morning sky, streaks of lemon-yellow and bright. Wispy clouds in the faraway distance had contrasted in shades of paler butter yellow. The continual peak of mountain ridge had been sharp and angled, a cut visible and snowy down to the horizon. Broad streaks of baby blue had reflected from the sky, highlighting the blanket of snow, interrupted in spots by the tan of exposed rock. Projections of rays from a rising sun had painted the east side of the silvery-blue mountain range. Gazing at those colors in March across the Rockies had reminded him of a colorful creature that might win the scuba magazine prize. He had been planning a diving trip six months from then.

The dive would start in a few hours.

A rare jellyfish often made an appearance each September, and Doss was convinced that with its singularly colorful radiation of lights and the notorious difficulty in capturing the creature with a camera, it could win. It would have to be encountered on a night dive, when the diffusion of bright sky neither distorted the water blue, nor diminished the intensity of colored lights emitting from the invertebrate. There could be no strobe flash. The shutter speed would be slow and the aperture of the camera lens, wide open. A remote firing device would prevent shaking the camera. The neon jellyfish would have to remain in almost perfect focus, and under 50 feet of salt water. Not easy. That's why so few of those creatures had been photographed. Doss wondered whether he could pull it off.

Unlike some Septembers, *Scyphozoa*—jellyfish, promised to be abundant this year. *Cnidaria* is a phylum thought of as the classic jellyfish. It's the one with a pulsating bell and flowing tentacles that trail so gracefully behind. It seemed the lowliest of sea creatures, without blood, brain, or extremities, save for an abundance of those long, wisp-like, stinging tentacles. To function without blood and brain, perhaps the creature was not so lowly at all. However, Doss was not after a *Cnidaria*. The colorful neon *Comb Jelly* he wanted to photograph was a jellyfish of a different phyla—*Ctenophora*. Instead of tentacles, they have stubby paddling combs that flash neon colors—shades of green, yellow, orange, lavender, pink, purple, and red. The bands of cilia are stacked along the comb rows so that when the cilia beat, those of each comb touch the comb below, creating a magical light show of vivid color. Unlike common jellyfish, the comb doesn't sting. It captures prey by means of sticky *colloblasts*. These creatures had been on Earth up to 700 million years, Doss had read.

––––––

The elementary school Doss had attended all those years ago, was gone. An overwhelming absence—the empty space of a huge open field—had shocked him yesterday in Belle Glade. Disquiet erupted from the mere space of nothingness where the old stucco building had stood. It was such a familiar and recognizable and essential part of his youth. Laughter and yelling had pierced the air in bursts. The cacophony of kids tagging and running, still echoed. The relative silence screamed in opposition.

The monstrous banyan tree still grew. The trunk's deep and sinuous crevices had always intrigued Doss. Passageways mysterious and eerie led into the very bowels of the leviathan. The roots of the Banyan—aerial ones—erupted downward from mature branches, some far out from the trunk, and in immature and dainty straightness, headed for soil. Once there, the sprouts grabbed black muck, sank within it, and multiplied roots, forming new trunks, to become woody and hard, expanding an already immense canopy. Between the north and south wings of what had been the school, that giant growth continued to flourish. It had been one-third as big five decades ago. But, only the tree still stood. Vacant field prevailed on all sides.

Some Buddhists contend that Buddha himself sat under a banyan tree to become enlightened. Doss hadn't known about any of that in 1959, the year to which his mind raced.

———

First day of first grade. White-haired and wearing silver cats-eye framed glasses featuring seven, small, black rhinestones on each corner, the matronly teacher in a powder-blue and white gingham dress announced instructions to her fledgling pupils. Doss had felt alienated in varying waves that initial day—the overwhelming unfamiliarity, leaving the comforts of home and mother. The teacher's announcement must have been clearly articulated, he later felt certain, requesting students come to the front of the room when their names were called. Doss wanted nothing more than to follow instructions flawlessly and with alacrity. So, the fledgling student jumped up when the first name, *Monica,* was called hurrying towards the front of the class, twenty-two pairs of eyes watching him intently.

Humiliated when the teacher asked sardonically "Is your name Monica?" Doss realized then the crushing angst of this new world. He wanted to be elsewhere. This milieu of regimentation might prove too brutal. The teacher's stinging castigation—"Follow instructions!"—sent him meekly back to his seat, embarrassed beyond measure, silently berating himself.

Chapter Two

Six weeks after school began, Doss had heard his mother telling a friend over the phone about a newspaper article she had read in the *Miami Herald*. The talk was of a family of four brutally murdered in their Kansas farmhouse by two ex-convicts. The pretty sixteen-year-old daughter, with smiling eyes, a strong chin, and hair curled at the ends, had been asked, earlier that morning, to demonstrate for Jolene, a younger classmate, exactly how she baked her blue-ribbon-winning cherry pie. Juice from hot cherries oozed through slits in the crust as it cooled. The prize-winning pie-baking Midwestern, all-American, lightly-freckled girl with friendly chestnut-brown eyes was named Nancy. She had an ambitious schedule. Her life was busy and bustling, full of anticipation, and no time to slow down and enjoy a warm slice with Jolene. After pie-baking, there was the clarinet lesson for yet another young apprentice. Life called—she answered. This time next year, she would be away in her own strange new environment-college-studying music and art.

It was not to be. Later that night, the award-winning pie-baker, who was abundantly generous with her time for everyone else, yet had not a second to waste, died. A shotgun of those bad men ended all Nancy's dreams. Her mother, father, and younger brother also died that night. At 16, she had become as grown-up as ever she would be.

Weeks later, a writer named *Truman* from a famous New York magazine would pay a visit to Jolene—the pie pupil's house to interview her about that last day. Since she had been one of the last to see members of the murdered family alive, the writer was especially interested in what Jolene remembered. An article about the senseless killing would be written—one that eventually evolved into a book whose sales would reach into the millions. The author had brought a female assistant—a fellow writer—to the town of the killing. She had been his friend since childhood and would soon write her own story—about a lawyer in the South.

Doss's teacher had read the same article in the Miami newspaper and discerned the whispering among Monica and one of the two Linda's in the class. During recess, word spread quickly even among first-graders, although the gory details were not known. Words like *robber, murder, shotgun,* and *massacre* were gently censored from first-grade ears.

"There are bad people," the teacher finally had to address the gossip which had been printed over the *Miami Herald's* front pages and seeped into her classroom. "Bad things happen, class. Good people doing good things is what we need to celebrate. That's Belle Glade people." She then moved on to arithmetic.

By late November the strangeness of school had largely worn away—the surreal ambience was replaced by a hum-drum of routine. Doss adjusted to the classroom, even made a couple of friends, and longed for his home less.

As Doss and his sons walked yesterday where his

first-grade classroom had stood, details and memories came flooding back. Doss remembered as a teenager reading *In Cold Blood*, the book about that family murdered right after he had started first grade. "How could his elementary school be gone? How could a nice Midwestern family be turned into nothing? The void of an abyss—maybe life is a nettlesome awakeness from otherwise dreamless sleep."

———

Hundreds of baby mangrove snapper vied for tidbits of meat near the dock at Key Largo. The whiteness of a maturing sun contrasted with a dark hammock of cypress trees. Doss tossed a small wad this way, one over there, toward the bullied and away from those bullying. His egalitarian practicality, tinged with a bit of idealism, condemned excess. Doss believed the right victim makes a bully of all of us.

Other feelings had cascaded into his mind yesterday at the elementary school. Standing in what had become empty space, he visualized the upper floors where he had paced countless steps, having climbed thousands of flights in the stairwell. He could smell chalk dust on a blackboard upon which he had written, 'I will not talk in class again,' over and over, on several occasions. Let's see, that classroom must have been right about there, on the top floor near the middle.

Closer to the west side of the former building was the room he spent fourth grade in. A prissy teacher with a spiteful temperament had been his teacher that grade. She had a prominent, jutting jawbone, dyed-black hair, blemished skin and stern grayish eyes. The teacher had told Doss "I'm so sorry," when he had gently announced to her "My stomach hurts." A pleading countenance combined with his hand covering his belly would surely prompt the unsympathetic teacher to ask him whether he needed to be excused. The teacher instead replied with that bullshit phony empathy. She knew what the child was asking, he thought, but she was plain mean. Probably unhappy at home. Even his fourth-grade mind had recognized her insensitivity. Her callousness on that and other occasions stayed with him. His mind realized as a nine-year-old: *Character is revealed in how one treats those under her power.*

Doss had to admit that the woman had been, despite her general demeanor, a quality teacher. Perhaps her sternness was the reason.

Chapter Three

Moon jellyfish are another interesting creature. They have a bluish-gray translucent center from which the animal's gonads—shaped like tiny horseshoes—can be clearly seen. Lacy, long fringes —the creature's tentacles—hang from its bell. For self-preservation, it can reduce its size to a tiny fraction when food is scarce, Doss had read in *Science Quarterly*. The divers had seen a few on the dive, but Doss hadn't encountered any Combs.

During the car ride yesterday, Todd, Doss's youngest son, 25, had asked about the timeframe in which jelly-fish had first made their appearance on Earth.

"They've existed for probably 500-700 million years," Doss had responded.

"Are they the oldest creatures?"

"Of multi-organ animals, yes."

"You mean the oldest fish?"

"They're not really a fish, they're invertebrates—no backbone. Fish are vertebrates. They have a spinal col-umn—a backbone. But, jellyfish don't have a brain.

"What doesn't have one? Besides jellyfish?" Aaron, his middle son, 27, queried.

"Starfish, octopuses, crabs, lobster, snails, and worms."

"Can't be an animal without a brain—couldn't think

to sting people," Todd remarked.

"Oh yes they are. While they have no brain, there are neurons that send nerve signals within and throughout the organism. It's a sort of net of nerves that permits motor activity. It can sense nearby obstacles. On top of that, they can navigate. They don't just float aimlessly, as appears. And, believe it or not, they have eyes that are fairly advanced. Sees a habitat that looks better than another, she heads right for it."

"So," Aaron concluded, "it can do all that without a brain? Some people I know *with* brains have trouble with those functions."

"That's probably correct," Doss conceded, "and, to top it off, they have only one hole—whether for intake or outgo—only one."

"Only one hole? That seems...how does that suffice?" Todd asked.

"Did you say seven million years?" Aaron asked.

"No, seven *hundred* million," Doss quickly corrected.

"But, that's really just yesterday. Almost four *billion* years transpired before jellyfish appeared."

"How long have humans existed?"

"It depends on what you mean by humans. Our ape-like ancestors have been around about six million years, but creatures that resemble us have been here for only a couple hundred thousand. And, civilization as we might think of it—pyramids, Stonehenge, cars, computers, iPhones—has existed only about six thousand years."

Aaron remarked, "So you're saying jellyfish have been on Earth for 700 million years, and men like us only a few thousand?"

"Right. The ratio would be roughly a grain of sand to

a basketball."

————

The barracuda that had lain suspended, seemingly for an hour, darted off. Baby minnows didn't notice its absence. A jerky group reaction occurred with every lob of meat. Doss smirked as he gestured the crowd this way, then that—pretending to fling the desired sustenance. He felt like an orchestra conductor. Such power. At first the small fry scattered quickly, diffusing meekly into the seaweed for a few feet—but, less so after each successive throw, no longer fooled. His feigned hurls were losing authenticity. Choppy waves in the bay gently tossed a passenger boat crossing in front of the huge cypress clump.

————

Doss thought of the lunchroom of his Belle Glade school where kids had congregated promptly at noon on Fridays, to eat fish sticks. When the bell rang, there was a consistent and predictable pandemonium that quickly morphed into regimentation when teachers halted a rush of famished appetites and straightened the line. No matter the tedium of arithmetic and writing, excitement lay in that cafeteria—and not just inside it, but heading for it, stomachs gurgling in the queue outside. An amnesty from the rigors of class. Sloppy joes and mashed potatoes with meat gravy had not been familiar to Doss at home, but were anticipated there—even hot dogs with that relish mustard. While lessons about Portuguese explorer Vasco Da Gama and arithmetic fractions seemed bewildering and unfathomable, the process of consuming a meal provided warm familiarity. In this large room of incessant murmur, a feast of comfort awaited. Spinach largely went uneaten, despite Popeye. Muscles which developed because *Popeye the Sailor Man* 'eats me spinach,' was not a top priority among first-graders.

Students noted that on the days when the mowing crew cut the grass with their big tractors, spinach was served, and that association made by a keen student had spread. No matter the impossibility of its reality—perhaps because of that impossibility—humor radiated throughout all five grades. Groups appreciate a shared experience. Among the lunchroom classmates, common traits were otherwise few. Doss believed that even when characteristics intersected, including friendship and love, a person is completely isolated—an individual, total and unique.

As an adult, he often thought about people who had a flair for gumption—clever associations like the mowing tractor and the spinach. Wit shouldn't be confused with mindless blather and nonsensical giggling. His father Cory often berated the shallow. frivolous programs on television-the 'boob tube'. As Cory had, Doss came to dislike asinine gibberish of popular culture. Wit-Johnny Carson, Jackie Mason wit-takes brains. Often, when staccato flashes of mindless imagery bombarded him as an adult, Doss thought about his father's distaste for television. How far-fetched those simulacra of pseudo-reality:—explosions, a bullet hitting someone, blood spurting, cars turning sideways on two wheels, a gun pointed in a robbery attempt. It was a rare person who would witness even one of those images in an entire lifetime.

———

As the man tossed bits of meat, his mind pondered

the wonder of water. What a blessed substance. That oxygen-laced hydrogen molecule—two atoms of one, and one of the other, H_2O. The precious liquid wasn't just part of life, but life itself. Those three atoms generated, in collectivity, a substance that was the Everglades, the Big Cypress Swamp, and Lake Okeechobee. Water in south Florida saturated over, under and above.

Doss's mind began to meld the imagery: offerings of turkey scraps to the small fish—life-sustaining remnants of former life thrown into life-giving water to sustain lives of these tiny creatures until their bodily existence could in turn be feasted upon. There was a unity for a brief moment.

Daydreams brought him back to Belle Glade and the visit yesterday. His mind fought to rebuild the school. In empty space floated a phantom school, that familiar cream gray stucco. The annex building way in the back had also been of the same material and color.

Doss contemplated his fifth-grade year and a particular date that had changed everything: Friday, November 22, 1963. The hedge, dark green, was shaggy and interwoven with moonvines of lighter green. Doss had heard a lanky boy—a classmate, returning from a restroom break around 2:30, right before school ended for the week: "Someone just said the President's been shot." The tall, skinny, handsome student with oily hair and black eyes, joked a great deal-sort of a class clown. He was given to mild outbursts of drama, rarely serious, and Doss mostly ignored what he had perceived to be an ill-advised and tasteless attempt at humor. The fifth-grade teacher was a man from Kentucky, Mr. Darby, hair black but thinning. He wore glasses framed with a thick, dark plastic. A moralizing docent, lacking in patience and obviously not well-suited for the classroom, he had been Doss's first male teacher. Class members had paid but scant attention to the lanky kid's remark about a shooting of the President—words that, if true, would mean history had been altered—radically and forever. The harsh reality soon was revealed: Earlier that day, about the time students in the lunchroom had been relishing fish sticks dipped in that creamy tartar sauce, a dastardly act had occurred in Dallas, Texas.

Class ended thirty minutes later. Mrs. Hooker, a school administrator, leaned over Mr. Darby's desk and Doss, the lone straggler in the classroom, still gathering his paraphernalia, overheard her hushed tones, "We just can't believe it." The kind, soft-spoken woman usually wore a warm smile that displayed depth of character and genuine dedication to students. But, she was not smiling at that moment, and the impact of her low, whispered tones became clear. Paying no attention to how Mr. Darby reacted at hearing her information, Doss had felt an icy fear strike deep within as he walked more rapidly toward the exit. Merger of the two statements turned what had seemed flippant foolishness into shock. A frivolous remark had now broadened out and blossomed into horrifying substance. The impossible seemed to be yielding to the inevitable.

"Mother, has President Kennedy been shot?" Doss, burst out, as he made his way to the family car, a white sedan, his face blanched ashen in anticipation of an affirmative response.

∞∞∞

Chapter Four

"Yes, and he's dead," was the blunt, unfiltered response from Doss's mother. Time stopped. Shock paralyzed. The boy stepped into the backseat of the car. "I heard Mike Backus saying something coming back from the restroom, but no one paid much attention. Class didn't stop—didn't even slow down. But, when I heard Mrs. Hooker speaking in a whisper, looking sad and gently shaking her head, leaning close towards Mr. Darby, my mind raced back to Mike's words."

Doss was not aware that his left hand moved to his face and made a wiping motion across his upper lip, almost as if erasing the question—as if that would negate the answer. Then he brought that same hand back to his mouth, while angling his dazed stare downward, glimpsing a glaring pink sparkle in the asphalt driveway. A particular rock in a million, which had loosened from the asphalt, was gazed upon, yet not really seen. Perhaps by infusing that inanimate object with mind-numbing meditation, time could be turned back a few minutes to a genuine reality—one of normalcy. One of fish sticks.

———

The silver flash of the barracuda, which had darted ten yards to Doss' right, removed his attention from the spindly mangrove roots curling down into the water. The largest of the mangrove snapper had vanished. Bits of turkey were almost gone. Minnow continued to jump towards the last of it, careful to refrain from straying too far from the safety of the group. "Ah, the security in numbers," Doss thought.

"Ever notice how in humans there seems to be a sense of mutuality and immortality," he had asked David, just yesterday, a son whose thinking was as astute as his own, maybe more so. "Just like those mourners after the students were shot." Four months earlier, thousands of mourners had crammed together west of Ft. Lauderdale, many with hands raised, holding white candles, yellow-orange flames bending gently from a light breeze. There had been another mass shooting. A premeditated frenzy by a former classmate, a lost creature complete in his cloistered alienation. It had happened not far north of the scuba diving—in fact he and the boys had passed within a mile of the school yesterday.

Fourteen high school students and three teachers were massacred by a military rifle near highway 27, which tracked a path parallel to the Everglades—the *River of Grass*. The swampy national park had first been called that in a popular book by Marjorie Stoneman Douglas after World War II, which described the importance of and threats to its delicate ecosystem. In fact, the shooting occurred at a school named for that author. Doss remembered watching the aftermath on television as grieving members of the community formed that tightly packed coalition of grief, heads bowed in sad disbelief. Others gazed inconsolably at the stage with papier-mâché angels representing each of the victims, blossoms of formerly vibrant youth. Congregants seemed to fancy themselves somehow more alive in that assemblage—a oneness of transcendence—while the unbalanced wretch, that lost soul who did the killing, likely saw community merely as an illusion—each person on his own, forlorn, forsaken, and friendless in a race towards death.

――――――

An upside-down jellyfish, rhythmically pulsing, threaded its way sluggishly through the sea grass. Was he supposed to be upside-down, or was the poor creature in distress, perhaps moribund? While of the general variety he had come to photograph, this one was smaller in its rotundity, tentacles shorter, not dragging lazily under, as spasms propelled water upward. And, no fluorescent color.

The invertebrate had moved a few feet, and now righted itself somewhere near the feasting mangrove snapper fry. It repositioned itself near the sea grass. Then, it moved again, and with fleetness—appeared to be fine. The turkey was now gone. Doss pushed himself up from the dock to go check on the boys. Maybe they should be wakened. The dive started in two hours. Doss tarried.

An adult female snapper was bloated with eggs, no doubt ready to spawn, and probably would do so that night. Seeing her, Doss thought of the little floating post office in Belle Glade ninety years earlier that his father Cory had told him about—one that doubled as a general store with a sampling of dry goods and groceries:

As a young teenager, Cory had gone into the floating post office one day for mail and some supplies for his grandfather's steamboat. There sat a baby girl, probably two years old, on the store display shelf happily smashing eggs—probably a dozen or more before she exhausted her supply. Next to the yolk-splashed infant, an elderly man, pushing 80, shaggy gray-haired and beard, lazily reclined on a cot, no doubt used for napping when not busy. His bare feet were painted in a thin residue of black muck, and of all places, propped up near where the butcher cut meat. The memory always brought a smile to Cory's—and Doss's— face.

Customers without shoes were common on this periphery of the Everglades in the 1920s. In fact, "Barefooted people—of whatever classification—were not uncommon, especially out near the lake," Cory had related to Doss years later. "The men who worked the dredge boats wore shoes, because they had to work the pedals, and those dredges were scattered abundantly throughout this frontier, for excavating underwater, whether to gather up bottom sediments or widen a canal," Cory explained.

Cory had aided his father Percy, and his grandfather Peter Neesh. Cory, even as a young teenager, made himself invaluable on the family steamboat—*Corona.* The craft was used as a freight hauler to transport produce across Lake Okeechobee. Three generations. Cory had worked alongside the two older men running the same boat near Cape Canaveral for five years. Merritt Island and the big Cape lay 150 miles north ofLake Okeechobee, and the two men and the boy had hauled citrus fruit for *Chase & Company.*

Cory told Doss about the menfolk in those days who would try to "date up with girls" in desolate Florida, particularly the swamp that had no roads and no railroads. Custard apple clusters grew wild, but were quickly disappearing—a swamp being bulldozed and burned, muck-bottom land cleared for growing winter vegetables. Girls were scarce. Especially the 'marrying kind'.

On their drive to Key Largo, Doss had asked Aaron whether he was going to 'date up' that pretty, red-haired girl who worked with him. Aaron largely ignored the question, allowing only that the girl was a "refined, up-standing young lady of Savannah gentry." A fancy girl. "No, sir, there weren't many of those a hundred years ago in the swamps of south Florida," Cory used to tell Doss. Those kind needed ice. In the early 1920s, "There was no ice in Florida's tropical, mosquito-laden swamps," Cory related. "And so, there were no 'fancy girls.'"

In 1922, there were two brothers, Germans, Mark and Mitch Crissman, desperate for money and women, who had come to Florida looking to establish them-selves in a business that would service communities near Lake Okeechobee. They decided to build an ice plant. Right after Christmas 1923, Cooter Cone, already a well-known boat captain, barged an ice-making facil-ity for the brothers, transporting it sixty miles down the Kissimmee River, across the big lake, and then up the Hillsboro Canal. The brothers drove a few pilings down to the limestone rock so that a brick furnace and then tubular mechanism for returning and recycling ammonia gas could be secured—all under a tin roof. The compressor and its tubes piped lake water from the canal to an elevated storage tank. At first, custard apple wood, freshly cut and cleared, was tried as fuel, but its heat was not sufficiently hot, so they resorted to oil. In those days even after the Great War had ended, oil was oftentimes unavailable. A young Navy veteran, Isadore Nachman, who had returned from that war knew about injectors and boilers. Before long, he had it running—hundred pound cakes of ice spitting out—the color of tobacco juice, but frozen and cold, nonetheless.

Chapter Five

President Kennedy's hotel room on his last night in Fort Worth featured paintings by Monet and Van Gogh, along with a Picasso sculpture—*Angry Owl*. The collection placed there by art aficionados, some of Ft. Worth's elite, included *The Swimming Hole*, Thomas Eakins's painted artistry of six nude men frolicking, swimming, diving near a rock jutting into a lake. Easkin's self-portrait appears on the right side of the painting where a signature would typically be placed. Another painting, *Lost in a Snowstorm* by Charles Marion Russell, featured two white colonists and five Blackfeet Indians, in brightly colored costumes and paraphernalia atop horses pointed in varying directions. There was an Appaloosa, a couple of Bays, a Buckskin, and a Roan, with the white riders in relative background obscurity. Had Kennedy even looked at them? Perhaps he had studied the dots and textured splotches of paint on canvas and wondered about the colorful message. Perhaps he had ignored them completely. It's possible he had glanced at them cursorily, but focused his mind on the critical fissure among Texas Democrats. After all, if the political rift couldn't be mended, all hope for JFK's reelection next year, 1964, was lost. Then there was the phone call to *Cactus Jack*—Jack Garner. In the 30s, when Kennedy was fifteen, Garner had been Franklin Roosevelt's vice-president. "Happy Birthday, Mister Vice-President," JFK greeted the 95-year-old man over the telephone. "November 22, 1963—your birth-day—and blessed you are with long life—congratula-tions. This is a day for celebration."

Doss remembered hearing about that final phone call of President Kennedy to a man who had almost become President instead of FDR. The shot had been aimed at President-elect Franklin Roosevelt, not far north of Key Largo, in Miami at Bayfront Park. A po-tential assassin took careful aim with his .38 caliber revolver, hoping to hit a man who would not officially become President for three months. In those days, the early 1930s, it was the month of March, not January, that inaugurations occurred. The bullet missed FDR, but hit the mayor of Chicago, causing a wound from which the man died three weeks later. How a bullet can change history. "Imagine no FDR," Doss had asked his sons, when telling a story that happened only seventy miles south of Belle Glade. Imagine no New Deal. Im-agine a history without that inaugural address whose promise was to reinvigorate a bankrupt nation—'The only thing we have to fear, is fear itself.' A brave woman, Mrs. Cross, jostled the assassin's arm there in Bayfront Park. If she hadn't, the country would have had Cactus Jack and not FDR.

Not an hour after the 1963 telephone call to Cactus Jack, President Kennedy was dead. Then, an hour after that, Doss would hear those whispered murmurings be-tween Mr. Darby, the man teacher and the lady school administrator. "The circularity and parallels of exist-ence."

Three months before Kennedy's assassination, Doss had cast ten-year old eyes on the handsome man's powerful face, color radiating from his tanned vitality, smoking a cigar, wearing tortoise-shell sunglasses, sailing aboard *Honey Fitz*, the huge yacht named after Mayor John Francis Fitzgerald, JFK's grandfather. On that family boat outing near Lake Worth, the boy had the pleasure of a quick, hand-pivoting wave from the nation's charismatic leader who momentarily gazed at Doss and the others on board. They gazed magnetically on the country's commander, who had only recently averted a missile crisis with Soviet Russia.

Chapter Six

A true Navy man, that JFK. So was Cory, who, when he learned in 1944 that he was about to be drafted—a friend who worked for the draft board had informed him—quickly enlisted. Where else but the Navy? Not only had Kennedy been a Navy man, but a Patrol Boat man at that—*PT-109*. "Those guys had guts," Cory thought, because unlike sailors lodged safely aboard large ships, even battleships and destroyers, the patrol boat men knew the enemy had them in sight, and aimed to destroy their crafts. Years later when Kennedy became president, Cory liked him better than he otherwise would have in view of the PT boat duty.

How could Cory not go Navy? Hadn't he been working on a steamboat since childhood and loved boats as much as girls—even as a kid? Hadn't he been given a little boat called *Dollar and a Half* by his grandfather? And, hadn't that same grandfather, Peter, let out a huge guffaw when as a four-year-old Cory remonstrated his kitty cat? "What the hell you doin' in my Dollar and a Half, ditty?"

"Yes, those Navy fellows were the best," Cory would insist. "And, speaking of Navy fellas, that ice those Crissman brothers began to produce, thanks to the shrewdness of the Navy man, was delivered block-by-block to customers along the canal, as the supply boat meandered between dredged banks," Cory had told Doss.

"Most landings did not have docks, so the skipper would swell his body like an alligator, and then blow a strong, forlorn note on his well-used, scruffy tin horn. That alerted the hearer that a hundred pound cake of ice had been dropped—oftentimes at the edge of the water where cattails and sawgrass grew from the shallows. If no one heard, it mattered not. Many blocks slowly melted, the afternoon sun dissolving them into canal water, before being discovered," Cory related.

Navy beans were a staple for Cory aboard the *Mona Island* in World War II. The enlisted man was an elder among youngsters-35. He longed to be with his family in Belle Glade between 1943 and 1945, instead of Saipan, Okinawa, Guam, and the Mariana Islands. At one point the man took a dip in the ocean above the Mariana Trench, 7-miles deep. His vessel had made a stop above the deepest part of the ocean in all the world. The Captain informed the men and offered for them to swim, if they didn't fear the sharks.

He made the best of life aboard the Navy repair ship. He had lain awake at nights worried about potential kamikaze attacks from the Japanese.

———

Back in Georgia, Doss thought about the comb jellyfish he had not seen. As he planned for his next expedition, he knew that diving at night was a necessary, but not sufficient, condition for spotting the creature. There had been an abundance of color below the waves that night. Maybe he didn't need to capture a Comb. Besides the pastel and bright coral shades, the reef teemed with spiny lobster. He had photographed them, along with a leatherback turtle, moray eel, and nurse shark. Maybe one of those would be good enough to submit to the magazine. The lobster, especially, were astir with revelry. Not a true lobster, he knew, since claws are absent—really a crayfish. Lobster, those associated with the state of Maine, the 'real' ones, have claws on the first three pairs of legs, with huge initial ones. What the Florida and Maine variety do share is a hard exoskeleton, but spiny antennae do not exist on lobster, as they do on the Florida critters. Some biologists have said the ones in the Keys might be more accurately called ocean crayfish. While Floridians refer to them as 'spiny lobster'—or 'rock lobster', that's a taxonomic misclassification. And, to confuse the contrast further, many zoologists contend the animal can't be called crayfish —or crawfish—because that term is reserved for freshwater creatures only. Whatever categorization is finally settled upon, many Floridians swear that the crayfish or lobster of the Keys are tastier than the exoskeletal varieties from Maine.

Chapter Seven

Doss remembered entering motel room 543 on the moonlit night to go to bed after the night dive. He had looked across the highway that terminated in Key West at mile marker 0. There was a group of dancers on a patio at a Mexican restaurant where salsa music blared loudly. He was about to sit on a plastic balcony chair, but, seeing the party across the way, instead went into the room to retrieve the binoculars. The two boys had gone to bed, Todd dozing, Aaron studying his chart with pictures of saltwater fish. Now armed with magnification, Doss spied a woman in a low-cut top with smallish but well-proportioned breasts. "Sure'd like to massage those," he thought. There was a muscular man in a tank top, ear piercings, and colorful tattoos, apparently deejaying for the patrons. The woman, probably forty, seemed to entangle herself with that fellow as he tried to take song requests from customers. He sipped what appeared to be a Margarita sporting a smattering of salt along the circumference of the glass. The deejay did not seem to desire that the hovering woman quit his presence.

There were four dancers, three women and a man. Two were dressed in colorful attire, swirls and paisleys, maize and blue and scarlet and maroon. The other two seemed drab in comparison. Swaying and tilting in a kind of ecstasy, heads cocked, eyes closed, then opened, they gyrated rhythmically. Doss thought of the primeval crustaceans—those spiny crayfish—he had seen an hour earlier on Sorghum Reef and wondered whether groupings of them orchestrated similar ritualistic pirouettes. Maybe the nighttime ceremony was instinctual. Perhaps creatures far and wide, even those below the waves, exhibited the dance. Did Dionysus have power under the sea? No. That was Poseidon's reign. Bacchus and Neptune for the Romans, of course.

But no, the lobster had exhibited no coordination, no systematic movement. Doss remembered one set of antennae protruding randomly, twitching back and forth with no apparent synchronization, from under a shipwrecked rudder. Another acted similarly ten feet away over near the pink coral. Bacchanalian revelry was exhibited in coordinated swaying inebriation, from drink or ecstasy or ritual. Was it not? Maybe it could be seen in a spasticity of inebriation. He wasn't sure.

The voyeur, for so Doss now was, carefully studied the countenance of motley faces, some scowling and serious, others engaged in levity and conversation, one man's eyes squinty, forehead furrowed, conveying a serious expression, others laughing uncontrollably.

Doss's thoughts ran to primordial jellyfish, a creature whose perfection made these variegated human shapes seem somehow deformed—or malformed. In fact, who determined that humans were so special in beauty and strength—declaring their position at the top of the food chain? Other humans—duh! Wasn't there a superiority of construction, a unified simplicity in the lowly jellyfish? Its self-contained survival mechanism —absent the distraction of arms and legs, faces and toes

—even brain and blood. Beauty resided in that easy, perfect symmetry. And, that one hole. One hole. How did that work? Speaking of symmetry, the woman with nice breasts was in his view again.

A streetlight out by the sidewalk cast a faint gleam across the planks of the motel's balcony, showing a slight lifting of dust, some of which passed in front of Doss's view, refracting colors off the neon sign, amplified by the binoculars. Doss could go over and see for himself.

He slowly laid the binoculars on a white wicker table next to the seashell-filled lamp, still looking across the highway, then descended two flights of the concrete stairwell and headed for the bar. Why was he going? He should be going to bed.

Chapter Eight

T hat next day in Key Largo, Todd had wanted another slice of key lime pie at lunch. As the three waited at the counter to pay, Doss saw a model steamboat with a red paddlewheel in the rear, sitting atop the ice cream freezer. His mind had wandered to Cory's tales over thirty years earlier about the three generations. He tried to imagine how his father, grandfather and great-grandfather relocated their steamboat to Lake Okeechobee from the big cape in Florida.

Captain Peter and his son Percy had gambled against odds that they could survive hauling winter produce grown from black muck across the lake's brown, shallow, and oftentimes choppy water. *Corona* would prove a worthy craft, faithfully cruising to the railroad terminus, thirty-five miles distant, time and again. Thinking about his father, Doss smiled inwardly. What it must have been like for him as a young kid to run a steamboat with his father and grandfather. Then, Doss remembered how Cory's sister a few years later had introduced her girlfriend Earlene to Cory. Love ensued briskly. Earlene wanted to go away from a father whose austere demands left her, she felt, no choice. They were married two years later. Cleo was happy her brother had found love with this girl who was a dear friend. The teenage girls' friendship had had its genesis in a poem

Cleo had written:

> *Time, thou thief of days,*
> *rushing existence into dust!*
> *Knowest not the grief diffused*
> *by thy incessant march?*
> *Robbing children of tenderest*
> *youth and parents of*
> *babies—left only with*
> *tattered toys.*
> *Think not dark hand that in*
> *thy fleeting thou art ignored,*
> *nor that thy ravages of magic*
> *moments go unheeded, despite*
> *momentary respites of mirth.*
> *Mortals cannot stop thine*
> *inexorable deeds, wilting the*
> *beauty of yesterday's prime.*
> *Why not halt thy rushing waves*
> *of brutal impulse—why not slow*
> *thy temporal engine to rest a bit?*
> *Mere seconds, if only, let time and*
> *tide pause—relish a few moments*
> *of joy or beauty or youth!*

Upon reading it, Cory's future wife and Doss's mother, was in disbelief. "Someone my age wrote that?" she wondered. Mesmerized by Cleo's prodigious thoughts, Earlene bolted over to the classmate's house. Cleo's literary gift was singular. Before reading those lines, Earlene had not realized this acquaintance loved to read incessantly, especially poetry. Earlene had no such talent, but appreciated it in others. Cory was there

at home, but the two hadn't yet been formally introduced. The boy was busy building a model ship. Earlier in the day, at school, Susan Burdeshaw had shown
Earlene the poem. A fusion of adolescent friendship
blossomed between Earlene and Cleo. Then a romance
between a girl and boy emerged. A poem set a great deal
in motion.

Earlene Thompson had come to Lake Okeechobee
from Georgia with her family just a year earlier. While
she had mildly complained about moving, her father reminded the family often of a *Readers' Digest* article he
had read about the rich soil. So, with dissension and
disgust from Earlene's mother, the family headed to
Pahokee, along the shores of the big Lake.

The stories from his mother and father about
their respective treks south, Doss found inspiring. But,
it was his father's tri-generational steamboat trek down
the Indian River, Doss found the more romantic. If
either odyssey had not occurred—that of Cory's, that
of Earlene's—what might have been? What might not
have been?

Earlene's expedition with her parents and siblings
from cotton fields in Georgia to the swamps of South
Florida, was as interesting in many ways as that of
Cory's. She recounted it frequently. Earlene, as had
Cory, loved home. Cory's area of comfort near Florida's
big cape, was as much a source of warmth as Earlene's
in Georgia. She had felt yanked by her father Lewis,
whom the children called "Pa," out of Georgia's red clay
to black, lake-bottom muckland. Both fathers, Peter and
Lewis, had gambled in the face of dark odds.

Chapter Nine

Tiny mists of cool water sprayed from the rear of the boat onto Rhetta's face as the boards on the big round paddle moved in a perpetual circle, plodding the steam-powered craft down the wide river to its new destination. The *Roarin' Twenties*—folks were getting rich on Wall Street—but not on a steamboat. As one blade of the giant red paddlewheel came up from the water's surface, another pushed down against it, causing a continual stirring, a deep, sonorous "slosh, slosh, slosh," in measured melodious beats. Slowly but steadily, each plank raised gallons of water, then returned it to the river. The slow, forward propulsion was initiated by a controlled, steady fire, fed by armloads of wood. Water for steam was contained in a large, stainless-steel reservoir, the pressure of which had to be controlled. If nothing else was watched assiduously, that was.

While the two men could not provide the maternal nurturing Cory's mother might have, there was Rhetta. His grandmother, Peter's wife Rhetta, was kind beyond measure. She wasn't often a passenger on *Corona*, but when she was, the title *Captain* belonged to her. The morning coolness strengthened the aroma of the aged teakwood in the cozy living quarters of the big steamboat, where canvas hammocks hung suspended from strong metal hooks. The lusty smell unique to teak took on added potency with the heaviness of cooler air, whose wintery blast had managed to push its way southward against the semi-tropical heat and humidity that permeated the big cape.

Cory was snoring lightly when the wood scent combined with that of frying bacon. His dream incorporated a twisted symbiosis of the two. A slender woman with brown bobbed hair, an apron tied around her waist, her index finger placed lightly over her lip, a worried look on her face, stood at the stoop of a little cottage. In his dream, she wondered where the boy was, why he wasn't yet home for supper. Hers was a face of angst, he discerned, as the conscious world began to invade his lofty wanderings. It was his distraught mother calling to him, anxiously awaiting his arrival at home before dusk. In dreams, she was a decent woman, who had baked cakes and cornbread for the boy, and for whom he had felt affection. The dream image was a letdown when he realized he had not seen the woman who had given him birth. Would he even know her face today?

Warmth and comfort was provided by an aging, tattered, but still brightly colored cotton quilt with alternating squares of cotton flour sack print. Percy had purchased the covering from a traveling evangelist with the ironic surname of *Lord*, whose tent had been pitched just up the river from the steamboat. Sometimes in dreams, Cory had to ease his mother's worry, erase the disquietude from her face. Sometimes the dream evolved into the bridgetender's wife. She was a nervous woman. But the stories they told about the high-strung woman obviously seeped into Cory and now found an outlet in his subconscious.

Cory liked to linger in that soporific state, his body rolled in conformity, intertwined with a muslin cover between his body and the quilt. He relished the hallucinatory escape his dreams afforded from the long hours hauling citrus from the cape to the mainland. Just a couple of mornings earlier, the *whooomp* of the whistle had been translated in his dream into a honking horn of a Model T his mother was driving. As she passed slowly down the dirt road that paralleled the river, a cloud of limestone dust rising behind, she gently and slowly waved her arm in a single motion and gazed at the boy steadily, neglecting to watch the road ahead, turning to see him even as she had long passed the spot where he stood waving. That dream seemed to have been a recurring one, a scene he had witnessed over and over. On second thought, maybe that was the first time he dreamed it. He strained to recall while rubbing his eyes.

The boat began to move, now freed from its mooring. The captain waved to his first mate son to acknowledge all clear. The loud steam whistle shrieked out the urgency of the day, and the dream was now thoroughly twisted as the sleeper tried to weave the concreteness of that din into his images.

Cory felt a gentle nudge on his arm which was comfortably tucked under his shabby feather pillow. The boy's face immediately turned away from the intruder. His grandfather, the captain of the steamboat, stood between the boy and the piercing ray of morning sunshine which rudely slashed into the cabin's sleeping quarters. The old man's flowing white beard and unkempt silvery-gray hair were illumined against the orange hue painted by the morning's sunrise and reflected back against the metal railing along the base of the window. The captain looked down for a moment, pondering whether to sternly and emphatically rouse the boy, knowing that only through "strict and consistent discipline would the boy amount to anything." Captain Peter wasn't fond of many people, but he dearly loved that grandson. Despite the softness in his heart towards the youngster whose surrogate parents were himself and his short, rotund wife, Rhetta, Peter wakened him gently.

If Peter was dour and austere, his son Percy was kind and genial. Vulnerability to liquor aside, the man was tender and curious, and a good father. Cuban rum could take control of his willpower, but he had a quick mind which copiously studied books, and avoided disagreement at all costs. The liquor provided a barrier between himself and unpleasant confrontation. His was a spirit of peace. He performed an invaluable service to his father by a quick willingness to accommodate the old captain's every wish and to obey every command with prompt response. Percy, an able first mate in his father's mind, assisted Captain Peter, in whatever task was asked, not least of which was as cook. His utility aboard *Corona* meant even the most exorbitant orders were carried out with little dissension. Percy's acquiescence, that yielding demeanor of his, stemmed from a desire to be at peace with the world—and himself. His passions ranged from history, philosophy, hard liquor and easy women. His handsome, sharp features—high cheekbones and light green, but saddish eyes—were weathered somewhat by liquor. There was also the constant exposure to a relentless, tropical sun whose intensity he endured while completing a thousand thankless tasks aboard the boat. His eyes appeared a bit sadder now than they had a decade earlier when they had laughed almost aloud during conversation. When his woman was still around, Percy had been intoxicated with life, drunk with the ecstasy of existence.

"Gotta make one last citrus run, Cory, so get up now, son," the boy heard his grandfather clearly now, thanks to the obliteration of his dream from the reverberating deep rumble of the steamboat's whistle. "I need some steam for the boilers. Your daddy's got some breakfast goin' for us," the old captain urged, turning away, confident in the boy's obedience.

The *Corona* team hauled tangerines, navel oranges, grapefruit, and *Lake tangelos* across the Banana River. As the whistle again belched its cacophonous steam, the boy resignedly pushed his feet onto the weathered teak planks lining the deck of the big boat. With his denim pants and cotton sweatshirt in hand, he headed for the little dining and cooking area, the dominion of his father. Had Rhetta been a part of the steamboat operation, it would have been she, not Percy, doing the cooking, for few, and no one in that family, could cook better. Her biscuits, meticulously rolled and cut from dough, were heavenly, especially when dripped with some cane syrup. Cory dressed before sitting down for breakfast, something he hesitated to do on warmer mornings when scrambled eggs and grits or home fried potatoes were his first priority.

The *Lake tangelo* the boat would be hauling, had been cultivated only a dozen or so years earlier by W.T. Swingle of the federal Department of Agriculture, and it was not an orange, as people erroneously believed, but a cross between a *Dancy tangerine* and a *Duncan grape-*

fruit. Those were Cory's favorite. Tangelos feature an abundance of juice and a lesser amount of flesh. And, they are sweet.

Soft tinges of coolness caressed Cory's face as the breeziness from the upper deck reached deep into the bowels of the boat. The nostalgic longing for his mother began to subside as the sizzling bacon released its sweet, sugar-cured aroma. His stomach lightly rumbled as he saw the fried eggs, one with its broken yolk drenched by pan-fried toast. A tiny puddle of melted butter filled an equally small crater atop a huge helping of grits sprinkled with pepper. The adoration he had for his father was intensified during those special mornings when the man seemed genuinely to enjoy preparing the boy's plate indulgently to his exact liking. Percy tailored the meal and added abundant servings of his son's favorite—what they both referred to as "round potatoes," nothing more really than potato chips still hot from frying in bacon grease.

The boy loved his father, though with less enthusiasm than he would have if not for the man's drinking. Moments of sullen moodiness diminished what could have been a gleaming camaraderie between the two. Stories from the father's history books comprised a source of education and entertainment for Cory, who listened for hours. His father, mildly inebriated oftentimes, but always fired with intensity in his narrations, recounted, in erudite detail, a rousing tale from some escapade. The narratives were inescapably laced with appropriate philosophical themes and embellished with a twist from Percy's imagination.

Toast from the iron skillet was light-brown on the edges, but less so towards the middle, where the melted butter preserved the whiteness of the bread, giving way to a creamy yellowness. Cory gobbled a piece of toast even before his father had served him his plate.

"Have some manners, son. I know you're hungry, but give me a minute and I'll have it for you. You know what he thinks about crumbs on his boat, so sit down," Percy's reminder presented itself more in a sense of mutual collaboration against the 'him' whose wrath could violate both their interests, rather than in a spirit of discipline.

"Yes, sir," Cory obediently responded.

Still sleepy, still daydreaming, his mind recovered. "How can that little piece of butter in the frying pan turn a plain slice of bread into such a treat? Gotta sop my yolk with it."

The ear-piercing whistle of the boat again interrupted reverie and reminded the cook and his sole cohort that this day would be their last one hauling citrus fruit. The *Southern Coast Railroad Company* had decided that for them. In two months, its tracks would extend across the river, thanks to a new bridge. *Corona's* services would no longer be needed on this stretch of water. The fruit could be more efficiently—and profitably—transported by rail. "Number one rule of the Capitalist," Percy would often recount: "Cut costs, boost profits. I'd like to see those damned capitalists do what we do. Fact is, I'd like to see them do anything worthwhile. All they're good at is counting their money."

When Captain Peter had received word of the train's extension, his response was quick and decisive. He was a shrewd businessman and, unlike his son, was not afraid of confrontation, nor even of an outright brawl. Staying ahead of any obstacle—that was his goal. Nothing he had control over, would limit his success. While he had no desire to take advantage of other men, other men—and that means no one at all—was going to take advantage of him. There was that one time as a young teenager when he had witnessed the Ogeechee River in south Georgia. It had been devastated from Sherman's Atlanta-to-Savannah war campaign. That's the only lesson he needed of life's brutality. Now, his steamboat wouldn't be needed any longer to haul citrus—no problem, he would utilize her services on Lake Okeechobee. "If ole Sherman, that sumbitch, and his Yankee soldier boys couldn't finish us off on the Ogeechee River in south Georgia, this railroad sure as hell ain't gonna ruin us now," he vowed. William Tecumseh Sherman's name was inevitably associated with the epithet 'sumbitch,' and not just by Peter.

At the moment, Captain Peter's hatred was aimed squarely at the railroad, not Sherman. Even then, the bridge over the Banana River was almost complete, and in traversing that body of water, it had, in all reality, compelled his decision. That's not to say he wasn't bitter—he was. Bitter towards them, towards it, towards something or someone who was causing him again to pull up stakes and go. With the railroad company's designs of crossing the river, he had no choice but to crank up the steamboat and migrate. There would be no crying or wringing of hands, no sentiment. Most especially, there would be no hesitating. They would pick up their belongings and find prosperity elsewhere. "If a man couldn't make a living in a place, that place wasn't worth living in," he reminded his son. He aimed to find a new place that would be. Bitterness was ameliorated greatly by his peripatetic propensity.

Chapter Ten

Steamboats ferrying vegetables, otter and coon skins, snowy egret feathers and alligator hides across the big lake down in the southern part of Florida, were featured in an article Peter had read a couple of years earlier in *South Life* magazine. Limited rail service across the lake translated into a need for haulers to get the goods to the railroad terminus that lay 35 miles across the lake, on its north side. He was convinced that three additional boatmen, along with his wife Rhetta, might be able to survive there. Survival was the sole aspiration. Aesthetics were not of concern to Peter, and luxuries were out of the question. Comfort was hit and miss. What the place looked like, or what the climate was, or whether an ease to his existence could be secured, were scarcely contemplated.

Without discussion, without consultation among family members, and with little more than perfunctory rumination with his own trusted counsel, he decided that his little group would relocate. About six weeks earlier he had come home to Rhetta, who kept their little cottage about a mile from the dock uncluttered and tidy, and announced, "we gotta take ole *Corona* south. "The railroad's fixin' to put us out here." His announcement to the family evinced no hostility, no 'what ifs,' no emotion, no regret, no second thoughts, and certainly no invitation for debate. It was a done deal, and all who would be part of the operation would willingly go along, and that included everyone in this family. Rhetta had said she'd "miss her brother," but no stronger protest issued forth.

As first mate and chief navigator, titles Peter had honored Percy with, the son's responsibilities included keeping the boat clear of hazards, docking and undocking, and maintaining the navigational charts stored neatly and in a waterproof packet. Rarely was the boat docked long before Percy started hosing down the big boat's decks, cooking a meal, or cleaning and drying the pots, pans, and dishes, or doing several of these simultaneously—all while sipping on some rum. Despite his drinking, he was industrious, as indeed his father demanded that he be. The two men wrangled occasionally, never for long though. To the extent Percy recognized and validated his father as the boss, and abided his decisions, the Captain rewarded his son with days off, money to spend when he truly needed it, and, most of all, the peace he craved in being left alone to read his books.

Gone were any hopes Percy had held in more youthful days of molding the world to conform to his reality or desires. He would trade any influence he might generate upon mankind for a few hours with the likes of Tolstoy or Melville. "Let me alone," he remarked to Peter once, "and let the world struggle to learn my secret to happiness." Early on in life, Percy had discounted happiness as a goal one day to be achieved through acquisition and worldly trophies—rather, he saw it in terms of a daily reward from performing well whatever task one undertook from moment to moment. He didn't lie to himself about his weakness for rum, and "The failed union with Cory's mother, was no doubt his own fault," he reasoned.

Percy knew fate had not been kind to him in many ways, given his woman's desertion, the ravage of family fortune owing to a brutal war between the states, the long, sleepless, guilt-laden nights about his son having no mother, and the days filled with onerous tasks and insurmountable responsibilities. He would have loved to be a professional baseball player like the "Georgia Peach", a man named Cobb, his hero from north Georgia. Percy didn't count himself fortunate, stoking fires on a steamboat to maintain pressure to fuel powerful boilers. Then again, many were not so lucky as he. He had a family-such as it was, and he was part of the family business. Yes, the job was toilsome, "but what worth doing is not?" Despite those moments of pensive reflection, his life endured, mostly fulfilled, and no problem existed for which his mother's gingerbread cookies or a swig of rum were not solutions.

Chapter Eleven

T he night Doss left Room 543 and entered the red-
and-white checkered tent in Key Largo, buzzing
chatter was pervasive. The unbroken hum reminded him of the Belle Glade school's lunchroom. It
represented the seemingly ubiquitous small talk that
floated about one's ears in places like this, completely
lacking in substance. Or, was it? Perhaps great ideas
were borne in such an environment. The future of civilization could well hinge upon some random remark ut-
tered - or a great discovery have its genesis.

One conversation seemed to question whether there
had been a play overruled in last week's football game.
A bar patron with tattooed muscles and a flat top hair-
cut shook his head emphatically, contradicting the as-
sertion by the long-haired blonde guy with blue-framed
glasses, who argued that the call had been reversed.

Another conversation involved what team had won
more baseball games in last year's playoffs—the Injuns
or the Coons. A woman in a tie-dyed T-shirt embla-
zoned in bright pink with the interrogatory text **Who
Cares?** defiantly asserted it was definitely the Coons, to
which a man with a red-haired Afro gently shook his
head in subdued disagreement. "Wrong." That was his
only oral response. He then pulled a cigarette to his thin
lips, inhaled deeply, blew it out while retaining a stern

look, and refocused his attention on the fifth inning of the game currently blaring from the TV. "Wrong," he repeated.

A couple nearer the edge of the patio by the canal used for boat traffic, argued fiercely but almost silently. The attractive, olive-skinned woman, probably 28, tightly drew in her lips and, in quick jerks, shook her head at her companion, a well-groomed man wearing a sport coat, who was sipping whiskey straight, consuming a couple of ounces in a single gulp.

Doss could decipher the woman's words "Says who? Says who? You have no idea of truth. You don't know truth from false. And, you're not true, either." The man only growled gruffly while staring intently into the woman's hazel eyes, which by now blazed savagely red. The target of her anger began gently scratching an itch on his tanned face, just to the left of his lips with his thumb, bringing that digit down three times quickly. Then he grabbed the glass and gulped down the brownish spirits.

Why did Doss feel the need to intermingle with these objects of his recent spying? The binoculars showed him all he needed. Hadn't he decided that partying hordes were not his scene? There must be something he needed there. The society of a crowd must have some merit. He knew loneliness - often. But, he hated bars. He hated second-hand smoke. He hated trivial small talk. Still he hated loneliness. He smoked sometimes. He loved to brag that he smoked OPs—'other peoples.' The L & M brand from the names Liggett and Myers were popular in the 1960's. His OP reference was lost on younger folks.

He also loved an occasional cigar, especially one

wrapped in shaded leaf tobacco, the kind grown in Connecticut. A couple of cigarettes a week were his limit —almost always bummed from a cashier at a convenience store where he routinely bought gas. Sometimes, feeling guilty, he would buy a pack from the big woman who was missing at least half of her top teeth, open it and pull out two—his allotment for that week, leaving her the rest of the pack. But, he didn't care for smoke from other people's cigarettes.

There were television screens, at least six, around which small groups of varying numbers were watching intently. Three other screens, off to the side were tuned to news and serious stuff. One featured an interview with a philosopher. No one watched. Another featured a concert by *Peter, Paul, and Mary.* Those folk singers had been a socially-conscious group back in the 1960s. The screen was largely ignored by the bar crowd.

Doss cared little for spectator sports, but loved historical programming, especially those which delved into substance. The *Theodore Roosevelt* documentary had grappled with substance, with issues, instead of hovering around the superficiality of sensationalism. Problem was, these days, even news programming seemed designed to entertain. On-air personnel with hands and heads bobbing continually, smiling, laughing. Always the damnable laughing. Did that somehow transform news into fun? What exactly about the war or plane crash or school shooting was humorous? Couldn't they just report the news? Why couldn't the talking heads, those news readers—for so they were, even though they fancied themselves celebrities—be more like Judy Woodruf? Why not deliver the day's events in a calm, non-dramatic manner, with little or no editorial commentary? Wasn't it the responsibility of viewers to participate just a little—by forming an opinion on a reported event?

Doss had always thought life too short to immerse oneself in watching sports on an electronic tube. Actually playing—ah, that was different. He had demanded his sons turn off the TV—go outside and play. A rare few make a good living by excelling in a sport. One could at least get a scholarship to help pay for college. Don't waste time watching—whether TV or other people. Get involved. Be competitive. Strive to be the best. You won't be the best always, maybe never, but strive to be. "It's the striving that's key," he reminded them often. "If you aim really high, you may land close." Todd, while still in high school, had even been awarded a scholarship to play football as a punter in college.

Chapter Twelve

Doss thought about Cory's many tales aboard the steamboat as he sat under the Key Largo tent drinking Irish whiskey. Since Peter was the unquestioned head of the boat and autocratic in its remaining viable as a livelihood, no one dared question his self-assured commands. He had consistently shown good judgment and a keen intellect. He was blessed with mechanical knack that contrasted sharply with his son's literary tastes. Peter seemed consumed with common sense, providing levelheaded answers to life's recurrent dilemmas. His talents had fit a marketable need in the desolate wilderness near the big cape. For the past seven years he had made a decent living hauling oranges and grapefruit across the Banana River. While he hadn't gotten rich, he had succeeded in feeding not only his stout little wife of Swedish heritage—with clear, blue eyes and the fairest skin he had ever seen—but also his son and grandson.

Rhetta lived in the cottage. She rarely ventured aboard *Corona*, nor did she care to. The men, in contrast, were rarely at the house. Their life was tied to the boat, and they slept aboard it countless more nights than at the cottage. Nevertheless, Rhetta devotedly waited for them, kept the abode clean--sheets washed, beds made, clothes ironed--ready if Peter decided at any moment to forego his wanderlust, which, she suspected, was stronger than any affection he felt for her.

Those customers in Key Largo sitting at the bar across from Room 543 - did any of them care in the least about that Asian country testing thermonuclear weapons? A report just ten days ago had warned of a possible, impending war with a power-hungry dictator in Europe that could destroy great swaths of humanity. As Doss felt the effects of the whiskey, he again thought of the sports screen as a damned distraction. The screen, period, was a distraction. The newscasters showed their whitened teeth, giggled every chance possible, no matter how inappropriate to the moment. News had become entertainment, pure and simple. Entertainment, including sports, had become asinine and shallow, distractions from even the hint of a formed thought. It seemed the clever lines of *I Love Lucy*, Jack Benny, and Rodney Dangerfield had dispersed forever.

There was a dancing couple over by the retro-looking jukebox lost in love and music, definite distractions. Doss too was distracted. The brightly lit beer sign was fuzzy and the reds and blues out-of-focus as he relaxed his eyes in a daydream. So many human activities seem to have only one purpose—distraction. But, from what?

A small group of bar patrons loitered by a screen featuring a reality show—about survival. Whoever could endure the greatest hardship, won. Even 'reality' shows seemed staged-the complete lack of authenticity was palpable. Hell, they displayed more fiction than sitcoms. "Hardship back in *Corona* days," Doss thought, "didn't have to be contrived." Hardship and privation were the norm. In contrast, modern conveniences made ease the norm. Or, at least modern humans interpreted it as such.

He heard one of the reality-show viewers say, "You know, that would be fun. Why don't we all go try our luck at surviving on a tropical desert island?" "Hell no," responded a member of the group, "that's not as much fun as it looks. I'll stay right here and watch someone else have fun surviving."

"But, it might be cool," another chimed in. "Sure would love to see that naked girl without her you know what blurred out," another viewer announced, quickly looking around to make sure his words were restricted to that little group. "They always blur that out," another added.

"They can't blur it out for fellow actors right there on set," the other retorted.

"I guess I'll never know about naked survival, no pun intended," the first man declared. "I'll take the comfort of sittin' right chere, sippin' my *Coors Lite* on a cushy barstool, enjoying breezy surroundings, and hope some girl will come snatch me away...kidnap me and take me to paradise. Not that there paradise there on the screen. More like the one over to the *Econo Lodge*," yet another, fourth viewer, proclaimed.

That folk concert being featured on the screen tuned to PBS, Doss thought, didn't fit in this bar. Doss saw that *Peter, Paul, and Mary* were belting out *If I Had a Hammer*, which Pete Seeger had written. Doss loved that group, and his attention was drawn to their music, playing lowly, but, "Why was that screen tuned to that?" he wondered. No one was watching. Hadn't folk music embodied an anchor of sanity in a 1960s drug-crazed, psychedelic-obsessed world of hippies and peace signs and black lights that illumined neon colors from *Make Love, Not War* and other flower-strewn, anti-establishment posters?

Peter, Paul, and Mary. Doss looked on his phone to research the group's origins: Paul Haajian, an Armenian immigrant to the United States, manufactured the *Mounds* candy bar in 1921. The *Almond Joy* came 27 years later. It featured milk chocolate instead of the dark chocolate of *Mounds*. Both Peter Paul's *Mounds* and *Almond Joy* bars became instant facets of Americana. Another Peter played a crucial role as a favorite follower of Jesus—was even the first Pope. Paul, the story goes, had formerly been *Saul of Tarsus*, a converted Jew, and wrote letters to early churches in and around the Greco-Roman world. Beyond chocolate bars and the Bible, there was alliteration in the two 'P' names. Mary's maternal role in Christianity needs no elaboration.

Mary Allin Travers, a lithe beauty born in Louisville, Kentucky was reared near Washington Square in Greenwich Village. Noel, who would become *Paul*, was a comedian at *The Bitter End* in the Village. He knew Peter Yarrow aspired to get a folk group together and introduced him to Mary. Her blonde femininity, hair-tossing, head-bobbing stage coolness, and crystal clear vocals would stand out in the middle of the beatnik-bearded guys—a nice balance. A musical group needed a musical name. And so *Peter, Paul, and Mary* became a folk group whose songs and singing would help bring about good things for America. Doss continued to watch that screen.

Chapter Thirteen

"The seduction of technology hides its poison," Doss contemplated as he sat and observed the TV. "The ease with which a math problem can be solved with a calculator dulls the brain with its substitutionary counting processes." Doss got truly inspired with Irish whiskey. Scotch, too. "The images on TV that flicker in a split-second from one chimerical scene to another even more improbable, relieves a viewer from creating mental pictures that would otherwise be required, say from reading a book or creating artwork." Was the whiskey thinking, or was Doss more astute when he imbibed?

"A washing machine dispenses with a ribbed washboard, but wasn't the rubbing on a bumpy surface part of the fun?" And, Doss thought "The entertainment afforded by leisure produces the boredom of free time. How to fill moments of leisure?" Doss wondered, now almost drunk. Drunk, but no longer lonely. Doss was incessantly thinking. His father had told him as a seven-year-old that his contemplations reminded Cory of Percy.

"If humankind had to grapple with survival, there would be no boredom. Mechanization has weakened mankind," Doss often told his own son, David, "to the point that it erases by sheer increases any comfort it formerly provided. Crises which modern humans perceive, our ancestors would have neither given a second thought to, nor been the least bothered by. Mainly because of the time they spent in brute survival." Doss thought "inventions and machinery have solved a few problems, but created many more. Technology demands slaves - human beings." Wasn't it Adorno who had said *No history leads from savagery to humanity, but there is one from the slingshot to the megaton bomb?*

Doss should be trying to talk to the comely brunette with nice breasts and olive-green eyes over near the salsa singer.

Maybe that was the problem with the boy who had shot his classmates a few weeks ago near the Everglades. Life was too easy. He was bored. Survival was a given. "Folks a hundred years had to struggle just to eat. Air conditioners and hot showers have made sissies of us all, even the girls," Doss concluded before staring intently at the lusty green-eyed beauty with ruby red lips and coal black hair.

As he contemplated bumming a cigarette from the woman, his mind raced again to the genesis of his existence—Belle Glade. The woman looked fine, and he didn't think she was with anyone. Surely the whiskey bolstered his courage to approach her. Now if he could just amble over there.

∞ ∞ ∞

Chapter Fourteen

As interesting as Corona's journey to the big lake, Doss thought his mother's story equally intriguing. After returning to Room 543, he lay awake thinking about the maternal comfort Earlene, the gregarious woman who loved people, and loved talking to them, provided. She was lonely, too. She had left with her family not long after Peter steered *Corona* towards the lake. The red clay of Georgia was a much more distant starting point for the Thompsons. The father in charge of her relocation lacked the compelling motivation that had prompted Peter's sojourn south. In a word, Lewis Thompson was relocating on a whim:

Particles of reddish dust were randomly lifted and dispersed from the road into a steady cloud behind the car and hung in dry, still, hot, hazy air for several moments before resettling. The family were oblivious to the machine's creation. On both sides of the road, fields of lifeless gray were strewn with summer's remains. Occasionally, a field covered in a late cotton crop appeared—scattered evidence of its white puffy fruit positioned among dark green leaves—a crop by which many in this region had been enriched and others enslaved. The tint of iridescent green from immature patches of young grass scattered irregularly across the bleak fields. Hopes of resurrection from poverty also rode in that machine by which the family was running, getting away while they could. Other families in Georgia talked about leaving, and some even seriously aspired to, but most were intimidated by such a complete uprooting —afraid to stay, afraid to go. In the *Roaring Twenties*, poverty was as rampant in south Georgia as it had been aboard *Corona*.

Beyond the dreary fields, naked trees showed their skeletons against a green backdrop. Pine trees with their clean distinct smell filled the girl's nostrils and reminded her of days playing in the *Little 'Hoopee* near her home. As the Ohopee River branched toward the south and east, a sizable tributary snaked across her grandfather's property. Clear water coursed along its banks. From an old dead chestnut tree hung a thick hemp rope. That had been a major source of escape for the kids from the dirt, from the cotton, from the dust and impoverishment.

Summer's intense heat was beginning to lose its oppressive grip, as occasional hints of cooler afternoon air drifted into the air vents of the black automobile. Earlene's father drove the *Star Car*, made by *Durant Motors Company*. It was a competitor to the *Ford Model T*. Focused intently, he watched the roadway in front of him. His chin was prominent and handsome and had a slight cleft that the girl had always admired. "Don't cut yourself shaving there by the little ridge, Pa," the girl had reminded her father years earlier.

She wondered what enchanting quest awaited her in the new place. Was her mother right? Could there be but misery and depression there? Already, Earlene had doubts. Tantalizing brightness was taking root, yanking sadness out of her spirits little by little. As the passing terrain eventually grew marshy, inner springs of excitement overflowed when she dared allowed. No matter how much her mother opposed moving way down in Florida, she detected the possibility of impending adventure. There were moments of delight—irregular waves of glee in this uprooting. The sadness thawed into uncertainty and then yielded to sporadic thoughts that this could be something good. Although respectful of her mother's displeasure and unhappiness, Earlene's own spirits just could not be toned down by those. She, too, perceived the costs of such distance from family and friends—remoteness from the familiar. Yet, like her father, she had an imagination for the possible—the 'What might be.'

The man's square jaw was full and muscular and darkened somewhat by short growths of graying stubble due to a dull razor he hadn't taken time to sharpen recently. The girl examined the small red veins running gently along the surface of her Pa's nose and cheeks—a blush suggesting health.

The man's eyes were amber, although his wife often told friends they were hazel. But, Pa's eyes did not shift color with the flecks and ripples present with hazel. No, his eyes were of brownish-gold hue. The tall, trim man was charitable, his aspect demonstrating strands of Cherokee blood, owing to his loving maternal grandmother, a princess in her native tribe. He was also an idealist—a dreamer.

∞∞∞

Chapter Fifteen

Along with the girl's mother and father, Earlene had a younger sister, two younger brothers, and an older brother. Needless to say, the car was crowded and tight. Her sister was five, therefore seven years younger than she. Earlene was perceptive, imbued with great wisdom for an adolescent. As she rode in the back seat, her eyes, which she kept intentionally locked on one spot of the horizon, enjoyed the staccato flitting of the fields with wooded areas. Brownish green of early autumn meadows was interrupted by the perpetual verdure of cypress trees set apart in watery fields. Cypress was adorned with dainty leaves of lacy needles and surrounded by knees of bark in circles around the trunk. That kept her consciousness subdued and emotions smothered.

The controversy and family strife regarding the wisdom of leaving Georgia had taken an emotional toll on the older children. It had torn asunder a faint hope of marital happiness for Lewis and Mabel. Since divorce was not an option in those early twentieth century days in rural Georgia, he and she would tolerate each other. The wife vowed not to like the man removing her from a beloved mother. Mabel had told Lewis six months before they left, spreading her hands out to encompass everything before her: "This is me."

Distance, and eventually, time, would combine to

quiet the laughter that had come so easily to all of them as brown water splashed from the *Little 'Hopee*. Cousins and the pecan pies they competed in baking, aunts who cooked butter beans with salt pork, and uncles who hand-rolled and smoked cigarettes, were 'back there'. Friends and late-afternoon games of *Halley Over*, in which a rubber ball was thrown over the rooftop, would be missed. At dusk, they had played *tag*, and then *hide and seek*. Bits of Mabel's soul could never be removed from that little village where monetary riches had been scarce, but wealth, in a spiritual sense, flourished in amplitude. Ray's existence, too, was formed from those relationships and part of him would remain right there —perpetually in that time and place.   Granddaddy's farm would be enjoyed no more, as would the goats Marie had named—*Bill* being her favorite. The little schoolhouse, badly in need of paint, worse on the west side than the east, and the incessant squeals at playtime —would also be dearly missed. Slowly, those would fade into distant memories.

For generations, foreparents had carved out a special niche in that spot—cleared land, planted peanut and cotton crops, sweated with the overwhelming labor of harvest, raised children and buried their dead. "An unspoken, fixed pattern followed too long, a way of life too set in its enduringness, displayed no good reason now to be amended," Mabel thought. While the mother was not an adventurer and certainly not a dreamer, as her husband most assuredly was, she did recognize an opportunity to advance their interests. But, this was not it, she felt certain. And she refused to stifle her better judgment or pretend to be happy at his hopes for affluence. "Some are destined to succeed while others must just get by," she was convinced. "Riches were to be feared way more than poverty," she had been taught by her father.

Lewis reminded her that "the children of Israel struggled to get out of Egypt." He had asked her several times: "Didn't they strive to make an exit?"

"People just don't uproot kids and replant them in some untamed swamp," she had instructed her husband several months earlier. "I don't care how rich the dirt is," she added. "Kids don't grow in black dirt and family love is more important than all those vegetables that supposedly do." She often wondered what the man was searching to find. "Why couldn't he be happy?" she often mused in the pure quiet of those late night moments. Besides, "Wasn't it the wilderness the Israelites were escaping from, not going to?" she asked herself.

She knew they would never be wealthy as share-croppers on her father-in-law's farm, but one day the land would be partly his, along with five of his brothers and sisters. Not a huge slice of the pie, to say the least. But they could survive, indeed they easily might have, "with the help and guidance of the Almighty," Mabel staunchly believed. "And besides, she reasoned: What is success? What is wealth, anyhow?"

Prosperity had not been abundant for anyone in peanuts over the past few years, but who could be so sure things would be any better, or even as good, down there? Weren't the mosquitoes oppressive? That's what she had heard from some cousins who went on a hunting expedition near the big lake two years ago. Didn't she remember something about cows dying from swarms of mosquitoes? Parasitic swarms crowding nostrils, blocking breathing?

This dutiful woman, comfortable in her homemade gingham attire, checkered handsewn quilts and chenille bedspreads, knew there were no Gardens of Eden. She steadfastly believed "you make the best of what you have into the world in which you've been thrown."

In the end, however, she knew her opposition was futile. A duty was owed her husband, whom she had vowed to obey, right or wrong. Her happiness was inextricably tied to his. If she couldn't love the man, she would at least try to be his friend.

Chapter Sixteen

Earlene noticed her baby brother's head bouncing gently while he slept, in rhythm with the rough surface of the unpaved road. She observed her older brother in the front seat between her mother and father, his eyelids heavy as he turned his head slowly to look sideways occasionally, discovering with a welling excitement, new terrain he hadn't seen before. At sixteen, Roger was becoming a man. He was permitted to drive the car. While he knew not to ask, he was confident his turn would soon come as the older man grew tired, something he did often. Roger was excited about the move. He had heard from cousins who had talked to friends. There was a wealth of catfish. The lake was full of largemouth bass, speck, bluegill. Pretty girls were moving down there from all over the South, and even the North, in search of a new life. There was little else he and Earlene agreed on. The girl was a little frightened of her brother as he had seemed to pay too close attention to her, especially in her growth towards adolescence, and she was cautious when he was around. But, he was her flesh and blood, and loyalty to family was everything, so she put the best face on an otherwise tentative relationship with this handsome young man whose full head of wavy brown hair and soft brown eyes belied his lack of innocence.

Chapter Seventeen

Aboard *Corona*, Cory watched his father while savoring the last few bites of yolk-sopped toast, a satisfied admiration on his face that Percy would have relished had he glanced at his son. Percy was busy drying the skillet when Cory spoke up.

"Is Pop Pop sure we'll make more money down there on that lake?" the boy asked his father with some concern in his voice. "I mean, isn't it gonna be a lot different haulin' those beans and stuff?

"Do you remember what I told you about Sherman burnin' us out in Georgia?" Percy asked Cory, in almost the same words and tone Peter had used. "When that bastard came down the Ogeechee River and the Hagins and Groovers got burned out, what did they do? They stayed put and rebuilt and replanted and survived. What did we do? Well, first we organized our kinfolk and shot a couple of them damned Yankees. That may have been the best thing we did. But our family didn't stay there," Percy continued in his father's dialect. "No, sir, our people had new frontiers to discover and conquer. We moved here to Florida and bought some land, cleared it, and grew oranges. Didn't get rich, but our people survived—survived a long time on citrus. Daddy's daddy, William Aaron, even became sheriff of

Volusia County—Daytona Beach," Percy proudly proclaimed to Cory. "That was forty-one years ago and
we're still goin' strong," Percy reminded the boy. Even
as a young man, you should decide right now-I'm going
to make it...I know life will throw adversity at me. I re-
fuse to be a victim.

Peter loved to tell Percy and Cory how, as a fourteen-
year-old, he had been a scout for the Confederacy. He
had wanted to join that Southern secessionist movement in an official capacity, but since he was younger
than 16, his entreaties were denied. He thought the
general from Ohio ferocious and merciless in his destruction of farmers' land that culminated in beautiful
Savannah. Peter remembered how the accursed Sherman 'gave' Savannah, along with 25,000 bales of cotton
to President Lincoln for a Christmas present: December
22, 1864. Fortunately for the people of Savannah, Sherman was enraptured by the charm of the town and the
civility and hospitality of its people, so refrained from
burning it as he had Atlanta. He headed to Columbia,
South Carolina, however, and instructed his soldiers to
burn it down.

"But can we make it on the lake?" Cory wisely interrogated, astutely noting the distinction between post-
Civil War days and hauling beans and vegetables now.
"When the Neesh family survived that brutish attack
from those Yankee animals, remember, none of us perished at their hands. I think it gave us an armor, an
armor of invincibility, you might say, at least in an emotional sense," Percy proudly reminded his son. What
he failed to tell him was that numerous crop failures
after the war nearly brought about an end to their clan,

forcing them to sell hundreds of acres of prime crop-land from the once wealthy estate. Those two drought-filled summers did more damage than Sherman and his men combined, at least to the Neesh family. That they had gone hungry following those dry spells was not as widely recounted by Percy as the Sherman story.

There would have been no steamboat had it not been for the reversal in fortunes wrought by the war. It had transformed Peter from a young, dashing scion of South Georgia gentry—the grandson of no less a man than wealthy land baron William and later his son Aaron—into a destitute, hard-working skipper. He eagerly learned nautical realities: navigation, tides, hauling schedules, tonnage. He loved boats and water. His father was William Aaron, and his grandfather was Robert. William Aaron was named after both Robert's father and grandfather. It was William Aaron, Peter's father, who wandered from Georgia to Florida, then over several little towns across the new state, including Merritt Island, Cedar Key, and Palatka. He forged this life from a position of absolute defeat and was proud of his accomplishment. No one had paved a path for him. Nothing had been handed to him. His own knife had carved this niche. His—and his forebears—had been a life of repose and plenty, and then suddenly, rudely—not. He had survived the transition, pride intact. And, no matter where, he would roam toward survival.

∞ ∞ ∞

Chapter Eighteen

Roger's big hands gripped the steering wheel, which seemed to sway, at times gently, and at others, with swiftness, to the rhythm of the roadway. Earlene perceived hushed muttering from her parents' mouths, a quiet monotone excerpt of a conversation that took place without either of them turning to face the other, Mabel sitting in the middle, Lewis on the right of the car. Earlene's Pa, was a proud, complex man. Despite lofty dreams, he had displayed a gutsy realism that translated into providing for a family. He didn't shun hard work when absolutely necessary, but preferably by someone else's hands. He readily admitted that, "Even if he was a dreamer, he believed in 'aiming high' for the better things of life." The expectation from his loved ones was that they play a role in his dreams. Lewis had a feature many dreamers do not - action. Rarely was he without a scheme for making lots of money, or making adequate money a lot easier. From the apprenticeship with the veterinarian to the goat farm—"the best milk for a person's health, by far,"—to a partnership that financed his cousin, Solomon's experiments to develop a more pest resistant black-eyed pea, his ambition was as admirable as his failures were abundant. It was not now surprising that he pursued an agricultural paradise in the untamed, uncultivated, unpopulated, undeveloped environment to which they were headed. Only a thousand years before, the land had lain completely underwater.

As the car jostled the sleeping bodies of her siblings, the girl's mind raced back to that day in early winter, a couple of years earlier when her father had clipped that *Readers' Digest* article about the land with black soil and a monstrously huge lake full of catfish. The article, which her father still carried in his billfold, was now tattered and yellow, but detailed the "winter vegetable potential while most of the country is buried in snow." The lake had a funny sounding name that she couldn't remember, but until just recently, Indians had lived near it and had buried their loved ones on its southeastern shores.

"They bury their dead with valuable artifacts and gold," 'Pa' had informed her. "Maybe we'll find some if we go there," he teased, with some hope of piquing her interest and ameliorate his wife's predicted resistance to any such dreams.

The article further mentioned soil "as black as tar at midnight," which it claimed would grow "most any vegetable year round." Some of the land had to be drained, according to the article, but there were plenty of Negro laborers available to assist. Lewis had assured Earlene's mother that there would be cheap workers when he later became serious about farming in Florida.

The yellowed article had gradually become a natural part of her father's possessions, and she could recall seeing him on several occasions fumbling for his reading glasses on the little table beside his chair late at night. When silence was pervasive, he would reach for his billfold so as to read, yet again, the promise of that land, and the fortune he began little by little to count on attaining. In fact, it was after he had studied the clipping thoroughly, late one night last winter that he decided. He announced to his family the next morning at breakfast, over a huge plate of scrambled eggs, country-cured ham, and golden-brown biscuits sopped with cane syrup diligently prepared by Mabel—"I'm going down there to see for myself!" He explained resolutely that he had worked long enough for someone else.

"Sharecropping," he declared, "is a great means of avoiding starvation, but a person can't get anywhere being a sharecropper. I can do better. Ole Abe Lincoln's freed everybody after the North South war, and even sharecroppers are now free," he kidded but with a degree of certitude about the destination that awaited.

"I'm tired of sharing," he declared, "We don't have enough to share. I'm gonna try keeping more for us," he resolved.

Keep on a-goin' if you got the least thought about moving us down to that swamp," Mabel had retorted and left the breakfast table that eventful morning. She headed quietly to her bedroom after refusing to hold her peace.

Before leaving, Pa walked slowly toward the bedroom where his wife was grieving and gently tried to turn the doorknob, but it was locked. He quietly moved away from the door when it did not open. After hugging his children one by one, the big man made them promise to behave and "mind your mama," and told them they could "start looking for me in about a week to ten days." He tried to comfort them: "Don't worry; I haven't decided anything definite about what we're gonna do," he explained. "But," he promised, "if we go, it will be because I'm absolutely convinced, beyond any doubt, that there is a great deal of hope for a better life there. It's a beautiful place, from all that I've heard, and the land might be a little wet, but a farmer like me, after all, can make a livin' there," he assured the children. "There's not a whole lotta people there," he added after hesitating and thinking for a moment, "and it may be sorta desolate, like your mama says, but there may be some real opportunities for us to better ourselves. I love y'all too much to sacrifice your comfort, but if we could live like the Deals and Brannens here in Georgia, wouldn't that be alright with y'all?"

He assured them that his was merely an expedition of sorts. Ray, the couple's 9-year-old son, had mixed emotions. He loved baseball and had recently joined a team, but he was the quiet one. He would be satisfied either way the decision fell. Thirteen-year-old Earlene thought she was excited to be going, but needed to know more about the place, and Roger felt sure it might be "a lot of fun." For a sixteen-year-old boy, adventure beckoned. Then, there would be those new girls and the fish in the lake. Those considerations naturally overtook any reluctance that oldest child might have had. Marie, the five-year-old, did not want to leave her grandmother, Hattie, and it was she whom Mabel commiserated with most closely.

"There's nothing final yet," he quietly reassured them, "I'm just exploring a possibility so that y'all can have what I wasn't able to when I was your age. So let me go now, and I'll be back in a week or so to give y'all a report. Give mama a big hug for me, and do what she tells you," he reminded his children.

When Lewis had returned two weeks later, he had

a twig he had broken off an orange tree. Earlene could still recall traces of sweet fragrance from the delicate, white orange blossoms in her nostrils. From the twig hung three, tiny, immature, green oranges which Pa gently flicked with his long, calloused fingers, patiently explaining that these would have grown many times their current size and would have turned bright orange when ripe. Even Mabel seemed to be interested in Pa's description of the rolling hills and row after row of citrus trees he had witnessed on his journey.

"You mean they grow in January and February?" Mabel asked with a modicum of amazement.

"Sweet Mabel, you wouldn't believe the crops of beans and celery and black-eyed peas they grow down there, I mean right in the middle of winter," he announced. "While we're up here piling on blankets and quilts to keep from freezin' to death, they're out farmin' and makin' money. I saw beans and peas of every description—besides the black eyes, there were limas, pole beans, butters, every kind of pea or bean you can think of, and I mean to say they were thick. Negroes by the hundreds out in the fields with heavy cotton clothes were covered with muck. Rich, I mean it's rich soil—it grows everything that can be grown. Muck, that's the name of that black soil. And I mean they were pickin,' just a-pickin,' fillin' their hampers as fast as their hands could go. It was something just to watch 'em!" he ranted with excitement. "They're blessed with good hand skills, you know. We couldn't pick beans the way they pick 'em. I want you to know I saw a couple of Nigra men in their early thirties pickin' butter beans, and they filled a three-foot high hamper in seven minutes sharp." There's plenty of labor to be had, and they work cheap."

———

Conscious of the car slowing to a stop, Earlene could see that ahead was a blacktop highway and what appeared to be the end of the dirt road upon which they had been riding for the past hour. A scattering of palmetto bushes lay not far to her right, as white sunlight scattered across swampy dark water. Circular pads of green growth floated lazily on the surface, one showing a pastel, light-pink water lily. As her father's foot eased off the gas pedal, she looked over at her brothers and sister, heads bent forward, sleeping, bouncing gently and rhythmically. Slowly, Marie, wearing pig-tails, raised her head off the back seat; shortly after, her baby brother roused, that curly hair piled in thick tufts on that high forehead. Their faces slowly turned from one side window to the other, studying their alien surroundings, searching for substance and meaning in this transition of uncertainty.

After rubbing his eyes, Roger quietly asked, "Where are we, Pa?"

"About 30 miles this side of Waycross, son. You ready to drive?"

The boy knew this was his father's diplomatic way of commanding him. He was thrilled to obey. It was Pa's way of telling Roger he was tired and needed relief. Pa rarely ordered or commanded this action or that, but deferred to diplomacy which promoted others' willingness to do as he wished. That was an admirable trait of his, Mabel had always thought. "Not a bully, that man," she decided when they were courting.

"We got pretty good road on down to there, so just stay on Highway One till you hit Waycross. We'll sleep there for the night. Keep your eyes open and be alert, son," he reminded the teenage boy he adored and whose interests might have been uppermost in his mind in deciding to move south.

Pa had confidence in Roger's driving. "The boy is careful and thoughtful behind the wheel," he had told Mabel several times. "He has quick hands for a sixteen-year-old, and, better than that, he's got a good feel for the road," Pa had bragged to the family when Roger was first learning to drive.

Chapter Nineteen

A s Percy watched the reddish face of his father, stern and austere, his light blue eyes were foreboding and steely. The old man steered the big pilot wheel to back the boat away from the Merritt Island dock for the last time. Percy often debated whether life at Ivanhoe near the Ogeechee River back in Georgia might have been preferable. "Maybe that's where they should be headed," Percy thought. How might family fortunes have been different if his great-grandfather William Aaron's plantation had continued to flourish with its cotton, peanuts, tobacco, and slaves?

Within a week's time, Percy would be reminding Cory, with a subdued, tight-lipped smile, "We gotta get down there to where the Seminoles live. I'm gonna be the first to see me a real live Seminole Injun," he boasted, with an implied challenge to his son.

As they cast off the ropes from the familiar dock, Captain Peter grimaced, though he was thankful that Percy had been willing to accompany him to the lake. Percy had not wanted to leave the Cape. If there was to be a relocation, Percy would have preferred the area called Cedar Key with its huge pencil factory, on the Gulf of Mexico in the bend where Florida's peninsula becomes the panhandle. It would be hard to imagine the *Corona* operating without Percy's contribution, particularly considering the pittance he was paid—a few dollars of spending money and an occasional bottle of quality rum. There were days when he had to force himself to work, enveloped as he became oftentimes in ruminations about the temporality and mystery of life. But a swig of rum did the trick every time. Contemplations of pleasure overcame the morose reality of a sad world-greed, poverty, hate, disease, wars. Gentle tugs of wisdom from vapors of rum brushed his soul. They stroked it with a rapture that returned in him a willingness to remain an essential cog in the steamboat's machinery.

With Peter, in contrast, a flame of quest flickered, and this move kindled the thrill. He hadn't any trepidation in the least. Despite the burden, despite the hardships demanded by the family's resettlement, despite Rhetta's quiet opposition to a sojourn that would mean goodbye to her brother, Peter discerned an enterprise being born. As he steered the big boat from atop the pilot house southward down the Banana River toward Melbourne, he reflected upon the opulent lifestyle granddaddy Aaron and his children had enjoyed a couple of generations ago in Georgia on the Ogeechee River. That had an attraction for him, and he often contemplated returning and farming peanuts, if for no other reason than to be finished with the rough life of a boatsman.

But no, Peter would not allow himself regrets leaving the Banana River and the Cape. He seemed to be immune to the maudlin moanings of other, he would argue, 'lesser men'. His was a world of reality, untainted by the 'what might have been' idealism--dreams and regrets and second-guessing--that stifle good judgment.

"Ideas are like tools--Never productive 'til put to use," he enjoyed preaching. "Even inferior ideas acted upon are better than genius ones lying dormant!"

Percy was certain Peter had developed that thought from a lesson he had taught the old man from Aristotle's admonition that a *race run to the finish with swiftness, yet on a futile mission, wasn't nearly so valuable as one run slowly and deliberately on a track towards a fruitful end.*

The boat plodded lazily down the river, the big paddlewheel turning slowly but deliberately in the rear, as the little family, this time with even Rhetta aboard, steered toward the canal waterway that would empty the Corona into the big lake, 100 miles to their south.

Chapter Twenty

After Roger and his father had exchanged seats yet again, Earlene watched her brother gently shift the Star into gear and ease out onto a newly-paved highway. She looked over at her father as he squirmed into a comfortable position and laid his head on the back of the seat to sleep. She studied her father's sharp, long nose, and saw the slight bend toward its tip which detracted from its perfect shape. Her Pa claimed he had always been kidded about his nose and how it had been handed down from one of his great, great, great-grandfathers, a duke in England with German blood, whose rebellious son had decided to seek his fortune in the New World.

"When you got royal blood," he would laugh, "You don't ask questions about your physical features. You take the bitter with the sweet. What's the ole sayin' about lookin' a gift horse in the mouth? It's crooked, a'right, there's no denyin' that, but it works real good. It smells Mabel's roast pork a quarter of a mile away," he bragged with a hearty smile, "so there can't be much wrong with it."

After motoring for an hour, the car slowed as it approached the main street in Waycross. Roger almost turned down the little dirt path that led to the Okefeenokee Swamp Preserve. Pa reminded Roger rather sharply "Son, we don't go down a dirt road once we hit Waycross. The place is over by the Baptist Church."

"Where's the Baptist Church?"

"I don't know, but I reckon it's near the center of town, don't you? Most folks around here are Baptist. You gotta few Pentacostals and Church of God folks, quite a few Methodists. By all logic, the Baptist Church should be purdy near the main section."

The little sign in front of the huge antebellum mansion read *Fountain's Tourist Home.* A rather large woman in a lightweight blue and pink striped cotton dress greeted the travelers. The woman, hair brownish-gray, had a dish towel in her hands, drying them to welcome her guests. A sweet disposition was reflected in her soft blue eyes, and a gracious smile on her oval face, jaw narrower than her cheekbones.

She reached out her hand to Lewis, the first to reach the front door stoop, "How are you sir, can I do something for y'all?"

"We're on our way south, Mrs. Fountain. Forgive me for presuming that you are Mrs. Fountain."

"You're quite safe to so presume. It is I. Dorothy Fountain is my name. Can I fix y'all up with a room?"

"We'd like to stay with you folks, if you have space. My brother was through here on a hunting trip about a year ago in the swamp, and his truck broke down tryin' to get back to Vidalia. You and your husband accommodated him overnight."

"Was he the fella who smoked cigars and had a couple of hound dogs?"

"That was him—and you might remember the blood on his overalls from the deer incident."

"Oh, how well I do. Poor man. We washed him up,

penned the dogs back in the yard, and put him up for the night. I didn't have the heart to charge him full price due to his car repair. Seems like it was fifty or so dollars he had to spend on his transmission."

"He still talks about that. You'd think that was the last fifty he had, the way he carried on about that transmission. He sure was grateful to you and Mr. Fountain."

"It was our pleasure. Hard luck hits us all at some point. And, he was such a pleasant man. Not much of a hunter, he told us. Just meetin' up with some of his buddies in the Okefenokee for a weekend of the menfolk as I recall."

"Yea, he idn't much when it comes to huntin.' He hates to kill things, but he's got that man image he's tryin to keep up, ya know," Lewis confirmed.

"He was covered in blood. Said the deer was shot in the neck near the main artery, and couldn't help but gettin' it all over him," Dorothy Fountain related.

About that time a tall, big-shouldered man wearing an olive plaid flannel shirt, walked from behind the house and stooped to talk to Marie.

"What's your name? Aren't you a purdy little thing? Look at those curls. And those big brown eyes."

Marie stood with her hands interlocked, turning them awkwardly inside out, fingers tightly gripping knuckles on both hands, twisting, rubbing, moving them up to hide her nose and mouth, trying desperately to avoid being the object of such profound admiration, yet proud of the splash of attention rarely obtained. The man stood to look eye-to-eye with Lewis, "Hello, friend, I'm Phil Fountain. Welcome. Where y'all from?

"We left outta Swainsboro this morning," Pa answered quickly, then thinking how he would describe his newly contemplated domicile, he added, "We're leavin' Georgia, goin' down to Lake Okeechobee. Gotta make a living. This is my wife Mabel, by the way. I hope Mabel makes it the whole way with us. She's not too happy to be leaving—she loves Georgia and I don't know but what we'll be back real soon," Pa said as a sorta apologetic defense to the family's up and abandoning a state whose devoted citizens included the two people to whom he was conversing. "I'm Lewis Thompson, friend, how are you?" This is my eldest daughter, Earlene, my eldest son, Roger—and I think you've already met Georgia Marie, my little girl. That rascal over yonder, pointing to Ray, "is my baseball player—and this is Baby Melrose, sort of showed up unexpected a few months back," Pa smiled sheepishly when indicating his unplanned, but certainly not unwelcome, newcomer to the family.

Mr. Fountain muttered "Hello," as he nodded to first one, then the others, and Dorothy, "Nice to know y'all," with a charitable smile and nod to the kids. Fountain then turned his attention to the baby whose black, curly hair was piled in waves on top of his long, handsome head, and whose olive skin looked different from the fairer skinned Mabel who had a few freckles dotting her fair complexion. "So you're the newest, are you?" the man asked Baby Melrose, who looked back at the man's big hand as he stuck it out to touch the baby. "Mama, that boy's gonna have a head of hair the girls will swoon over one day. Kinda like you did mine thirty years ago," as Phil looked at Dorothy, smiling. "Look at that baby's hair," the man commanded his wife. "Purdy—I mean purdy." She responded with a gentle nod, gazing lovingly at the curls. "She tells me I got wavy hair. One waves at the other," the balding Phil, obviously a self-deprecating, humble man, joked. The crowd, his wife chief among them, had a light chuckle that engendered camaraderie.

"So you goin' catfishin' down to the big lake?" Phil inquired, obviously intrigued by a family trek of this sort, and of such great distance.

"Yea, you know peanuts hadn't done much up in Emanuel County last few years. I been workin' with my daddy, but between the credit man at the mercantile store and the county tax man, there's not a whole lotta profit once the harvest is done. I been croppin' with him for six years now. Started out workin' with a mechanic over in Vidalia, but that wudn't for me. Didn't have the patience to work on a car. No future in that 'cept for greasy hands. No, sir. Got outta that, fast. You gotta be born to fix things, I don't care what it is, and the good Lord didn't bless me with that talent. Daddy talked me into croppin' with him. We did a'right some years, but there's got to be a more lucrative way. Got three brothers and my two sisters' husbands tryin' to eat off the family farm. This place's got promise down there—this Lake. You been down there?" Pa asked, obviously self-conscious of his prattling, anxious to relinquish conversation to his host.

"No, I haven't, but a cousin of mine named Rich Cowart—he's down somewhere near there. He's done good, real good," Fountain reported as Pa listened now more intently than ever. "I got a letter from ole Rich about a month ago. "Said they were fixin' to try and drain some huge—I forget how many acres he said—some big chunks of land to farm watermelon. "Said that land was real good for watermelons."

"That's around Immokalee," Pa answered immediately, obviously up on his research of the area. "They grow some big watermelon around Immokalee," he reiterated. "The area we're goin to is just east and somewhat north of there. We're literally on the banks of the big lake. There's catfish, there's bream and there's largemouth bass. Brother, if you like to fish, it's a paradise!" And then, there's the Atlantic ocean forty-three miles east and the Gulf of Mexico eighty miles west. Lord only knows what fish are in those!" Lewis exclaimed.

"You know, I just thought about it, my wife's got a cousin down there works on a dredge. Dot, what's the name of that Cape ole' Boatright's workin' on?" Phil asked his wife, interrupting her as she and Mabel compared cornbread recipes, he contemplating with furrowed brow, his teeth gently biting his lower lip.

"Sabel," Mrs. Fountain answered swiftly and with certainty in her voice.

"Cape Sabel is right," Mr. Fountain quickly confirmed. "Anyway, her cousin Boatright is a digger on a dredge boat. It's a floating dredge. It's not like a regular crane or dragline, it's like a boat actually floating in the water but with this big huge scooper that digs ahead of it to burrow all those canals they're trying to drain the water into. It's a big ole boom they use to reclaim swampland. They're draining all that land, sellin' it for big money. Developers gettin' rich. He's the head man on the crane operation. Told me last time he was up to Georgia they stayed out with the most God-awful mosquitoes in the middle of these islands, I think he called 'em hammocks. Clump after clump of cypress trees a lot like we have right here in the Okefenokee. Said the roads down there, if that's what you wanna call 'em, are this grayish mess, like clay—marl. Said it's slick as greased oil. A car could slide all over the place when it's wet," Fountain related.

"That sure sounds like our Georgia clay," Lewis added.

"Her cousin, if I'm remembering right, lives out there on that thing for two days at a time, then he's off for a couple of days. The workers ferry themselves back-and-forth from the dredge in a little rowboat to a hotel with these bunks he said are rough as corn cobs, about six miles away through this sawgrass, half water, half land. He said he heard tell of an ole settler around there say 'hit's too wet for farmin' and too dry for fishing.'

"That 'bout sums it up from what I saw," Lewis confirmed.

"Takes half a day to get to-and-fro the dredge boat to the hotel; that's the reason for the long shifts when they do work. He was tellin' me that they have these iron frames that come out like an 'A' shape on each side of the boom to anchor to shore—supports the boat while they're dredging the land to make a channel—a canal. Operates on steam, y' know. Got these big ole locomotive boilers to power the machinery and an electric generator to give 'em lights. Said his crane man, I think he called it a crane man, was his assistant. His job was to control that big ole dipper—that huge scoop that digs up the dirt and puts it over on the bank. He's called a crane man because of the bird, the crane that stands on one foot. Seems he has to use one of his feet as well as his hands to pull his shifter lever back and forth," Fountain rambled, relating as best his memory served from

talking to his wife's cousin a couple of years earlier.
"Let me tell you, brother," Lewis interjected, "there's
swamp land to be reclaimed. It's not gonna be too
long before you see folks movin' down there in droves.
They're clearin' land, sellin' off the wood, drainin' the
wetlands, buildin' canals just like you're talkin' about.
A lot of travel though is still by boat. They have these
boatsmen and fishermen that practically own the lake
area. Get around the south edge of the big lake by
riverboat or steamboat. And their mail. Haul vegetables
'cross the lake. Trappers get their skins across by steamboat. They're tryin' to put in some roads, but it's just
too plag-gone wet. Got a lot more drainin' to do before
any roads other than the kind you just mentioned are in
place," Lewis explained. "I've even heard tell of some big
plan to channel all the water by drainin' it with these
huge pumps into the canals, and then control the water
level with floodgates or dams of sorts. They release
the water into Lake Okeechobee durin' the rainy season
when water gets too high."

"I remember my wife's cousin talkin about these real
bright colored tree snails," Fountain remembered.
"Unusual creatures. Then, the orchids—purple, red,
yellow, some all mixed—growin' in lots of places. All
kinds of tropical plants. Fruit trees with peach-like
fruit, mangrove, or mango, I think he called them. Said
not only was the fruit delicious, but it cured his ulcers in
two weeks."

"Mango," Lewis nodded, adding "delicious fruit."

"Your mangrove are these thick bushes that grow in
the salt water," Lewis added. "There's a river called *Alligator River* littered with islands of mangrove clumps.
Roots grow above and below water. 'Em waters full of

gators. Course that's nothin' for y'all around here, y'all see gators all the time in the Okefenokee Swamp.

"If I'm not badly mistaken, he mentioned something about crocodiles down there, too," Fountain recalled. "You know gators we got aren't like those crocodile gators around the Amazon River."

"They're a lot more vicious than your American alligators," Lewis instructed, adding, "They say some of them are man-eaters."

"But I'm sure ole Boatright said they got 'em down there. Man, I think you better do some real thinkin' fore you up and leave," Fountain warned. "Our good peaches. Our pecans. Boiled peanuts. You thought about our boiled peanuts? You gonna be able to get good Georgia stuff like that down there?" Mr. Fountain asked in a lighthearted manner, but with a measure of concern for the family and this monumental expedition.

"Civilization's movin' in there. Two nights a week, mailboat services the local post office," Lewis altered the conversation with subtlety.

"Postmaster's purdy smart too, 'cause she also owns a grocery and dry goods store. Customer comes for his mail, buys a month's supply of groceries. And, don't forget, purdy much anything grows in that muck," Lewis added.

"She, did you say?" Fountain reacted to the pronoun Lewis had just referenced.

"Yeah, and I hear no man better ever cross her or mess with her livelihood," Lewis laughed.

"Yes sir, and those trappers and farmers make money," he added. "And, she can do business with the roughest of them. There's otter, coon, and gator skins that require shipping, not to mention the crates of bell peppers and hampers of pole beans. The early settlers live right next to the lake on what's known as bottom land. They and the island residents are slowly becoming outnumbered by those on the mainland."

After a night of convivial togetherness, including a table laden with bowls of sweet potatoes, corn-on-the cob, lima beans, rice with tomato gravy, a platter of fried chicken, and plates of cornbread, the family all seemingly slept soundly, all, that is, except Lewis. Remembering Mr. Fountain's admonitions, he wondered whether he should turn the car around, head back to Swainsboro, and plant that crop of sweet onions his uncle Walter was planning to grow in the spring. They are the "crop of the future," Walter had proclaimed, "owing to the mildness due to that soil around Toombs, Emanuel, Tattnall, Bulloch, and Candler counties. Lots of men gonna get rich off them sweet onions," he concluded. If Walter knew Lewis wanted to grow onions, he'd gladly put him to work.

Before he dozed, Lewis forbade his mind to ponder further on sweet onions. He was set on that frontier wilderness with its sawgrass, mangrove swamps, slippery marl roads, canals, steamboats, dredges and huge scoopers, cypress hammocks, catfish, black muck, butterbeans and pole beans all year round. Somehow, he would deal with alligators that dive underwater, suddenly to confront a man at the canal bank, and the bloodsucking mosquitoes, whose voracious appetites killed cattle—suffocated them by crowding their nostrils. Lewis imagined, as he drifted to sleep, a mosquito biting though that thick and bumpy reptilian hide.

This was his adventure. It was true that he might be

caging himself into a predicament from which escape would be impossible. But, he believed a wise bird happily accepts imprisonment over the perils of nature's freedom. His life could be better than it had been or else he wouldn't be moving. He wouldn't have kept that little tattered, yellowed article from the magazine. He sure would not have packed a family he adored into the old Star and headed even as far as Waycross, down a road of no return. Lewis had more than a modicum of hope for a more prosperous existence, despite the protestations of a wife whose equal certainty was for a life filled with greater despair than the one they were departing. He knew the heart is overly full in most people, while their heads are comparatively empty. He hoped that wasn't true of him.

Chapter Twenty-one

Next day, driving, Pa related news about some of the earlier settlers by telling whoever was listening that "the lake farmers didn't own land. They were squatters. They sharecrop the Negroes," he continued. "The squatter furnishes a few acres and a mule. Might throw in some seed and beat-up equipment, and then go in halves. Course, squatters had their shotguns loaded just in case the law fell through."

The pioneers truly had begun to own the land through the process of adverse possession, especially Hans Rhine, a native of Courland on the Bay of Riga, an inland area of water connected to the Baltic Sea. Many of the colonists to overseas lands had come from this tiny European nation. Hans Rhine had known that a better life awaited him across the vast Atlantic.

———

Packing his buoyancy compensator and regulator, Doss was ready to head back to the Keys. Since Aaron and he competed for the prize, he was thrilled the boy could make the trip.

Doss still dreamed of one day photographing a comb jelly, but he was told about another marine life that would surely win, if caught in the right light and at a propitious angle: The *Royal Star,* a starfish, another invertebrate, was foremost in his mind this trip. Doss thought as he drove how nice to be living in south Georgia—within a day's drive of Key Largo. Such a variety of marine life was visible in that clear water, and he only wished he had appreciated the proximity of *Pennekamp* marine wildlife refuge when he was growing up in Belle Glade all those years ago—why hadn't he dived then?

To see the Royal starfish—in its native habitat—that would be a treat. Any hope of a comb jelly was out, since the season was a little late for it. Doss took his middle son Aaron as his dive buddy, hoping David could join the two.

As he had matured, Doss focused less on girls, cars, and football. Worldly interests had yielded to ones of profundity.

His attention these days tended towards three diverse, yet somehow interrelated concepts: molecular life, geologic time, and interstellar distance. He was kinda OCD—wasn't that the acronym for obsessive people? Especially about *Proxima Centauri*. "The word *proxima* means "nearest" in Latin, and it is a red dwarf star that lies closest to Earth--a mere 4.25 light years away," he explained to Aaron. "While it's small and faint and can't even be seen with the naked eye—it's about 15% the size of the Sun—it does occasionally get brighter due to a magnetic field that allows it to appear to fade in and out. Its close companions are *Alpha Centauri A* and *Alpha Centauri B*, considered binary stars. *Proxima* is a third star within the Alpha Centauri system and since it's a fifth of a light year from the other two, or, a distance of three and a half light months, many scientists wonder if it's correctly categorized as even part of the Alpha system," he explained.

"Astronomers are not sure that Proxima is bound by gravitation to the other two, and if it's not, it may wander off and leave the twins in a few million years," Doss continued. "Our Sun is eight light *minutes* from Earth, and it would take months to reach it, traveling the speed Apollo Ten did, roughly 25,000 miles per hour. At that same speed, Proxima could be arrived at in 80,000 years," Doss related to David. "The Great Pyramids in Egypt were built roughly 7,000 years ago. If a traveler had left Earth then, only a mere 73,000 years would remain before arrival. The *nearest* star. "Then, what about the furthest star? How long to get there? Did stars exist in perpetuity? Did space?" he often cogitated. Only creatures trapped by finitude worried themselves with infinity, the man thought. 'But' Doss reassured himself, 'only smart people pondered such imponderables, right?'

Then there were the small things. Doss's mind wandered to those too. Viruses, bacteria, and protozoa. He had read recently that some bacteria were smaller than some viruses. That single-cell form of life, bacteria, represents life at its most basic. And the earliest of those was anaerobic, Doss had learned, meaning that oxygen was unnecessary for survival, and probably would have proved toxic. It's the *aerobic* form of life that breathes oxygen and expels carbon dioxide. That great symbiosis between plants and animals probably came about due to the waste of plants—oxygen. Then, the virus. Not even one cell. Not even living. No metabolic system. Just a bundle of genes within a protective protein shell. Dependent on a host's cells to reproduce. Doss's mind drifted to the atom. How big? The nucleus of an atom would be akin to a flea in the middle of a giant cathedral, and that cathedral would be the outer electron shell. Everything besides the flea and the cathedral would be empty space: Nothing. "So, the great majority of everything is nothing. Mere empty space," Doss Neesh concluded.

Doss also knew that the vast preponderance of life forms that had existed at some point, were now extinct —over 99% in fact. Five billion, 300 million forms of existence had now disappeared from Earth forever. And, of the thirteen million forms of life currently in existence, nearly 90% have never been described—roughly 11 million species never identified.

Just over a million forms of life have been named and categorized according to *domain, kingdom, phylum, subphylum, class, order, family, genus,* and *species.* Human beings are of the kingdom *Animalia*, phylum *Chordata,* subphylum *Vertebrata,* class *Mammalia,* order *Primates,* family *Homininæ,* genus *Homo,* species *Homo sapiens.* The first and broadest category for humans and other animals is *Eukaryota*, a grouping that requires genetic material—DNA—be enclosed in a nuclear membrane. In contrast, the *Prokarycote,* such as bacterium, lack the membrane around the all-important DNA. There were prokaryotic microbes found in deep-water volcanic plumes of hot water, *smokers,* one of the most inhospitable places that existence could be imagined.

The taxonomy for dogs tracks that of humans, but diverges as it funnels downward: *Eukaryota, Animalia, Chordata, Vertebrata, Mammalia, Carnivora, Canidae, Canus, Canus Lupus, Canus lupus, familiaris.*

———

En route to the dive, Doss passed over a bridge

from which Lake Okeechobee could be seen, headed toward Belle Glade. He thought about the star-shaped Royal Star-the echinoderm he hoped to take a picture of. It belonged to the class *Asteroidea*—starfish. There were over a thousand species on Earth and their habitat ranged from tropical waters, which most of the Indian Ocean is comprised of, to those that flow around Antarctica, where the coldest deep ocean water has been recorded. Cod and Tuna survive in abundant schools in cold water, thanks to the phosphorus and nitrogen-fueled phytoplankton upon which zooplankton eat. And, there is dissolved oxygen and other gases that warm water just can't hold, thanks to the fast-moving molecules that zigzag hither and thither, literally jostling the murky gas from the water. Because of phytoplankton, those tiny plants, and zooplankton, those minute animals, the cold waters of northern climes are rarely clear, and in fact, are abundantly cloudy—but not the Keys.

Tropical green clear seas have few of those cold water plankton, either photo- or zoo- hanging around in the water—that was Keys water. In fact, the clarity of the salty, turquoise liquid owes much to a poverty of nutrients. Coral, in all its beauty with its deep purples, bright oranges, scarlet reds, and lime greens, abound in sediment-free water, and can't live in oceans with phosphates or nitrates. In fact, scuba divers curse pollution and its nutrients that seep into crystal waters, because algae then explode. Algae has chlorophyll, a green pigment that permits a transformation of photosynthetic light energy into chemical energy to fuel the activity of the algae. They range from one-celled aquarium and swimming pool nuisances (that have to be scraped periodically) to the multi-cellular kelp off the coast of California. While necessary in small amounts, blooms of green algae threaten to overtake and strangle coral.

———

Adult starfish are marine invertebrates, as are jellyfish. They are found at every depth of the ocean—from intertidal to abyssal zones. Along with its central disc, there are usually five arms with the upper surface or aboral being rough or smooth, oftentimes spiny. Some starfish have more than five arms—one has nine—and is called the Nine-Armed Sea Star, *Luidia senegalensi.* One starfish has forty arms. Arms can be shed defensively when a predator threatens, and can typically regenerate.

Aaron, too, wanted to see a Royal Starfish—an *Astropecten articulatus*—with its vivid purple and yellow-orange coloration. They can survive at depths exceeding 500 feet. Most can be found between 50 and 90 feet. Its favorite diet, mollusks, are consumed whole. Doss had promised David that they would dive a wreck, the *Janice,* upon which a Royal had been spotted by a diver a week ago.

"What we don't want to see," Doss told David, "is a starfish such as ones between southern California and Alaska that are afflicted with 'wasting disease', taking a toll on starfish along Pacific coastlines," he explained to the boys. "Detached arms can be seen crawling away from a creature's body." Doss had read about this disease described in an article he had read by a biologist. A ghoulish image. "Reminds you of the cattle of Helios, that both Tiresias and Circe had warned Odysseus about in Homer's epic story," Doss related to Aaron. "Disregarding orders, Odysseus's company enjoyed the beef roasted on the spit, with skins that began to creep and flesh that began to bellow "moos." Meat dead, cut up, and cooked but still moving and speaking. Ugh."

After seeing the big lake, Doss wandered into a trance thinking about his mother and father. His imagination began to visualize scenes that might have taken place when Cory, Percy, and Peter, had scurried across Lake Okeechobee nearly a century earlier. The stories Cory had told Doss all his life, still reverberated: *Corona* wasn't the only steamboat on the Lake in the early 1920's--far from it. There were the *Belle of Myers, Free Lance, Alice Howard, Floridelphia, Arbuckle, Poinsettia, Uneeda, Norma, Floweree, Chindy, Planter Success, Thomas A. Edison, Grey Eagle, Suwane*e. Steamboats were already abundant on Lake Okeechobee.

From Peter's chubby left cheek, a small brown mole protruded, one that Cory always seemed to notice when he looked at the old man's face. His complexion was ruddy with tiny red veins coursing and crisscrossing near the surface of his cheeks and nose from too many sun-drenched days on the boat. Percy's complexion, in contrast, was aged and gray. It was lined and weathered. Excessive liquor, excessive sun. Percy's was darker but somehow redder at the same time. That the son drank heavily was not surprising. Peter's rantings practically demanded strong drink, although Percy imbibed from other stresses, one of which was the angst engendered by deep thought. Ideas and theories seldom, if ever, left his pondering. Another was his desire for a woman—a woman he had no time for, given his maritime duties.

Chapter Twenty-two

Light streamed more darkly now from the late after-noon sun, the kind that brings memories of things done and undone—all those sunsets—days dead and moments past. One particular beam glared semi-brightly and shone on the red oak cabinet. Percy noticed a wavy pattern repeated in the wood grain that resembled an upside-down mountain laid with purpose but whose intentionality was negated by its randomness. A small speck of dust floated into the bright ray, disrupting his daydream.

Percy's laughter and smile did not come often to Peter's stern face. Peter had a sense of humor and appreciated a good laugh—mostly in the form of a bawdy joke. Captain Peter worked hard at keeping this floating freight hauler moving and productive. But it was Percy who rose early, loaded heavy fruit crates, unloaded them, washed and scrubbed the deck. Peter, on the other hand, negotiated rates and routes, and tolerated little silliness. Both men lived and breathed mariners' terms and lingo, but it was Percy who could still be a kid. He would join a game of work-up baseball on those rare occasions when he could be lured off the boat.

———

As he drove through Belle Glade, Doss reminisced about his days as a young teenager when Lawrence

E. Will had written all those great books about the Lake and its steamboats, skippers, hurricanes, natural beauty, ways and customs. Will was continually writing, then speaking to public groups about what he had written, and Doss had absorbed those thoughts. He particularly loved that Will had included his daddy's family and their steamboat trade in the book *Okeechobee Boats & Skippers*.

"We had more boats here than Carter had liver pills, and we had some skippers who were legends in their own day and time," Will wrote. "Lake Okeechobee was the last stomping grounds for steamboats in Florida. Those smoke boats once had splashed their way on every watercourse in the state, always just one jump ahead of civilization, but when water was drained off these Everglades and folks started to settle here, those wet-ass (Will had used the term 'wet-tail') boats were the first to bring them in across the lake and down those new dug canals," Will recounted.

In one of the several books that Doss had read, and which Will had even autographed to him, Will told the story of how "Lake Okeechobee was plumb surrounded by the impassible Everglades on its southern half, by swamps and marshes on its other sides. It was only in a few places on its north side that horseback or ox team travel was possible at all. Catfishing was the only business on the big lake in those early days, but then Everglades land was put on sale and 'hard-hatted Yankee tourists' came here to view the 'Everglades Promised Land,' and every blessed one of them came by boat. It wasn't long before settlements began to spring up along the shore and on those Glades canals. For a right long spell of years, boats were the only transportation for these settlers and for the tomatoes and beans and peppers which they raised," Will recorded.

Doss remembered asking Will one day near Christmas 1966, when the two passed walking on the sidewalk, why steamboats had become obsolete.

"Steamboats needed big crews because the boiler and engine were at opposite ends of the deck. There had to be both a fireman and an engineer, as well as the pilot in the wheelhouse overhead," Will explained. "A gasoline engine boat, on the other hand, needed only a pilot and an engineer."

"So gas was more efficient?" Doss affirmed.

"Much more so," Will emphasized. "And, you wanna know something, son? No skipper was ever called 'Captain' unless he had a passenger run, and mighty few even wore a boatman's cap. They didn't want those country folks to think they put on airs because they ran a boat."

"However," Will recalled, "steam engines were as reliable as could be. It's true that it took a plumb good fireman to keep a head of steam. Those ungodly early gasoline engines, in comparison, were big one or two cylinder heavy duty jobs—two cycle types. A cylinder would fire each time the piston came up. The firing points were inside the cylinder, and the electricity was furnished by five dry batteries and a low tension coil —nothing more than turns and twists of copper wire around an iron core. Water posed no danger with this ignition system as it would with later four cycle versions. So, gas power was popular, especially in open launches. But, until the four-cycle engines, with valves and spark plugs, timers and high tension coils, even a religious man would want to cuss—or cry," Will remembered. "The four cycles were a heap of improvement, though you had to keep that engine dry. Most of them had only a single cylinder and a huge and heavy flywheel. You'd hear the exhaust explode with an ear-shattering 'Pow!'" the balding, intellectual, bespectacled Will remembered, scratching his head as he looked up to the lower part of the sky talking to Doss as the two stood in Belle Glade those many years before. "Later on, we had two, three, and four cylinder engines, and after awhile, some sixes, but I recollect only a couple of Diesels on the lake—a dredge company's tug and a freighter."

Lawrence Will told the story in one of his books of the *Bertha Lee*, a 130-foot steamboat, the biggest ever on the Lake, which had been brought from New Orleans:

"As fur as you could see, thar weren't nothing but wet prairie both here and yonder in the fur distance, a trifling cypress hammock, and a clump of swamp cabbage trees," the author related, slipping into his mostly acquired native dialect, for he had come originally from Maine or one of those New England states. "Strange lookin' water plants crowded along each river bank, whilst ducks and cranes and pond birds by the hundreds, stalked and swum and flew off in plumb clouds as the boat would approach. There was all them by-channels, cutoffs, and dead rivers a-ziggin' and a-zaggin' among the water bonnets and flags and reeds, with a narrow channel crookeder than 'ary snake, and with a current so sluggish that you couldn't tell which the main channel was. This river was the beatenest that ole Captain Hall of the *Bertha Lee* had ever seed. Further up it narrowed some, but thar was some of the most bodacious long bends where you could steam ahead an hour or two to gain a hundred yards. Yes, Siree," Will continued, "this was a new kind of river to Cap'n Hall, and he soon begun to wish that he and that monstrosity of a boat was back on the good ole Mississippi."

So, Peter had been wise to avoid a big boat, and aim instead for speed. His boat was thirty-three feet in length, and with 120 pounds of steam, it could move six miles an hour. A couple of brothers had the vast majority of the river business, but they didn't have it all. Peter and Percy had carved a niche for themselves and their steamboat, despite sullen glances from already established skippers who resented any competition. The men worked—and played—with enthusiasm and steadfastness.

The work-up baseball game Percy loved to indulge in when he could snatch himself from the toil of the boat, involved picking numbers, one through seven or eight. The number one player got to bat, then after scoring a run or striking out, move himself to the highest number defensive spot, typically right field, all the while working himself up to again becoming a batter, while playing increasingly more desirable positions —pitcher, first base, catcher. Cory's cousins typically talked the old man and Percy into playing the game on their monthly family get-togethers. In later years, Peter demurred more frequently.

Percy was a kid in many ways. Rhetta wasn't sure he ever wanted to grow up—or old. Not only did he love baseball with the boys, the respite from hauling cargo he found immensely refreshing. Percy's life philosophy revolved around leaving the world a better place— 'more edified and enlightened,' much as 'Aristotle, Newton and John Locke had done,' the man would intone. Always pulling for the underdog, the disadvantaged, or anyone he thought of as such, Percy craved abundance of wisdom and minimal material wealth. The man had nothing but antipathy for the robber barons, a term that originally applied to German lords of medieval times who demanded toll on any pathway traversing their land. A lack of ethics had permeated Cornelius Vanderbilt's business around the turn of the twentieth century, according to many. Vanderbilt, Carnegie and Astor, were all monopolists who loved to crush any hint of competition. They rigged markets and did all they could to corrupt politicians. Percy thought of them as conniving, greedy rascals who in their avarice cheated and robbed in a predatory rat race comprised of a combination robber-rat and a baron-rat. A baron, of course, was "illegitimate in an anti-monarchial republic—what the USA was supposed to be," Percy would preach.

His ancestors in the post-slavery South had adapted to war's tumultuous aftermath. That was an admirable feat, Percy believed. He felt both former Confederates and former slaves overcame great hardships and humiliating adversity after the war. Percy admired the way his great-grandparents revamped a semblance of community in the face of carpetbaggers' malicious stunts. Vicious acts of ridicule and oppression with which the Northerners seemed to enjoy torturing them, had been met with a gentile stoicism. He lacked the vitriolic hatred for that group that his father still proudly harbored. Nonetheless, he believed that Southern society of that time lay utterly destroyed by a systematic rebellion of Northern outsiders and troublemakers. Percy had no appreciation for the realities of the system of slavery. He never profited in any commercial enterprise perpetrated by selling Negroes. Percy wondered if what he had heard was true: that slaves had been destined to work in the industrialized world of factories up North. Supposedly, they were not practical workers in that mechanized environment for which they were initially intended. If true, and slaves had succeeded in the North's mechanization, Percy imagined a reversal of history in which he would have fought with the Confederacy to free them.

Cory remembered one of Peter's heated tirades to Percy, strongly asserting that, "Slaves orta be appreciative of their white captors whose acts of snatching them onto ships, freed them from an inhumane savagery. And never did one of my granddaddy's slaves want for food, shelter, medicine, or comfort," he swore. "No one" Peter told Percy, "at least in my family, ever mistreated a slave in the way depicted by books written by those damned Yankees, most of whom have never been south of southern Ohio." It was Peter's firm belief that those books delighted in painting the Southerner as a crude, cruel, ignorant and sadistic misanthrope. Percy knew that some slave owners did engage in acts of bullying and cruelty, but was proud that he had neither seen nor heard of such from his family—even from distant relatives. Percy made a conscious effort to treat with kindness former slaves with whom he interacted, owing to an innate judgment that the institution was illegitimate.

While indeed an empathetic supporter of the less well off in society, Percy was convinced that Negroes had been better off in a system of benevolent indentured servitude than they were in post-slavery times, trapped as they were in what he called "invisible bars" owing to unspoken Jim Crow rules denying them basic rights. After all, he thought, they had no access to power, education, or the means to succeed. "Thrown into an alien environment unprepared to be free citizens, was harsh on the race" he conjectured. Not to mention the relative safety and prosperity from a tribal existence replete with barbarity, from which they had been "salvaged," as he was wont to say—making their escape aboard slave ships leaving Africa.

Despite these opinions, Percy had told Cory on several occasions, "Indians were victims of the white man, way more than kidnapped Africans." He would always conclude with, "White man should have kept his ass in Europe."

Peter still held deep grudges and was proud and satisfied in his prejudices, unlike Percy, who accepted, admitted, and even analyzed his frailties and resolved to better himself and to mitigate through copious reading any bias he held.

"After all," he once conjectured to his father, "hadn't so many great participants of history been significantly flawed? "'Hadn't Napoleon overcome short stature and an inferiority complex, and Jefferson the loss of several children and a wife? Hadn't Lincoln overcome severe bouts of depression to find success in politics?" he asked his father one day when Peter had demanded that he "leave the rum alone."

"Don't you ever mention that scalawag's name in my presence," Peter scolded.

"Who you talkin' about?" Percy demanded, surprised.

"That damned Lincoln. Do you realize he ruined

us? He ravaged the South. You should have seen what things were like before that sumbitch devastated it. He pillaged Georgia—that damned Sherman did, anyway. He burnt Ivanhoe—ruined my Mama and Papa. "Don't quote me no damned Abraham Lincoln," Peter ranted vociferously. He had disowned a niece who married a man with the first name of Sherman—Sherman Taylor. "Never will I talk to that little bitch again," he had vowed.

The old Captain's white beard covered those rounded, seemingly benevolent, baby-faced cheeks and a square jaw whose slight twitching betrayed underlying feelings of indignation and bitterness at the loss of his ancestral homestead—remnants of memories in tattered fragments. Distant recollections of the Antebellum South he lived as a little boy were vague, but the strong hatred among his beloved kinfolks whom he remembered as kind and loving, lived on vicariously through their tales of defeat. He often thought about how pre-war prosperity had been replaced by misery and scourge.

Percy should have known better than to mention Lincoln. The old man had a temper and Percy knew he resented Yankees—resented Lincoln as the very emblem of that tribe. Most of all, Percy durst not mention Sherman—"that son-of-a-bitchin' animal," in Peter's mind. Then, Percy's mind drifted to the beautiful signature and handwriting of William Tecumseh Sherman. Percy read the letter Sherman had written to Lincoln. Big words. Fancy phrases. Beautiful calligraphy. He was an educated and cultivated 'son-of-a-bitchin' animal', who had famously portrayed war as hell, and nothing to be romanticized about, and something to be avoided at all costs. But, "If it came to war," Percy had read, the General intended to "make it as brutal and hurtful as can be on the other side." Percy silently admired that about the man—about any man who did his job to the utmost. Sherman had a mission, no matter how ill-advised to men like Peter, and he executed it cunningly and masterfully, though with dreadful consequences for those Southerners in his path. In a word, Percy didn't share his father's complete detestation against Lincoln, or the Yankees, or even against Sherman, though that latter name could rouse mild discomfiture in even Percy's imperturbable temperament.

Percy was determined to be content and live in peace. He perceived life's evanescence. Happiness wasn't a destination, but rather, a manner of traveling. And, he knew that enjoyment in small, commonplace endeavors was the height of happiness. Even in rare displays of anger, there seemed little threat from this kind man with a nicely shaped nose, a handsome head full of hair, and laughing green eyes.

Percy's father Peter had not been a captain from any military service. His great-great-grandfather William most certainly had been—a Revolutionary War hero whose raid on the Tories in a battle near Yorktown helped wear down the resistance of the British. Peter enjoyed bragging about the bridge across the Ogeechee River in Georgia that had been named for his famous ancestor. As a youngster, Peter enjoyed hearing stories from his grandfather Robert about Captain William and his exploits on and off the battlefield. "Captain did this, or that," or "What would Captain have thought or done? "Hadn't Captain been handpicked by God, or at least by someone high in his command?" Peter decided early on that 'Captain' before his name would sound right nice, so he honored himself accordingly when he passed his navigational course and purchased *Corona* nearly a decade earlier.

After he determined that the boat was well under control and that his services wouldn't be needed for a time, Percy settled back to read *A History of the American People* by Woodrow Wilson. Wilson had only a couple years earlier been replaced as President of the United States by Warren G. Harding, who had died even more recently. Calvin Coolidge was now President. Percy read in the book's introduction that Wilson had lived in Augusta, Georgia, and married in Savannah.

Chapter Twenty-three

D oss thought about the sports bar he had visited a year earlier, having left his two sons asleep in room 543, exhausted from a rigorous day of scuba diving, followed by a night dive with underwater flashlights.

He had heard about a new place that had opened since his visit, and it was touted as having the best key lime pie in the entire Keys. The *Conch* version, no less—egg whites used for a meringue topping. The *Citrus aurantifolia* "Swingle" is abundant in the Florida Keys, and while the bush is thorny, the fruit have an aroma that far exceeds the more common Persian limes, whose acid level is not nearly high enough to make a superb key lime pie. Key lime rind is yellow and not as thick as the green Persians. As such, yellow filling was de rigueur, and the natives were wary if not dismissive of a pie whose filling was green.

In the old days, the reaction between the juice of the Key lime and condensed milk did away with having to bake the pie. The chemical reaction thickens raw eggs, but Doss knew that those could be unsafe. Because of that, it was common, even for the Conch natives in the Keys, to bake the pie for a short time. After all, sponge fishermen, the first Anglo-Europeans to settle the Keys, spent days on end upon their fishing boats, with food stored onboard and neither refrigeration nor oven. It all made sense, Doss thought. He had to have the Conch variety. He'd take his chances. And, the biological name, *Citrus aurantifolia*, often called by its nickname 'Swingle,' sounded familiar. Almost surely the same Walter Tennyson Swingle who had put Kansas State Agricultural College on the map with his genius for agriculture—and produced the *Lake tangelo* that Peter, Percy, and Cory had hauled bushels of near the Cape.

Doss thought of *Bugsy's*, a home-style restaurant in the Alapattah section of Miami that his mother and father used to frequent on their weekly excursions to the big city for their paint store inventory. Its classic dessert feature was Key lime pie, and no matter what else his parents ordered (usually Salisbury steak, roast beef, or chicken paprika), the pie was a must. Doss used to see high school students playing across the street at *Miami Jackson High School*, one of the biggest in Miami, where his brother, from tiny Belle Glade High, had caught three touchdown passes fourteen years earlier to beat the mighty team from the big city. The head-lines of the *Miami Herald* even screamed out the feat in *Golden Rams' Neesh and Flanders Hook up for Triple TD Connections to Overcome the Mighty Generals of Jackson High*. Miami's oldest hospital, not a half mile away, was *Jackson Memorial*, and it was there that an elected, though not yet inaugurated, Franklin D. Roosevelt had been taken twenty-five years earlier after a bullet had missed him but hit and later killed the mayor of Chicago, Anton Cermak.

Andrew Jackson, that Indian-hating, Indian-hunting believer—nay, promoter—of *Manifest Destiny*, was popular in Florida, as was Zachary Taylor, his chief lieutenant. The Euro-Americans owed their settlement in the lower peninsula to those Indian-removers.

Chapter Twenty-four

I n 1960, six-year old Doss watched the Jackson High School students chasing, tagging, and wrestling one another on the playground across the street from *Bugsy's*. Some were squealing, others moving randomly across the way, some carrying textbooks. Doss's mother remembered a story about their travels from Georgia to Florida to resettle in 1924. As Doss's mother cut and then ate a piece of her chicken-fried steak, she reminisced about the trip. Her family had stopped at a boarding house to spend the night, and eaten supper—at which she had also dined on chicken-fried steak. On that dreary occasion, so many decades ago, her heart heavy and somber at leaving her grandmother in Georgia, she remembered a great deal more: The Georgia family had been driving for almost an hour when their Pa reminded them to look for the 'Welcome to Florida' sign.

Breakfast had consisted of milk gravy and biscuits for the Georgia travelers, and even baby Melrose had eaten heartily, his face and hands slathered with white slop. Earlene alone had ordered chicken fried steak with grits and toast. The breaded cutlet was coated with flour and seasoning and then fried. There was, in fact, no chicken. Rather, cube steak was coated much like fried chicken - so popular in the South. It had a similar taste and texture to *wiener schnitzel*, the pride of Viennese cuisine, though Austrians use veal cutlet. Another similar dish is the Italian *milanesa*, which can be coated veal, pork or beef. The Scots consume a dish quite regularly called *collops*, which is either beef, lamb, or venison. Collops, a dish Robert Louis Stevenson mentioned in his book *Kidnapped*, is typically garnished with a thin toast and oftentimes accompanied by mashed potatoes.

Thinking back to how courteous and hospitable the Fountains had been as hosts, welcoming them into their tourist home, Earlene lamented that she had forgotten her dress. Mabel later berated the teenager for leaving behind the brown-spotted gingham garment, but then relented and told her instead, "Forget about it, what's done is done, and we're sure not going back for that." Earlene remembered the way Mr. Fountain had described the place to which they were headed and was appreciative that her father had received from those hosts what he needed most of all—conversation.

After the visit, Lewis subdued any misgivings about their move, and the swamps and mosquitoes, the possible crocodiles, the slippery marl roads, and God knows what else. Some passengers riding in the car had trepidation, some, enthusiasm, and one held definite reservations and disappointment. Of that clan, despite disparate attitudes of uncertainty, "we still headed south," Earlene remembered over the Miami lunch.

She remembered Pa telling the kids: "If y'all keep your eyes open, you'll see the state sign here directly."

"Who cares about a sign? I just wanna know when we're gonna get there, Pa," said Marie, with more than a hint of impatience.

"Honey, this idn't a trip like over to Soperton or

somethin.' It's gonna take all of today, and we may have to spend another night."

"Well I certainly hope we don't have to spend another night," Mabel piped up, "I thought we'd be there by tonight," she added.

"We're gonna be there by tonight, I was tryin' to let her know it's a long way."

"It's an eternity," Mabel complained, claiming the last word.

"Let me tell y'all a story that might help pass the time," Lewis suggested, looking halfway back at his two smaller children, then watching their reactions in his rearview mirror.

"That land down there where we're goin' is real wet, like I told y'all. There's these big ole tall stalks like sugarcane that they call sawgrass, that has saw-like teeth on the edges."

"That sounds real inviting," Mabel interjected sourly.

"No, this is out in the uncultivated, wilderness type areas where they haven't reclaimed the land yet," he assured his still skeptical wife.

"Anyway, there's this wild grass called maidencane, I reckon it's an offshoot of our chewin' cane in Georgia, but it's smaller and you don't chew it. It's just a bigger version of your Johnson grass, sort of a cousin to the sorghum plant. Well, clumps of this sawgrass-like maidencane grow around wet areas on out towards the lake where the ground is this kind of peat soil. The farmers want to get rid of it. It actually grows in the water. If the water were to dry up, the grass would die. Well anyway, there's just enough water for it to live, and that's what the farmers are up against. They can't fish because the water's too shallow, and they can't grow anything because there's too much water."

"Well if it's wet, how can they grow anything at all?" Marie wisely asked.

"Good question, Little Bit, good question. You know, this is a smart girl we got here Mama," Lewis reminded Mabel they had something of great value in common, even if it wasn't her approval of this move.

"I was gonna ask you that before she cut me off," Earlene interjected.

"Good. Smart girls. I'm prouda' both o' ya. Well, the answer is that once these big huge pumps drain the wetlands, the land will be dry. Maidencane vegetative stems and rhizomes lie underneath the muck. Once they yank those weeds out, get the water gone, the land will be ready to be plowed and start growin' pole beans an' other vegetables. That's one reason the muck is so rich. It's been sittin' under a little layer of water and vegetation all these years. When stalks of this grass eventually die, they lie there and rot, while new stalks shoot out to take their place. Just a continuous feeding of the soil. Nutrients produced in that life and death cycle. That's what makes for its superb growing capacity. It will eventually be prime farmland."

"Why don't they just go out with sling blades or somethin', Pa and hack it up?" Roger asked his father, reminiscing earlier about the weeds he had just trimmed around the old barn in Georgia.

"The problem, son, is their thick roots. They're just like rope. I mean just like rope! And those connecting roots run all over the place. They even call them runners. You gotta get 'em with one of these special tractors, not the one's with regular tires like you see on a tractor in Georgia, but with crawler tracks like on an Army tank. They have this sort of horizontal shaft that goes around underneath with knife-like blades, that not only get the roots, but plows and pulverizes the land all at the same time. I read that it's known as a *whirling knife attachment*. That little invention is what they hope will conquer the Everglades."

"Pa, just what is the Everglades?" Marie asked, hoping for the same affirmation her other query garnered.

"There's a huge sea of grass down there, honey, where no one lives. It's a lot like the Okefenokee Swamp we came through. It's mostly all water with this sawgrass I been tellin' you about. There's these beautiful pink birds that stand on long legs in the shallow water, and these purdy big white birds that wade around and eat small fish from a pond. They're not like our little sparrows and mockingbirds and kildeers you see on the farm in Georgia. They're big. They stand on those long legs and watch and wait for a fish to come along. Fancy women up North love to wear the big white feathers tucked in their ornate hats."

"Oh," Marie responded, satisfied.

"Rivers flow down through this big ole river of grass and move through it and over it and empty into the ocean near the Keys, down there where Florida ends," he added.

"You means Florida ends near where we're going?" Marie asked.

"Well, every state has its border, where it gives way to another state, like how we're fixin' to leave Georgia and come into Florida." Florida is a peninsula, kinda like an island that sits by itself all surrounded by water, but instead of being surrounded on all sides by water,

Florida juts out into the ocean. There's ocean water all around most of it, but not all. That's what makes it a peninsula. And just to think, all those miles of real purdy beaches."

"You mean we're gonna have beaches where we'll be living, Pa?" Earlene asked, daring to let her excitement show itself now and then.

"Don't count on it, kids," Mabel interrupted.

"Well, there's no beach right where we're goin', but there is that lake I told y'all about. It's fresh water, though, not salt water like the ocean. But Lake Okeechobee has a beautiful little beach there near where we'll be, and the water is clear as crystal."

Roger was sound asleep sitting between his mother and father, with a small dribble of drool easing from his lower lip.

Doss had asked Earlene at Bugsy's whether she was excited about moving. "Roger and I had mixed emotions," she told Doss. "We were sad on one hand, yet had anticipation for all the good things Pa had told us about." No one felt completely elated or dejected," Earlene remembered. "Pa made a remark something along the lines of, 'you gain somethin' in every move in life you make, and you lose somethin' too.'"

∞ ∞ ∞

Chapter Twenty-five

Roger had harbored excitement, but doubted any real family prosperity would result from relocating to Florida. He recognized even as a teenager that his father was an idealist whose dreams usually had not translated into any great monetary reward. Roger had an evenness, a uniformity in his attitude towards the world. He figured both great things and terrible things were neither as great nor terrible as they seemed in the moment. Besides, he had sworn fealty to his first girlfriend about three months before Pa decided to move, a girl who swore to him in return that she would love him forever.

The couple had experienced sex in the barn, just a month before the move, he panting with excitement as he fondled her breasts. The girl stroked his upper legs in heated arousal. Soon there were powerful longings and lustful thrusts. In that bundled straw, the teenager proved to himself that while timid, he was adequate as a young lover. She told him how 'luscious' that "first time" had been. It was only later that he wondered, "what did she know, if he had truly been her first lover?" Earlene, hearing the moanings and groanings, had been drawn to where the two were making love, yet said nothing, ever.

Melrose was fussing between his two sisters, and

Earlene's job was to pacify him anytime he needed a bottle or his diaper changed, which seemed to be now.

"Mama, I think the baby needs a fresh one," Earlene gently tapped her mother's arm.

"I think you're right," Mabel noted almost before the girl could get the words out of her mouth.

"Pull over, and let's change the baby," Mabel commanded Lewis, more sternly than she probably would have if she weren't sacrificing so much at his request. She knew who held the upper hand for the next few days, and maybe even months. The moral high ground was hers for awhile, and she intended to take full advantage of it.

Pa obediently pulled the car over at a small dirt driveway, seemingly abandoned and largely grown over with grassy weeds. The little shack at the end of the path seemed abandoned, but almost immediately, a thirty-ish or so African-American woman came out the front door and started over to the stopped car, to offer help.

"Y'all all right?" the slender black woman wearing a paisley bandana on her head asked.

"Hey, we're fine, thank you for asking. We didn't know anyone lived here, we just saw this little road and need to change my baby's diaper, if you don't mind," Mabel responded as the woman now made her way up close to the car, without coming all the way over.

"Honey, you go right ahead, is there anything I can get for you?" the seemingly kind stranger asked.

"Could I trouble you for some water to rinse out the diaper?" Mabel asked, with a request that was probably anticipated by the black woman, whose children, five at least, began to appear from behind the screen door as it opened and shut with a loud bang several times within a couple of minutes.

"No trouble at all. Bring it right over here," the woman gently commanded. "Here, let me have it, I'll do it for you." The woman swiftly and without hesitation grabbed the soiled diaper, ready to empty it and do whatever was necessary to help these travelers.

"Where ya'll headed, if I may ask?"

"My husband's got some kinfolks down the road we're gonna' visit," Mabel answered, not wanting to explain or acknowledge, the true nature of their travel, figuring, quite correctly, that this abridged version of events would suffice to satisfy the helpful woman's curiosity.

The woman pumped a few times on the well handle to prime the pump and then, when a trickle of water finally appeared, began scrubbing the fabric back and forth against itself to rid it of the soiled residue, taking extra care to help these strangers in need.

"There," she said, as she started to hand the wet diaper back to Mabel, then thinking further, she pulled the white cloth back. "Let me wrap this in a bag or something for you," she offered, not waiting for any sign of approval, instead turning to perform a task as though she should have thought of it before.

"No, you don't need to do that," Mabel quickly stopped the woman's movement toward the rundown wooden shack. The screen door still popped like a gun going off every few seconds, with each of the woman's children going in and out, as they scrutinized these interlopers. When satisfied of their innocuous presence, the little black children headed back inside, one following another. "We'll be where we're goin' in just a few minutes," Mabel said, thanking her and perpetuating the harmless deceit.

"You sure? It's no trouble. I'd be happy to get you a bag or cloth of some kind to wrap it in," the black woman continued, eager to display hospitality to visitors.

"You're so kind. Thank you, honey," Mabel added. "We surely appreciate your kindness and we're so sorry to bother you like this, especially with a dirty diaper of all things," the mother apologized. "Thank you so much, and God bless you."

"God bless you, and thank you for stoppin' to visit," the owner of the property responded as Pa began slowly to exit the weeded drive.

Mabel waved again in gratitude as the car moved away from the little shack with the overgrown driveway. Even Roger, who had awakened by now, waved with an appreciative smile as a little cloud of dust lingered where the blacktop intersected with the dirt path.

"Well, wadn't she precious," Mabel praised. "I tell you there's some good ones," she declared, obviously affirming a fact she knew already. "Lord, bless her good," the woman muttered in an undertone voice, stated as a prayer for the helpful black woman.

"That sure was nice of her," Lewis agreed. "Yes, I tell you people are people. Just the time you think you can label a group all good or all bad, you make yourself a fool. Show me ten people of whatever group and you'll find one is a saint, one closer to a demon, and the other eight, well, they're somewhere in between. And I imagine most of your Nigras would have helped us just like that woman did, don't you?" he asked Mabel, eager to continue on an area of agreement.

"I sure do. Oh yea, there's no doubt," Mabel agreed. "There's some sorry ones, but there's plenty of sorry white people I don't want anything to do with, too."

"Daddy, tell us more about the Everglades," Marie requested.

Chapter Twenty-six

Percy recalled the very first day of *Corona's* business on the lake. The Neesh family had arrived just over three weeks earlier. Cory, Percy, Peter, and Rhetta. It took those few weeks to get the steamboat ready. The first working day began rather routinely. The crew and steamboat had docked here-and-there around the southeastern shore of the Lake over the past 23 days. There were various mooring points they had tied up to. Peter and Percy surveyed the new terrain. Two large and verdant fingers of land jutted from the bay on the south—veritable peninsulas—ones Percy had known about, having carefully studied his charts. Without those, the lake would have been a complete, unbroken circle. Percy had explained to Cory that the men were orienting themselves to "the lay of the land."

The manager of the one business near this part of the Lake was a man named Palmer Chancey. He could be found at almost any time—literally, from the earliest streaks of daylight Monday morning until, typically, late after the dance on Saturday night—manning the dusty little general store, with its creaking cypress-plank flooring, sagging shelves of canned foods, oatmeal and cereals, smaller shelves with countless jars of ointments, balms, salves, creams, lotions and potions. Bagged wheat and corn flour lay in 50-pound burlap

sacks on the floor. Rugged pioneers could be seen saun-
tering in, purchasing necessaries for the week, many
laden with those cumbersome bags of flour, or others
containing rice or corn meal. One customer even then
slowly waddled off, the weight burdening his slight
frame as he struggled to a boat. Sometimes, the mer-
chandise would be toted to a Model-T, or even a wagon
drawn by horse or mule, but, most often, it would be
lugged towards a boat tethered to the long, rickety,
wooden dock along a canal.

The placement of *Chancey's Dry Goods* was ideal, as
it lay a half-mile east of the southeastern edge of Lake
Okeechobee, down the Hillsboro Canal, a manmade
waterway dug by a huge crane ten years before. At that
point lay a little settlement of 300 souls, most of whom
came there from diverse places—Georgia, Alabama, Germany. There was even a Latvian family and another of
Slavic émigrés—but nonetheless it was a homogenous
little village in one sense: The belief that they were "The
Chosen of God."

Many in that community would survive a monstrous hurricane three years later, one which would
rumble its bullying will and shrieking winds reck-
lessly over their loving, carefully husbanded terrain.
The cyclonic winds and surging water would rip over
the southernmost portion of the Florida peninsula, and
up the huge lake, crippling nascent communities. The
deafening roar and hideous gusts and unyielding tide
gave way to an unearthly quiet and placid calmness.
Such quiet seemed genuine peace after a storm so ferocious, one in which most living beings were amazed to
be spared of their lives. That is, all but a handful. Hundreds, mostly black laborers in low-lying areas, had per-

ished, and been cremated in piles of bodies. A dozen or so white settlers in that little village had lost their lives as well, a couple drowned while climbing into an attic to escape rising waters. Those who survived dogmatically insisted that it was owing to a smile from Providence that any were delivered. Their little hamlet on the canal still stood. It deserved a name none other than *Chosen*.

Peter set up a credit account with Palmer Chancey to purchase dry goods and staples he anticipated the family would need routinely. He laid down 25 cents for the first two month's rent on post office box number 53. Not that he expected to hear from his kinfolks, either in North Florida nor his grandparents back in Georgia. Having put his hand to the plow, as it were, he was not one to look back and pine nostalgically for fond memories of days past, nor would he even once revisit his decision to ply a steam trade on the big lake.

Palmer Chancey was a small man, eyes close-set and furrowed brow. His upper lip seemed occasionally to be curled into a scowl. He had an elastic band encircling his head, long brimmed green shaded visor in front covering his face when tasks took him outside in the scorching sun. The band lightly pinched tufts of silvery-gray hair, causing them to rise from the periphery of his scalp, revealing sunburned skin in the middle, which a full cap would have concealed. He was neatly shaven, clean in his appearance, and had a quickness about his movements that affirmed a meticulous astuteness in shuffling his chores. Although his mien was mostly pleasant, it was businesslike. His was a personality not predisposed to spend excess time welcoming these or any other newcomers, as he moved efficiently from this labor to that. His sharp face and pasty complexion had a slight smile when called for, but his was not an animated countenance. It became clear that his disposition was as accommodating and amiable as was called for in the circumstances. No more, no less.

After exchanging greetings and completing the business tasks, including the purchase of ten pounds of flour, some eggs, and a side of beef, a brief conversation ensued about what led the familial foursome to combine their resources in a maritime commerce such as theirs. The diminutive clerk lost a modicum of austerity in his countenance at last, assured that the boatmen were embarking on a final desperate effort to make a living with the steamboat. Realizing the precarious beginnings of a business venture in what must have been to them a strange, desolate locale, and feeling some pity for the displaced boatmen, and more than a little empathy for the woman among them, he decided to confide some information to the Captain that would prove propitious.

"Haul all the vegetables you want, Mr. Neesh, cause Lord knows these farmers need a means by which to get their pole beans across the lake, but you gotta remember, you got some competition; a lotta fish goin' for the same bait, as the catfishers say. Tell you what I'd do. Go over here to Sewauwee, a little Indian village over on Locha Hatchee 'bout two miles west, with about twenty families of Seminoles livin' there, and set up a trade with them. They got gator hides, coon and otter skins, and these bright beads and clothes their wives make, that they say sell good in the big city and with tourists down in Miami. And, word has it from my wife's cousin up in New Jersey that gator shoes and belts and women's purses are becomin' a real fashionable thing in the big city. Tyger, one of the head Injuns over there, even tried talkin' me into marketing them to the distributors who's been a-wheelin' and a-dealin' so's he could sell 'em up there."

"Don't the locals trade with them?" the Captain asked, following up inquisitively on this tip from a man whose laconic nature signaled to him the generosity and potential accuracy of the information.

"Not much." They's been hard feelins' between them and the white man goin' back to Andrew Jackson's *Indian Removal Act,* where *ole Rough and Ready* literally tried to get all redskins out of here to west of the Mississippi. You know why he wasn't more successful?" The Captain shook his head in rapid jerks to indicate he did not.

"It was because of maps, or I should say, the lack of maps. They needed maps a whole lot more than they did ole Sam Colt's six guns, and without them, they were no match for the Seminoles, who had never seen a map," Chancey explained.

"More recently, they've been feudin' and fightin' with some of our people here in Chosen, these German fellas, the Meyerhoffers, who grow beans and celery. First, it seems, the Seminoles agreed to lease them some of their land over there on the island for farming. Then after a couple of years, the Germans tried to persuade 'em to give up more and more land for less and less lease money. Well, ended up the Indians finally decided the lease terms were not to their likin' nor benefit, and gently asked them for permission to rescind the lease. To top it off, some roughneck trappers and fishermen kept on pushin' 'em for more and more rights on and around their island, sort of demanding this or that amount of acreage for a pittance, or else 'There'd be trouble' and so on. So, they're quite understandably wary of dealin' with the likes of our kind."

"By jingoes!" the Captain responded, interested in the seemingly reticent man's newfound verbosity.

"Don't forget, the first white people down here in the swamps was your Indian chasers who rounded 'em up for a good bounty for Jacksons's bunch." Got rich."

"Do they own that island land?"

"Evidentially, the government granted them a patent to the acreage in exchange for their willingness to leave the mainland. Thought they'd be no threat out there. And, was a good way just to get 'em out from under foot of the white man." Trouble is, they's talk now of floodin' that land cause the government wants to raise the lake level. The chiefs and their squaws been raisin' hell at that idea, as you can imagine. That hadn't helped matters."

"I thought the idea down here was to drain the land so it could be reclaimed, not raise the water level?" Peter queried, puzzled.

"It was. Seems they went too far, though. Miami's growin' down south of here. Must be 50,000 souls living there now, including the beach. Lauderdale's got that Navy base, and a bunch movin' in there, and not to mention the Yankees flockin' over to Palm Beach with all their money from up North." They figure by raising the lake level, drinking water will be more available, plus they've decided muck needs a certain amount of moisture so it won't oxidate or deteriorate. Don't forget, the whole area was completely submerged until a few hundred years ago."

"I thought it was closer to a thousand years ago,"

Peter shot back. You sure 'bout that?"

"No, Sir, Mr. Neesh. Used to be sure of purdy much everything when I was a young man, but as an old man I'm not sure of much of anything," Chancey responded.

Captain Peter recognized an opportunity when he saw it. Percy recognized his father's unspoken thoughts.

Chapter Twenty-seven

The Georgia family was making good progress in the Star rolling down Highway One. Lewis thought of a story he had heard when he visited the Lake a year earlier: "There was this big ole tractor to clear the muck. Most of the farmers don't have a lotta money, so they use an old Model T car that they convert into tractors. They work real good because they're light and don't sink down in the soil."

"Oh, Lord, now we're gonna bog down in some kind of mess," Mabel complained.

"Instead of rubber wheels, which are worse in muck, they will install ones of sectioned steel for traction. A lot of the tractors are handmade by each farmer. Those Ford cars or trucks pull the plow or disc behind. They take whatever car they have and put somethin' together that'll do the job—pull a plow, tear up those ole sawgrass roots. The rich farmers buy new Fordsons straight from the factory, but they're heavy, and they sink in the soft dirt."

"What about the 'big ole tractor' you started to tell about?" Ray asked.

"There was this man who used to be a gold prospector up in Alaska. When the gold rush hit, he left California and headed north," Lewis began.

The children were listening with rapt attention at

the mention of Alaska and gold.

"It seems he ran a newspaper up in Alaska when he didn't strike it rich, and he made more money doin' that than he had lookin' for gold. After a while he made so much money and got bored up there, and he heard about this place where we're goin'. A friend of his told him about the reclamation efforts goin' on in the Everglades and he decided that was for him, so he and the friend formed a company, moved down there and bought a section or so of land they planned to clear and grow crops on. Since he had money, he decided that all those custard apple trees that grow thick in wild groves would be hard to clear by hand, with just an axe and a regular tractor. See, they gotta chop down the trees, and dig out their roots, but once they're chopped down, a tractor pulls them over into wind rows, piles of dead brush, like our hay, set out in a straight line. Then a man comes along and sets them on fire; after that, the men, they go to grubbin' the roots outta the ground."

"What happened then, Pa," Ray asked.

"Anyway, this man from Alaska comes down with his buddy, and they arranged for a big ole huge steam-driven tractor to be shipped from California, where it had been specially built. I think the fella told me it weighed around 30 tons. It was some kind of monstrosity, to hear them tell it. The rear wheels were seven or eight feet tall and I think he said five feet in width. I mean, it was a big 'un," Lewis recalled, happy now having even his wife's full attention in the form of her looking at him, as best he could tell, out of the corner of his eye. "Said the driver was sittin' up there so high he could look in a two-story window."

"Why didn't it bog down?" Earlene asked, daring to

use that word her father had shunned.

"I'm fixin' to tell you the whole story," her Pa quickly assured her. "You had to have a licensed steam engine man operating the machinery and a fireman to keep the fire under control, besides the operator of the tractor. There was this wagon thing pulled behind the tractor, which they kept full of wood. They used the wood from custard apple trees they had plowed to fuel the steam engine, and it had some kind of power. But, the wood burned up real quick—it wadn't like oak where a log'll sit on a fire all day. This fireman fellow had to constantly feed the little firebox to produce steam with this custard apple wood. It seems the constant opening and closing of the little door to the firebox kept cool air going into the boiler which messed it up somehow."

"Did it bog down, Pa?" Earlene persisted.

"As this monster rolled along, people said the ground just shook, just rumbled under all that weight moving along," Lewis continued to relate, ignoring his daughter's question. "And then because of the steam engine and the wood burning, an ember would get out and catch the ground on fire. That muck soil burns."

"Keep talking, Lewis Thompson, and you're gonna put me on a bus back to Georgia," his wife warned, anxious at this news about the volatile soil.

"No, no, not like that," Lewis couldn't resist defending on this one. "It's just so rich and organic that when it gets dry, it's like peat moss when it dries out—you can light it on fire. How do you think it grows those beautiful vegetables all year round," Lewis tried to remind Mabel of the more positive attributes of the frontier.

"Did they put the fire out, Pa?" Marie inquired, oblivious to any nuance of disagreement between her parents.

"Yea—I'm about to tell you," Pa answered while turning his head toward his wife with a glance of disgust to repay her sarcasm, a glance she did not see as her eyes were fixed in a stolid stare down the road. "There was a separate group of men who carried water buckets to keep the fire from takin' hold. One time, they didn't put the fire out, and it burned up several feet of the muck—went all the way down to the limestone subsoil underneath. But, back to the tractor. That was some kind of powerful machine. In some places, it did the trick. I mean, it would clear out those custard apple groves by the tons, but with the weight and the wood burnin' up too fast, it just didn't pan out. And the bad thing was the fella from Alaska had spent a couple thousand dollars just gettin' it there from California. If I'm right, that was more money than the thing had cost to build in the first place. The fellow tellin' me about it said it finally got stuck in some soft muck and they had to take it apart in little pieces," Lewis related, carefully avoiding the phrase 'bog down', which, indeed, is exactly what it had done, and "in such a way that it could not be budged an inch."

"There was another tractor that played a part in the story, and this one had first been used at what they called the *Secret Ranch*. Worked even in soft muck that would have completely swallowed the monster one from California. Its back wheels were connected to a series of wide boards that moved along and made contact with the ground. That distributed most of the weight from off its wheels. It was like it had pads that walked on the ground right beside the wheel, and when you got several boards contacting the ground at any time, the weight got distributed over a broader area and that kept the thing from sinking. This man, Mr. Love, kept going on about the inventor of that contraption being 'right smart.'"

"What was the *Secret Ranch*," Earlene queried. "Tell us about that."

Chapter Twenty-eight

A warm breeze wafted through the vents of the car as miles of cypress trees, interspersed with pines stood on either side of Highway One. The family had arrived in Florida. The day seemed alive with moist thick air.

"This is so much flatter than Swainsboro," Mabel noted. "Gracious! Aren't there any hills?"

"Actually, on my way back to Georgia last spring, I came through the middle part of the state. Didn't come this way. Over there, you'd see one hill right after another. But, it's flatter nearer the coast, where we are now," Lewis noted. "Wait till y'all get down there. I haven't even described the palm trees with their huge, long-flowing and feathery branches. It's like you see in those drawings about Hawaii. Just like that. You have 'em all over where we're goin'," he assured them.

Roger was perusing the map of Florida he had unfolded a half-hour before, squinting to look at the fine print to identify the names of the little towns around the big lake. He had been laughing at some of the funny names such as *Coot Bay, Bear Lake, Tishimingo, Pelican Island, Vinegar Bend, Pahokee, Chosen, Alligator River, Port Mayaca.* "How in the world do you pronounce these?" he asked, pronouncing Mayaca like 'My'-Ah-Cuh', stressing the last syllable, instead of its correct pronunciation 'My-Ah'-Cuh' with the accent on the middle syllable. "Bacon, oh, I guess that's *Bacom Point*," he decided.

All of a sudden, there was a loud detonation from the rear of the car. Lewis fought the steering wheel, jerking it first to the right, then sharply back to the left, finally slowing it down by veering onto the narrow, grassy shoulder of the highway.

"What in Sam Hill?" Roger was startled away from the map, throwing it to the floorboard.

"Son, don't cuss, how 'bout it?" his Pa warned while fighting the steering wheel to keep control, knowing clearly that the boy had not used any profanity.

"I didn't cuss," Roger argued.

"It sounds too much like the real thing," the man retorted, less vigorous in his protestations than he otherwise might have been in view of the tire blowout.

"Plag-gonit! A flat!" Pa exclaimed, using his strongest, and most favorite exclamation. As Earlene heard him say it, her mind raced back to last summer when her cat scratched her arm next to the wrist after she picked it up a little too roughly. She'd yelped out a "doggonit" loud enough for her father, who was beating out a hot horseshoe on his anvil in the nearby barn, to hear. He quickly summoned her to the barn where he proceeded to "wear her out" with a horse bridle, leaving little red stripes on her bare legs. "We're not gonna have any cussin', Young Lady, especially not from a purdy lil' thing like yourself, not even yet dry behind the ears. You look like cussin'. I'll do the cussin' for now, hear?"

It was the left rear tire on the Star that had blown, and Pa had done an admirable job bringing the black automobile to a stop and getting off the road so that he could begin replacing the defective tire with the spare.

"Roger, get me the jack, how 'bout it?" Pa demanded.

"Here," as Roger returned from the rear of the car, handing the device to his father.

"How old are you now, son?" his father demanded.

Understanding the message his Pa was relaying, the boy dutifully knelt down by the frayed and flat tire and began to unloosen the lug nuts.

"I can't get this last one undone, Pa," Roger proclaimed. "Can you help me with it?"

"Slide over a little, son," Pa commanded, placing the wrench on the lug.

"I want you to take a lesson from that blowout, son. See, the car wants to leap out of control, so you gotta hold the wheel tight, stay with it and keep it on the road, in your lane," Lewis warned.

"I wouldn't have no problem doin' that, Pa. You know how strong I am and how my reflexes are good and quick. You don't have to worry about me lettin' it go —in fact, you don't have to worry about me ever behind the wheel," the boy assured his dad.

After the tire was changed, Roger relieved Pa from driving, looking carefully to his left before pulling out onto the blacktop. Ray, the nine-year-old son, hadn't been asked to help, much to his thrill.

"Looks all clear, son," Lewis reported, turning back to see down the road behind them while sitting directly behind his son in the back seat with the two girls. The baby began to fall asleep on his lap with that big head of curly black hair resting against the tall man's chest.

The clear blue sky glowed with a brightness Mabel had not seen in Georgia. Gone was any hint of summer haze. White clouds in puffs layered three and four atop the other, reminded her of bolls of Georgia cotton. The brightness resounded sharply in all sectors of the light-blue sky. The glare in places bounced off scattered bushes and vegetation, which seemed strangely shorter and less vertical than she had known, but had a thickness of dense tropical jungle.

A wide river meandered slowly, and a few scattered houses separated by a half mile or so, lay in the distance, some with docks stretching out to the water. No doubt, the trees were different from Georgia's. There was a strangeness to them that Mabel noticed, but couldn't articulate. Vines of a strange variety grew into trees and their wide, waxy leaves didn't resemble wisteria or any ivy or Confederate Jasmine or honeysuckle that she was used to.

"That's the St. Johns River," Lewis pointed to his right, resting his other hand gently and briefly across Mabel's shoulder. "It's wider over younder than the big ole Mississippi River. It flows towards and all around Jacksonville, and what's unusual, it flows north. Some smaller tributaries that branch off, such as the Kissimmee River, flow into Lake Okeechobee and into the Everglades," he proudly educated his captive pupils.

"You see that boat out there in the middle?" That's one of those low-slung, freight-hauling boats like they have down there in the Hillsboro Settlement. There's a little cabin with a roof on top to keep you dry in the rain, or to keep the sun off on a hot day, and you can carry a right goodly amount of stuff to Ft. Lauderdale or Miami down the canals. Everything down where we're going is built around the canal system. It's not like it is back home. We have roads in Georgia, but down there, people get around as much by boat," he announced.

"I hope you're teasin'," Mabel retorted in disgust. "But I know you're not. Enjoy it mister. For as long as it lasts, I hope you have fun," she said rather menacingly.

"You know what I mean, there's streets and all, but to get to the big towns, like Miami or west of Palm Beach, those folks have to go by boat down the canal. There aren't any roads. It's just too blamed wet to build roads all over the place." There'll come a day when they have roads, but they're still reclaiming the land," he explained patiently.

"I'm gonna' give it six months," Mabel stoically explained. "And then I'm headin' back to Georgia, with my kids," she added matter-of-factly. "You better hope there's some roads and a way to get around Lewis Thompson, or you'll be stuck down there all by yourself," Mabel warned.

Chapter Twenty-nine

C ory was proud of his grandfather, even admired the way the old man had begged as a fourteen-year-old to fight for the Confederacy. He was told by officials that he was too young—he could be a scout, and that was it. Short for Cornelius, a name his mother had loved, 'Cory' had evolved after his third birthday. Rhetta found Cornelius to be too long, and too strong a reminder of his mother. Percy agreed to the name, but later found it too strong a reminder of the capitalist Vanderbilt. *Cory,* it would be, but not before they had called him *Stumper* for a time while a toddler. There had been an incident involving a bait box shortly after his mother deserted him. Peter told about the little boy stumping his toe on the box while learning how to fish; in reality, the old man had accidentally allowed the box to slip from his grasp, hitting Cory's toe. Guilt, and a measure of self-deception, had modified the tale, but Percy knew it was his father's fault. He allowed the proud man to save face by not challenging him when the Captain later told Rhetta how the boy had "accidently" stumped his toe "not lookin' where he was goin'."

"Why, he stumped his toe just the other day on the dock!" Rhetta quickly remembered, suggesting a pattern of vulnerability. "Stumped it on Pop Pop's boat, stumped it on the dock. We may have to call you *Stumper* you keep this up." Percy smiled inwardly at the name, but he was really amusing himself with Peter's lie —his sham version of events. "Was the tough, old Captain too scared to own up to the truth, assuming he perceived it himself?" Percy mused. The name lasted but a short time. As he approached adolescence, Cory was Cory—nothing more or less.

Rhetta kept Captain Peter humble. She was a short woman, seemingly as big around as she was tall. With a strong sense of rectitude, she was quiet, reverent and possessed good judgment. But Rhetta was tough as nails with her family. If anyone could, it was she who could cool Peter down quickly when he allowed his vicious temper to flare. Percy always admired the way his mother could exercise her will and not subvert Peter's in the process.

"I'll run the steamboat, and you run the house— and me. Thataway, we'll all be okay," the captain liked to remind his wife of their pact from time to time.

The couple had been sympathetic when Percy's woman left him. They couldn't completely blame her. There was his drinking. His was a curious intellect— hers, shallow and focused on the commonplace. The only good resulting from their match was Cory. Neither Peter nor Rhetta knew whether the two had married. There certainly was no ceremony they attended. While they hadn't blamed the mother's intolerance for the man's lack of sobriety, they had condemned her for leaving the baby. Any court would award custody to the father, almost invariably, and Cory's mother was pretty well aware that she didn't stand a chance of "gettin' the baby." She didn't seem to have the will to mount a legal fight, for, given Percy's adoration of the child, not to mention Rhetta's and Peter's, a battle surely would have been waged. Nor was Cory's mother's a strong or stable mental presence, in their opinion, and her abandonment was probably the best course for them all. She was proof that, as they had always suspected, Percy's taste in women was not good.

At first, Percy was quite heartbroken over the woman's decision to leave him and the boy, but he fought through his disquietude, and eventually became resigned to his role as sole parent. While he had never felt great love for the mother of his son, he had enjoyed her sexual prowess and longed for it even now. He came to recognize that the enduring prize of their union was this boy—his existence—an invaluable and appreciated fruit of her womb.

Before coming to work full-time on the steamboat near Merritt Island, Percy had farmed several acres of land that Peter had helped him buy shortly after the doomed relationship. He tried to produce potatoes, and then squash, but on the nutrient-poor sandy soil, he had only moderate success with either. He was then convinced by a drinking buddy to try his hand at growing grapefruit, which he did, and with greater success for several years once the trees matured to produce fruit. In fact, for two years, the trees yielded a decent living, but a bitter and unusual frost during one winter badly damaged the young trees and dashed his hopes of even moderate prosperity. When success eluded him, both in money and in love, it was almost a relief for him to go home to his father, work the steamboat according to the Captain's will, and in the true sense of the repenting prodigal, yield to his guidance and care.

In rare moments of leisure, relaxing in his favorite chair from Canada on the deck of *Corona*, Percy reflected in moments of melancholic contemplation, the vicissitudes of life. After a day's run, he loved puffing on a meerschaum pipe carved in the likeness of Bacchus, enjoying deep breaths of Virginia tobacco along with salty, moist air. Celebrated in Roman times, *Bacchus—Dionysus* to the Greeks—was the god of the vine, in a word, the grape, and most importantly, its fermentation. The domain of Bacchus also included vegetation in general. Wild, drunken frenzy, even downright madness was under his rule. Romans must have thought humans needed moments of pandemonium and bedlam as a pleasant retreat from the ennui of rationality and boring normalcy.

Percy would miss this river, and he was apprehensive about the lake. His father's temper tantrums aboard the boat created angst in Percy's otherwise rational and boring normalcy. Peter could cuss a blue streak—and would to the utmost degree—and it didn't take much to set that off, and it would last and it would be overwrought and edgy and tense. Percy didn't like that kind of madness—those downright frenzies of Captain Peter.

The father and son team worked well and promoted both family unity and prosperity, despite the Captain's temper and Percy's drinking binges. Cory's addition to the boat duo could be either a benefit or liability, depending upon whom you asked, and when. While most boys his age lived in a regular house with both parents and went to school with classmates and a teacher, he did neither, yet longed for both.

Given Peter's sternness in insisting on hard work, it wasn't surprising that his was a religion which made allowance for God and profanity, interchangeably during the course of a day, whichever best served the ends of an honest living in the moment.

"God's will be done," he preached, then added in an undertone "with a healthy dose of self-initiative from his creatures."

Chapter Thirty

After driving for close to five hours, most of the Thompson family were tired or sleeping. Marie must have asked first her mother, then her father, "How much longer till we'll be there?" or "Where are we now?" or "When we gonna' be at our new home?" and a hundred other similar queries. "Kids have no concept of distance or travel," Lewis thought to himself, remembering the mule-pulled buggy he had traveled upon with his mother and father as a young boy near Kemp, Georgia. Going into the closest large town, Swainsboro, and then back to the tiny village of Kemp had consumed eight miles and nearly the whole of a day.

"Lewis, these kids are tired, we gotta' stop next town we come to," Mabel demanded.

"Lake Placid is just ahead, why don't we stop and eat lunch there?" Pa suggested.

Within five minutes, a little sign read *Lake Placid City Limits*. Almost immediately upon coming into the municipality they saw a little white two-story building on the left side of the road with several cars parked in front. There was gingerbread trim in front. Lewis craned his neck, angling it sideways to read a little sign out front.

Howard's Tourist Home and Dixiana Grille. Open.

"Looks like they could put up a sign big enough for ya to read," complained Mabel.

"Yea," Pa responded, nonchalantly. "You kids ready to eat?" he asked.

"I sure am," reported Earlene, "I'm starvin'!"

"Me, too," Marie added, "I'm starvin', too!"

"This looks nice," Mabel declared. "Gosh, I'm hungrier than I thought."

'Don't say it,' Pa thought to himself, laughing at the potential for a good verbal poke at his wife.

'Musn't remind her 'you're always hungry, honey,' especially not now—in fact, not at any other time, either.' He had said it before, and it had always proved good for a laugh, even from her, who, given her weight problem, could be a good sport, or so thought Lewis, about her affection for eating. But Lewis loved to joke and kid, even when he knew a price might be paid for his levity.

A petite, brunette-haired waitress approached the family. She had a small, upturned nose, straight along the bridge, with small nostrils that were neither flared nor pinched. Her smallish mouth was coated in too much red lipstick. Grayish smiling eyes looked from one Thompson to another. As she sprang over to their table, she carried two glasses of iced tea.

"Oh, thank you, a cold glass of good ole iced tea. Hope it's sweet. How did you know?" Lewis asked.

"I see that Georgia tag on the front of your car, and my grandmama is from Georgia, and I know how much they love iced tea, and sweetened at that!" the waitress answered with a cheery sound to her voice, obviously delighted that she had guessed correctly, and that someone had appreciated her intuition. "I knew at least a couple of y'all would want sweet tea," she added.

"Honey, he could drink a gallon at a time," Mabel told the congenial little waitress, fixing her stare hard and fast upon Lewis. "And, the sweeter, the better. In fact, I think you did drink a gallon at that last family nose-rubbin' we had," she added.

"Nose-rubbin," the waitress quickly responded, "I haven't heard that since my grandmama died two years ago. "She used to say that all the time. "Idn't that like a family reunion or get-together?" she asked.

"Exactly right. A family get-together or reunion is a 'nose-rubbin', yes," Mabel quickly confirmed, smiling at her own use of a provincial phrase she quickly realized was not universal.

"Well," the waitress with the cute personality asked, what can I get for y'all to eat at this little nose rubbin'?" As the girl's eyes smiled towards the family, her pencil was poised to write in her order book.

"Gosh, it all looks so good. I think I'll have the roast beef and gravy with mashed potatoes," Mabel declared, still perusing the menu for alternatives. "Have 'em put some extra gravy on my meat, will you, hon?" she added.

"Corn bread or dinner roll?" the waitress wanted to know.

"I'll have the corn bread, please."

"I'd like the fried catfish with grits and tomato gravy," Pa spoke up.

"I want some chicken and dumplings," Roger declared.

"I want that too," Ray piped up.

"Better make it two of those," Mabel said to the waitress, ordering for Roger, knowing that he was too shy to speak up for himself. She expected reticence from Ray, a mere child, but Mabel had answered for Roger, now a teenager, for she couldn't remember how long. Each time she promised herself it would be the last. "That boy simply has to start speaking up for himself and telling people what he wants!" she told Lewis on more than one occasion. "I gotta get him outta that."

"I want a hamburger and french fries," Earlene announced.

"Me, too," Marie agreed.

"I'll tell y'all what, we're gonna get one hamburger and one order of fries, and you two girls can split them, and then if you're still hungry, we'll order another," Mabel stated.

"Mama, I'm old enough to have a hamburger and french fries by myself without having to split it with some little child," Earlene stressed emphatically.

"Well, Miss—do tell. I guess you can have one by yourself if you're that big," Mabel agreed. "I thought you sorta liked sharing with little sister."

"I'm grown now Mama, and I need stuff by myself. And I hope she's not gonna be sleepin' with me any longer when we get to our new house," Earlene informed her mother.

"Don't go getting' too grown up, Miss. You belong to me for a little longer," her mother reminded her.

After bringing a high chair for the baby, the waitress asked whether everything was okay.

"If you have a napkin that you'll put a little water on, so I can wipe the baby's face, I sure would appreciate it," Mabel requested.

"Where in Georgia are y'all from?" the waitress asked as she returned with the napkin, slightly damp.

"We're visitin' from Swainsboro, honey, northwest of Savannah" Mabel responded, still denying the permanency of the transition. "My husband's found a place down south of here where he thinks he can farm and grow some crops," she added, not relating that she might not be a part of his adventure.

"Oh, where are y'all goin' to?" the waitress wanted to know.

"It's down on Lake Okeechobee," Lewis answered this time, "On down the state a ways in the wetlands area."

"I have an uncle that catfishes down there," she quickly revealed, surprised. "He runs a catfish camp along the rim of that lake. I never been down there, but my daddy says he lives out in the middle of nowhere, and that he lives to catch those catfish. You know it's a big business. 'Specially now that ice can be produced and they can ship 'em. People think of men sittin' out there on the bank, relaxin' with a fishin pole in their hand, you know, kindly whilin' away their time, waitin' for one to bite. But daddy tells me that's not that way it is. They rig up these big long nets that they pull behind a motor boat, then have another boat that goes to get ice and keeps the fish fresh." Lewis nodded and Mabel listened. "Then, they'll haul the nets in the boat later to see what they've caught," the garrulous waitress informed the family.

"It's gettin' to be a big deal," Lewis affirmed. "I heard tell of the brothers who got a commercial ice machine 'cause too many loads would spoil before they could get 'em over to the railroad. Fella I met when I was down there a while back said those ole boys rigged up a huge ice-making operation so they can ship 'em. Judging from how these taste on my plate, I'd say his machine works. These catfish are outta this world!" Lewis praised.

"Well, thank you, Sir," the young girl responded appreciatively. "Can I get you some more?"

"We're fine, honey, thank you so much for helping us. You're a lovely little person," Mabel announced.

"Aw, you're so sweet," the lipsticked waitress blushed in return.

"Come to think of it--do y'all have any banana pudding?" Mabel asked the waitress.

"Let me check for you," the nice girl responded.

After the meal was over and the Star smoked and rumbled down the highway, Melrose laid his head against the back of the seat to sleep. Roger followed him into a slumber a few minutes later, his head falling forward as he began to dream. Ray was proud that he had consumed the same meal as his older brother, and their Pa had promised Earlene and Marie before leaving the restaurant that he'd tell them about a Secret Ranch he had heard about on his trip, if they could be quiet and let their brother Roger get some rest.

∞∞∞

Chapter Thirty-one

Cory leaned over the left railing on the rear of the boat's deck, head protruding beyond its side, to spit some orange seeds into the river. His grandmother, sitting nearby, her gray hair blowing with the boat's movement, warned him to be careful. She then remembered how steadfastly and diligently the young boy had worked on the boat as the chief assistant to her son, the first mate. He could skillfully maneuver his youthful body in myriad angles and configurations about its slippery decks. She quickly realized her fears were groundless. A tempered dose of maternal discipline, however, was healthy for him.

"Keep an eye on the gauges," his father warned Cory about an hour down the river. "I mean keep your eyes peeled, son, hear?" he cautioned.

"Yes, sir," Cory answered dutifully.

"When you get finished, bring up some wood from the engine room, will you?" Percy asked, more as a formality to soften the command, than as an entreaty. "When you do that, come sit down, I gotta story for you about the Indians that live down where we're goin'," he promised.

Percy often chronicled tales from his copious reading. He often embroidered details and elaborated facts to suit his audience. The concoctions, partly from fact, partly from imaginative improvisation, were as much as part of him as his selfless devotion to Captain Peter. Truly, the stories were replete with vivid imagery and credible mystery, and the boy's appetite for the tales increased the older he became.

After completing his tasks, Cory eagerly came over to the little map table where Percy had spread out a worn nautical chart, its edges torn, folded creases frayed. This was his directional blueprint with its arcane symbols and numbers, compass angles, and lines of latitude and longitude, weighted with a sextant and protractor on top. He especially, being a talented navigator, knew how to use them. As Percy stood, slowly rubbing the bearded stubble on his chin, pulling his thumb and forefinger together, he studied the river route and contemplated a transition to the canal. Its man-made, calculated direction was the shortest, quickest, most profitable route to the big lake.

"How much you know about the Seminole Indians?" Percy asked, without ever looking up from his chart.

"Not a lot," Cory answered honestly, "but I know about Osceola."

"Sit down, I wanna tell you about 'em," Percy commanded, turning from the maps to retrieve a cup of coffee next to the stove. Your Seminoles are nothing more than Georgia Creek Indians, some from Alabama —an agricultural tribe. Raised livestock and farmed. For the most part, they were a real peaceful group. But, a few hunted for a living, and they tended to be aggressive and warlike. Those hunting Creeks were the ones that came south. They banded together with Miccosukees, warriors who were spiteful and ruthless. Now, mind you, these were not the native Indian tribes who inhabited Florida for hundreds of years, although the Creeks intermixed with the remnants of some of those natives. Those original tribes were the *Tekestas* and *Mayaimis*, along with the *Apalachees* and *Timucuas*. Most of them had been killed by disease and raids. You also had *Calusas*. People called them Spanish Indians. They headed even further south, down to the Keys— some even went to Cuba."

"Did those hunting Creeks fight?" Cory inquired. "Those meaner ones that didn't farm?"

"Eventually there was a war, but not really due to their own belligerence. The fightin' was on account mostly of the white man messin' with 'em, tryin' to get 'em out of here. They began to live real civil, even had houses, which were these little thatched huts they called *chickees*, with steeply-angled roofs almost to the ground, made from huge, wide leaves called palmetto fans. There's a short, shrubby tree called a palmetto or cabbage palm that grows wild on high, dry ground. It shoots out wide with pleated branches. Those branches were what Indians used for the roof of their chickee. They dressed in regular clothes, like us white men, but with shirts and dresses made of narrow strips of red, yellow, turquoise—all kinds of colored cloth, which are stitched in horizontal bands. Got that from the Spanish. I mean they're a colorful bunch. In earlier times they wore tunics for clothes, turbans on their heads, and had buckskin boots up to their knees. They hunted and trapped for a living. A lot of them even owned slaves," he apprised Cory, who was surprised at this information.

"You mean slaves like white people owned in the South?"

"Exactly, but the relationship between slave and master was different," he emphasized. "It seems the Nigras liked their Indian masters who in turn trusted them a great deal and gave them a lot of freedom to come and go and do this or that, as they pleased. They even intermarried sometimes."

"What did the slaves help the Indians do?"

"A few of your Seminoles raised hogs in those days, like a lot of 'em do still. But most were trappers, out for coon and otter skins. Slaves would be right in there with 'em. They'd pole the canoes along the shores of Lake Okeechobee in ankle-deep shoal waters. After the Indians would catch em, the slaves'd skin 'em, then they'd ship pelts up north to be sewn into coats. Even still, these days, some of the more adventurous ones trap alligators and skin 'em. Women up north like purses made from gator hide, the under belly section-- that's the highest grade 'cause it has no scars. Your men up there like alligator shoes. Gettin' more and more popular among the fancy types.

"Why'd they quit huntin'?"

"Startin' about four or five years ago, these get-rich land developers started drainin' the swamps and cuttin' down the piney woods. Since those are the Indians' huntin' grounds, they had to give it up, and a lot of 'em have gone to raisin' hogs. Some of them are raisin' cattle.

"Did Osceola come from that group?"

"Yea, and Tallahassee, too. A lot of people came to know them as *Tallahassees* because of the Chief by that name. Some called them *Cow Creeks* because they were living in that little settlement north of Lake Okeechobee when an 1880 census was taken."

"Tallahassee, like the capital?"

"That's right. They lived near that area of the state at one time. See, before Tallahassee took over the tribe around 1884, his uncle, the Chief they called Chipco, brought 'em from near where the state capitol is now on down to the Big Cypress Swamp, west of Lake Okeechobee. That was primitive country. No one, they thought, would root 'em outta that swamp."

"Are these Seminoles still livin' there, where we're goin'?" Cory asked.

"There aren't as many as there were a few years ago. Only a couple hundred left, but there wouldn't be any at all, like I say, if it hadn't been for ole Chipco. Oh, and don't forget the biggest name of 'em all, you just mentioned him, the warrior Osceola."

"What is it he did, exactly?" Cory wondered.

"He was a Creek, well, a Seminole. They say he had some English or Scottish blood. I think maybe a grandparent was white. Anyway, he wouldn't go along with the treaty that tried to move all the Creeks out west. He got up a band of his Creek brothers who all said "No". That infuriated the white man. Osceola later paid with his life, but not before he had caused some trouble. This little group were determined they were not goin' out west. Even called themselves by the Creek phrase *Esta Semoli*, from which they get the name *Seminole*, which translates into 'Wild People' or 'runaways'. The Spanish government, which had authority over parts of Florida, encouraged them to come south, to defy what they thought was an American revolutionary government that was immature and could be toppled. The Spanish even protected them against the white man."

"Why didn't the white man want 'em around here?"

Cory wondered.

"The government uprooted most all the Creeks from their homes in Georgia and Alabama, due to a notion that they were gonna impede progress in one way or another. Thought of them as savages and a threat to law and order. A group who didn't share the white man's ideas. Didn't share his rules of law and ordered government. Wouldn't mix in; in fact, really didn't want them mixin' in. Decided Indians had to be moved out west—get 'em outta here. What the government leaders didn't realize, this particular tribe of Creeks, mixed with your *Muskogees*, and *Tallasis*, weren't nearly as hostile as the *Sioux* and *Apache*, and other tribes out west. Now brother, those were some ruthless, brutal bastards. But the white man categorized them all in one bucket. In his greed, had a fear that they would stand in the way of those white dreams. Most of 'em ended up captured and headin' down the 'Trail of Tears' to what is now called Arkansas and Oklahoma. Only a few succeeded in stayin' behind. Those are your *Esta Semoli*--Seminoles."

"Did they actually cry goin' out there?" Cory asked.

"I'm sure they did. Wouldn't you, if someone made you up and leave a place you hold dear?"

"Well, idn't that what we're doin' right now?" he observed.

"And aren't you sad in your heart, leavin' your friends, the Banana River, Uncle Cooter-Miser, your cousins Joe and Seth, and all the things we used to do?" Percy interrogated.

"But, I ain't cryin'."

"Well, there's different kinds of cryin'. There's cryin' on the outside, where everybody can see ya, and then there's cryin' on the inside. Everybody's crying about something, nearbout always. I sure am cryin' on the inside over leavin' our little village and the cape and the river, now aren't you?"

"I suppose," the boy admitted.

"Anyway," Percy quickly changed the subject, "Chief Chipco brought this little band of Seminoles, as they began to call themselves, down to the Big Cypress Swamp. Chipco was Tallahassee's uncle. Both his and Tallahasee's father were later killed by Andrew Jackson's troops in a battle near the Suwannee River. The Federals were determined not to let even this small number get a foothold in Florida, but instead wanted them gone."

"What did they do?" Cory inquired.

"What could they do? Percy responded sadly, obviously commiserating again with the plight of the underdogs.

"Jackson hated Indians. He saw it as one of his key missions, first as the military governor of Florida, then later as President of the United States, to do away with them. He was largely responsible for passage of the *Indian Removal Act*, which would get them out of the civilized part of the country, out to west of the Mississippi River," Percy explained. "But there was this one battle, I'm tellin' you, where the Indian had the final say," Percy proudly proclaimed on behalf of his mistreated brethern.

"Did the Indians beat the white man?" Cory inquired, excitedly.

"Not once, but a couple of times. Twice, the Indian got the upper hand," his father replied. "War Chief Halpatter killed Major Dade—by the way, Halpatter's name was derived from *alla-patta*, a Seminole word for alligator—anyway, ole Alligator and his warriors killed Major

Dade and most of Dade's soldiers east of Tampa."

"How many men died?"

"Almost all of Dade's 110 soldiers were killed. I think a couple were spared."

"But where the Indian really snookered the white man was in another battle a couple years later. I mean it took some white men by surprise," Percy related with pride, in vicariously reliving the rare show of victory for the downtrodden.

"Was that Major Dade fella after the Indians?"

"Sure was. That was at the beginning of the Second Seminole War, when General Winfield Scott was fightin' to get all the Seminoles outta this area around 1835 or so. Osceola was makin' noise, and trouble was astir. After Scott was relieved of duty because of his lack of success, and sent out to fight the Mexicans in Texas, General Jesup took over and lured them into capture using flags of truce."

"What's a flag of truce?" Cory innocently demanded.

Turning the yellowed pages of an old, dusty, mildew-covered book, Percy traced his finger down the columns, studying the words, then said, "Here, *truce*; the dictionary calls it a *cessation of hostilities*."

"And, hostilities means war, right? Cory confirmed.

His father nodded and continued, "Well, anyway, Jesup's men got Coacoochee the Wildcat and Chief Osceola, who really wasn't ever a Chief. He was a great warrior who fought for his people. Jesup had 'em both shipped to Ft. Marion at St. Augustine. That's the same place Geronimo ended up, by the way. He even died there. Anyway, Osceola was later taken to and died near Charleston, I think, but not until after he killed General Thompson in a battle near Ocala."

"You mean Osceola killed a white general?"

"I mean he did. That bugger hated ole General Wiley Thompson for capturing him and his wife and selling his wife into slavery. He vowed to get the General and I mean he finally did, sometime in the 1830s."

"But he later got captured again?" Cory questioned.

"Yea, he and Caocoochee both got sent to that fort at St. Augustine, you know the one I took you to?"

"What happened to the Wildcat?"

"Story has it that Caocoochee and a lot of his men quit eatin' and got skinny enough to escape through their jail bars. Then he got a band of some warrior Creeks and Miccosukees and went down to the Kissimmee River near Lake Okeechobee. The Colonel of this operation, none less than Zachary Taylor, had a regiment of a thousand or so men, some regulars, some volunteers, and even some Indians, I'm told. Anyway, on Christmas Day of 1837, Taylor surrounded a thick, wet cypress hammock where Caocoochee's bunch was supposed to be, but as Taylor's men approached to attack, all deployed around the Indian encampment, they discovered to their surprise that the cypresses were deserted. Fires were still burning, but the Redskins had disappeared."

"Where had they gone?" Cory asked, fascinated.

"You know they're wily—sly. "It seems they had cut a wide swath, 50 yards or so, and 300 yards long, through a thicket of high sawgrass in a foreboding, marshy, wetland area leading up to a dense jungle, an oasis of high ground where the Seminoles were hiding. There, poised and ready, the Indians waited to do battle. Some were sittin' like snipers in trees, others carefully hidden behind bushes and logs, guns loaded, resting, notched on the tree branches, keeping a vigilant look-out, carefully and quietly, hoping the white men would take their bait."

"How did Zachary Taylor's men know where they were hidin'?" Cory inquired.

"One captured a young Indian warrior who was keeping watch over several hundred head of cattle near the site. He was obviously planted by the Indians to lure the Federal men over. When Taylor's man asked him where the warriors were, and threatened to hang him if he didn't tell, he pointed, seemingly reluctantly, to another thick grove of bright green cypress growth, some two miles westward."

"Was it a setup?" Cory wondered.

"Seems obvious. Taylor ordered horses and equipment moved onto high ground and decided to conduct a direct attack right smack through that tempting swath the Indians had cut to an easy quarry. One of his officers suggested that Taylor flank the Indians from either side, perceiving a possible trap. Taylor said no. As the company began its march, trudging slowly through the cold, wet, swampy, muddy, sawgrass-covered terrain, a barrage of gunfire attacked the federal troopers, catching them completely off their guard, unprepared. The Colonel who suggested the flank attack was killed immediately, his suspicion obviously validated. His son, one of the volunteers, fell wounded, along with a total of 111 others as Caocochee's rifles loudly cracked in that fusillade of bullets and gunpowder. Twenty-six Americans were ultimately killed, including a lieutenant colonel, a key lieutenant, and Captain VanSwearingen, a personal friend of Zachary Taylor's. Well, needless to say, Taylor greatly mourned his friend's loss on that fateful Christmas near the little catfishin' village north of Lake Okeechobee."

"Golly, the Indians sure pulled one over on them, didn't they?" the boy asked.

"I'll say they did, by jingoes!" Percy crisply responded, "and of the 300 some odd Indians, only 9 or 10 were killed, and about that many injured. Federal troops outnumbered them by almost three to one. And while I guess you could say the government won, the Indians still pride that battle as one of their noblest."

"Did Taylor survive?"

"Oh yea, even went on to become President of the United States, but his nickname, 'Old Rough and Ready,' was not earned from that battle on that day with Caocochee."

Chapter Thirty-two

U p in the pilot house were Peter's living quarters, with a cot at its center. His lavatory was a wide hole in the floor with a drain pipe leading to the bottom of the boat. Stained muslin curtains hung over the little windows, one of which was broken, arranged in a semi-circle around the upper station from which the Captain guided the big boat.

Looking nervously down at his gauges, then looking up, his vista of the river complete and unimpeded, he yelled to the others. "Y'all check the pressure, I'm showing excess."

Percy, hearing the yelling, yet not perceiving the content of it, bolted over to the pressure gauges, realizing the sole motivation in the old man's insistence. The pressure indeed was excessive. At 270 pounds per square inch, the boiler's limit was on the verge of blowing.

"I'm shuttin' down, Pop," Percy yelled up to his father. "Back it down, we're stoppin," he added, this time a little louder. Peter hobbled down the stairs in a frenzied rage. "What the hell you doin?" he demanded. "What's goin' on? Y'all not watching my damned pressure?"

"Calm down, Pop. I was talkin' to the boy, got a little carried away. Everything's gonna be okay," Percy assured his father.

"Okay?" the man retorted, "Son, we gotta have somebody keepin' an eye on the dials. I can't steer up top and be down here at the same time," he screamed. "Son of a bitch!" he muttered loudly as he strode over to check the boiler for himself, knowing not to push his luck with his rabid expostulations.

"I'm droppin' anchor," Percy loudly shouted. With a flair for drama, he loved to articulate with full adornments, any nautical lingo.

"It'll be at least three hours before we can get underway again," Cory explained to his grandmother, who knew nothing about the boat or how it operated. "Once that thing overheats, it takes awhile for it to cool down and be restarted."

"What'll we do in the meantime?" she inquired.

"Oh, we'll just anchor here in the channel and sit it out."

"Well, how do you like that?" she responded with a slight chuckle, a smirk on her face.

Rhetta had heard her husband's outburst, and she didn't say anything to him, but was poised to do combat if he had kept it up. She would tolerate some of his rage and raving, but, at some point, "enough was enough" she would tell him, and Peter didn't dare cross her.

"Honey, everything okay?" she asked her son as he quickly moved across the deck, still trying to secure the anchor lines, which required more rope than he expected, owing to the depth of the river.

"It's fine, Momma, don't you worry a bit," he encouraged as he moved hurriedly about his duties.

"You got enough line, son?" Peter yelled with his two hands cupping his mouth.

"I think so, Pop, but it's deep," Percy replied. "What's our depth here?"

"It's right at 8 fathoms in some spots," he assured him. "You probably gonna need some more rope."

As Cory studied his aging grandmother's round features, her clear, blue eyes, he noticed the countenance of a kind, almost saintly woman, whose skin was still unblemished, even at the age of 65. Her equanimity was a welcome contrast to the red, fiery, stormy temperament of her husband, whose tempests of outrage scared the boy, despite the adoration Peter lavished on him in moments of calm. Had it not been for the boy's father, who was an obstacle - although a feeble one - to the Captain's rage, Rhetta would not have acceded to Cory's desires to work with the duo.

"You'd better not ruin that child," she had warned Peter one day after a string of perceived misfortunes plagued his comfort. "He's been through enough, and I mean you better think twice, Mr. Neesh. Think twice," she warned, with all four feet, ten inches of her steadfast resoluteness looking up to the full measure of Peter's six-foot frame with its scowling physiognomy, daring him to protest her demands.

Rhetta called Cory over to her, "Son, when I was a little girl growing up over on the island, there were black bears all over the place."

"Did any ever bother you?" he inquired.

"No, but my grandfather got chased up a tree once," she related. "They was a-huntin' in the woods over by the cape, him and his brother, I think it was, and they got too close to the bear's food—this big blackberry bush, and the female had a cub, I believe he said. Anyway, she chased him for close to half a mile, he claimed, and while his brother took off the other way, daddy climbed up a crabapple tree as far as he could. The bear waited on the ground for him near 'bout an hour, then sauntered off' and left him alone. He came home, told us kids and Mama about it, scared to death, but tried to act all brave. We knew he had been terrified. That's all we heard for a month."

"Did he get injured?" Cory asked.

"No, just embarrassed the fool out of him. I'm surprised he told anybody about it, but I guess it was too exciting to keep to himself. I can assure you they didn't get near any black bears and their blackberry bushes anymore, nor did they go huntin' near that spot ever again. Your daddy was about 14 then. There's still bears over there."

So, black bears like blackberries, the boy thought, noticing the alliteration and the rhyme. Cory was clever. His gift for grammar and writing was high, even though his schooling was procured completely in lessons his father and grandmother provided. He would eventually graduate eighth grade, even receive a diploma, but, both before and after that, his services were needed on the boat. Cory was strong and sinewy, although of medium height, weight, and build. Too great utility lay in his contribution aboard the vessel to be wasted in formal schooling. Percy was assured, almost cocky, that given the depth of his own studies and reading, the boy would never want for knowledge.

"That wadn't too smart of his brother, runnin' the other way when the bear was chasin', was it grandma?" Cory asked Rhetta.

"No, they shoulda stuck together, but you wanna know something, son? Everybody is always alone. I mean you may be here with me and your daddy and Pop Pop, or you may even go to a dance when you get older, but you're always alone in this world," she told Cory.

"What about your friends?" Cory asked.

"They can make you feel you're not alone," Rhetta responded, "but no matter how many people there are around you, when it's all said and done, it's just you. I'm telling you that not to scare you, but to make you real, Cory. It's being real that's more important than anything. I've found in my old age that I can count on myself and that's pretty much it. And, I'm sayin' that while lovin' you, your daddy and Pop Pop. We're just all of us alone in this world. We're born alone, and we die alone. Don't ever pity anyone who seems to have it worse than you do, and don't ever envy another who seems to have it better, because that aloneness in all of us is to be pitied. Remember that always, honey."

"I will grandma."

"And, one other thing, when we're alone and when we're faced with trouble, like this engine that won't start, we're more alive than ever."

"What does that mean—we're more alive?"

"It means that trouble or crisis or turmoil may not be the most fun moments of life, but that is when people's lives take on the most meaning. My Swedish grandmother used to tell me that when she'd talk about her family immigrating to America back before the Civil War," Rhetta explained. "Times were tough, but her daddy and mama were determined to make it in Wrightsville, Georgia. She'd had enough snow and cold and Lord knows those mountains over there in Sweden don't grow nothin'. When I was a little girl she'd say 'we're most alive when our trials are the most intense.'

And, you wanna know something? I think she may have been on to something.'"

"Oh," was all Cory said.

Hours passed while the boat's little family stayed put.

"We ready to fire this thing up?" Peter yelled to Percy.

"It should be cool, let's try it," Percy replied.

"What's your pressure readin'?" the Captain inquired of his son.

"It's right at 150 per square," Percy informed him.

"Okay, release a few pounds and let's kick her up," Peter commanded.

Percy toyed with a shut off valve, turning it to the left to release some steam pressure, then flipped a toggle switch to start the powerful engine. Nothing happened. He tried it twice more.

"Nothing doin'," he yelled to his father.

"What the hell?" Peter demanded.

"Peter Neesh!" Retta yelled at her husband.

"Yes, M'am," Peter responded.

"Our grandson is aboard and listening to what you say," she cautioned.

"Thank you, M'am," he responded.

The boat was still at anchor in the wide, deep river, and the steam engine remained silent.

∞ ∞ ∞

Chapter Thirty-three

As Todd and Doss meandered through first the superstructure and then some of the lower hatches of the shipwrecked *Janice*, the state of preservation, Doss noticed, was excellent. He knew that the material from which ships were constructed largely determined the vessel's underwater condition. A ship covered in silt would fare better than one lying exposed. The level of salinity was a factor, and so was depth. Octopuses and crustaceans tend to seek refuge from tidal current at wreck sites, and those creatures typically break items, appurtenances of a ship, in their path of movement. A marine archaeologist would be challenged when attempting to piece together that giant puzzle.

The *Janice* had been a Coast Guard Cutter commissioned in 1936 and had served patrol as well as convoy escort duty during her days atop the waves. In 1942, she had been a flagship for *Operation Dragoon* during the D-Day invasion.

The launching of the *Janice* had occurred one year earlier, in 1935, giving the hull its name and identity. Before commissioning, there were electronic systems to be tested, completion of the galley, weapons configuration and the engineering equipment whose addition would convert her hull into an operational warship ready for habitation.

Her crow's nest—the topmost point—lay under fifty feet of seawater, while her deck lay at 97 feet. Hordes of reef fish, turquoise, pinks, blues, greens and yellows, meandered near the wreck. Not far off were a couple of silver dotted Great Barracuda with their menacing, exposed teeth. There was also a Bull Shark.

As the two men dove the wreck, Doss noticed Todd thirty feet deeper than himself, inspecting the few extant wooden components. Wood exposed to the salinity and tidal flow was first to decay, with preservation reserved for those portions buried in silt or sand. Shipworms are more abundant in waters that are particularly salty, such as those of the Caribbean, and, along with other wood-boring sea critters, can destroy a wooden hull in short order. Ships built from steel, a ferrous metal, particularly if the material is thick, may be preserved unaltered for a long time. Eventually, corrosion, when added to the tides and weather, conspire to collapse a wreck's structure. Items of thickest ferrous material, such as a steam boiler or cannon, are spared for a time. Since most propellers, portholes and hinges are fashioned out of non-ferrous metals, such as brass and bronze, they rarely corrode.

Two favorable factors for preservation are fresh water and low salinity. The USS Hamilton, lying at the bottom of Lake Ontario in about 300 feet of icy cold freshwater from a storm in 1813, is extremely well preserved. Its masts are relatively pristine and cannonballs are orderly piled aboard the ship. Salt - sodium and chloride ions - lead to an accelerated chemical oxidation which inevitably results in rust, even rusticles, as seen in deep-water shipwrecks such as the Titanic, Lusitania and Bismarck.

Doss examined the gunwale of the port side. He knew that the gunwale, a/k/a *gun ridge*, was a band or wale—a thick wooden plank—added above the gun deck so that the explosive stress of artillery fire would not tear the ship asunder. There is a similar reinforcing hunk of wood often placed next the keel, the fin-like item on the underside, which must endure a great deal of stress. It's called a *garboard*.

Doss, as a scholar of law, contemplated the legalities of a shipwreck. He recognized that the wreck itself was separate from the cargo carried. The remains of a vessel are owned by insurance underwriters who are subrogated to the proceeds of any policy paid out. Since the company has paid for the loss, anything that remains, now belongs to it. It works the same way with a car wreck. The insurance company pays the owner for loss, and subsequently owns both the car and the claim against the at-fault party. The cargo, in comparison, property aboard a wreck, belongs to its owners. If a military vessel, it's owned by the government that lost the ship. Only Doss would be thinking about law during a scuba trip.

As Todd continued to explore the capstan and starboard bulkhead of the *Janice* at about a hundred feet, Doss recalled that salvage hunters, are entitled to a proportion of a ship's cargo. In fact, a salvor's rights may supersede those of the original owners and, if the shipwreck is a civilian one, and if it's not associated with an historic event, it's fair game. And, for wrecks beyond a certain number of years, there may be no legitimate claim by the original owner to the cargo. The salvor files a salvage claim, places a lien and then commences recovering booty. All legal stuff. Doss would be dwelling on liens and writs and motions when his students returned for class in a couple of weeks. Todd's interest in scuba diving came as a thrill to Doss, especially in light of this youngest son's disappointment in the college football program that had not utilized his talents. Doss had special empathy and was largely motivated by that when he brought his son to dive in the Keys. Some of Todd's stories strained credibility. "Coaches could be downright vile," Doss concluded.

Hail to the Victorious Ones! Now, get your ass ready for the lifting workouts with coach Mort Gitelman," the offensive coordinator barked. Gitelman, the weight trainer and coach had been an inspirational mentor for the punter when he arrived to play two years earlier. Generally, Todd did not associate Jews he knew with weight training—but Mort defied the stereotype. His muscles were huge. He and Todd kidded each other about Yiddish words the two of them shared some small knowledge of. Gitelman even told his Beth Shalom rabbi about the time Todd confused mazel tov with matzo. It seems that the punter had asked for mazel soup at training table, doubting that was ever on the menu. Gitelman overheard the player and almost hyperventilated from laughing so hard. Todd loved the book by Leo Rosten called *The Joys of Yiddish.* He found it a colorful, amusing language.

As a high school football player, Todd had seen his name in lights back in Georgia—and on the front page of most of the newspapers. His team had even competed for a championship once.

In contrast to sunny south Georgia, the college in the north was cold and overcast, with sunless days seemingly without end. Todd had been thrust further down the depth chart, now ranked behind two other players. In pensive moments, he wondered how these seemingly less talented players had surpassed him. He knew he could not 'bulk-up' as much as trainers would have liked, but that had posed no problem to the coaches recruiting him, who practically begged him to come play at their college.

"Neesh, get over here, I've got a new number for you," one of the assistant coaches commanded.

"For right now, you're number 43," the coach barked at the player, whose stoic demeanor belied the indignation he felt having his number peremptorily snatched away from him with no consultation or discussion. He neither desired nor had ever worn 43 in the twelve years he had played the sport, beginning in fourth grade.

"Coach, I'm happy to wear whatever number. "Hell, give me 143, just let me get some reps," was Todd's response. He had but a modicum of dignity after a couple of years being ignored, overlooked, and pretty much discarded.

An hour after practice, Todd requested some one-on-one time with the coach in his office. After demurring, the brusque team mentor agreed to give the athlete ten minutes. Cautiously, the boy from Georgia entered the coach's office paneled in birdseye maple. In the middle was an ornate desk trimmed in pink ivory and African blackwood, carved and blended delicately. Preaching already, the coach, with books titled *Managing the Clock, Blitzing versus Covering*, and *How to Make Your Opponent Eat Dirt*, had a spiel--no doubt well rehearsed:

"Whether you play or not, boy, you're a *Grizzly*, just remember that. What could be better?"

Have a seat," the coach barked, half hospitable, half demanding. "You are family now and will continue to be a member of a great legend. What young man wouldn't want to be a member of a fraternity that includes some great American leaders and a host of NFL greats?"

"That's awesome, Coach, but I want to play some football."

"Don't forget, Neesh, you're a meaningful and contributing part of this team whether you're out there punting on fourth and four, running up the middle on a keeper, or simply standing on the sideline rooting your teammates to victory."

"My *family members* to victory," the boy thought.

"There's nothing like actual playing time, which is what I've sorta' gotten used to over the years. I was on the first-team squad over a hundred games in fourteen years.

"Hell, boy, that's why we awarded you a full scholarship. Books paid in full. Free tuition and courses—what more could you ask?" he continued. "Plus," the coach added as an afterthought, "at least a chance at any girl on campus."

"The only thing more I would ask, Coach, is to play."

"Well, you know we've got these blue chippers coming in from California and Texas, and both of 'em can kick and run the football."

"But, I also know when y'all recruited me, you told me I was gonna play," Todd responded gently but assertively.

"Son," the coach, squinting as his eyes were drawn tight now in a serious 'hear what I have to say manner': "Gonna let you in on a lil' secret if you promise you can keep it: We tell every kid and every mother and father what they wanna hear. We gotta get a kid before some other school does. It's competition from start to finish, even before there's a kickoff."

"Is my jersey number going to be worn by one of those blue chippers you're bringing in?"

"Yep. This kid will be a huge plus for the program and he wants the number he had in high school—which just so happens to be the number you wore in high school. We gotta give it to him, because we promised. What kinda coach would I be if I lied to this kid after promising him he could wear number 7?"

"Yea, coach. You're right."

Silence was palpable.

"I mean, how would we be perceived if we didn't do what we said," seemingly not conscious of irony that bounced off the birdseye maple walls and back again.

"That boy asked for number 7. Wouldn't agree to come here until I promised it several months ago. I'd a-like to talk'd to you first, but son, you got to remember that in this business, you do what it takes to entice a top-notch player. Then you turn right around and do whatever it takes to find someone even better, all the while promising both of them the moon," the coach reported in stunning frankness.

"I see."

"That doesn't mean you're not a real fine kid. Good work ethic, good raisings, fine family, God-fearing parents, and someone that always puts himself second to the interests of the team. Given those traits, I knew you wouldn't mind me taking your number and giving it to this new kid coming on board. No doubt he'll be homesick; they all are," the coach decided resolutely.

"I never was, Coach. I s'pose I could have been, but too much of my time was occupied with honing my skills to play. No time to get homesick."

"Son, I believe that about you. You're a man. It's time all these little turds became a man. Let me tell you a little secret that really isn't too secret: if snatching a recruit means tempting him away from some other college program that he's already committed to, that's so rewarding. To grab a recruit away from an arch-rival, especially if the kid looks like he's gonna get some really good play time...say what you will, we're gonna do it. That's the cold, hard facts of collegiate football. You see, in reality, it's not a game at all, it's a business—a big business...hell, it's more than that—this here's a billion dollar industry. We got boosters whose contributions diminish proportionally to our losing games; and those same people don't mind shelling out thousands of those little green babies when we're winning," the coach ranted.

"Hell, there's even stories of big-money boosters calling the athletic director and college president, threatening to withhold their donations if things don't suit 'em. No coach would ever admit to being influenced by the boosters. Coaches typically say 'we'll listen politely, then do exactly as we please.' Yea, until the money starts drying up. I'm earnin' big money just to get this program out of the shithole. Can't let the hurt feelings of a couple of players, or hell, the whole team, stand in the way of my job. Got a family to feed. This is my career on the line. We're gonna win if it hairlips ole Granny. I can't mollycoddle some little turd and let that stand in the way of this enterprise. If it's between me and a kid's hurt feelings, well, you know how that's gonna go down," he added with no apology.

"Know what you orta' do? You're smart. You orta' get into coaching and work your way up to a big school. Who ever thought I myself would be here? Hell, I wadn't worf' a shit as a player, but I've enjoyed every freakin' minute on this runaway train—and made a good livin' in the process."

"I know about ambition, Coach," Todd finally got in a word.

"Pursue something you can be successful at, like coaching. Hell, look at what you got. You got a full ride."

"Look at how I did perform when I was out there for a couple of scrimmages," the player reminded the coach.

"You done good. I was proud of you. You ran for a twelve-yard gain right over our big logo letter in the middle of the field. That made my heart skip a little, seeing you trouncing over that emblem of pride and glory. Holy ground. Not only that, you were running against the first-string defense."

"Maybe with a couple of plays like that I could get some play time?"

"Get a good education. We're paying for it, after all. We're a good school. And, never forget: you're a man of the North now—part of the family."

After weight lifting, Todd spotted his position coach Willy Alvarez standing between the training room and the treatment center where a whirlpool, massage device, hydro-electric apparatus, and other physical therapy gadgets awaited sore players. The boy sauntered over to the stainless steel montage of 'feel-good' mechanisms and told him: "Perhaps, coach, I'm not the player I think I am."

He proceeded to ruefully recount the jersey-snatching episode to Alvarez, who assured him it was nothing personal. "Neesh, you know how things work at this level. This ain't Pop Warner. It's not even high school. This is football at its most heroic—maybe even a bigger enterprise than the pros. And, without those million dollar player salaries. You know any of them would gladly play for a tenth as much. You know that...let it go.... Hell, we just switched shoe brands from *Scooters* to *Jumpers*...wanna know what *Jumpers* paid us? Ten million dollars. Just to wear their damned shoes. Big business. Big money," he brusquely asserted. "If *Mercury* wants us to wear their damned shoes next year and pays us twelve mill, we'll be wearing *Mercuries*, without a doubt."

"I don't know, Coach, I'm from the South. People are gentler, more humane there, I'm afraid."

"Bullshit, Neesh! It's the same everywhere. The system, the way it works, the dog-eat-dog' brutality—civility be damned. This isn't a 'chuck 'em under the chin' or 'stroke 'em till they feel good' operation that tries to please—'cept fans and boosters. We gotta win football games, or we don't keep our jobs. I'm making ten times more than I did as a police officer. The head coach is making a couple million. We can't lose that money—that's more than our fathers and their fathers earned put together—and we're not going to be deprived of those lucrative salaries. Wanna know something? If we didn't coach, you know what we'd be doing for a living? Most of us would be selling used cars, life insurance or shoes. A few would be cops, like I was," he concluded.

Diving on the shipwreck presented a welcome respite from the turmoil and humiliation Todd had been part of. What had started out a hundred years ago as a group of school boys entertaining themselves with sports after class, had devolved into a base form of commercialism. Nonetheless, the athletic scholarship had provided a wonderful opportunity for students to receive a quality education. That was a definite plus, no doubt.

Chapter Thirty-four

Moments of quiet while driving, headsets covering the boys' ears, listening to music, or dozing —didn't bother Doss. In fact, his mind was drawn, in moments such as this, to the multitude of stories his father Cory had told him 40 years ago—stories which had their origins 50 years before that. One he remembered and snickered at was of an event aboard *Corona,* both calamitous and hilarious. Cory had just turned 15 when it happened. He had awakened, startled, by the strident sound of a foot stomping on the deck above, undoubtedly from Peter, accompanied by his—and only his—rhythm of swearing.

"Son of a bitch, I'll be a son of a bitch—you stupid... . You've let the—what the hell have you done?" That was what Cory thought he heard through the thick teak deck. Snippets of such ravings were not uncommon, asleep or awake, above deck, or below. Rantings of that kind could be expected, especially when a barge was being towed. It seemed that bad things happened when those flat-bottomed transport vessels for heavy goods, trailed behind, tethered to the steamboat. But, they proved useful in hauling produce. In fact, as the American West was conquered by settlers, barges could be navigated downriver, and tenders of the craft would pole with muscular arms upriver against heavy Mississippi River currents. That method proved faster than proceeding over the primitive dirt roads, which were not abundant.

That tirade alone might not have wakened the boy, but the stomping in double time, heavy and urgent, did alarm him into consciousness. Cory looked around the sleeping quarters as he raised his head from the soft down pillow, still warm from his head. As he focused his eyes and mind, he tried to surmise the complication which had prompted his grandfather's tantrum, remembering the barge, laden with hampers of beans. The scene was not visible from his narrow quarters. He saw only the vast lake and slight chops of wave activity upon its surface. He thought he saw a gator's head surface some fifty feet west of the boat, but as he squinted his eyes to confirm the reptile's presence, whatever may have been there, was no longer. Still tired from loading hampers the night before, Cory debated the reasons favoring and opposing his attendance at the rant above.

Otis, a black man whom Peter had hired, had dozed, causing the barge to list, in turn resulting in a slow seeping of lake water into its hull. Otis was a big man, with big, calloused hands, and had a habit of napping when he served as a security watchman on the boat, oftentimes when it was docked. Near the pier in Pahokee, Peter felt the boat was in a less secure open area and often paid Otis fifty cents a week to sleep aboard at night. Fortunately, his siestas had not previously been an issue, since had any prowlers come aboard, or even near the craft, Otis presumably would have awakened. In fact, even the big man's very presence was enough to dissuade would-be trespassers. He would slouch down in that comfortable Muskoka plank chair that Percy had brought back from Lake Couchiching north of Toronto, when he visited Canada two summers ago. Much like an Adirondack, the plank chair has five boards angled backwards, and wide armrests.

On this occasion, however, several hundred hampers of pole beans were being transported from the loading dock to the railroad terminus in Lakeport. Sleeping by a hired hand should not have occurred. During Otis's moments of inattention, the barge began to yaw just enough that over the course of ten or so minutes, water inundated the bilge. Doss tried hard to remember the subtleties of the story Cory had related that both he and Doss cackled over. Assuredly, as a young teenager, Cory, witnessing the event firsthand didn't find anything funny, especially when Peter dressed the man down.

When Peter saw that the barge had become waterlogged, he yelled to Otis: "Shit! Shitfire, boy! Did you fall asleep? What in hell were you doing? We paid you a half dollar—a brand new 1924 Walkin' Liberty half dollar—to watch the barge. Most 'yo Nigra buddies are lucky to earn half that much today—and your sorry ass falls asleep and lets the barge track adrift."

Grabbing this man twice his size, Peter, a blue artery bulging on the side of his reddening forehead, mouth tight, lips pursed, yanked Otis by the collar, then turned him sideways by grabbing his slack, worn belt. The dark man could have easily manhandled the white-bearded captain whose back was hunched and legs bowed, yet he calmly abided the old man's ravings, aware that his brief, ill-timed shut-eye had allowed the stern of the barge to swing, dip, and ultimately take on water. He owned it was "all my fault." Even mild-mannered Percy cussed and moaned and screamed insults as the big man hemmed and hawed in a faltering stammer, half-heartedly defending himself.

Percy was of kind heart and gentle spirit in most situations, slow to denigrate others, especially based on differentness in general. Having read a great deal of history, and studied modern civilizations, as well as those of antiquity, and being an admirer of cultural nuance, Percy knew the ancient Egyptians and Persians were not fair-skinned people. They had remarkable achievements in architecture, engineering, construction, and mathematics. Percy's Ku Klux Klan father, possessed a bigotry Percy neither admired, nor desired to emulate. But, this load of beans, Percy had worked—and worked hard—for. In fact, upon harvesting the beans, two days earlier, he had noticed an aspect about them, whether their plumpness or depth of color, or both, he couldn't pinpoint, but this crop was special, and, "They'll bring a purdy penny," he had told Peter.

Percy dove overboard to salvage what he could of the lost cargo. He knew as he plunged into the dark water that half their bean crop was drifting toward the bottom or already lay twenty-two feet below. As he submerged himself, flailing his hands to grab a bean pod here and one there, Percy recognized the futility of his efforts. He surfaced after diving a few times, his face red and flustered, squirting water from his mouth. Some beans were floating, but they wouldn't be for long. The final time Percy rose above the water, Cory seemed to discern a resignation in his countenance indicating any further diving or thrashing or bemoaning the loss, would be pointless. Percy paddled his body through the water back to the steamboat, having surrendered any notion of retrieving the produce.

The hours of labor plowing ground, planting seed, fertilizing and harvesting the crop, had yielded no tonnage for the railroad this trip. The produce broker in New York who casually awaited loads from countless areas of the country, was nonchalant about any single load, and equally indifferent to whatever woes that load's farmer or transporter suffered. That a barge laden with gorgeous plump green beans lay beneath Lake Okeechobee water owing to a sleeping grandson of slaves being paid a half dollar to "keep an eye out", but who then ignored that exhortation, was of little concern to the big city broker. He would rest secure in handsome profit, and that margin had little association with the price beans were "bringing".

Percy perceived a stocky, squat figure standing on the bank just beyond the upraised corner of the submerged barge. The man was Billy Tyger, one of the local Sewawee tribal men, who had heard the commotion from the canal bank. It wasn't uncommon for Seminoles to scout alligators for later capture, as the hides commanded five to ten dollars. Boots and shoes were fashionable, but the gators were also harvested for their oil to lubricate steam engines. Confederate troops during the Civil War had used gator hides, and as tanning became a reality, thanks to inventors in New York, the skin could be worked into a softer and more durable product. Demand for the hides had been up and down for the past hundred years, but at the present, it was soaring.

Peter hollered back and forth to Tyger, with a "much obliged," and "appreciate your concern, Billy," for many natives on Sewawee were known by name around Lake

Okeechobee. As the two men tried to converse, Peter's anger began to abate, thanks in large part to Tyger's appearance. The *Withlacochee* dredge huffed and hissed, nearly a quarter mile distant. With its large bucket clanking, big engine roaring and straining, custard apple groves rocked and swayed, creating little ripples which radiated outward from the waterbound trunks of the small indigenous trees.

Percy turned to look behind as he began to climb up near the stern, using a little ledge on the side of the steamboat to raise himself. "Looks like we lost about a whole load of beans, Chief," was Percy's greeting to Tyger as the Seminole native stood ready to jump in to help recover the overturned produce. "I got some fellas here can help you if you need," Billy graciously offered.

"Much obliged," Percy responded, "But Hell, there ain't no way...this Nigra here." Then he recalled his audience and felt embarrassment. He knew Tyger was aware that white settlers made little distinction between the relative worth of Negroes and Indians, feeling that both were valueless obstacles to white mans' progress. Otis looked toward his feet. Billy Tyger looked toward his.

"Sure appreciate it, though, Chief," Percy added, thankful that the focus had switched from the merits of race to assertions of gratitude. "Anything we can do for you while we're right here?" Percy asked Tyger.

"Not unless you got some fever medicine, Captain," Tyger replied to Percy, for he called most white men on a boat by that designation, not knowing Percy was merely the first-mate. Peter jealously guarded the title Captain for himself. "My cousin Red Osceola, his lil' girl is sick," the native reported, seemingly distressed over the child's condition. "Cat scratched her real bad, and arm's all red and swollen."

Percy shook his head sadly to indicate they had no fever medicine, but lowered his head in melancholy commiseration and yelled back his best wishes for "little miss to recover." Tyger yelled something to Peter that the man didn't hear, as he merely waved a final thank you. Still upset about the beans, Peter hit his knee on a bulkhead, and that reignited the cussing and stamping frustration—all those days of paid labor, not to mention five hundred hampers of pole beans.

Peter was in a quandary about whether to cut the barge loose and hope it would stay afloat until he could come back with some help to raise it, or make an effort to tow it the three miles back. The man was still red-faced, mumbling curses about "idiot stupidity," and other like rantings.

After deciding to cut the barge loose and return to Chosen, Peter Percy, Cory, and Otis, that "sorry Nigra," as he was even still being derided, jumped down from the boat onto the rickety dock, Otis stammering something to the effect he would find a way "to make it right."

All of a sudden, Percy blurted out to Peter, "Pop, now's our chance! Remember Chancey's advice? We got a reason to pay a visit to the little island of Sewawee." Peter said nothing, but Percy could tell he was thinking.

∞∞∞

Chapter Thirty-five

As the hot afternoon blew warm into the car, Earlene saw little beads of sweat pop out on Ray's forehead in tiny, almost imperceptible droplets —and next to Pa's nose and above Marie's eyebrows. The baby was crying, louder now than before he got his bottle ten minutes earlier. His face was bright red and sweaty, with half milk, half saliva dribble moving down his chin, coming from both sides of his contorted, angry mouth.

"He's not happy, mama," Earlene reported to her mother.

"He's not alone, honey," Mabel responded, never moving her gaze, looking straight ahead.

"Put that wet washcloth on his forehead, wipe it a little, see if that'll cool him off," she quietly commanded. "Lord, I can't believe it's this hot in September."

"Daddy, what about that Secret Ranch you mentioned earlier?" Earlene inquired.

"The Secret Ranch?" Pa instructed the children that if they would behave he would regale them with the story of Mr. Love's operation, hoping even baby Melrose might take an interest, or that at least by hearing a soothing murmur from his voice, would suspend his fretting.

"On my visit to the lake several months ago, I took an excursion boat," he started.

"What's that?" Marie asked.

"An excursion is a trip, a tour to someplace," he gently explained. "There was this man, I'll never forget his name, L.L. Love. His logotype, his little symbol for his business, was a big red heart. I thought, at the time, how appropriate for a man named Love!"

"You mean his initials were L.L.L.?" Earlene wanted to know. "Little lost lamb," she quickly theorized. "Live like lions," she continued having fun with alliteration. "Like em, love em, then" she hesitated, thinking for a moment on this one, " lose em," she persevered in her nonsensical sequence of possibilities.

"Love the Lord and live by his word," her mother reminded her, joining the parody.

"A man named Love...was he a lovely fella, Pa?" Earlene asked sarcastically.

"Alright, be silly and act like a monkey," he responded. "You wanna hear the story? And to answer your question, Lil' Miss, yes, if you were buyin' a big parcel of land from him, I suppose he could be right lovely," her father retorted. "He sure was hard-favored though, poor fellow. Hadda real rough face, with moles and blemishes, and a bulbous, bumpy nose that didn't quite fit his round, tarnished face. No, come to think of it, he didn't look too awful lovely," Pa critiqued, with an excessive concern over the man's appearance.

"Lord, Lewis Thompson, listen to you—is this the man who's always carrying on about a person's intellect, kindness, and compassion, and downplaying 'looks'?" Mabel retorted. Her husband thought before answering.

"Every single human being is flawed one way or another - we're all to be pitied," he finally asserted.

"Anyhow, this fella had a boat with a high roof, not like that one we saw back there on the river you had to stoop over to get in. This one had a roof made of a canvas type of material like a tarpaulin. It lay flat on a steel ribbed framework across the top to keep rain and sun off the passengers. They sat on long cushions which covered a bench, one runnin' continuously down each side of the boat. A person could hang his head out and see real good. Some of the tourists were throwing bread out to the fish and birds. I saw this big mama gator carrying some baby gators in her mouth. The passengers were sittin' way up high off the water, and down underneath was the cabin where the skipper sat and steered the boat from. I think he lived on board, cause I saw some bunks and pillows and a little stove in the middle of the cabin," Lewis recounted.

"Did you go on the boat, Pa?" Roger wanted to know.

"Not only did I go aboard, I took an excursion!" he announced, being careful to use the word he had just taught them. "I took an excursion to several places around the big lake, including out to where the Secret Ranch was," he proudly noted. "This man Love, he was a real estate speculator. A bunch of businessmen at the get-go bought up section after section of this land, which they realized could be a good investment. Thought it would command a premium price later to people like us movin' there. Love was one of those land speculation fellas, or at least he worked as a salesman for them. His job was to take people out on the boat and talk real big about all the great things soon gonna happen and how buyer's would surely get rich. Well, a lot of what he said's true," Lewis caught himself in his skepticism, reminding his listeners, especially his wife, that there was indeed great promise in that budding development that would flower into prosperity for a hard worker such as himself who was willing to persevere.

"We went down the one big canal that runs from the lake clear over to Palm Beach," he continued.

"You went to Palm Beach where all the rich people live?" Earlene interrupted with excitement.

"No, I didn't make it over to the rich folks' mansions, but we did go out several miles down the Hillsboro Canal, past the little village of Chosen to the main street of the settlement. It's named after the canal, *Hillsboro Settlement*. "There's no real town there, yet, but it's comin' soon. They're tryin' to get it off the ground. There's a few businesses—dry goods store, a grocery store combined with the post office, a little mercantile store that has mostly furniture, and the city hall."

"You mean the post office is there with the store—all the cans and stuff?" Earlene asked.

"Right. People who live close drive their buggy or Model T, while others living miles away trek down the canal by boat, buy a week's supply, pick up their mail and head back home," he explained.

"I wanna hear about the Secret Ranch, Pa," Marie interjected after listening patiently about a future town that would one day be named *Belle Glade*--information she didn't care anything about.

"Well, anyway, there were these two men from Minnesota, or somewhere up there who believed they could grow this stuff they call *ramie*, a plant that originated in China. It grows real high into a straight stalk that's hard like wood, not green and bendable. Anyway, the men erected buildings out about 12 miles from town, on a 3,000-acre plot of land and posted *No Trespassing* signs near the entrances. The foreman would meet the mail or delivery boat at the canal to keep anyone from venturing too close to the operation and discoverin' their secrets about growing ramie. Anytime a boat would stop or slow down, they'd be out there with their shotguns, inquiring into motives."

"Rainy?" Earlene asked.

"No. It's pronounced ramie, with an '*m*', not rainy," Pa smirked, with a slight nasal snort.

"It's a fiber. "Tell you what I heard. "Egyptian civilization from thousands of years ago used it as a fabric to wrap mummies in. "But today they use it in makin' twine, and even rope or feed bags. "It doesn't rot in wet climates, it's strong, and you can't tear it up, they say."

"Why were they so secret about it," Earlene wanted to know.

"No one knows. They even had a real fast *Hacker* runabout with a V-bottom that would skim atop the water's surface - hydroplane - at 35 miles an hour, when most of the boats are lucky to do 10, and big steamboats do six. "That boat, they said, was beautiful. "Its hull was made of mahogany which they kept lacquered and buffed. "They had rails and lights and horns made of brass and chrome, shiny all over, and a 75-horsepower engine."

"Now, you tell me, why did they need all that?" Mabel, to Lewis' surprise, chimed in to inquire.

"I don't rightly know. I asked a fella that, and he said he didn't know either."

"They must have been up to no good," Mabel continued to show interest in the topic.

"No one knows why they kept everything so hush-hush." Lewis reiterated. "Probably because if this stuff did well, if it was a success, they didn't want every farmer down there tryin' to grow it. There's just so much of it can be produced before the market's flooded, and I'm guessin' they didn't want competition. Their speedboat, they called her the *Margaret James*, was named after the mother of Horace James, one of the owners of the company. They were so secretive that all the farm's employees had to live there on the farm—couldn't venture off and mix and mingle with the rest of the people. Had to swear never to talk about any business that was transacted, nor what was grown, nor how," he related.

"Is anyone sure what they grew there or is that still a secret?" Earlene wanted to know, anxiously hoping to keep the story going, the secrets pouring out.

"They aren't sure. Another fella used to sneak on the farm with a couple of his buddies and once brought back a leaf of it to the agricultural people who were in the know. Those men studied the leaf and came to the conclusion that it was a plant called *sisal*, I think they said. S-I-S-, yea, that's what they called it, sisal. It too is used as a fiber. It's like the plant they use in Mexico for makin' that whiskey they drink, what's it called? I can't think of its name. But it has these broad, waxy leaves that taper to a point at the end with sharp spikes on the very tip. It's in that same family, and it's from Mexico. That, too, was speculated as the type of plant they were growin', but the agriculture men said it wadn't exactly like that either, though it was real similar. Sisal is used to make cord. A lot like jute, which makes the stuff you wrap packages in—you know, twine," he explained.

"Did the Love man tell you all this?" Earlene demanded.

"No, some man after the tour ended was tellin' me all about the farm, but Love did relate a tale about some tourists he once took over there: While some freight from the tourist boat was being unloaded for the farm, the people on board started askin' the foreman questions about the little metal sheds over across the bank that had these rows of baby plants, growin' in wooden crates. The foreman finally told em 'Look, I ain't here as your tour guide, and I ain't answerin' no questions. If your man there knows anything about it, why don't you ask him,'" Lewis explained.

"Well, that sorta surprised the travelers on board, one of whom got real indignant and began to come outta the boat to take a picture of the operation," Lewis related. "The foreman stuck up his hand and said 'Whoa there, par'dna, you ain't comin out.'"

"So this Yankee tourist fella yelled at him, 'You can't prevent my exiting this vessel, and you can't prevent my snapping a photograph—I'm not on your land.' Well, it seems he began lookin' at that little hole in his camera and was fixin' to take a picture when the farm man told him, 'If'n you push that button, I'll smash it along with yo' head. 'Put it away, ya hear?'"

"Well this Love fellow, bein' their tour guide, and them payin' all that money to have a good time, he was mad," Lewis continued. "But, he had to stay in good with the ranch people. 'cause he delivered quite a bit of stuff out to that secret place, so he kept his mouth shut and later apologized all over himself to his guests after high-tailin' it outta there."

"Do you think the secretive man was really gonna

shoot the Yankee?" Earlene wondered.

"Could ya blame him?" Mabel couldn't resist asking, but then immediately recanted "Lord, forgive me, I shouldn't talk like that. That's my Georgia granddaddy talkin'."

"Pa, I gotta pee," Roger said bluntly.

"Urinate. It's urinate," Mabel corrected him.

"No, myinate…it's me that's gotta pee," Roger said in a silly attempt at humor.

"Okay, UR-IH-NATE," the teenager said, pronouncing each syllable carefully to satisfy his mother."

"Just go right out there," Pa commanded, pointing to some tall maiden cane weeds.

The heat was oppressive, especially for this late in the season. Blasts of hot air rolled in waves. In one area of the sky, the baby blue with white circles of cotton clouds had given way to angry shades of darkening gray. In the distance hazy light gray streaks of water fell in torrents from a particularly ominous thundercloud. The car was quiet, and even the baby too hot to voice any discontent. Loud, sharp claps of thunder reverberated in booming echoes across the flat, mostly treeless landscape.

In the distance, a huge, lifeless trunk of a tree stood, its bare and skeletal branches, protruding in countless directions. Mabel wondered whether it had been struck by lightning. Just then, a bright flash shot forth in a fiery display—a blinding bolt from sky to ground, stabbing—and then instantly disappeared.

Fat drops of water began falling on the windshield as Roger hurried back, trying to avoid getting soaked, struggling, both hands with his zipper as he ran towards them. Water drenched car and ground nearby within two minutes, and in that time, an inch covered the asphalt. A small leak just over the left rear window allowed water to drip in. It fell in quick, successive drops onto the rear seat and floorboard. Less than ten minutes from the first sign of gray sky, there seemed to be a flood in the making. The anger of the heavens visited them with a vicious dominance. Wetness covered them both from within and without as the rolled up windows created a hot and humid container.

Just as quickly as it had begun, the sky was again silent and peaceful. The rain had quit. The violence of the storm gave way to an eerie quiet as its ejaculation left no more than a vaporous residue, lifting, rising in misty clouds. The steam rose from a green plant with big broad leaves. It lifted from a cypress tree, and from the asphalt pavement, and, closest to them, from the hood of the car.

"What kind of tree is that?" Mabel's question was directed to no one and to anyone. "Do y'all see that thing?" she asked, pointing over to the unusual growth.

All heads and eyes peered to the right of the car, about 20 feet beyond. Lewis opened his door and raised his body up to peer over the top of the car for a better look.

"That's a banana plant. A banana tree. You see 'em all over these parts—anywhere in the tropics," he informed her.

The tree had wide, long leaves, some as big as a person's torso, waxy and tattered on the edges. Rib-like creases ran perpendicular to the main stem the length of the huge, light-green leaf. Shoots of young stalks of bananas, green and small but with the characteristic shape, grew out from the center with a knobby stem connecting the top to the trunk. A large, purple blossom with peels, reminiscent of a flower petal, shot from its center.

"Are they the eatin' kind?" she inquired

"Oh, yes," Lewis assured her. "But they aren't the big bananas they import from South America. They call 'em finger bananas, and people down here say they make the best banana puddin' you've ever tasted. My favorite, by far."

After quickly checking the oil and radiator, Roger looked over at an unpainted, large, two-story house that stood to the west with a seemingly abandoned car in the front yard, rusted and twisted, missing its two right wheels. A small, gray-haired man with a roundish head and face and a pair of frameless glasses pulled down on the tip of his prominent nose walked from just beyond the front steps and prepared to cross the road. He sauntered slowly toward the family's car, calling out something indistinguishable and waving his left hand to get the driver's attention. Mabel rolled down the left rear window, poking her husband gently to inform of the stranger's approach.

"How do you do, sir," the elderly man, who appeared to be in his eighties, asked Lewis.

"We're fine, neighbor," Pa quickly responded. "We saw lightning and thought it best to pull off and let the storm pass," he explained, not mentioning Roger's predicament that had prompted the stop in the first place.

"Good idea. These gullywashers ain't made for drivin' through. Good thing is though, they over 'bout as soon as they begin.

"So I've been told," Lewis answered. "Can you tell me how far it is to Canal Point?" Lewis had been wondering for the past hour. "You got a good two hours to go. You right at Yeehaw Junction just up there 'bout ten mile," the elderly man pointed down the road, "And you know the road ends at Port Mayaca, right? Whatcha goin' ther fer?"

"That's where you catch the ferry on over to Pahokee and the Hillsboro Canal community, isn't it?" Lewis asked, to confirm information, yet not answering the man's question.

"That's right. Y'all goin' all the way down there?" the man asked, eyeing the suitcases tied to the top of the car, and boxes piled under the feet of passengers.

"We're goin' down there, leavin' our farm in Georgia, to try and grow some vegetables," Pa nodded.

"You leavin' Georgia for good to go there, are ya?" he asked

"Well, you know, everyone's entitled to make a mistake or two in life," Lewis answered, chuckling apologetically for any sanity the old man perceived he lacked owing to such relocation."

"I been across over there once—Brother, it's wet. Sawgrass, alligators, but plenty of catfish. Plenty of 'em," the stranger promised.

"Yessir, and some of the most beautiful vegetables you ever seen, and you can grow 'em nearbout year round," Pa bragged, a chance to show off his vision of a better future.

"Well, I don't know about all that, but time and tide wait for no man," the old man graciously declared, pulling his index finger gently under Marie's chin as she leaned out the rear window towards him over her mother's lap. "Aren't you a purdy lil' thing? Hey there, Honey," he said, and then slowly turned without further conversation and shuffled back across the road from whence he had come.

"Nice ole man," Lewis acknowledged, adding, "These people down here seem to care about each other, checkin' on people, ready to help out."

Sure was nice of that ole fella to come over and offer help," Roger agreed.

"There's good and evil in every single one of us. They fight and fight to bear fruit in our actions. Takes a stronger person to beat back the evil - the good is beaten back real easy," Mabel observed.

"The way I got it figured, these folks bein' pioneers in a frontier, they have to work together—to cooperate." There's no room for people who don't have something to contribute," Lewis insisted. "Being a loner is a luxury of specialization; but here, everybody's got to know how to do pretty much a little of everything."

Melrose had settled down and was asleep on Marie's shoulder, who was also dozing, her head resting lightly next to the baby's. Roger turned around and smiled at his two little siblings in that configuration. Earlene could not sleep. She, like her older brother, was too excited in anticipation of the ferry Pa had told them they might have to take down the road, though neither knew what kind of floating contraption awaited them to convey their car across.

∞ ∞ ∞

Chapter Thirty-six

*S*ewauwee. The tribe of native men and women who had settled on the island near the big lake around 1860, called it *Locha Hatchee*. The word *Locha* meaning turtle, and *hatchee*, the Miccosukee translation for creek. Lieutenant Ives had looked for the place fifty years earlier, but Seminole families desperately wanted a place the white man could not find. Seminoles wanted no interaction with whites whom they felt brought nothing but destruction.

Ive's map was a good one—it showed Lake Okeechobee, and the monstrous swamps now called the Everglades and the Big Cypress Swamp—in great detail, but it didn't reveal the quarry of Seminoles to the bounty hunters. Even the southernmost Keys, south of the peninsula, and the cypress hammocks of the lower glades, adjacent to the tip, uninhabitable in its wilderness, were included in the sketches of Ive's map. A tiny community called *Sewauwee* had been the cultural and habitation hub of the island for roughly 32 family members. Many families lived scattered over Locha Hatchee in tar paper shacks and teepee-type huts or chickees, those thatch-roofed abodes.

Despite the uninviting nature of this swampy wasteland with overflowing wetness, a vast and seemingly useless marsh that cried out to would-be settlers to stay away, the charts encouraged settlement. It was on maps such as these that the white man's boundary lines, in the form of *Range 37, Township 41*, were drawn, and that included this secreted nook, remote from the world, a utopian refuge from what Indians perceived as European barbarians and savage marauders. Located on the southern edge of a gigantic body of water - big water - they felt safe.

The Hitchiti natives from what is now western Georgia named the lake *oki*--water, and *chobi*--big. Calusa Indians, who resided around the lake from the time of Christ until the 1700s, gave it another name: *Mayami*, also meaning 'big water' in their tongue.

Tribal members on Locha Hatchee sustained themselves by fishing for bream and catfish, trapping gator and otter, and growing corn and beans. Citrus fruit was something Captain Peter was pretty sure the group would savor. While they grew some citrus, they hadn't tasted tangelos, that hybrid between a tangerine and grapefruit. He had a huge bag of them that had lain in the cooler of the steamboat for two days, ever since a crew on a tug had come through the St. Lucie Canal by way of the Indian River.

Peter had thought about, on several occasions, carrying a large bag of the fruit to the Seminoles, and thereby, potentially, establishing a rapport with the tribal elders and leaders. Encouraged by Chancey's words regarding a potential trade with the Indians, Peter was, at the same time, skeptical of trading with men of such dissimilar customs and mindset. But encouraged by his son's advise, Peter agreed that perhaps indeed the time had come to visit Sewauwee. When made aware of the little girl's infection two days ago, his contemplation of visiting was acted upon.

"Come on over," Tony Barefoot, an acquaintance of Percy's, encouraged. "You all are welcome in the village," he assured. "We brought y'all something you might could use," Percy explained, stooping to nudge the huge bag of citrus fruit over the edge of *Corona*. Seeing Percy tendering the back of Tangelos over to their wagon, he quickly added, "I can see already that y'all must be good meanin' fellas to bring total strangers, something I know my people will love."

"It's clear that we all are of a like mind," Percy remarked, endeavoring to bring a confluence to two cultures that were clearly and historically divergent, and that not in a small measure.

"Come on with us, Mister Neesh," Barefoot repeated to Percy, not daring to call him by his first name. Percy, not wanting to appear indecisive for the several moments it would take to observe another's countenance, quickly declined the welcoming words by reporting that he had some little things to do before they could get underway again in a boat "whose age is tellin' on her." In fact, Percy was buying time, trying to decide whether or not to remain behind on the boat, with no repairs really necessary. He was merely tweaking a pressure gauge that could have waited. Finally, he acquiesced and agreed to go to Sewauwee.

"Last time I saw you in Chosen, you was adjustin' on that steam valve," the Native kiddingly reminded him. "It can't need that much adjusting. Get yourself over on this little island village of ours," he commanded. You're welcome here.

Barefoot, whose grandmother was English, had straight black hair that spiked up in places, with reddish-brown skin. After chatting with Percy briefly, Barefoot welcomed *Corona's* captain with a quick soft handshake and crisp hello, spoken just as plainly as anyone would on the mainland, with a hint of deference as he refrained from staring directly at the white man. Peter, who had alone walked down the dock towards the mule-pulled buggy, heard Percy calling him to wait as the groaning wooden vehicle slowly began to ease forward. Percy would go too.

Vibrating in tempo with the rocky, potholed limestone road, big spoke wheels rolled northward, parallel to the southeast shore of Lake Okeechobee. A small ferry about a mile further waited to usher the men across Pelican Bay to Sewauwee, the little village on Locha Hatchee that was home to several families of Seminole Indians. The island jutted in a northwesterly direction about two miles. Its width was half that distance. The rock road was ten-feet wide and cut a path through the middle of the island. Other, more primitive paths had been hewn out by hunters and fishermen with boats or canoes. The lightweight carriage, creaking, rocked gently onto the thick wooden ramps which permitted access to the ferry—a broad, sideless craft that could transport two such vehicles. On many days, the little steam-powered ferry never made a crossing. As it traversed the narrow channel, a brisk wind moved the brown lake water against itself in small, choppy waves that rocked the boat steadily but non-menacingly.

Before disembarking, Percy, turning his neck slowly around and up, eyed the hues of nature: variegated greens - olive, myrtle, phthalo, forest, shamrock; there were also shades of brown - chestnut, chocolate, umber, burnt sienna, tan. Particularly prevalent were patches of *strap fern*, which grew on dead trees along with green-blue *lichens* in cypress hammocks. For years, local white hunters knew Locca Hatchee was a mecca for game—turkey, deer, wild pigs, and quail—and had been welcomed by the natives.

A huge banyan tree grew tall and strong with branches that spread outward like a monstrous umbrella. Hundreds of thin rope-like appendages dangled toward the ground, where, upon contact, roots would form. Custard apple trees surrounded the giant banyan like dwarfs. Black-green *shoestring fern* and *ladder brake* radiated in imperfect circles from the ground as twisting vines in thick, tangled cords took advantage of neighboring trees to aid their climb upward. Elephant-ear plants with huge lime-green leaves grew in dense clusters around moist, low areas, and orchids held tight to the branches of rough-bark, mostly on cypress. Vanilla orchids roosted two or three on many branches, and a few butterfly orchids and other air plants—*epiphytes*—grew amid Spanish moss. Peter saw a mule ear orchid with thick, dark leaves and a flower stalk five feet long. Those were rare. Its flowers were yellow, spotted with brown. He pointed out the seldom seen bloom to Percy, poking his index finger towards a bald cypress tree twenty feet to the west.

On the northern portion of the island, a thousand more greens contrasted, yet melded, to paint a verdant vibrance of jungle growth. Then, suddenly, a clearing. In its midst stood Sewauwee and its twelve wood-framed houses, some stucco sided, some poised on stilt foundations. Whitish veneer was powdery and crumbling in areas and in others, flourishing patches of mildew darkened the stucco with fungal growth. A jagged tin roof torn by wind from the big hurricane, no doubt, curled rearward like a bent tin can lid. A window shutter hung crooked on one of the tiny dwellings, the once-bright orange and turquoise paint now oxidized into a dull patina.

Two rusty cars sat abandoned at an unusual angle, one with a windshield resembling a huge spider web from its cracked glass, the other with no front end, just a motor and fan blade. The *Sewauwee General Store*, its door ajar, stood unabashedly with asbestos-sided pride. It had functioned as a communal gathering place for mostly elders. A plant known as *Zamia* - known also as *coontie* - ran across bermuda grass. Zamia is used to make flour. Natives use the underground stems, grind it and soak it overnight. The concoction is rinsed to remove *cycasin*, a toxin that would otherwise make the root inedible. The resulting paste from coontie is left to ferment and then dried into a powder. Seminoles used the resulting powder to make a bread-like substance.

Sewauwee was dotted with *coreopsis* or *tickseed* in some areas, and a*rrowhead*, in others. *Wild poinsettia*, that native relative of the famed Christmas plant could be seen in patches on dry ground. Plugs of grass shot up through broken areas of the narrow sidewalks, lost territory being reclaimed from the concrete. Sawgrass and rubber vine, also known as *wild allamanda*, bulged upward through weaker spots in the bleached-gray asphalt of the only paved street.

Scattered around the front yard of one of the little island's cottages, Percy noticed children's toys lying marooned—a doll with a leg and an arm missing, a deflated, moldy football devoid of strings, a rust-consumed wagon with a hint of the bright red it once sported, had but a single wheel attached. He saw broken chunks of green soda-pop bottles which he thought glimmered like sparkling emeralds around front steps where afternoon gatherings of friends and family had been the highlight of daily life.

As he looked up, Peter suddenly saw the squatty, stocky man. "Welcome to the island," Sammy Tyger greeted him. "What in the world can we do for you, Captain Peter?" he queried, having known Peter and Percy both from town, seeing them at the post office and dry goods store, among other places. Most everyone around that area of the Lake either knew—or knew of—most other residents, including Natives from Locha Hatchee and its little village, Sewauwee. In some instances, there was even a measure of fraternization among many disparate folks.

"Billy told me him and his boys helped y'all with some beans that spilt out over in the Rim Canal a day or so back," Sammy said.

"Yea, we sure appreciate him and his boy's willingness to help us. Had a Nigra man s'posed to be watching, but decided to take a nap," Peter lamented.

Tyger was a young tribal elder, not at all the gray-haired, red and wrinkled, stooping old man a stranger might expect to encounter. He was probably in his mid-forties, around Percy's age, and attired in a shirt comprised of bright strips of cloth in reds, greens, yellows, blues, and turquoise. Their trousers were dungaree, that coarse thick calico cloth from India much like the Germans over in Chosen wore. Pretty much on any occasion Percy had encountered Natives in town, they were wearing what they had last been. Little about

Sammy's features revealed him as a Native American Indian. He could have been Portuguese or Mexican, but he clearly was not Caucasian. His reddish-dark complexion, the bright colored stips he wore, and a little string of small seashells about his neck, mostly concealed, were emblematic of natives.

"Chief Sammy, I understand one of your little girls over here needs medicine," Peter stated, with little salutation or formality. Not waiting for the response, the Captain greeted a child—or perhaps grandchild who appeared from behind Tyger. "I hear you got a sick lil' one," the old captain reiterated, sticking to the theme of his visit. To allay fears of an ulterior motive that would not be of benefit to the Natives, he quickly added "I brought y'all some oranges from off my steamboat."

"Sammy, is it you or Billy that's head of the tribe?" Peter asked.

"I guess you could call me the *head* leader," Tyger proudly, but with a slight sense of levity, proclaimed. "But, Billy'd tell you the same thing," as Sammy, Percy, and Peter all laughed.

"My father Daniel Tyger's really the head man, truth be told, but he's gettin' up in years. He's over in the village, reaping his lil' garden crop of corn, gettin' ready to plant some beans," Tyger announced, with no trace of foreign tones or accents in his voice. "I was fixin' to go over to Chosen to get some flour and lard, but I'll be glad to give you a ride over to where my father and Billy and Red is at."

"I'm really just interested in getting your little girl some medicine," Peter had forgotten the exact kinship between Sammy and Billy and Red and the girl, although he knew they were all somehow related.

"I got a friend over on the northwest side of the lake, a doctor. He's got medicine, and I reckon he oughta have a look at her," Peter offered. "I've been meaning to get out here for a right smart while, after Palmer said y'all might possibly be interested in doin' some trading," he added.

"You mean Palmer Chancey?" Tyger inquired. "Yea, I've known ole Palmer many a long year, quite a fella. We all trade with him. He's like family, and if he don't have it, he'll sure find it fer ya," the man claimed, praising the proprietor's diligence and business skill.

"Here, jump in the wagon, and I'll take you and brother Percy over there where my cousin and his little girl are at—it'll only take five minutes, and I'm sure they would be appreciative that you came," Tyger ensured the Captain. They's been a few of 'em over there we've been hesitant to deal with," Tyger said carefully and discreetly, as the three men rode, though with no hint of malice or ill feeling towards those Peter already knew had dealt harshly with the Seminoles.

Peter had ridden in a horse and buggy a handful of times since he left Bulloch County, Georgia in 1917. Once was on Cedar Key, a beautiful, but desolate little cypress hammock tenuously attached to the west coast of the North Florida peninsula. He had been visiting Percy and Cory's mother. Another was a year before. It occurred in a parade down the main street of a little town of 500 or so residents by the name of *Daytona*, not long after his father William Aaron had been sworn in as sheriff of Volusia County. That was about the time Peter had purchased his steamboat and begun his citrus run on the Banana River.

As the wagon vibrated in cadence, the rock road

gently swaying the men, Tyger again thanked Peter for his caring, not realizing the Captain had ideas for possible business ventures. Despite trade aspirations, both Peter and Percy cared sincerely about the little girl.

Stepping down from the wagon, a young fellow, who looked to be in his teenage years, said, "Let me grab that. Hello," the young man said to Peter, then Percy, nodding his head toward them, quickly pushing his hand toward the Captain, who after introducing himself, greeted the old chieftan—the elder tribesman —and others standing around, one of whom, a little girl, Percy assumed, was the one with the infection.

"You know, it's good when we as humans, no matter what our backgrounds, can share what we have with others. Seems like people did that more when my father and grandfather were young. We Indians have a real belief that the more one gives, especially if he doesn't look for a favor in return, the more he will be provided for. I'm sure your people have some of the same ideas, too," Billy Tyger declared, hurrying to bring himself and his culture into a kindred mindset with these white men, careful to articulate and refrain from contrasting what might be seen as divisive.

"With the possible exception," he continued, "that we don't wait for birth anniversaries or holy days to exchange gifts. No, we try to give up some possession to others as a sort of sacrifice that brings peace to our inner spirits," the man explained, then continued as an afterthought, "it's a sort of every day denial of material things whose cravings can bind like a rope" he declared.

After a brief conference with some of the tribal members who seemed appreciative of Peter's time spent on behalf of the little girl, Percy inspected the girl's streaked arm, obviously infected with some microbial organism. About to make their way back to the steamboat, Peter, then Percy said their goodbyes, Percy ending with, "Let us see what we can do. We'll be back...and, what you said about giving to others, Billy, is completely true. Let me add: It's only what you give away that you truly keep."

Chapter Thirty-seven

ROAD ENDS THREE MILES AHEAD, the sign read. "Uh-oh," Mabel thought of the irony in the message, "This is the end of us, too—or, at least me. It's not too late," she reminded herself. "We got here from Waycross in one day—one long, hard-driving, hot and sweaty day, but it was within the dimensions of 24 hours. We could just as easily turn around, head towards home, and we'd be back where we started the next. Back to familiar terrain. Back to Georgia. Back to the Fountains and their kind hospitality. We must go back!" her confused mind seemed to scream. Yet, not one word did she utter. Somehow, her resolution to go along, to get along, was complete. She would grudgingly trudge onward, even cross the wide channel on the floating bridge that carried cars, toward the swampy wilderness. He promised her that while rough-hewn, it was a soon-to-be paradise. She was reluctant, but despite grave doubts, how could she abandon the mission at this point? It was earlier in the year that she should have quashed any such endeavor, if she had ever intended to. Why hadn't she?

As the car came to a halt, Earlene asked her father if she could walk over to take a look at the lake, while he studied his map. He nodded his head, and Mabel added, "Be careful, honey."

It looked like an ocean. The big lake might easily have stretched into infinity, but she allowed herself to envision, across its waves, the topography of an alien land. This vast expanse of open, placid, clear water lay sensually before the girl, as if it were hers alone. The right of possession seemed unconditional and absolute. All others could be excluded. From the little sandy beach, no obstacles stood, except for one tree - a bald cypress - with lacy layers of fresh new green. In her thirteen years, a forest of pine trees, a barn, a cow pasture, a field of cotton or peanuts, had seemed to stand between her and the horizon. But, not now. For the first time, she could see across the way to the distant edge, and the big water was all hers for the mere taking.

"How could mother object to this paradise?" Earlene wondered. "This could be, would be, our home." As she dipped her hand slowly into the clear water, she saw small rocks lying inside crevices of ancient coral on the shallow bottom. The pure, transparent liquid slowly dribbled in tiny traces around her fingers, then cascaded into drops, gently splashing back down to reunite with a seemingly endless body of water.

The tingling of nostalgia for a faraway home seemed less palpable now, and while those memories would remain thick upon and within her soul, they would come to be surpassed—gradually—by the edge of newness, by an idyllic tomorrow.

Reality might warp a hoped-for utopia, but inherent in any reality are small dabs of beauty. Earlene had once read a poem that jumped into her mind: *Reality is bombarded by imperfection, but perfect cannot be corrupted by real.*

Here, she realized, even at her young age, there would be trials and difficulties aplenty, but there would be good times, and the sweet could not be undone, nor significantly lessened, by the bitter. The girl realized the primitive lack of conveniences. But, that had been true in Georgia, hadn't it? She seemed to intuit the drudgery that taming a swamp would entail. So, no, it wouldn't be a perfect place to live, but she—at least she —was determined to make the best of it, and to drink generously from the beauty unique to this tropical land.

Here lay a potential for newfound freedom. The power from that would provide choices. That reality fired her adolescent psyche to new heights. She looked around at a darkening horizon and visualized an abstracted, grownup image of herself. Her spirit soared, laced with alien feelings of romantic visions.

The area around this big lake, it seemed to her at that moment, had been destined to be her home. Memories of her Georgia home, her grandmother, and her friends, remained sweet and rich. But right then, her soul held a lusty promise of newness and anticipation of what might be, and what might come.

"How could her mother continue to bellyache," Earlene wondered. "Wherein lay, when all opposition was put out there, the substance of her discontent?" Near this vast pond, Earlene envisioned multitudes of people establishing businesses, making their homes. She was going to be content, and her mother—well, she hoped for her contentment.

Trees along the lake's edge could be seen for miles as the coastline curved to the northwest. Gradually, and ever so gradually, the trees began to get smaller, then finally, disappear. Then the lake and coast gradually faded and disappeared. The green of Australian pines gave way to a grayish haze, which passed into a dull whiteness that blended with the sky's dull blue. High clouds in narrow wisps slowly became tinged with setting sun reddish-orange.

Chapter Thirty-eight

As the asphalt pavement came to an end, just south of the little village they had traveled through, the dirt road began, and comprised the remainder of their travel leading to the boat ramp. An aged sign was barely visible due to its faded lettering. It read *Port Mayaca,* and an arrow beneath pointed down the road accompanied by the words *Canal Point 4 miles. Mayaca* was a Spanish term for a Native American tribe in central Florida in the 1560s. As dusk was almost upon them, and the car rolled to a stop, Mabel felt a slight stinging on her ankles. Mosquitoes. She was not unfamiliar with a mosquito bite. Georgia had them in abundance, especially after a good rain, she thought to herself. She immediately began to wonder whether they were about to be attacked on a larger scale as the sunset was complete and darkness began to creep forth.

"Oh, Lord," she exclaimed, "I feel mosquitoes. Watch the baby. You kids brush them off your ankles," she warned.

"Mosquitoes ain't gonna hurt us Mama," Earlene scoffed.

"I said to keep them off that baby, you hear?" she reiterated.

All the children were now awake and Marie was straining to see the boat dock and what kind of craft awaited them, while Ray looked in the other direction.

Both kids felt tied to this adventure—not a sight to be missed.

"Where's the ferry boat thing, Pa?" Roger asked.

"I don't see it, son," Lewis replied, somewhat anxiously.

At about that same time, a big man dressed in grubby, unwashed overalls, one strap unbuttoned and hanging, waved them forward with a red cotton rag in his right hand. Pa eased the car toward him.

"Waitin for the ferry, mister?" the man inquired.

"Yessir, I hope we're not too late."

"I'm afeared the last ferry's gone. Left well before sunset. Won't be operatin' again till sunrise. He quit early today...supposed to operate right up till dusk. That's his usual hours," the man reported matter of factly.

"Lord, we were supposed to get over there. Had a room waitin' for me and the family. We're movin' down here with y'all for good."

"You goin' to the sawgrass swamps? You can have my share of 'em. I live up over younder a piece on dry ground," he seemed to brag. "Ain't too late to change y'all's minds—it's dry here," he insisted.

"We don't need your wise comments, mister," Pa thought and almost said, "here we are, all of us with doubts about whether we're doing the right thing, mosquitoes stinging, and this man's sarcasm on top of it all."

"Well, good thing the road runs back to Georgia, just as it does to the swamp. Thank the Lord we can always turn around and head back," Lewis responded instead.

"Listen, I used to be a catfisherman. I still do that a little, but these days I'm a-helpin' my brother-in-law. I'm doin' his job while he's temporarily indisposed of.

A little problem between him and the law. I got a little shack back down this dirt road next to the bridge, right on the edge of the big lake, if y'all'd like to stay with me and the missus fer the night. Y'all'd be welcome to be our house guests," he invited.

Pa didn't know what to say. He needed to confer with Mabel, but there was no time or space nor courteous protocol to do so. What should they do? He's got a brother-in-law in jail, what kind of family is this?

"We can't put y'all out like that. That's mighty thoughtful of you to offer, but we'll just go back to the little village we came through, what's the name of it?" Pa inquired.

"Okeechobee. But there ain't no tourist rooms there that I know of," the man related.

"Well," Mabel said to Lewis in a hushed voice, "let's go with him, just be for a few hours."

"Sir, I hate to impose on y'all."

"Not a 'tall," the prospective host assured.

"Well, we sure would appreciate it. We'll be gone quick as we can. Outta your way in the wee hours.

"I'm Bobby O'Steen," the man announced, sticking out his hand for Pa's, the traveling man from Georgia thanking him again. "Y'all more than welcome. Here, follow me. I'll carry you over yonder and introduce you to my wife," pointing over by the bridge. "Let me close things up 'round here."

He headed for a rickety Ford Model *Double T* wood-paneled truck, with its tires low on air. After four attempts the ignition fired up worn pistons and little bursts of light colored smoke puffed out the tailpipe.

"Just follow me," he motioned toward the rock road.

Earlene's father, cranking the Star, followed the

man to a large, wooden-planked bridge which crossed a waterway resembling a river. On second glance, the river had a manmade appearance. A rude interruption not from nature had created it, had cut steep, sheer edges, exposing tree roots, chopped, convenient...promoting commerce. Not a river - a wide canal.

A slender woman—quite skinny really—ambled over with a slight limp. There was a weathered cottage set close to a drawbridge that opened to allow boat traffic to pass. The house was high on poles, as they later learned, stilts, with a large empty space underneath.

Mr. O'Steen yelled to the woman, "Inez, we got comp'ny! They tired, and Wilder's ferry's done quit fer the night."

The adults and children disembarked from the car, one-by-one. Holding back a little were Mabel and Earlene, a little less so Marie and Ray, all of them not knowing what this situation presented. The slender woman with graying hair tangled and lopsided, hurried over to the group, chuckin' Ray under the chin, complimenting him for his friendliness as he held his hand up in greeting.

Mrs. O'Steen's squeaky voice yelled out, her prominent chin and nose protruding from a narrow face. "Y'all been travelin' a right smart distance, I take it." "Don't fret about that ole bridge. It gets stuck 'bout half the time, and to heap up trouble, the ferry boat's left y'all stranded. Come five o'clock, Woody Wilder's gone. By ten after, he's outta sight. That man do not stick around. And, he don't care about people he leaves behind neither. If'n the bridge ain't workin' that ole ferry boat comes in right handy. I don't think Wilder's nary toted one passenger what comes a minute late. He's plumb down to Lauderdale by now in that water-sobbed, ramshackle, catfishing boat of his. Man stops, shuts down the ferryboat, then quick as he can, jumps in that used-up swamp-donkey of his'n. I'm sorry fer' carryin' on, but it riles me how he complains he got no bidness, catfishin's off, then a passel of nice folks like y'all comes along, and he's nowhere to be found. He purt near lost everything he had last year, and he would have excusing for his papa's comin' to his rescue. I can't tell you how many times the law's been out here huntin' that man, owing' to this or that trouble Woody's stuck his nose in."

"Well, looks like we're stuck right along with the bridge," Mabel nodded politely.

"Oh, no you're not," Mrs. O'Steen responded. "Not on account of that bootlegger."

"Really?" Mabel responded.

"Yea. Lord, I shouldn't gossip like this, but we kindly think the man's runnin' illegal whiskey from over in the islands. Says he's haulin' catfish to Lauderdale," the frail woman explained. "That might be the reason he's so quick to leave outta here, I've told Herman."

"Well, that's interesting," Mabel asserted, wondering nervously again about the wisdom of this family adventure she was a part of. "Do y'all have a lot of that goin' on down here?"

"Honey, they's scoundrels a' plenty here and everywhere else, I 'spose. Only problem is, around this place, the law ain't overly quick to jump in against someone who has money or a name for hisself. Seems like folks team up with the bigshot. Little man gets to know someone with money, then first thing you know, they's illegal gambling, illegal rum-running, illegal girls. Lord, what's this ole world a-comin' to?" Mrs. O'Steen wondered. "You know, they's one or two in every crowd that's never satisfied—could never get enough, never have enough—I think those folks die more savagely than the rest of us," she insisted, abstract thoughts from a woman whose surface appearance was simple and shallow.

"Lord, you're right on that," Mabel agreed.

"Well, doggone that puny ole bridge, anyway," she quickly shifted to the here and now.

The thin wife of the catfisherman wore light blue plastic-rimmed eyeglasses slightly askew on her face, the left lens thinly cracked near the edge closest to her long straight nose. There was a safety pin holding one arm of the glasses affixed to the scruffy frame. Her faded, tan-and-yellow gingham dress had not been ironed, Mabel could tell by looking at the garment's rumpled simplicity. Gray hair, piled up and disheveled, had some strands escaping the security of a rusted barrette, and hung straight on both sides of her smallish head. Beady dark eyes squinted at her listeners.

Mabel thought to herself "maybe it's good the bridge wasn't working, otherwise, this hospitable woman and man would have been passed by." She visualized the Thompson family moving along, rolling inside their car past the stilted shack, heading over a drawbridge not stuck, recipients of a casual wave, perhaps. Fate can lead to complex, unforeseeable events.

Mrs. O'Steen seemed to savor the information she had teased Mabel with a minute or so earlier, in order to have the whole family hear her announcement, "Y'all ain't a-stuck nowhere. Come on. I'll fry y'all up some catfish and corn dodgers," without wasting a great deal of time to catch her breath, she continued, "Then, y'all gon' bed down with us for the night," boldly assuming an acceptance of her invitation.   She quickly added, "They's always some catfish and corn meal around this house—and grits. Not to mention pork and beans."

Mabel, feeling a bit of shame, tried to relieve the emaciated woman from the onus of a carload of company, "Honey, I hate for you to go to any trouble for us, but we sure appreciate you offering. I know you weren't counting on a load of travelers from Georgia barging in on y'all, but I sure would appreciate a little milk, if you have any, for my baby's bottle. Otherwise, we'll be fine right here in the car till the morning ferry."

"Sweetheart, no trouble at all. 'Sides, them mersquiters would eat you alive. They come out at dark, I'm a-tellin' ya. Fact is, I insist. Herman and me, well, we get lonely out here by ourselves, and I got a cousin in Woodbine, Georgia, near the Florida line," she proudly proclaimed as though a camaraderie arose through the geographic association of kinfolk. "Plus, my grandmama was from Georgia - Folkston," she reported. "And, yes, I've got some goat's milk - now y'all gon' march yourselves right into our humble shack and stay with us the night. Besides, whether I was plannin' for y'all or not, I'm not gonna let any family the good Lord sends my way go hungry or without shelter, if they's anything I can do to stop it," she proudly announced, with a hint of righteous indignation that they might even consider refusing her hospitality.

"Y'all know in the Old Testament it was a custom to feed anyone who stopped over to somebody's house. In fact, the man of the house would even pour their glass of iced tea to where it spilt over on the table, if'n he didn't mind the traveler stayin' fer the night. But now, mind you, if that cup was not poured to overflowing, then the traveler knew that after the meal, his time was up," Inez explained.

"Matter of fact, you hear about 'my cup runneth over' in the Psalms? Remember, it's all about pourin' that iced tea 'til it overflows." Mrs. O'Steen was didactic and bold in her explanation. "It's what they done," she added belatedly, gently throwing forth her hands, cocking her tilted head forward, beady eyes squinted in a 'matter of fact—that's the way it was' end of the lesson. "Learned that in Sunday school," she admitted, seemingly to dispel any pomposity the guests might impute to her too comfortable knowledge of esoteric Hebrew tradition.

"I declare," responded Mabel.

"Didn't know that," Lewis added.

"We don't go to church near as much as we orta," the squeaky woman blurted, changing the subject only a little, while staying near it on a religious continuum. "Used to go purt' near ever Sabbath," she added. "But, he's been sick right much here lately," her head and thumb casually directed towards her husband. "Says he don't feel like a-goin' but I keep remindin' him they's a roll gonna be called up younder. That ole judgment day ledger's bein' tallied."

"That's certainly something we all should be thinkin' 'bout," Lewis interjected. "I just worry, though. Heaven's supposed to be pure and perfect. Trouble is, most of life down here is messy and ugly and full of trouble. But, a lot of excitement comes outta those. Ever thought 'bout that? Heaven'll be a lot more interesting if there's a little fussin' and arguing," he chuckled, hoping his observation was not offensive to the O'Steens.

Herman pointed a thumb to a dark reddish chair, upholstery tattered on the edges of its arms, gesturing for Lewis to sit down, after the tall father of the Georgia crowd returned from the restroom.

"Have a seat ri'chere, neighbor," the stocky, full-faced man with little hair, a graying ring surrounding the back of his head, offered.

"Whew!" Lewis exclaimed, glancing around quickly to assure everyone in his family was as comfortable as time and place afforded. "Sure appreciate it. I won't say no to a plush chair like that, not with that ole car's rough seat," he added, quickly apologizing for "putting y'all out like this. Y'all sure it's okay for us to stay? I know you didn't count on a whole passel of wayfarin' strangers," he continued.

"Don't mind a bit. You know these mechanical systems devised by human hands don't always work the way they supposed to. Trouble with technology is that it creates way more problems than it solves." Herman answered quickly, seemingly pleased to have a group—even one this big—to interrupt the O'Steen's lack of social interaction.

"I've said ole Woody orta run that ferry past dark, but he's always a-hightailin' it with his brother's run-boat to fetch a load of ice fer his run down to Lauder-dale," the host explained. "Or so he says. The law is always out here askin' questions. Don't know, don't wanna know, what that man's up to," Herman added.

While her man talked, Mrs. O'Steen crept into the

kitchen to prepare some semblance of a meal for the travelers. Loose boards on the floor creaked loudly, frustrating her stealthy exist. As the loudest creak rang out, she simultaneously, as if on cue, managed to squeal out: "Herman, tell 'em 'bout the catfish' nets and how they made 'em against the law," she commanded with authority."

"When you gonna have some vittles ready for us?" Herman demanded right back, showing his authority.

"We gon' be eatin' in less than ten minutes. Y'all might wanna wash your hands, and the bathroom's right over there," pointing to a little door, paint curled and missing in various spots, loose at the top hinge, causing it to hang at a slight angle.

Chapter Thirty-nine

"I'm glad for us y'all missed ole Woody's ferry. We don't get much house company, even when we're helpin' his brother run the bridge. Lots of cars goes by," she declared, seemingly not mindful that she had barely learned anything of her new guests given her steady babble.

"Herman's always-and-a-day talkin' to new folks and makin' friends," she continued on at a clip, gulping new air to vibrate her larynx, seemingly uncaring that the conversation had been almost exclusively a monologue, with her its sole participant.

"I hope y'all'll come back up to see us after you get set up there to the muckland. I hear tell that black dirt grows stuff real good. Herman's got some kin there, come to see us, I reckon a year ago now; said they was a-growin' pole beans three times a year. I ain't a-talkin' 'bout no puny little things, neither."

"Well, we are hopin' and a-prayin' that's the case," Lewis interjected.

"Herman, we orta go down there, I reckon, and try our hand at farmin'," Mrs. O'Steen continued quickly before he could even answer, "but, Herman, he's too lazy to farm. Tendin' this here bridge don't take a lotta sense, and that's good, cause he's not real smart, bless his heart," she continued, Mabel her audience, as the two men conversed gingerly. "A good man, mind ye, but I've had to make 'm work. They's been times I thought he was almost sorry, but I finally just realized, no, the man's just plain-out lazy. Lazy don't wanna work, sorry refuses to. Works because he has to. Wouldn't starve or let me, but enjoys his ease. Wouldn't hitch a plow to a mule to pull his mama outta' ditch, and definitely not on the Sabbath," Mrs. O'Steen leaned close to Mabel who threw her head back in mock laughter, eyes closed, smiling grandly, careful not to emit a sound, probably out of slight embarrassment for the man who was sitting right there, and probably heard every word. She suspected this was but a recurrent skit the couple played out. "I'll have to say he was right smart with his catfishin' though."

"Why did Mr. O'Steen give up the catfishing business?" Mabel questioned, trying to avoid any talk of the man's slovenly nature.

"Well, we lived up at Taylor's Creek, with no neighbor for six or seven mile, for near 'bout twelve year. Among some of the purtiest woods and grassland you ever seen. That there Taylor fella, I understand, was a big deal in the army, and fought a right big battle against these here Florida Indians, what we call Seminoles. Later, got to be President of the country," the loquacious woman related, while Mabel struggled to appear attentive, as, one-by-one, the children yawned or looked around the big room, its wooden floor uneven and dusty, surveilling a pump organ with figurines on its shelves and a picture on the wall of an old bearded man praying over a loaf of bread. Marie eyed a Raggedy Ann doll across the room. Roger looked at a Buddy L delivery truck made of pressed steel, and Ray spied a swingset made from tinker toys.

"The ole-timers thought of these catfish like Yankees do them salmon fish up north. They's a livin' in 'em. First men to make any money started out with trot lines. Just ole hunters livin' in the woods, with nary a roof o'er they heads. And I mean they wadn't nobody livin' along the shore of the lake but them hoboes. It was plain sad," Inez explained. "Anyway, a barge boat come down the river with a refrigerated box stocked full of ice. I believe it was ole man Ben Carnegie come down the Kissimmee River. He'd promise these local hunter fellers he'd buy all the cats they could sucker onto them there trot lines. Well, to keep it short, Lord, y'all don't let me ramble and bore y'all to death," she said apologetically, but then unrelentingly plunged on, "before you knew it, the man went to using seines, a kinda, I don't know, Herman, whatcha call them things - them net things?" with not enough pause to give Herman any chance of helping her explain, even if he had wanted to.

"That thing would fetch dozens of 'em at a time instead of haulin' 'em up one-by-one on them lines. It wudn't long 'fore they was a million dollar bidness carryin' on at the mouth of ole Taylor's Creek," Mrs. O'Steen's face took on a nostalgic expression longing for the days when she and Herman were but a young couple "just a-startin' out with nothing."

"So that's how the catfishin' business got started," Lewis remarked. "How does that compare with growing beans and crops?" "I mean, as far as percentage of folks making a living with each?" he clarified.

"Herman, I don't know, do you?" Mrs. O'Steen glanced at her husband, who merely shook his head, knowing the futility of trying to interject any part of his knowledge into her tale.

"I reckon they just about even, far as income goes," Inez stated. "Cattles gettin' big too. Ranches springin' up north of the lake."

Herman, to erase any potential notion of rudeness owing to his willingness to allow Inez to dominate the conversation, explained the seine nets in some detail: "Them seine nets she mentioned, was a couple hundred yards wide. I mean wide! Some of 'em more than t'others, and ole man Hill knowed he was onto something, by jingoes, when he caught sight of a big ole ice box full up with catfish. I mean plumb full!" he related, as his wife hung on every word, ready to jump in at any moment. "Problem was, he couldn't depend on some of the fellas he had workin'. They was always pitching a drunk—makin' a few dollars and drinkin' it right up, even 'fore their wives got holt of a penny, so it wadn't long till he hired me to keep an eye on his boys."

"And Herman was a right good supervisor," his wife jumped in. "Wadn't ya, Herman? As long as he didn't have to get his hands dirty and clean fish, he could do that job. He was right smart at watchin' the men and a-keepin' 'em straight," Mrs. O'Steen told her audience, with a little smiling peek at Herman when the part about 'getting his hands dirty' was mentioned.

Herman jumped in again, "They was fish camps sprung up over every part of the lake, from Pelican Point to Moore Haven. You had 'em to Sand Cut and East Beach, clear on over to Fisheatin' Creek, and even right there under our nose in Tantie. That's the town y'all just come through. They've now renamed it after the lake - *Okeechobee*, but first it was named after a Miss Tantie, uhh, Lord I can't think of her last name, can you Inez? What was it? Anyway, she was a right good school teacher there around Taylor Creek and wandered round these here parts a smart while, and taught for the longest time in a little ole palmetto shack—the main schoolhouse. Then, by jingoes, she fought the school board for a nice new modern frame building. She was a right nice lookin' woman, but Lord she had a cousin who taught school there, too, and bless her heart, she was hard-favored as Miss Tantie was purdy."

"Course, you know what they say, 'purdy is as purdy does,'" Inez quickly jumped in to assert her belief that inner beauty surpassed outward physicality.

"And," Inez continued, "the townsfolk loved her and 'fore ye knew it, she done had the town named after her. And, it became the catfish capital if ever there was one."

"Dub Boon and his brother, ole one-eyed Phil, soon took over the business with their steamboat—a plumb beauty, a 52-foot stern wheeler called *Prosperity*. It come a-sailin' down the Kissismmee River, and after a spell, set up some fish camps from the mouth of that river right on down to Taylor's Creek. I bet you there were forty all told. Five cent a pound," Herman remembered. "That's what they was a-bringin'. Well, anyhow, ole Dub and Phil hauled, Lord, I believe it was six thousand pounds of fish over to the west coast one February morning, on account of that's where the closest railroad was. They had 'em a gold mine, I'm here to tell ya, them and ole O.K. Taylor, till finally word got out 'bout how much money they was a-rakin' in. Some Yankee fellas got wind of their operation and went into competition with 'em. Wadn't long after that they cut the *North New River Canal* down to Lauderdale, and Lord, I'm here to tell you, that made a catfish town outta that place.

They was shippin' catfish everywhere you could think of. It was a lot more profit goin' down there than up the Kissimmee River! Seine nets solved one problem, but you know how it is - every problem solved creates three more that need solving."

Chapter Forty

E arlene, remembering her earlier flight of ecstasy interacting with the big lake, daydreamed about cupping its water in her hands, confirming its realness. She was only now and then conscious of the O'Steen's house and its mundane reality, which contrasted starkly with her sublime encounter. She heard vague talk about fishing for a living—for catfish specifically—and of fish camps that had sprung up, like 'water starved weeds,' to supply the country 'cravings for a delectable treat.' In this setting, she began to lose any lingering visions, and was rudely snatched back from those open waters into a reality where her stomach growled. Despite her bashfulness, and given her heartfelt assessment that these folks were kind, she asked Mr. O'Steen about catfish. Inez ambled towards the supper table, laden with colored plates, each one chipped or cracked somewhere. Around the table, painted light blue, stood worn chairs, smudges of grime on edges.

"Why do people want catfish? What makes 'em so special?" Earlene inquired of the man who had been a catfisher. The girl had an obvious disbelief in the quick willingness of men, and some women, to leave home and drag their families to the 'big water' in pursuit of 'those whiskered creatures,' as Mr. O'Steen had called the curious fish.

"To answer your question, Lil' Miss," Herman responded, "They's good eatin'—mild flavor an' all. Meat is sweet and when human beins' ain't aimin' to eat 'em, some animal or bird, or other livin' creature is after 'em fer food. A lot of these fellas here catchin' 'em, why, they former crooks hidin' from the law," he reported.

"Former?" Mrs. O'Steen questioned, dishrag in one hand, slowly wiping the top of a what-not shelf next to the food-laden table.

Herman chuckled at her. "Well, most of 'em have changed their bad ways, but a whole passel of 'em is fugitives, I guess you could say a-runnin' from the law. Now, not all of em's bad fellas, but somes as wild as a bunch of hares let loose from a cage. Just made mistakes in life, like all of us. Some of us gets caught, some gets away. But they here now, and these camps they settin' up, they ain't no tellin' how many'll be here when it's all said and done. They ain't a-runnin' from the law no more, cause they here to work. They here to man those huge, big ole seine nets, most of 'em. Changed men who've decided to obey the law."

"Most of all, they here to make lots of money by supplying all them Yankees with this here kind of fish meat we been a-talkin' 'bout, on account of it's as sweet and clean as any little girl could ever chomp down on," Mrs. O'Steen added. "And, this ole lake here, thirdy-five miles runnin' one way and right at thirty't'other, is plumb loaded full of 'em," she explained in probably more detail than Earlene desired, wondering only if they tasted good.

"Come on up here, Lil' Miss. You first, then your brother is gonna have a plate of catfish, since you ain't never tasted it before. I don't think your mama or papa's gonna mind you bein' front of the line," Herman's eyes twinkled with delight as he looked toward Lewis and winked. This rite of initiation, this thoughtfulness, spoken with such insistence and graciousness on Mr. O'Steen's behalf, ingratiated the young teenager to the host.

Her faced reddened, as she ran her tongue over her lips and said simply "thank you, sir."

"What's his name?" Mrs. O'Steen asked, nodding her head toward and looking at the middle son.

"That's Ray," Mabel quickly responded.

"Okay, Ray, you next."

The group began to seat themselves, and the teenage son, three years older than his sister, scooped his plate full of catfish, fried squash, and steamed okra.

"Don't forget the corn dodgers," the woman exhorted. Roger quickly grabbed a couple, while exclaiming how much they reminded him of 'hush-puppies' back in Georgia."

"Same thing," Mr. O'Steen quickly informed him. "They's people around here calls 'em both."

During the meal, Earlene, trying to pick clean the meaty skeleton of catfish at her mouth, exclaimed, "They sure have lots of bones!" Quickly, she glanced at her mother, who cocked her head a little down and sideways, giving the girl a gentle reprimanding look, from which Earlene cringed in mild embarrassment.

"They do have that, sweetheart," Mrs. O'Steen agreed.

"Yea, that's the only thing keeps 'em from bein' perfect," Herman added. "They are bony. Just gotta work your mouth around 'em and get to that white meat," he added with a friendly nod and smile, probably to lessen any shame the child might have felt as the import of her words settled in.

"Can't nothing be perfect," Inez suddenly inter-jected. "In this life, gotta be something bitter in even the sweetest of things." Leastways, that's what my momma told me when I was little."

Earlene quickly attempted to redeem what she thought might have been a lack of table manners by adding "They sure are good fish. Mama, I think I like this about as good as chicken fried steak!" Anxious to assuage any vexation she might have caused, Earlene complimented the hostess on the dainty flavor of the mild meat.

Bowls of seconds were passed clockwise around the weathered table, remnants of paint having rubbed off over the years.

"She was mentioning them seine nets a little bit ago," Mr. O'Steen began to relate, quickly tilting his head in his wife's direction remembering she had demanded he "tell the story 'bout how the seines were outlawed."

"That ole boy, Dub, I was tellin' y'all about, at one point, he owned close to a dozen boats and employed 52 men. Really, you might as well say, financed near 'bout all the fish camps 'round the lake. He owned three or four refrigerated cars, to boot, and was shippin' at least two, sometimes three a day to points up north and out west. Big cities like St. Louis, Chicago, Cincinnati. I'm here to tell ya' they was bringin' more money per pound than salmon. Some folks even started callin' 'em Okee-chobee Salmon!" O'Steen explained.

"Was that the first lucrative venture, as far as people makin' real money down here?" Lewis asked.

"To tell ya the truth, huntin' Redskins was the first

big thing," O'Steen recounted to the surprise of the two teenagers, both of whom eagerly awaited this tale.

"The guvment had placed a bounty on the head of every Seminole. Squaws and pickaninnies brought a couple hundred dollars, while bucks fetched close to five hundred. They hounded 'em buggers up and down the peninsula, but wadn't nobody gettin' rich bountyin' for redskins. Course, that was years before settlers really started comin' here. They was a few folks herdin' cattle on the northern prairies beyond the lake," motioning to a point north of where they sat, "others trappin' otters or alligators. But, the real tale was a passel of rascals that hightailed it down here to yank the feathers outta them there big white birds for the high falutin' women up North. They got to wearin' white feathers in their hats. The bigger, the better. They was at one point bringin' more money per ounce than gold, I'm told. Course, you hear tall tales, ya know. True or not, the nests were left with the babies just a-squallin' for their mamas, left to die. Sad, in a way."

Mr. O'Steen was referring to the snowy egret, somewhat smaller than the great egret whose plumes don't splay out in a diffuse scattering of tattered remnants, as do those of the snowy. In the late 1800s, hats worn by women, especially those of means and desiring fashionable wear, could be seen sporting the luminous, dainty plumes of white. During breeding, the feathers of the beautiful bird with heads that looked wind-blown, assumed gossamer wisps that milliners lusted after. Once hunters discovered that the feathers truly were selling ounce for ounce as much as solid gold, they came to Lake Okeechobee and swampy areas south, to first kill, and then skin adult birds. The squealing orphaned hatchlings echoed in canopy after canopy for miles, starving to death. Not only did the hunters not spare a rookery, they hunted the once bountiful creatures almost to the point of extinction. In a tragically short time, the brilliant white plumage so barbarously pilfered from nature, thanks to the greed of millinery centers in New York and London, resulted in the deaths of more than 100,000 of the awe-inspiring egrets. And, the snowy egret was only one of 50 or so species almost slaughtered to extinction, thanks to "sticking a feather in one's cap."

Two socialites of Boston, Harriet Hemenway and Minna Hall held tea parties, inviting friends and acquaintances in order to educate them. The women related how sordid mass slaughter of these birds was occurring and urged them to refrain from wearing feathers in their hats. Word spread to their friends, and the federal legislature was appealed to. Great numbers of women joined the noble crusade, and after the deaths of countless adults and nestlings, Congress eventually passed the *Migratory Bird Act of 1913*, which forbade shipment in interstate commerce of birds or their feathers. Guy Bradley, a Florida game warden was shot and killed by plume hunters in the early 1900s. It seemed that a law with a similar goal, the *Lacey Act*, which proscribed transporting birds or feathers across state lines, was futile. In the end, both federal statutes, along with stricter state law enforcement, combined to forestall further killing of these glorious winged creatures with their head-tousled feathers of radiant white. Despite the dastardly greed and thoughtless plunder, the majestic birds have largely recovered from near extinction.

"Talkin' 'bout them seine nets, they proved awful effective at gatherin' in a heap of catfish, and for years, this here was a boom area for 'em, but right about, I don't know, I guess the late teens, right up till the early twenties, fish was a-gettin' scarce," Mr. O'Steen remembered. "The water level of the lake was steady bein' lowered, and the sawgrass areas where the fish spawned were bein' cleared out and drained by farmers and roadmen, not to mention the fact that no game or fish organization existed to close the season for a spell to give 'em a chance to catch up.' Finally, a summer off-season was put into law, and the mesh on them there seine nets was regulated, as was the length of 'em. I remember 'em talking about ole Ad Peck and how he bought someone's fish house and a couple of boats on the rumor that seining would be outlawed in another couple of years."

"Okeechobee, that town y'all come through up the road, the one used to be called Tantie," Herman reminded Lewis, "As I say, that became the town for catfish. It was, and will forever be, associated with that delicacy because at one point, for nearbout ten year, railroad shipments from there averaged six or seven carloads a week."

"In the early 1920's, the local paper proclaimed that over six million pounds of cats had been fished from the big lake, with a profit to hundreds of fishermen of nearbout a million dollars. Be that as it may, in the mid-twenties, the sports fishers pushed through laws that completely outlawed seining in fresh water lakes and rivers. As good as nets was at catchin' fish, it was really a lowering of the water table done 'em in. Several years drought and a drainin' of the sawgrass spawning areas led to 'em disappearing," Herman continued.

"You gotta remember that a big industry in this here state is tourism, and every dadburned tourist wants a bass on a hook to take a picture of or tell his friends back up North about. I'm not sure how the seines affected the bass, but they said all game fish was bein' destroyed by them nets, and got enough bigshot politicians to go along with 'em. But commercial catfishermen, at least the responsible ones, was all for a closed season to give the cats a chance to recover," he proudly explained as he obviously included himself in that 'responsible' category.

"In fact, one ole boy done a study where he found the seines caught aright many ole predatory fish, like them there alligator garfish and mudfish, which nothing would eat 'ceptin' a ole gator or maybe a Seminole. And they was a-takin' over the bass and catfish, which, if the politicians had left things alone, the seines would have caught them bad ones and the fishermen would have got rid of 'em. As it is now, the gars and the mudfish takin' over out there," he sadly reported. "Like I say, solving one problem seems to lead to a bunch of others."

"Tell 'em about the mudfish Indian name," Mrs. O'Steen gently commanded her husband, turning toward him, wiping hands on her apron at the first instance of silence, as she washed dishes with Mabel at her side.

"The Florida East Coast Railway was thinkin' bout runnin' a line down to Tantie to haul lumber and turpentine from the piney woods north and east of there," Herman explained. This high-falutin' little biddy thing, high styled though she was, the daughter of some railroad baron, come in here bound and determined to rename our Taylor Creek where me and her lived when we was first married. The original Seminole name, *Catch Big Mudfish Creek*, was sumpin' like *onosho-lecha-ko-hatchee*. Well, that didn't sit too well with Miss Fancy on account of she thought *Mudfish* ought'n be part of the name. She wanted it just *Catch Big Fish Creek*, but the locals didn't take a likin' to her idea, nor to her big shootin' ways, and run her outta here, along with her daddy's railroad. Kept the name *Taylor's Creek.* The railroad did have the final laugh, I reckon, on account of it's here to stay," he announced with an air of resignation born of the inveterate progress upon a frontier.

"I'm gonna bore you good folks with one more story, then I gotta get to bed," Herman announced. His wife would no doubt keep any who would listen, company. "The state began drainage operations in the early years of the twentieth century and dredges from Ft. Lauderdale had fared poorly in digging canals, so eventually a company from Maryland, near Baltimore, took over. The soft mud and water hyacinths were difficult for a normal dipper to handle and at some point a hydraulic dredge with dual anchors was utilized," Herman related. He continued with his story for another ten minutes before excusing himself and heading to his bedroom.

∞∞∞

Chapter Forty-one

On the day after the barge had upset, *Corona* would have to make three runs to Lakeport to compensate for that loss, but Peter was determined to deliver what he promised. Still ornery, and certainly in no mood for levity, Peter told Percy "Don't you even think of getting that boy to come," referring to Otis. In time, the big black man might return to the old man's good graces, being handy and typically dependable, but not today.

"In fact, why don't y'all just stay here and let me get these damned beans over to the man.

"You sure you don't need me?" Percy asked.

"I've got it."

Percy didn't mind letting his father go alone, though he knew Peter needed, and probably secretly desired, his help. In fact, he welcomed a day to drink some rum and read some *Nietzsche*. Percy agreed with his notion of perspectivism, the concept that a 'unified truth did not exist because each person's interaction with the real world is so different from all others.' In his rum-instilled meditations, Percy contemplated Nietzsche's claim that morality attempted to create a one-size-fits-all model, and that didn't work due to the disparity of genetic composition among groups, not to mention a person's cultural upbringing and experience with others. Then, there were differing conclusions and theories as well as humankind's captivity in a set time. One moral code to fit all situations, seemed problematic. Percy tended to agree that framing one morality was difficult, given the variations in outlooks and backgrounds, but disliked the resulting moral relativism that seemed to argue there is no right or wrong.

Percy felt the philosopher Jean-Paul Sartre was wrong in thinking humans are free - that humans' very existence was freedom. "As long as spermatozoa are swimming around in my testicles, havin' a fit to get out, I'm definitely not free. I have some choice, but it's limited. That's determinism. As long as a person's genes direct cells for generation after generation, there is determinism," he concluded. "Also, my limitations—and my talents—dictate what I can do. Would that I were truly free," he often said. "Hell, human beings inevitably gravitate towards what is pleasurable and away from what is painful. Tell me again how much freedom we have," he added.

Cory wondered at his daddy's wisdom, understanding little. "Freedom," Percy summarized, "is tenuous and limited at best." Cory wasn't sure what any of that meant in the steamboat days, but he too had an appreciation for history and philosophy, and, later in life, would read as copiously as had his father, though mostly fiction.

———

Returning from the dock, Cory headed to the round house with the lookout roof on top brought south on *Corona's* bow when the three generation-family had relocated to the Lake. Percy had been fretting about the little Sewauwee girl. Then, he suddenly remembered a little jar of medicine used for Cory—*ammoniated mercury*. After a hog roasting, three months earlier, Cory had developed an infection after burning his foot walking over some hot coals lightly covered with sand. Percy had worried. He loved the boy greatly.

The thought of the little Indian girl Billy Tyger had mentioned—'was it his niece or cousin?'—Percy wasn't sure. That white cream had seemed to cure his son's foot. Percy remembered how nonchalant Peter had seemed about Cory, then, on a run up to Lakeport, hauling some bell peppers, Peter had docked *Corona* at Doctor Tabb's big house. The steamboat was also laden with hampers of potatoes. Peter knew that Percy was worried about the boy. So was he. While the captain truly didn't fret about too much, except the goings on aboard the boat and its cargo, he had a sense for when to take appropriate action.

The two-story house with a wrap-around porch on the bottom floor, fronted the lake. Three large royal palms standing next the water's edge came into view, their angled and spiking fronds gently waving in a light breeze. A section of palmetto fronds scattered white sunlight across the edge of swampy waters, an inlet that led into Tabb's estate. Flat water lilies floated lazily on the surface of a large pond, one featuring a white flower protruding from the middle, petals pointed and sharp. But it was the palms Percy routinely marveled at, and knew the names of—*date, windmill, zombie, sonoran, foxtail, carandy, spindle, king, Florida thatch, palmetto, cabbage, pindo, sago, bismarck, masari*—didn't matter, he knew and loved them all. Swordlike blades from drooping branches dangled lazily in a circle around the trunks, some scaly and rough, others spiky and sharp, still others smooth with circles climbing ever upward. Lake Okeechobee was a land of custard apple, cypress, and palm trees.

In ancient Rome, triumph in athletics had been symbolized by the palm. Rome venerated the tree itself, but Romans were especially enchanted by the frond as an embodiment of victory. In Judaism, the closed frond from date palms is known as the *lulav*, a part of *Sukkot*, a holiday of feasts on the fifteenth day of *Tishrei*, the seventh month of the ecclesiastical year of the Hebrew calendar, which falls in September or October of the Gregorian calendar. Sukkot has an agricultural genesis, representing the end of harvest. Myrtle, willow, and citron— known respectively as hadass, aravah, and etrog —are also part of the festivity.

Percy knew the palm branch in ancient Egypt represented immortality. Across the Near East and Mediterranean, including Mesopotamia, the palm tree also reigned supreme.   For Christians, the branches were special because numerous ones had been waved by followers of Jesus in a gauntlet as he rode atop a donkey on his final procession—the destination of his execution. In the iconography of Christianity, the palm frond came to personify a conquest of flesh by spirit. In Islam, Percy had studied, palms became symbols for a termination of war—in a word, peace.

In addition to weeping palms of seven varieties, Dr. Tabb's expansive estate featured six species of banana plants, some with curved, traditional, yellow fruit, while other bananas were brown, purple or red. Stalks hung in clusters from the top of the tall but largely hollow stems. The trunk-like stem is situated upon a base known as a corm, often called a bulbotuber—though really neither a bulb nor a tuber—short and vertical, swollen with winter-preserving nutrients. Cormous plants—those that grow from corms—like bananas, crocuses, and gladiolus, are different from the tuberous plants. Plants from tubers include yams, potatoes, cassava. Plants from bulbs feature garlic, amaryllis, tulips, daffodils, and lilies.

A huge mango tree loaded with fruit—reds, greens and yellows in assorted patterns—dripped with sap. Percy once told Cory that both the peel and sap of mango can be toxic, containing as they do *urushiol*, the same substance in poison ivy and poison oak that causes rash, itching, and sometimes even a severe allergic reaction.

Tabb had a charitable reputation around the lake. He was a man of average build with handsome features, hair graying but fairly thick, clear blue eyes serious and sure. Folks who were able to, would come to his little peninsula. If not, the doctor would trek to the patient's house. He handed Percy a small tube of metallic, 'miracle' ointment, as many of Tabb's patients called it.

"Captain," Tabb looked to Peter while conveying the medicine to Percy, "have the boy soak his foot three times a day in some warm water with epsom salts. That's the most important thing." *Magnesium sulfate* indeed seemed a panacea for infections, and its more common name originated from a spring, high in salinity, called *Epsom*, near Surrey, England. For use internally or externally, doctors readily prescribed it as a potential cure.

"He should soak for at least four or five days, then afterwards, you wanna spread a thin smear of this cream over the blistered area."

"Much obliged, Dr. Tabb," Peter respected this learned man of science, and after just a short minute of small talk, Percy waved his appreciation and headed for the day's mission.

Rhetta had made sure Dr. Tabb's treatment instructions were followed precisely, and in a matter of three days, Cory's infection abated. Perhaps the cream had anti-bacterial properties, or maybe it commenced an inflammatory stimulus to the patient's immune system, causing it to form antibodies, thereby checking microbial invasions by its own natural defense—even Dr. Tabb couldn't be sure—but Cory's wound had healed.

As Percy thought about the words of Tyger regarding Red's daughter, remembering the Natives' willingness to help collect bean pods floating in water, he wondered how serious the little girl's infection was and whether Tabb's ointment might help. Able to commiserate with the unease of the little girl's father and uncle, seeing how Cory had recently had infection himself, he was worried about the girl and wanted to get some of Tabb's cream to her. Percy was kind that way, as he was in so many facets of his personality. He loved stray dogs —stray anything—and had a soft spot even for people, especially "ne'er-do-wells or ones a little lost or living near the edge," as he often described. "After all, aren't we all?" Percy would ask.

∞ ∞ ∞

Chapter Forty-two

Early next morning, Percy awoke and headed over to the real estate office owned by Sterling Moore, a pioneer from a tiny sawgrass village on Will Island, which lay on the south side of the big lake. Moore's farming had yielded profitable crops, and his cabbage, especially over the past seven years, had sold well. Enough profit had been saved that the farmer, turned real estate developer, was able to establish a sales operations where prospects could be ferried out from Miami over to Ft. Lauderdale and then up the dredged canal northwesterly to the lake. As a fledgling entrepreneur, Moore recognized the potential for land speculation and himself came to Lake Okeechobee from Walla Walla, Washington, for yet another frontier adventure. Moore was no idealist, but cognizant that land prospecting needed sizable capital investment and didn't mind a bit being sidetracked into growing pole beans and cabbage for a full decade before having the means to invest in his dream. Realistic to the core, this diligent working man loved to say "Hell, if I got time to kill, I'm 'onna work'kit to death." One huge investment the industrious man had made was a speedboat.

The craft had sides and tops of mahogany polished to a radiant sheen, the straight grain lightly visible in the darkness of the rich, reddish-brown wood. The big, open boat could slide over freshwater waves at 30 knots, a speed many in cars only dreamed of—24 knots was their average. Shining brightly in the sunlight and loaded with prospective land buyers of Lake Okeechobee property, mostly Northerners from Miami, the boat ferried passengers to see in person the black farmland Moore touted in his flashy brochures.

Percy knocked on the office door, but no one responded, even though it was after eight o'clock. A neighbor from across the street saw the man and informed him that Moore was busy in Palm Beach and wouldn't be back until the next day. He crossed the street to talk more intimately to the neighbor woman. Percy was like that: face-to-face, whenever possible. He seldom corresponded in writing, sent a wire, or talked over the telephone because he liked "to look in a person's eyes I'm talking to."

Percy informed the neighbor of the need to hire Moore's agile craft to get out to Dr. Tabb's then over to Sewauwee and tender the magical medicine to the girl's caretakers. The woman seemed surprised that Percy would concern himself with an Indian child on Sewauwee. That was obvious from her subtle but palpably startled reaction, as she drew her small hand next to her chin. She slowly explained that Jimmy, Moore's seventeen-year-old son, was coming by "directly to take some of the kids on a picnic," and offered that he might "run him out there real quick."

Within twenty minutes, Jimmy and Percy having briefly chatted, the teenager headed briskly toward the polished craft, even as Percy continued to describe the situation. Jimmy petted 'Ole Dash', his white bulldog with a "black dash and a mean streak," then set off with Percy for Dr. Tabb's house.

Chapter Forty-three

The young Seminole girl recovered in less than a week, and Red Osceola, Billy and Sammy's cousin, left a note for Percy a couple of weeks later, at Grace Gaskin's post office. He again referred to Percy as 'Captain', though Captain Peter would hardly bear usurpation as boss of his steamboat. Nonetheless, upon the next visit to Grace's post office and store, that letter was awaiting him, words misspelled, *PURSEY*, for one. Since Red couldn't write English—not well, anyhow—he had dictated the note as best he could to Grace, who helped him articulate his thankfulness for the medicine, and to inform Percy that his daughter was "now cured up." This caused a tear to stand in Percy's eye that he preferred Grace not see, averting his face to look out towards the mail dock.

Grace had built the store two years earlier after she landed the post office contract from the federal government. As a little girl growing up in Nebraska Territory, she had dreamed of a different kind of frontier life, one near water. No doubt, Nebraska filled the frontier role, but obviously lacked the water. She was a single woman 34 years old, who continued to crave both adventure and solitude. Her life was clearly compartmentalized between the excitement of dealing with the mail run and her colorful customers—white and Seminole—yet she longed for moments of quiescence to reflect and "hold to a measure of inner authenticity," as she liked to say. "Damned big city life with slaves to a money-worshipping system...scurrying like rats, never happy —never satisfied," she repeated those exact words routinely. "Let the rats have it!—Roof overhead and some vittles for a gurglin' belly's good enough for me," Grace insisted.

When Doss heard about Grace many years after she died, he felt a spiritual connectedness that 'might have been,' but for the prison of time. After all, "We are captives of this age and strangers to any other," Doss used to say. He believed that death—each person's life lived to its own end—was what many dreaded. In seeking comfort, individuals join groups and teams, swear allegiances and alliances. That cluster of aliveness, that shared association, provides an illusion of immortality. Rhetta had introduced Cory to those sentiments years before aboard the steamboat.

Six months before applying for the post office contract, Grace had purchased a houseboat from a man whose brother was serving time for rum-running. When he was released, he owed four hundred dollars to the government as a fine. The convicted man's brother was made agent—been given a power of attorney—and sold the boat to Grace for about half its value. The lien from the fine would be satisfied with proceeds of the sale.

The water level of the lake had been falling over the previous five years and Grace saw a need to get the post office out nearer the water's edge so the mail boats could reach her with the sacks and bundles that currently were able to come no closer than a quarter mile from her enterprise. In fact, a competitor named

Booth Ralles, who was the owner of the first hotel in that area, an elegant structure two miles away, wrote the federal government, asking officials to appropriate Grace's contract to him, due to complaints from men who had rights to run mail. Several had complained. One even told Ralles about the "mud and sawgrass we gotta trudge through to get to Grace's."

When the post office officials forwarded the letter to Grace, she packed her six-shooter rifle and went to visit Ralles. Samuel Colt had brought a couple dozen revolving rifles to the area sixty years earlier during the Seminole War and had demonstrated them to the United States military leaders at Ft. Basinger. The guns tended to be water resistant and featured an unusual cartridge configured from cloth sack that had tremendous penetrating capability. They were superior to the muzzle loaders of common issue to Jackson's soldiers— the ones who rounded up Seminoles. Colt had been determined to interest some of the Generals in the unique design and firepower of the novel weapon. No luck. The Feds had only recently made a switch from flintlocks to muzzle loaders. How Grace ended up with the unusual gun is anybody's guess.

With the revolver rifle barrel pointed squarely at the ground, Grace boldly traipsed into Ralle's walnut-paneled office. Ralles managed the hotel he owned, and sat comfortably in his full-grain leather chair of deep burgundy. A toupee was perched squarely atop his head and a gold pince-nez gently squeezed his humped nose. Booth quickly drew in a sniffle of air, startled at Grace's sudden appearance, especially carrying the Colt six-shooter rifle.

The rich man was proud of his hotel, the first on the

lake, he liked to brag, and he thought by having the postal service for himself, he could become even richer. He stammered as Grace slowly and calmly approached his elegant baroque desk.

"Grace, uh hello. What in....by jingoes! What you got there?" "You alright?" he managed to get the words out. "Who you locking horns with?"

"This your letter?" was all the woman responded, slowly unrolling a curled corner lightly soiled, never looking away from Ralles' face.

"Ye—Yeah, I wrote it," the man stammered again, obviously unsettled, "but they can't get mail to you, hon. You know how the lake's down, and several mail boats have run hard aground trying to get up yo' place. And, it's happened a right smart number of times," he continued, still hesitantly uttering stammered words that a rural person would appreciate, to assuage the no-nonsense woman carrying the unusual weapon. "I just believed strongly that a deeper draft was needed to get boats in and out."

"Belief is different from knowing," she retorted. "People believes a lot of things that t'ain't so."

As Ralles searched in his mind for some way to soothe the irritated post-mistress who was proud of her position and duties, Grace muttered strongly, "Leave my mail alone."

"Hate to see you eat that letter, or worse." She looked defiantly down at the revolving part of the gun while turning to take leave of the neatly dressed man in a dark gray woolen suit and waistcoat covering a light silk shirt. He was adorned with a gold-plated Waltham pocket watch and chain, its fob inserted through a middle buttonhole.

Ralles seemed to search the curled woodgrain on his maple-trimmed desk as he sat and said nothing. The woman walked towards the door as Ralles reflected on the time the strong woman had peeled off her dress in front of the mailboat man and two other fellows, jumped in the deep mud and pushed a heavy grounded craft to deeper water. Those men probably blushed, but not Grace. She knew what had to be done, and woman or not, stripped down to her skivvies.

The fun-loving, tough, but kind woman had dealt with the Seminoles whose trust she had gained early on by treating them fairly. Only a month after setting up her houseboat store, some Natives came looking for spirits. Grace rarely paid them in dollars for hides, beads, moccasins, or dolls, neither did she give them change in dollars for fear of the whiskey they would almost certainly purchase with cash. Bright cloth, little trinkets, and figurines held a special place for Natives, so it was with these the lady merchant and proud postmaster was inclined to remunerate.

Chapter Forty-four

Seminoles were an interesting concretion of several native groups. The term itself derived from *Esta Seminoli* meaning 'wild people' or 'runaways' in the Creek tongue. While Seminoles were comprised of mostly Creek, an agricultural group of natives, they also included an amalgamation of the *Yemasees* and *Yuchis*, who hunted and sometimes fought against whites, but farmed very little. Then, there were the fierce and battle-hardened *Miccosukees*.

Scattered fragments of those groups had headed south from Georgia to the Everglades, an area most white settlers avoided. Even after Billy Bowlegs was offered a couple hundred thousand dollars from the federal government to relocate with other natives to Arkansas, he refused. Bowlegs opted to make a stand in these swamps that he felt were safe from the white man.

The region that would one day be called *Florida* had some original tribes, namely, the *Appalachees* and *Timucuas* of the panhandle and *Tekestas* and *Mayaimis* in the center and further south. Seminoles, so long associated with that state, were from areas far removed from Florida. Not only disease, but also slave raids and war, had eventually annihilated the original Florida natives. The *Calusas*, often called 'Spanish Indians', were another Florida tribe. Many of them headed to the Keys on the southern tip, and some to the Bahamas and Cuba. Seminoles arrived in Florida much later.

Grace Gaskins loved the native peoples. She detested General Taylor and his bloodhounds. On Christmas 1837, *Holata Micco*, better known as Billy Bowlegs, and Zachary Taylor squared off on the banks of the lake, and from his victory there, Taylor was promoted to brigadier general. 'Old Rough and Ready' had earned his nickname largely as a result of that rout, even though his use of the hounds purchased from Cuba, had been repulsive even to those who wanted Indians gone.

Another source of extreme repulsion to Grace was Issac Striker, a dark-complexioned poker player from St. Augustine, an enigmatic rogue whose sentiments lay with Taylor's mission of ridding the swamps of Seminoles. Striker wore white linen suits and a two-carat diamond solitaire ring, his large round head covered with long wavy black hair topped with a Panama hat. Black patent leather shoes with glossy coating that mirrored the man's attire were worn over red silk stockings. When hunting, Striker would often shift his outfit to beaded leggings with a shot pouch to match and a flamingo feather protruding nine inches from his straw hat of Ecuadorian origin. The delicately woven hat Striker wore was made from the plaited leaves of a paja toquilla straw plant, indigenous to Ecuador. As early as the seventeenth century, hat weaving was a specialty for artisans along the Ecuadorian coast, and numerous villages within the Andean Mountain Range. Hats of the best quality were produced in the province of Manabí, then shipped first to the Isthmus of Panama before sailing to Asia and other destinations. The point of origin for the goods, Panama, stuck. Thus, the *Panama Hat*.

Boat companies had later been employed when the bloodhounds from Cuba hadn't panned out in finding all the Indians. Striker was the civilian head of a group that continually scoured the sawgrass hammocks, wading in mud, looking for Indians, his henchmen often covered in red, festering sores.

The boat companies would round up entire villages of natives—braves, squaws, pickaninnys—like fugitive escapees from a prison chain gang. For each brave captured and brought to headquarters alive, $400 was paid —$250 for squaws, while a pickaninny was worth $100. Black slaves, who were leaders in many Native villages, commanded a whopping $1,000 each.

A United States Army Major held charge of each company boat and Striker at one point in late spring of that year demanded the officer let him ashore, claiming he saw signs of Indian presence. Major Askew had little respect for the flamboyant poker player and refused. The Army officer didn't realize the colorful creature had been a rugged surveyor and ruthless hunter for a dozen years east of the St. John's River, south of Jacksonville. When Striker pulled out his six-shooter and pointed it at Askew, the Major backed down, complied with the demand. Off went Striker through the thick swamp grass to scout the suspicious signs.

∞ ∞ ∞

Chapter Forty-five

Ray, now 28 and Melrose, 21, both found jobs as surveyors of the Everglades during the years after atomic bombs had been dropped on Japan. Sam Walls from Jacksonville had hired them immediately after receiving their applications, sight unseen, after learning they were former Marines. Ray had promised Mabel he would "take good care of Melrose," seven years his junior, and make sure to "keep him 'way from any gators." The team was planning a two-month survey from the Loxahatchee Slough, about twenty miles east of the lake, to Canal Point, on its eastern shore. The twelve-man crew would work from daylight until dark, and for those 20 miles and 68 days, sleep as best they could in a variety of positions and environs. There were wet bogs, clumps of sawgrass, and areas of dry sandy land. They slept often on top of sawgrass, cut stalks stacked above the water, and sometimes in their glade boats. All the while, the team would establish a 'traverse,' a line or path of travel, a survey base from which the next point could be observed. Glade boats had been brought to the edge of the wetlands by large oxen-pulled wagons that had come as far as the primitive sand road, which ran from West Palm Beach to the Loxahatchee Slough, 18 miles inland. Up to that point, pine trees and level ground prevailed. West of the Slough, closer to the lake, cypress trees, twisted and stunted, seemed to outnumber pines as the periphery of the Everglades with its muck and sawgrass began. Hammocks of magnolia and myrtle rose from the water just enough to form small islands. There would be no more dry ground for the team, including axe and machete men, a transit man and his rod cohort. All of these were followed by chain men carrying measuring tape and the pegs with which they marked key points. They were followed by level men whose services had not been needed on the high, flat pine land.

Ray was a member of the axe team, and his fellows cut through the thickets, some with machetes to create a trail for transit and rod men. After a mile or so, the terrain evolved into sawgrass and marsh, with its bogs, sloughs and floating clumps. Sloughs were five feet wide and about as deep, with no sawgrass or other growth, probably carved out by alligators, eyes shining red on a full-moon night. The primordial creatures watched from every direction. Melrose wondered how there was sufficient food for all the leathery-backed reptiles, feasting methodically on fish and turtles, in between their long, patient, watchful waits.

At points westward, the elevation rose perceptibly, and the sawgrass was taller. Sometimes reaching seven or eight feet in height, the Everglades grass yielded only to machetes. Axes were useless against the sharp-edged, sawtooth leaves, as determined surveyors, always scratched, cut and bleeding from somewhere, forced a path through. The transit and level tripod had extensions that would penetrate the soft muck easily, but because of the pliable ground, a slight breeze could upset the adjustment, interfering with an accurate measurement. Melrose, an assistant to Wink Hood, was continually urged on by his boss—threats and cajoling —as they walked ahead aiming their binoculars—aligning men setting stakes behind.

To get an accurate level of the lake, a graduated rod was topped with a level, then turned 180 degrees to sight new elevation ahead. The instrument personnel couldn't move a millimeter, for fear of throwing off the readings, so instead of trying to sight aft and fore, three men would dedicate their attention to the critical instrument. One would sight on the rod behind while another swiveled the level on its pivot, looking forward to the rod in front. A 'bubble man' watched the all-important magic globule of air in the level, gently rocking, finally centering between the indicator which would lead the bubble man—who on this expedition was a big man, corpulent in his roundness, called Bacon, no less—to yell "Mark!"

———

Melrose told Ray about Biddle Greer's chickens, "Seems his *Buff Orph-ing-tons*," Melrose emphasized the syllables to mock Greer's emphasis on the superior nature of that variety, "were losing their feed. His peanuts kept getting' dug up by some coons, as they later found out. Ole Biddle put a hunting light on his head, and along with a box of shells, killed 26 of those boogers, skint 'em and sold those to Trapper Sam, then cooked the coons in a big ole iron kettle he borrowed from that abandoned moonshine still. Then he fed the cooked coons to his hens, and I mean those ole girls laid some eggs." Ray responded with a subdued "zat so?"

"Remember that thing Biddle's daddy built back after World War I?" Melrose asked, to which Ray replied a mumbled "uh-huh"—"Well, that big monstrosity he called a hotel, you ain't never saw so many duck hunters come up from Lauderdale and Miami," Melrose went on.

"Ole Yankee guy from Miami asked Biddle's daddy for a key to his room, and Ole man Biddle said 'Mister, they's nothing but honest people here—you don't need a key.' Turns out there wasn't no lock on the doors for a key. Fact, there was a huge room upstairs that old man Greer had partitioned with half-inch boards, studs exposed, and chicken wire tacked a'top all those—good ventilation, and the hunters got a great view of the roof rafters overhead. Two light bulbs, one at each end of the hall," Melrose continued, Ray beginning to nod off on the checkered cotton quilt topping a sawgrass mattress.

"Ole Spence Wilson was gonna spend the night there to be ready early the following morning to leave with the group. Said women couldn't stop talking next cubby over—he heard all the details about their husbands. One husband didn't drink much, but when he did, he would 'sull up and get plumb mean as hell.' The other's husband wanted to get lovey-dovey with just a swig or two, and if he had four swigs, fell asleep," Melrose continued. "His wife, according to ole Spence, said either one would suit her just fine."

"Then, one of the more philosophically-inclined women started on a contemplation something like: 'Love is basically selfish. When he loves her, it's because she has something to offer him. And, it's his desire that keeps him around—he gets bored, or she loses the attraction he used to crave in her—he's gone. Yet, there is a mutuality to the arrangement—after all, that runs both ways,' " pensive woman declared.

"Through the night, the thumpin' against the walls and clatter of washin' pots and pans, and the stompin' back and forth to the one toilet—Spence didn't get a damn wink of sleep. One ole lightning-struck rascal was moaning, passed out from too much hooch, then within ten minutes, just before Spence started to doze off, the staccato cracking of an unmuffled boat motor bounced in waves off the thin partitions and reverberated out to the bank of custard apple trees," Melrose rambled.

"Uh," was the only response from Ray.

"Ole Travis Reeves had to get up early for work— pulling levers on his dredge for eight hours—poor sumbitch was tryin' to get a little shut-eye. Spence said he never saw one man so mad, cussin' those shotgun-happy city dudes as well as the locals who 'didn't give a shit about sleepin,'" Melrose continued. Although Ray now dreaming deeply, his story-telling brother was oblivious to the lack of reception or comprehension of his story.

"One weekend, Lodi, Biddle's middle boy, guided some big-shot English governor of the Bahamas on a duck shoot. Lodi noticed the man's shotgun was some kinda fancy—with some fancy cursive name carved on the barrel, but Lodi couldn't make it out. Young guy, said he couldna' been thirty, had two fellers with him —his aides, by all appearances on account of they kowtowed to his every whim. All had fancy shotguns, or what they referred to as 'fowling pieces'. The big-shot man, or kid, really, had a *Peter Hofer* side-by-side 12-bore sidelock, engraved with ducks in flight. The one aide, feller with one of them twisted up mustaches on each end, had a *Holland & Holland* over and under, and the other, a short bald feller with a accent so thick," Melrose now twisted up his mouth, screwing, tightening his lips, and uttering throaty sounds to mimic the character he was mimicking, "that one had a *Purdey* side-by-side with Damas steel barrels. Lodi said the three of them guns would cost as much as the castle that prince feller lived in over there in England."

"Anyway, come to find out not long ago this English bloke Lodi took out duck huntin', was the damn Prince of Windsor, the one who years later give up bein' king for that American woman. Even at the duck hunt, Lodi knew the man was a Prince. Every word outta they mouth was 'prince this, and prince that—does prince need his bloody arse wiped?' and later ole Lodi learned he had been guide to royalty," Melrose droned on, not missing a beat, probably not caring that Ray was now hard asleep.

"It was sometime during the Depression; man's daddy—the King—died and Prince So and So took his place. Damn if ole Lodi hadn't taken the future king on a duck hunt right here on Lake Okeechobee," Melrose told Ray, who rousing, mumbled "I'll be damned," then promptly laid his head back, on the musty quilt inter-mixed with the clean, verdant smell of sawgrass, a small string of drool descending from the left corner of his mouth.

Ray's momentary resuscitation prompted Melrose to keep talking, seemingly not needing sleep: "Yea... said the prince couldn't shoot worf a shit, but the two aides were excellent shots. "Knew the range of their fowling pieces, and killed any they aimed at outright—never crippled one."

∞∞∞

Chapter Forty-six

Next morning, it was Ray's turn to talk. "Hope you know, lil' brother, you kept me awake half the night talkin' 'bout Lodi and his duck guiding escapades," he reprimanded his younger brother.

"Just thought you'd wanna know 'bout them fancy shotguns," Melrose responded.

As the two men trudged along trying to get the survey completed in the period of time the state had allotted, Ray told Melrose a story of his own.

"Balls Hotel, two and a half stories of it, balconies on all sides, fancy thing, had a observation tower where sightseers could look out. It was built right in the middle of custard apple groves on Cramer Island. Wet as hell. When ole man Ball built it, the shores of Lake Okeechobee were untamed and desolate. Mind you, they was a few catfish camps scattered around, mostly up near Okeechobee city, but down here in the south, you had five fellows, mostly squatters. Besides the crew of that huge dredge *Caloosahatchee* that was dredging the access canal, you had two hunters, two trappers, and a catfisherman," Ray related down to the finest detail.

"Why the hell did he build a damn hotel on that swampy island?" Melrose wondered aloud.

"Damned if I know, I guess cause Broward kept

promisin' to 'drain the Everglades.' Now that he's governor, money's run out," Ray informed.

"Wadn't ole Bob Balls a promoter out in Oregon before he came here?

"Yea, had what he called the *Oregon Valley Land Company*, and after he made a killin' out there, he heard about this land around the lake—had the state's word it would provide irrigation. So, here's this man, richer 'en hell from his Oregon sales, leaves the West and heads down here, oh, I guess it must have been 1910 or thereabouts. Paid $2 an acre and just about every inch of it was swamp—at least two foot of water on top—contracted to sell thousands of little farms to these Yankee folks, mostly from Indiana, Illinois, a few from Ohio. Now you talk about sell—that sumbitch was a helluva salesman. Broward personally promised to survey, then drain the sawgrass. Somebody said the state of Florida put half of Ball's huge purchase money payment towards reclamation. Hell, ends up, Ball was as much a victim as the buyers. Here he goes and sets up a company like he had in Oregon, called it *Florida Fruit Lands Company*, relying on Broward's and the state's promise to drain. Anyway, others like him showed up, bought section after section, trying to copy what he done," Ray remembered.

"Wasn't he the one who sold 20 acre tracts right out of his office to speculators?"

"That sounds right...yea, musta been," Ray scratched a rough spot on his head, cap in his other hand, fumbling on the details. "But he sure as hell didn't have any offices around here. Kept his offices up there" Ray added, waving his hand and index finger in a northerly direction, the scratched area now bleeding slightly. "What he done was sold folks an option. They had first dibs if they chose to exercise it. Lost their earnest money if they didn't. Some of them plots was a whole section, at least the ones over near Big Cypress Swamp."

"Had they even dredged canals at that time?" Melrose inquired.

"Hell no. Guy'd pay $10 a month for two, three years, not even know where his tract would be. None of it explored, none surveyed," Ray recalled.

"And that was about the time they were dredging canals over from Palm Beach and up from Lauderdale, right?" Melrose asked.

"Yep. Then, after Ball's company sold all the tracts, the buyers, or some agent would make their way up to Lauderdale from Miami for what they called a convention."

"Didn't they have some kinda auction?"

"They did. They'd read each buyer's name, then someone'd draw a piece of paper outta' hat that told how many acres that buyer got and give a legal description. Some buyers had multiple contracts, multiple tracts...some of them found out that one plot might be miles from another. Course, they knew all that from the get-go. Some lucky ones drew a tract that sat on a canal —stuck a feather in his cap. Even so, after the canal easement, the right of way, was dug, outta 20 acres, you might end up with 12," Ray explained.

"Then wadn't there some Everglades Land outfit?"

"Oh hell, they was a bunch of them damn land companies. One you're talking about was ole Bland Holmes outfit *Everglades Land Sales Company,* then you had Gumble & Blackston's *Florida Everglades Land Com-*

*pany...*hell they musta sold over 50,000 acres. 'Member, ole man Broward started drainage there at Lauderdale, so lots near there was first to go. Holmes copied him. Did the same thing."

"Yea, what I heard, Blackston and Ball would alternate their square miles, like a checkerboard. Seems like it was ten miles in width, or thereabouts, and went from the lake down 'bout twenty miles south."

"You right. Then you had some lots over west by the edge of Big Cypress. Ball had another company for that area: the *Okeechobee Fruit Lands Company.*"

"Seems like I remember the *Florida Reclaimed Land Company*. Wadn't they the ones who sold over by the Hillsboro Canal?"

"I think they were," Ray responded, nodding his head slightly, and inhaled a draw from his cigarette, now down to a mere butt. Eyes skyward, Ray continued to recount his tale about land sales operations. He loved to first squeeze the tobacco and paper remnants between his index finger and thumb then aim and flick the remnants out beyond where he squatted on his hams.

"But, they wadn't a whole lotta buyers saw their land, and even fewer folks than that actually set up stakes and tried to reside there. Few that did had to leave during the '28 hurricane," Ray remembered clearly while kicking some mud off his rubber wading boots.

"Some of them ole boys got rich down in Lauderdale," Melrose added, more of a question than a comment.

"Damn sure did. Turns out, as fate would have it, old man Ball set up some town sites. One of 'em I remember, Progresso, was right in the middle of what's now

Lauderdale. He would give a lil' bonus to the buyers who had put a down payment on a huge tract. Those damn lil' ole town lots brought a helluva lot more than huge tracts—a purdy penny. Gumble and Blackston had the same idea. They had your *First Lauderdale Addition* town lots—proved way more valuable than that tract land—acre after acre of underwater swamp land they had such high hopes for. I 'member *Everglades Plantation Company* had farms out in the Everglades 'bout seven miles inland from the coast, that even today are selling for thousands a dollars for even a half acre. Those were prosperous subdivisions out from Lauderdale," Ray added.

"Sumbitches got rich," was Melrose's response, echoing in subdued admiration, the foresight of the land speculators.

"Oh yea. And, 'member, five years before that, before he'd bring sales prospects to Lauderdale, Ball would summon 'em Yankees over on the west coast, to Ft. Myers on the Gulf. Fact, ole Bub Summers quit his job down to the ice plant and started selling for Ball, and Summers was makin' good money with the ice."

"When was it he started operating out of Lauderdale?"

"That was...Lord, like I say, that would have been a good five years later, after the canal was finished," Ray scratched again, not his head this time, but just above his right eyebrow. But, go back to when he was bringin' 'em in from the Gulf of Mexico side. First, he'd ferry 'em down to Ft. Myers, then quickly herd 'em on Ball's boat *Dixieland*, over a hundred footer, with twin decks 'fore they could get to talkin' to locals. Ole man Ball had ole Pal Freedman dolled out in an oopsy-poopsy, fancy pants uniform, looked like a merchant navy feller. Had gold lace and braid insignia on his costume and cap, even down to the the executive curl, you know that *Elliot's Eye* we called it in the Marines? Landed 'em in *Everett Hotel* there in LaBelle, then finally get 'em to old man Ball's hotel on Cramer Island. They'd go a-shinnyin' up to that lookout cupola smack dab in the middle of the hotel, and ole Summers would poke his index finger over yonder this way, or over yonder that-away, then he'd fancy up his voice real deep and formal and inform 'em—the customer—that the land he'd purchased was 'over thataways,' they, all smiles, eyes a-gleamin'."

"Customers would then scoot back down the ladder, then go high-tailin' it over to the *Innovative Eden*, name for Ball's row after row of citrus and beans, squash, eggplants, you name it...even had some banana trees in luxuriant huge green leaf, loaded with fruit. By then, Yankees were plumb hypnotized as he would walk up and down like a fast-talkin' auctioneer. Show 'em strawberries, watermelons, name off each one. Told 'em when it was he had put seed in the ground, and then how fast it had grown, how much a buyer could expect per plot, not to mention what the vegetable or fruit was bringin' in the marketplace, and then to top it off, proudly brag that he hadn't used nary an ounce of pesticide or manure. You think you talk?" Ray asked Melrose. "Hell yea, we know that, kept my ass awake half the night with the Prince's fancy-ass and his shotguns," Ray laughed "...anyway, ole Summers could run on and on, never miss a beat, never let 'em get in a word edgewise. Good thing, too, 'cause he didn't want them Yankees asking for too much explaining." Ray took a breath and continued, "Hell, he'd promise 'em this muck was richer than the Garden of Eden, more fertile than the damn Fertile Crescent—the Nile—in Egypt. Course, what they was seein' was only the good stuff. He'd take 'em only far as that thick custard apple ridge—dry land, ya' know. Wund't take 'em over to the sawgrass, swampy and wet. Told 'em you can make it big on between five to ten acres, thirty'd make ya' plumb rich, then let them just assume Broward would go forward with drainage."

"And you mean to tell me the folks from up North bought all that bullshit?" Melrose asked.

"Oh hell yea. They chests bulged out," Ray related, swaying his torso left and right, shoulders back, chest out, in mimicry, "Thought they'd found gold, with that ole underwater swampland that they knew fer sure would one day be as fertile as land he was a-showin' 'em rightchere on the shore of the lake," the older brother added.

"Who ran that boat *Queen of the Glades* up from Lauderdale?" Melrose wondered.

"Don't 'member his name, but that was a shorter route, and they'd make two treks a week—at least. Went on for five, hell maybe seven years 'fore lawsuits started croppin' up. Land buyers plus the U.S. government was hot on the asses of them land companies. Fact, that was about when Ball's Hotel dried up. Them big-shot land boys went to scrambling for a legal defense. And, some of them had a good leg to stand on. One was that the information they had told the buyers had been guaranteed by the state, at least through word of mouth. State of Florida told Ball and them boys this and that, so they relied on the state's word and that was all they told the buyers—no more, no less," Ray said.

"Well, that's kinda true, since the state had assured them it would finish reclamation in few years time," Melrose added.

"Yea, and on top of that, you had the United States

weather bureau saying things like it was a "frostproof environment, except on rare occasions," and even went so far as to say "even the most delicate vegetation had withstood what little bit of frost there had been." Hell, some of them fellers—company head honchos— even argued in court that they had tried to hold people back from movin' in. Had tried to restrain folks from makin' drastic moves until reclamation was complete. Trouble was, they knew too many company salesmen had stepped way out on a limb—said more than they should have 'bout what a paradise this was."

"Hell, you gotta figure anybody plops down money for land he's never set eyes on, is a simpleton. That's just actin' like a monkey," Melrose laughed.

"Time it was all over with, Dr. Chamberlain and some of 'em was indicted and convicted. Think his law-yers were able to keep 'em outta prison. Then, damned if ole Ball up and had a heart attack. Right before he could be indicted, fella fell dead."

"Everglades from that time after was associated with 'If you believe that, I got some land in Florida I wanna sell ya.'"

"Sellin' of land dried up after that, I take it."

"Sure did. That and the land bust 'round 1925, ended that happy party," Ray stated flatly. "And you know, what was funny, people who'd put down earnest money just walked away—defaulted on their payments —let 'em lapse. Some poor bastards who had paid off the note and mortgage, had deeds in hand, they just quit payin' taxes—land reverted to state on account of tax liens."

Chapter Forty-seven

"Lewis Thompson, I'm proud of you," Mabel approached her husband, opened her arms. "I gotta say—those are the purtiest head of cabbage I've 'bout ever seen.

"Ever see a head like that in Georgia?" Lewis asked with obvious pride in the crop he had just harvested the day before, after having moved to the Lake 22 years earlier. "I mean we grew some nice ones, even some big 'uns, but tell me right here and now if that idn't the nicest cabbage ever? Go ahead and admit it. And, while you're at it, go ahead and admit just how smart it was to move here."

"That's some beautiful cabbage," was all she would allow.

"So tell me now how desolate and lonely this mosquito-ridden swamp wilderness is," he remarked proudly, complimenting himself indirectly for his prescience at moving the family there.

"Don't go a-pushin' your luck, mister. You know my mama lived and died back in Georgia, pining for us the whole time. I hadn't forgotten how often you said we'd get back there and see her. Hadn't been back half that many times," she mildly rebuffed her husband. "Lord, I miss her 'bout every minute," she added, a mild rebuke of refusal to permit Lewis to wallow in pride for the move to frontier Florida that she disliked only a little less than she had those two decades earlier.

"I know, May, and Lord knows I hated to pull all us away from there, but I gotta make a livin'. Man's got to provide, but wives don't, at least not out there in the hot and sun. Hungry mouths to feed, and all five head of our young'uns has fared safe and sound, nary a hair on their heads touched by misfortune, healthy and safe. And judging by the letter I just got from my sister Bertie, two of my brothers, Ira and George, are headin' this way, directly. Fact, Ira's already lined up a job!" Bertie told me in her letter.

"Yea, but my Mama never would have traveled an inch 'less all her young'uns were together."

"She was always welcome here in my abode, and I don't mean just in Pahokee, May. Your mama was my mama, and she could have lived right here with us under this roof," he proclaimed.

"Certainly no doubt this has been good for us financially. You've made lots of money, Lewis, and I'm proud of you. I always say riches should never be counted in money, least not money alone, but I guess these days that's what most people measure success by, sadly," Mabel sighed and pensively stared down at her folded hands.

"You know they wadn't nothing for these kids up there. Forget about us, what would they have done? Chop cotton? Grow peanuts? Like five struggling generations before us? Guess they could have, but here, the two youngest boys got good jobs—surveying—working for the state. Then, you got Roger doin' even better with that sales job in Palm Beach—and moonlightin' with the truck-driving delivery job. Said next week he's getting' a raise on that."

"They coulda grown cotton and tobacco and peanuts," Mabel rejoined. Our folks did alright before us, and we weren't starving ourselves in Georgia," she added.

"But, May, you know what hard work that is—didn't our foreparents pave the way? And I mean that literally and figuratively. A road was paved that led us all the way down here, and we drove on it all those years ago—took a big chance, but everything paid off. And it was those forebears paved the way by eking out a living so we had just enough money to take that chance. Our kids have an opportunity. Look at the rich folks over in Palm Beach. Look at the big town Miami is becoming. There's opportunity here, and you know it well as I."

"Sure hope you know. Lord, I pray so. I do know you made right at $3,000 our last year in Georgia, and this year, which is three months from over, you've already made $6,000 on this purdy cabbage. Mighty proud of you for that," Mabel believed in giving due where it was rightly earned.

"Like I've always told you, what I know, I doubt. What I doubt, I'm pretty sure I don't know," he waxed philosophically. "We always just shootin' in the dark, hoping for the best."

"What you know, Lewis Thompson is lots of things, but knowing something doesn't make it so," she smirked slyly, a mild gleam in her eyes.

∞∞∞

Chapter Forty-eight

Roger and his co-worker Ralph had one more stop for the auto parts delivery business, where Roger moonlighted on the weekends. He drove the 1940 Ford Panel Delivery truck, while Ralph, his manager, rode on the passenger side. After the truck crossed over the big bridge at Twenty Mile Bend, a rare morning drizzle, especially so for that time of year, fell steadily. As Roger held tightly to the steering wheel, just as Lewis had for years exhorted him, Ralph looked back startled at a loud thudding in the rear. A box of tire supplies had fallen off the middle shelf. Roger's head followed Ralph's in turning towards the thunderous sound. He turned too much, and with his eyes averted from the road, the delivery van swerved away from the pavement onto the steep shoulder. As he quickly fought to jerk the wheel back onto the highway, the right front tire became trapped in a rut of wet mud, causing the truck to flip, and roll over twice, throwing Roger out onto the side of the highway.

Ralph was tossed toward the bulkhead separating passengers from cargo on the second roll and hit his head, gashing it severely, but managed to clamber to his feet when the sideways momentum ceased. Dizzy and disoriented though he was, the manager of the delivery truck stumbled away from the upset vehicle. He hobbled and tried to run to his employee who was lying motionless along the rocky shoulder interspersed with weeds, twenty-five feet away, over by the canal bank. Just above Roger's right eyebrow, an area on his forehead the size of a silver dollar was gushing blood, and a copious amount of the life-sustaining red liquid was already pooling in the grass. Kneeling beside him, Ralph tried to rouse Roger. Despite frantic tapping, poking, and gently shaking his prostrate co-worker, there was no response. The severely injured man's breathing seemed sporadic and labored. Breaths of air came at grossly irregular, long intervals between one and the next.

Ralph realized after fully fifteen minutes of panic and fervent and impassioned resuscitation efforts, that Roger was not, as Ralph had desperately hoped, merely unconscious. The boy whom his Pa trusted as 'the best driver in the family, with the steadiest hands at the wheel,' was dead.

Two cars had now stopped and pulled off the highway, the drivers rushing over to the man's lifeless body, to find Ralph silently weeping, turning his head gently from side to side, mumbling something about 'never should have looked back' and 'those asinine boxes...calling Roger's attention to the noise.' Ralph asked one of the motorists to "please head over to a house about two miles up the road, to call the funeral home for an ambulance—and tell them it's the hearse they'll need, I'm afraid, not the emergency station wagon." As Ralph continued to mumble through tears and a remorseful choking, the passersby began to console him. He had not been a close friend of Roger's—merely a co-worker —but had nonetheless come to admire the man's industry and willingness to work two jobs to feed himself and his wife. She liked to spend money.

Melrose, the youngest son, would have to break the news of the death of their eldest son, to Mabel and Lewis, a task he fiercely dreaded. Roger, the first-born of the five children, was favored— those rich dark features. His piercing, handsome eyes were rather close to his nose, and that had given him a countenance of innocence, yet a mildly mischievous one. His hair dark and wavy had been slicked back and consistently well-groomed. Roger's posture had always been upright, a bearing of assurance revealing a cocksure attitude. The whole of the man was what his redheaded wife Texie from Rye, New York had fallen in love with—practically worshipped. And now, his life of thirty-eight years, was over. This man who had possessed a notable joie de vivre—partying after a day's hard work, enjoying the Palm Beach social scene, losing all his troubles in festivity and society, had passed into eternal silence.

Melrose remembered stories Earlene had told him about their mother being fiercely opposed to leaving Georgia. "What would she think about the swamp now?" he wondered. He could hear her thoughts, it seemed: "I'll never forgive that crazy fool for draggin' me to this God-forsaken swampy hell." After a mournful but cathartic display of tears and emotions, he headed to his parents' house to inform them of Roger's death.

∞ ∞ ∞

Chapter Forty-nine

A aron had picked up a brochure at the motel lobby the day before. After first balking, his boss had relented and given him a couple days off—his employer was an amiable but sometimes stern man. Finally, he told Aaron "I know how badly you want to win that magazine prize, and beat your old man to it." So, with an 'aw shucks' dismissal of Aaron's absence for a couple of days, the man had acquiesced. Doss's beloved middle son seemed always willing to go skiing in the Rockies, or diving, anywhere—magazine photo contest or not. David and Doss had been surprised when he showed up, because Aaron had told them both that the boss would surely say no, given his newness on the job. Aaron was probably the best diver among the family, and he certainly was the best skier. How he could turn on a dime and race down those Rockies, was incredible. And, on the Nintendo game *Pilot Wings*, he could land the man with the rocket pack on his back squarely on the moving target, something neither Doss, David, nor Todd could do.

David slowly unfolded sections of the information packed leaflet and read about the tropical hammock and mangrove trails. It had pictures of wading birds—cormorants, herons, egrets and coots. The text described the mangrove forests and showed illustrations of the close-packed, mangled and matted roots, above water level, capable of accommodating tides that flow and ebb with inexorable certainty. While mangrove jungles seem to be resting atop the water, in fact, the anchored roots keep tides, waves, and currents from destabilizing and eroding coasts. Besides providing marine creatures a sanctuary from predators, the slowing of tides creates mud and silt from which mangrove roots extract nutrients.

The dock had an angled bend about a third of its length out into the water, and a morning sun rose over the horizon. Pinkish-orange painted a lower cloud, clear and defined, while wispy ones more distant and out of focus featured a monochromatic gray, bordered by bright white. The blue of an otherwise clear sky highlighted a central yellow of brightness—morning rays diffusing outward, all of which reflected an intensified mirror image upon the brown, brackish water of the bay.

A television blared from inside the caretaker's cottage, not twenty yards away, with snickering chortles of mostly female voices. A male voice interjected a guffaw on occasion, seemingly to tease a continuation of half-witted triviality from the vacuous prattling and cackling of the women. Doss hated it. He praised the day the mute button had been invented to transform mindless, chowderheaded drivel to silence. Why did they do that? Laugh like that? Always levity. Always silliness. Giggles. Did viewers see that as entertainment? Another way of dodging reality? It seemed the more significant the world's events—the graver the consequences—the more senseless was the product of the medium. Did audiences escape some perceived ruination by a distraction of such nonsense?

"I know, right," was one bit of conversation Doss could construe. "And she went back three times to change her hair color—couldn't get it right," was another. "From a blonde to a blonder blonde, and not a single date....that's how a raven-haired brunette emerged," were other words issuing from the TV, more in stammered dribbles, than perceptible speech.

The man, this scuba diver, a student and teacher of law and its history, rather than suffer through any further asinine 'tee-hees,' ambled disgustedly away, straightening his stiff back, still tired from yesterday's dive.

"Maybe it's me," Doss thought. "Perhaps I'm out of synch. Isn't the caliber of programming geared to viewers' tastes? What's wrong with Spring Break orgies at Daytona and Panama City Beach? 'Students blowing their parents' money, sex with anyone willing—puking and drinking, pissing and passing out. These young kids in the prime of their lives when—if there was a time for fulfillment—this should be it. But, no—a simulated counterfeit of reality was what they craved," he concluded. "Hell," he thought, "forget counterfeit—an outright escape from reality. Been that way a long time. Used to be milder, years ago in Ft. Lauderdale, but still vacuous, vomit-filled drinking and sexual conquests," Doss recalled from his teenage years. He never went to Lauderdale, no sir, not this boy who aspired to get to law school with an average intellect at best. And, he easily could have traveled the distance to that party city. It was only 65 miles from Belle Glade.

"Who am I to judge today's world as lowbrow or out of touch, or immoral?" the man thought. "Then again, no, it wasn't that," he quickly protested to himself. Doss understood wit. He understood clever discourse and the repartee of wordplay. "It's more the grim reality of a sober world juxtaposed with the superficial and gratuitous triviality. Harmony of the two seemed aimless," he concluded. Maybe he took life too seriously. The kids at Spring Break may be enjoying their own once-in-a-lifetime feast—perhaps the highlight of their entire existence.

———

The queen angelfish, six in a small school, had an electric blue stripe outlining lemon yellow near the pectoral fins of its central torso, shading to a canary yellow nearer its twin pelvic fins. The blue stripes ran vertically on either side of its eye, and terminated in a patch of equally vivid blue below and to the rear of its mouth. One of the six fish had four irregular streaks of a brighter, but more turquoise shade along its body, the final streak much shorter, fanning out near its translucent tail, interspersed with light gray streaks. Doss remembered the neon quality of that blue, along with the splotches of gray on a black grouper, and the irregular stripes and squiggles of the smaller Nassau grouper. Those underwater vistas combined with a plentitude of rainbow and blue parrotfish, helped calm his fretting disquietude over the nonsense on TV.

Years earlier, while still a baby, Doss's father Cory had wanted to dive. Couldn't get his wife to go, so that notion waned. Unlike his father, Doss convinced his wife Daisy to get certified with him. She did—she was always a good sport, although scuba diving wasn't at the top of her list of vacation jaunts. But Cory's wife, Doss's mother, loved one thing around water, and one thing only—fishing. Weird as it was, she detested the taste of fish, didn't matter which way it was prepared. Didn't matter how mild the fish. Loved oyster stew, but only after the oysters were removed. Loved the broth...loved to fish. In fact, before her family left Georgia, fishing was the one enticing activity Lewis had promised the kids they would engage in. Doss had loved his mother, and remembered her peculiarities with tenderness.

Chapter Fifty

Aaron urged Doss to venture on a shark dive the next day, since that would be their last day in the Keys, but David was wary. He had seen the media portrayals of big sharks—Whites, Tigers, Bulls—that required divers to be in cages. He knew they could be vicious. Aaron assured both men that Caribbean reef sharks, *Carcharhinus perezii*, were of little threat to humans. "Their long, slender bodies can move through caves and other openings in coral reefs, which, despite the rough surface, does not discourage the animal. Some shark experts think the scratching may promote a narcotic pleasure in the fish, while others are convinced the removal of parasites is a more likely explanation," Aaron asserted.

"Caribbean reef sharks love to hunt, even in close quarters, and yellowtail snapper are a particular favorite. A shark typically makes lazy turns around the snapper, seemingly nonchalant about the prospective meal, lulling the prey fraudulently into a sense of security—before darting full speed, head cocked at an unusual angle to grab the unwitting meal at the corner of his sharp-toothed, hungry jaw," Aaron's speech quickened with the drama of sharp teeth and stealthy hunting.

"You know the Caribbean reef is a requiem shark, right?" Aaron asked David.

"What's that even mean?" asked David.

"Dudn't have to swim constantly," Aaron responded. "Most sharks have to keep moving or die, but the requiems are different. "They can rest on the bottom, take a nap and chill out."

"Why do the other ones have to swim all the time?" David queried.

"Way to get air—oxygen," Aaron informed. "Otherwise they suffocate. "Caribbean reefs are unusual in that they can rest, and that's true of the dusky and silky shark, not to mention *Triaenodon Obesus*—the Whitetip shark in the Indo-Pacific region's oceans. They, along with the Blacktip Reef and Gray Reef are common in those oceans. "A lot of the reefs are requiems," Aaron educated his older brother, thanks to his years of studying pictures and reading stories beginning when he was 12, after watching a classic movie about sharks.

In fact, the 'reefs' were distinguishable thanks to their sporadic swimming in stops and starts, almost seeming to propel themselves in a waving pattern, white tips prominently featured on both dorsal and tail fins towards the ends.

Their snouts are blunt, with a Bulldog-like flattened jaw area, brow ridges protruding with ovoid eyes, and especially "that mouth formed in a half-circle that makes the fish look serious and grouchy," Aaron continued educating on shark esoterica.

"The Caribbean reefs can turn their stomachs inside out. Instead of vomiting stuff they can't digest, or other junk like parasites. That's how they clean their digestive tracts. Anyway, I was hoping y'all might want to go on a shark feed. Somebody told me you could pet them when they swim by you, but you're not supposed to—

they tell you to keep your hands tucked in so they don't mistake it for a fish. There's thirty or more in a group that the dive master tends to, from what I read in the magazine article."

"What do they feed on," Todd asked.

"The much larger tiger and bulls make meals off the smaller reef sharks, which themselves feed on fish, shrimp, and crabs."

"That's all they do--eat, David added. "Never sleep."

"The requiems can rest their robust, slender bodies in caves at the bottom for long periods of time, much like the nurse shark—those notorious bottom dwellers of the shark family. But, they don't actually sleep, at least as measured by experts who have carefully noted that their eyes continue to move and watch for predators" during such moments of repose."

"Ah, those moments when nobody's eyeballing you," Doss interjected, quickly remembering one of his favorite gems of wisdom: "It's the things you do when no one's looking that most clearly illustrates who you are on the deepest level," a truism he durst not bore these boys with, distracted as they were with videos, electronic games, and music, typically loud and unintelligible, especially while riding on long trips.

———

On this their next to last dive of the scuba trip, the colors were unsurpassed. The coral, here a light green, over there dark pink, was comprised of countless tiny animals known as polyps, which—like a starfish, squid, or jellyfish—has no backbone, and is no smaller than a pin head. Coral, of whatever variety or shape—*staghorn, elkhorn, sea pen, black, blue, pillar, antipathies*—are not plant life. Anchored to the bottom of an ocean by roots, it would be easy to think they are. Plants manufacture their own food via photosynthesis—coral do not. The tiny animals are not rock, either, as could be supposed. They are living organisms.

Each polyp's mouth is encircled by tentacles that pack a stinging punch. Prey passing near stunned by toxin from nematocysts. Of course, the prey by necessity must be smaller than the coral polyp. And, only one hole. The polyp eats its prey and expels waste through that one opening. Then, the majestic mounds of celestial color formed—the coral reef—a creation of billions of polyps. A kingdom of dazzling beauty that any individual polyp probably never appreciates. An opulent kingdom of hues and shades enjoyed never by its subjects. Subjects exist, objects observe and admire.

Suddenly, exploring aft of a sunken ship's rudder, there it was: Doss caught a glimpse of blue, star-spangled color. The Royal Starfish, with five appendages of Egyptian blue, not quite as dark as cobalt, had one arm arched flexibly and lazily over a side of rock upon which it lay. Bordering the blue was a vanilla, almost flax colored ribbed edge running parallel on either side of each arm, from which hung delicately lined protrusions that resembled vacuum cleaner bristles of a much lighter Alice blue. Doss snapped three pictures of the starfish.

At the foredeck, on the port side, there was a hatch. Not six feet away, near a large area—rusted, pitted, and open—lay another. This starfish was olive, at least proximal to its central disc, with shades of army green, almost a rifle green at the far ends of its extensions. It was topped by nine or ten orange nodules, spaced evenly down each arm, which also dotted the lower edges of the creature near its bottom. The central disc was army-green, shading towards the Feldgrau of a gray-green.

The scuba tank had only 500 pounds of pressure —almost time to resurface—as Doss took a long look at the wreck and tried to envision its wholeness. His mind drifted back to the steamboat that his father, grandfather and great-grandfather had operated. His mind recalled nautical terms the three generations had used so effortlessly, and which he had learned through conversations with Cory. Doss remembered with a tinge of sadness how *Corona* had met her demise in the Banana River, not far from its west shore, with only her helm and a portion of quarterdeck protruding. Doss lived life aboard the steamboat vicariously. Memorable moments of great-granddaddy Peter's antics, were eagerly related by Cory to Doss on countless occasions. Percy, too, always had lively tales about life aboard the beloved boat, but Doss was born after Percy's death. Cory had passed the narrataives on to Doss. And Cory's version took on added color because he lived the events twofold. Cory had been an integral part of the steamboat operation for many of the momentous events, however his youthful mind remembered on a child's level. Percy had recounted to an adult Cory what had happened on an adult level, with subtlety and texture that Cory's callow mind could not absorb while a child. Percy's accounts were in many ways new to Cory, at least to the extent and scope of what had transpired.

After the steamboat days, Percy and Cory worked together in an entirely different venture, and some of those episodes were more colorful even than the steamboat capers. In this new venture, Cory was a grown-up right along with Percy.

Chapter Fifty-one

Doss and his sons went on a night dive, and a starfish Aaron spotted and pointed out to David, made the whole trip worthwhile. The intensity of the coral, tropical fish, anemones, starfish, and jellyfish is not tamped down and skewed as in daylight dives. At night, with no sunlight diffused into ocean water that distorts otherwise vivid colors with a bluish tinge, the object shone upon by a diver's light beam revealed true shades of each remarkable creature.

Near the pedestal of the 'Touchdown Jesus'—*Christ of the Abyss* statue—twenty feet beneath the ocean surface near Sorghum Reef, lay a starfish garbed in its purple attire. Fully sixteen appendages radiated from its central disc of light lavender. A dark, African-violet colored the length of its arms with a pinkish-purple running along the edges of each. In addition, the dazzling creature featured tiny spikes, not sharp, but seemingly rubber-like, protruding from its bodily structure. Its center, its extensions, was a textured richness, almost abstract in beauty and luminescence. Doss snapped a picture. So did Aaron, but from a different angle. "What did Aaron see in that angle?" Doss wondered.

Then—another. About seven yards away, over near

a corroded boiler, lay a five-appendage starfish. Its arms were stubby and short, featuring cherry-red splotches on a white background radiating from the central disc. The splotches continued halfway out to the distal portion of its limbs, which abruptly showed only white, save for the bottom side of each extension, where one last red daub appeared. The two again snapped pictures, several of them, from varying angles. The strobe flash was a must to capture colorful scenes underwater, even in daytime dives.

As the three men drove through Belle Glade, headed back to Georgia, Doss chided Aaron about winning the contest in *The Fin*. Aaron demurred, saying merely, "We'll see. What about that stupid book you wrote, that *Our Story*, to teach us big words? You said that was gonna be a bestseller - well, we're still waiting for it to get published," Aaron reminded Doss. Aaron began to quote from a portion he had memorized:

> The youngest of the three boys is Todd, an unusual young man, obsessed as he is with flatulence and eructations and when he burps or passes gas, is insistent that all in his presence be aware of the din he has created, assuming the malodor associated with the expulsion would not otherwise inform, and one of his recent acquisitions is a device with the crude and somewhat uncooth appellation of *Fart Machine* with which the lad is able to place an electronic speaker device near a seated, unsuspecting individual, and then with a gentle touch of the bright red button placed on the operating

remote control of a cheap green plastic mechanism, activate a blaaaaaaaat sound that both surprises and embarrasses. Normal?

"Sorry Mr. Doss Neesh, that ain't funny at all. Now, it's crude silly and I guess some moron might laugh. But, to have a bestseller, you've got to have funny - irony funny - plus a plot," David informed.

"Well, ain't you a big dick...you know it all, don't you, smartass. It's got big words that you two dummies should know," Doss challenged.

"Maybe if dad paid THEM they would publish it," Aaron told David.

"No. It'd cost a fortune," David added. "He ain't got it."

"Laugh you clowns. As your great uncle Melrose used to say, act like monkeys, but don't you doubt for one second about ole Doss writing a bestseller. Hell, forget a bestseller. I really don't care how many it sells, just as long as it becomes a classic. How many li'l smartasses like y'all would read *Moby Dick* or *Grapes of Wrath* if they came out today?" Couldn't spare time away from 'shoot and kill' video games or the ones where the hero steals cars. Couldn't spare time from *March Madness* or *Keeping Up With the Sluts*, or twerking Silly Myrus or some stupid ass TV show where the girl jumps from one rubber cog to the platform without falling in the pink goop. Yeah, y'all should be reading the big words, but you never will. Y'all should read *This Tide Waits*, but you never will. No, sir - too much work to learn new stuff and better yourself. Learning requires work. Entertainment exacts a price - both money and gray matter. Education might mean success and a good future. Too scary for y'all, right? Yes, sir...success is scary," Doss decided.

After sarcastic chuckles from travel-monotony banter,

David asked Aaron again about sharks. "Exactly which ones are the most dangerous to humans?"

"Whites get the most blame," Aaron told David, "but the Bull shark is probably your most dangerous. "They're big, round, solid, and will attack even when unprovoked," he added.

"What about the White?" David queried.

"They get awfully big, especially females. Average up to 15 feet."

"You mean the males are smaller?"

"Yep, and usually by five feet. "They average around ten, eleven foot," Aaron informed his elder brother.

"But," Aaron added, "one of the most to be feared is the Oceanic Whitetip. It's the first responder to a ship-wreck. The *Nova Scotia* was sunk during World War II, and out of 1,000 men or more, only about a hundred were rescued, mostly due to the oceanic whitetip, which one survivor said 'fed in a frenzy on the distressed sailors,'" Aaron concluded.

"You mean those whitetips we glimpsed on our dive in the Bahamas," David asked.

"No, no. Those are reef sharks—a lot smaller and not nearly as aggressive as your Oceanic," Aaron explained. "Two completely different animals, with the commonality being the white tip on their fin."

"But, I'll tell you another one I wouldn't want to mess around with," Aaron added, "and that's your Shortfin Mako. That and the Tiger will both put a hur-tin' on ya' if you get too close. The mako is fast, strong, has powerful jaws, and is plenty aggressive," Aaron in-formed them. "It's probably the fastest, clocked at over 20 miles per hour, and swims in a figure eight before attacking, its big ole mouth wide open right till it sinks its pearly whites into your flesh," Aaron added dramatically. "And, number two in attacks on humans is the Tiger. It has a huge appetite and will eat almost anything, even things that are not edible, like neoprene wetsuits," Aaron told the others.

"Next year, I want to see an octopus," Doss told the boys. "You know, those are some strange critters," he added. "Way they can camouflage themselves and become almost impossible to spot."

Chapter Fifty-two

Peter had died at the height of the Great Depression
—died of a sudden heart attack, no doubt during
one of his impassioned rants—and *Corona* had
been sunk back near her old stomping grounds, the Banana River. Cory was never sure why his daddy had
made that trip back just to sink the craft during the
middle of World War II, but it seemed to have something to do with the reverence Peter felt for the vessel,
and a need to give it a proper burial. Rhetta had died
just three years later, and that had been devastating to
Percy, but with no steamboat or mother to look after,
that freed Percy–and Cory—to branch out into other
ventures. The two of them, plus Emit, Marie's husband,
were now operating a labor bus whose purpose was to
haul bean pickers out to muck fields where pole bean
vines, ripe for plucking, would be loaded.

The three men had purchased a flatbed truck, with
wooded slats for sides, and at 5 a.m. every morning,
Monday through Saturday, Cory or Percy would drive
the vehicle to Fifth Street of 'colored town' to collect
Negro workers. Needless to say, the drudgery of filling
hamper after hamper of beans was strenuous and pro-
tracted—back-aching misery pure and simple—but a
decent living could be earned in those twelve-hour days.
Not only men, but also women, many with children

tagging along, trudged up and down the rows, sweating and exerting themselves, hands tugging and pulling in mindless but quick repetition for the fifty cents each hamper commanded for their pocket.

There was no contract, and a worker may labor one day and sit home the next. Or, labor for one farmer or broker one day and then switch to a different one the next. It was highly libertarian because showing up at one of the many labor trucks or buses was not compulsory. For certain highly productive workers—typically women with a couple of children helping—a labor contractor would be disappointed or maybe even slightly annoyed with one who failed to show.

The modified school buses would often feature a yelling barker, whose fluidity with words cajoled and enticed workers to one vehicle over another. Samuel 'Sleepy' O'Neal and Emit 'Loco' Murphy were talented that way. Neither Percy nor Cory was facile with words, so Sleepy and Loco were paid well. Howard 'Trouble' Moses was another, but he was better at business than barking up laborers. It was common for some of the laborers to become loyal to a single contractor. Oftentimes, because of some slight by a boss, or a better paying opportunity from another truck, an otherwise devoted picker would switch allegiance and head towards a truck going to a different farm. Today's farm might be miles from the acreage worked the day before. There were, after all, seventeen farms from which to choose. That made for a true free market which screamed in an egalitarian voice. Labor contractors, that is, those who owned transport vehicles, or served as barkers by the truck, as well as field supervisors, were mindful of pickers' liberty to choose. Therefore, they treated the migrants who toiled so steadfastly, with cold water or iced, sweet tea, or lemonade, not to mention snacks and goodies sprinkled with a copious dose of kindness and goodwill.

Radios became popular in later years, and the contractors allowed them—pickers scrunching up shoulders to hold the device next to their ears, all while swiftly and adroitly picking pole beans. Some of the labor contractors or farmers even went so far as to provide hearty meals or a comfortable rest station with clean rest rooms. Meals were typically prepared by a supervisor's wife, whom farmers paid for culinary talents.

All sorts of tactics and shenanigans would be employed by Trouble, Sleepy, and Loco, especially with wavering employees, or those who were new, or not strongly committed to a particular supervisor or farm.

One such subterfuge Loco used involved paying a shill to join a huge crowd of prospective workers already loaded onto a truck. He would have Sleepy give an apparent laborer fifty cents, then whisper in his ears the plan, for it varied week to week. The shill, ostensibly loaded and ready to head for the farm, would ask the identity of the owner of the bean farm to which the vehicle was headed. Upon hearing the name, the impostor would throw up his hands with vociferous protestations, moanings and other such demonstrations of disapproval. The actor would then promptly jump down from the truck, vigorously shaking his head declaring "No, sir, won't be goin' there," oftentimes pulling half or more of the gullible group from that truck towards Loco's modified school bus. After all, Loco was the labor contractor who had paid for this skit. Some workers knew the true picture--what was really happening, and would try to convince those deserters that it was but an act, but many refused to believe so, the thespian's remonstrations being so convincing.

Few laborers were willing to brave an overbearing taskmaster. So, most briskly jumped down and headed towards the imposter's barker instead, in this case, Loco, ready with praise of his farm boss's generosity, kindness, and docility. The trick worked amazingly often, despite the repetition of it over the season.

"They's a-jumpin' in the hampers," Loco Murphy would bark when a field's loaded vines would yield easy pickings. Pickers loved hearing that, knowing that while not literally true, the fruit was abundant and the wooden-slatted hampers would be quick to fill. And, it was the manner in which Loco echoed 'juuuuuuump'.....kind of a growling sound at the start, morphing into an extended and ringing song, that would tickle hesitant workers. With sheer hilarity they would quickly move over to Loco's truck. Trouble Moses, another witty labor recruiter, would squawk something similar, yet in a more subdued monotone. Even laborers who weren't convinced to go with Sleepy, Loco or Trouble, would be clutching their bellies, out of breath in laughter, some rolling on the sidewalk, so replete was the merriment. Needless to say Percy and Cory kept Loco and Sleepy and Trouble well paid. Beyond the comedic antics of the showmen, their work habits were anemic—the lone exception being Trouble, who kept books for the labor brokers.

Loco had often wondered whether life wouldn't be easier growing the beans instead of brokering the laborers to pick them. He was a good man, but had little sense for practical affairs. He loved to talk, and it didn't much matter to whom, as long as the topic was politics. He hated Debs, the Socialist candidate promising equality of wealth distribution in the Great Depression. "Deb's ambition was well nigh impossible in a political system that treasured liberty over equality," Loco expostulated. "He knew that to promote wealth equality, certain freedoms had to be tamped down, because a government empowered to mandate taxes that redistributed wealth, had power to subdue, if not stifle, avenues of freedom." Loco's idea was that government should never curtail liberty. If there were big-shots who seemed to have more than their share, well it was because they were blessed, or had worked harder, or were more deserving. What others thought of as obscene riches, Loco was willing to tolerate as honestly earned, even if by a corrupt system where insider trading and rigged financing permitted the rich to grow richer, while leaving poor men like him only the hope of 'one day.'

Sleepy had tried fishing for three years with Percy and Cory, and only through pity from the two men had he lasted over a week. As for Loco, he had tried to grow cabbage for Percy, and the two even enjoyed a measure of success, practically gettin' rich one year when other farmers had bet on celery and tomatoes. Through his friendship with Earlene, Cory's wife, Loco had been introduced to Marie, the baby sister who had never taken to Lake Okeechobee as Earlene had. In fact, Marie had moved back to Georgia to reside with her grandmother, Mabel's mother. She stayed long enough to fall in love with a clumsy, lanky, but handsome dark fellow, really a big kid. Marie discovered that she was pregnant. Her lanky Georgia husband began to display a hostile, sometimes vicious demeanor. That prompted Marie impulsively to gather up her three-month old baby girl, Hope, and make the long trek back south to rejoin her mother and father and sister and brothers in the muckland.

Chapter Fifty-three

By 1960, Mabel and Percy had been dead a little over a decade. Percy had died in 1948 and Mabel a year later. The mother who had given birth to Cory had died about that same time, it seems in early 1950. Her death occurred in Chattahoochee, at the Florida state institution for the insane. No one much noticed her death, nor celebrated nor mourned it in any but the most superficial way. On a spring day in the mid-1960s, Ray was dead at 50. Pa would live until age 90, two more years after Ray died. Ray was the uncle Doss had mourned before school started. It was Melrose's daughter who had noticed Doss's teary eyes.

As the second oldest son, Ray had felt a nudge from his daddy especially in the months following his older brother, Roger's death. Roger had been highly ambitious and an entrepreneur, much as Lewis fancied himself to be—great ideas for profit, although most were idealistic and therefore in vain. He was a man of the world, a ladies' fellow who worked diligently to remain on at least the outer periphery of Palm Beach social circles. His debonair and cosmopolitan personality blended with a practical, hard-working resolve, a combination not common. Ray was nothing like his older brother. He had no interest in dressing up in suits with fancy accoutrements; in fact, he hated the idea of attire fancier than his well-worn short-sleeved cotton shirts —one, faded plaid, the other displaying nautical themes barely visible—and denim work trousers. He simply refused to be impressed by the big-shots, even those wannabes around Pahokee. Some muckland entrepreneurs thought of themselves among the elite—you know, the ones who got rich farming and brokering and shipping vegetables. Many figured they would one day own property over in Palm Beach. Ray felt an utter disdain for that crowd and eschewed even the appearance of prosperity. No show-off, he. Conversation even among his baseball-playing, country-music-loving buddies, was sparse. The machismo rituals among those tobacco-spitting rough-hewn characters was strictly limited to like-minded brethren whose initiation into that club was ironclad.

Nor was Ray anything like his younger brother Melrose. The youngest of the five siblings, Melrose grew up to be critical and bellicose, disgruntled to the nth degree. He had no intellectual curiosity like Ray, nor did he read anything more profound than a pulp-fiction cowboy story, and that, only rarely. Ray was gentler. He had helped spoil Melrose as a small child, just as Earlene had Marie. It was no surprise that after his Marine Corps days, Melrose's belly-aching got worse, and became veritably incessant, while Ray tended to take both good and bad times with equanimity. Unlike Melrose, a hard-working, industrious, what Georgia folks called a 'smart' worker, Ray didn't enjoy tasks nearly as much, at least not on a steady basis. Both men had joined the Marine Corps, and both loved sports, Ray much more than Melrose. After playing baseball, then softball, into his late-40's, Ray coached his two sons in baseball, and rarely missed a game they, or any of the other young people around Pahokee, competed in. Ray could be seen at every game squatted on his hams, smoking an unfiltered Pell Mell down to the stub, where it began to burn his fingers, then with his middle finger, flicked it, aimed it almost, out beyond where he crouched.

Melrose loved a dollar bill, but to his infinite credit, he didn't mind peddling a bicycle mile-upon-mile through sun, heat, fog, or rain to deliver mail. Packages and leather-strap bound letters by the dozens overflowed in his oversized front basket attached to the handlebars. The red and blue industrial bike was U.S. government issue and bore *United States Postal Service* on its side flanges. A sturdy metal bar under the front tire rather than a kick stand made sure the heavy duty bicycle remained standing when unattended, so that mail did not spill out. After ten years, Melrose graduated up to a gas powered three-wheeled cart, but missed the exercise of the bicycle, and asked the postmaster for it back.

Doss could do nothing to win praise from Melrose, although Doss had to grudgingly admire the man's daring and bravado - even his stoic no-nonsense, sullen demeanor. Melody, Melrose's daughter, Doss's first cousin, finally prevailed upon the man to go to Disney World, and after coming home, he told Doss: I been twice't..."my first and last." Doss kidded Melrose by asking whether he wanted to "go back and visit Mickey the Mouse?" - to which Melrose responded: "not only no, but hell no!" When this youngest of Lewis and Mabel's children finally advanced from the bicycle up to a motorized mail cart, he had allowed a young Doss to ride down the street a couple of houses. The uncle jumping out at each stop bolted hurriedly to front doors to place letters and bills in mailboxes. Earlene had asked Melrose if Doss could have a little ride in the cart. Melrose worked - and sweated. He was 'smart'. After he had once purchased a fan blade for his Ford Bronco's radiator, he bemoaned the fact that the accessory had cost 15 dollars...he had asked Cory a week or so later whether he could believe he had had to "pay fi'teen dollahs" - except he stressed the 'd-o-l-l' into a long guttural squeal and then spat out 'ahs', to emphasize his displeasure at what he believed to be an exhorbitant amount. When some wiseguy kids had laughed at him for peddling a bicycle all over town, he finally had enough and told one particularly obnoxious young man "get the hell outta my way, how 'bout it!" The boy quickly realized Melrose had had enough of the mockery, especially when the man bore down on the "'bout" portion of the reprimand in that husky growl of his, spitting out the 't' of 'it' for emphasis.

Measured against Melrose, Ray was not smart. The older uncle was never perceived by Doss as shiftless. Anyone who hybridized orchids, bred parakeets, and worked those perilous catfish lines, could hardly be called slothful, Doss believed. It was true his house was in a constant state of disrepair, unpainted, an overhang of a porch falling in, storm shutters dangling at a significant slant. Inside the house, faucets dripped continually, doors squeaked from uneven frames, dust rose in slight waves when someone walked on the groaning, creaking floors, and an aquarium with its resident fan-tailed guppies featuring a *Keep Your Cotton-Picking Hands Off* decal, bubbled with air from a little pump. Ray and his wife were indifferent housekeepers. Dead roaches could be seen flipped on their backs, legs sticking up from rigor mortis, carcasses weeks old. White tablets that looked like aspirin were scattered at various points behind a tattered chair and a stained light blue couch - set out as bait to kill more. And, that strong musty odor inside the house. Despite that, Doss refrained from picturing 'Unka Ray' as lazy, although his parents had always characterized the man as such. Doss viewed him as someone who wasn't a steady worker on a schedule answering to a boss who demanded answers.

A couple of Ray's siblings had been workaholics. Besides Melrose, there was Marie. It was really she who ran Cory and Earlene's paint store. And, before he had been killed, Roger had been fairly 'smart'. Ray was a different kind of worker, no doubt. He wasn't overly fond of hard work. He preferred labor on his own terms and at his own pace. He had rebelled against authority ever since his days of regimentation and discipline in the Marine Corps. The yelling of orders in his face hadn't set well with his placid demeanor. Maybe Ray was lazy, but Doss admired his authenticity. A lazy person who goes to work is to be admired. Not so a workaholic - that person enjoys toil. For a lazy person to pull out of bed, get dressed and head to onerous chores - now that, Doss thought, was true triumph over adversity.

Ray could get angry, but it took a great deal of goading for him to do so. In contrast, Melrose seemed to stay angry. His tanned, wrinkled brow was furrowed, and his squinty blue eyes pulled tight as he gritted his teeth to bemoan something wrong in most every situation. Ray had been but a mediocre Marine except on one occasion. A dishonorable discharge disappointed Lewis and Mabel. It was owing to an impetuous weekend rendezvous to visit a girl he had met not far from Quantico, after which he faced an AWOL charge.

A tough and swift fullback at Swainsboro High School, Ray had fancied himself sufficiently, if not overly, motivated. Whatever job in life he might have would not include yelled commands of higher-ups. He had rescued two fallen comrades at a battle right after Iwo Jima, all without the exhortation of a thundering drill sergeant's nose touching his. That satisfied his curiosity. He had what it took, he knew, after that valor. He had acquitted himself bravely when it mattered most. He was awarded multiple combat medals for his bravery. Then he took off stupidly and impulsively without that damned leave. Figured he'd earned some R-and-R, for the show of courage back in the Pacific a year earlier.

As a civilian, years later in Pahokee, he had raised gorgeous orchids of varying shapes and colors and sizes. Some varieties he grew, were rarely seen. Many went for society bids in ritzy Palm Beach, a world completely alien to his. He bred turquoise, yellow, and green budgies which Pyes, the local pet store sold as exotic parakeets for $5 each, and, most adroitly, fished catfish. Doss was at Unka Ray's house for a day when his parents had gone to Miami for business, and Ray patiently, but not with an overabaundance of nurturing, answered the boy's many questions. One was about the parakeets. Doss asked whether the birds were easy to raise.

"Yea," Ray answered, "nature takes its course and does the work for you. Besides, every species except for humans sees glory in propagating. Not true of us. I hear tell of some French woman in Paris who thinks children are but a form of entertainment for stupid people not capable of finding life's enriching wisdom without kids. Was just reading 'bout that. Some of those Frenchmen —Existentialists they call theirselves—all screwed up," Ray's voice trailed off, giving the lad far more information than he had asked for or could probably comprehend. And, Ray read—copiously. He was smart and wise, and reminded his brother-in-law Cory much of Percy on the steamboat.

Ray began reminiscing about his visits to the *Smithsonian Institution* in Washington, D.C. As a young Marine at Quantico, Ray had visited the museum four or five times in his three-month stay. Doss's incessant queries were answered readily. Ray would go into great detail on some subject, usually pertaining to nature or science -geology, physics or astronomy.

"There was a meteorite the size of a baseball that because of its atomic makeup, was heavy. Meteorites have nickel and iron, metal content that rocks on Earth lack. "So, this one, the size of a baseball had such a high density, it weighed a great more than you'd think," Ray explained.

"Melrose could not have cared less about any of those visits when he was stationed with me a couple months at Quantico. In fact, I think he only went with me once to the big museum, then said 'I been twice't— my first and last.' I still remember him saying that. He just wasn't interested in the way I was," Ray explained - the exhibits, culture, knowledge, glimpses of wisdom that the massive museum offered, most of whose contents were kept in safe vaults and locked storage, not displayed to the public.

Chapter Fifty-four

Baiting catfish trotlines was tedious. Doss watched in the afternoon as his uncle sliced off small chunks of soap. The bait was not a little fish, not a chunk of meat cut from mullet—not a grasshopper or a worm, but soap. Ray would patiently and methodically thread a hook through each one. Wooden racks were stacked four or five high, had hooks hanging down an inch or so, a dozen to a side, on all four sides. How the whole contraption worked to haul in catfish, Doss knew not, and he was hesitant to ask.

Finally, after the two had driven over to the lake in Ray's 1949 Ford truck, not far from the wharf at Pahokee, Doss summoned his courage, "Unka Ray, what's that you're working on?" The wharf's wood was dark brown and aged, and smelled of creosote, that unmistakably pungent, noxious-smelling substance slathered over poles near water to treat them and retard decay. A streak of twilight replaced the brightness of sunlight as the last semi-circle of a huge orange sun seemed to dip into Lake Okeechobee's westernmost waters. Waves in their blackness constantly lapped the shore just beyond the wharf. Within thirty minutes, the sky began to show light purple of a darkening night sky. Ray's face appeared sallow and wrinkled, a sort of off-white which contrasted with two smudges of grime, another of blood, where he had picked at a scab repeatedly. From another angle, the man appeared dark from age, although he was just 47. He had a pack of cigarettes, *Pell Mells*, Doss recalled. Money earned from catfishing, coins all, created a muffled jingle in his shirt pocket where the logo from the pack could be clearly seen through the threadbare cotton shirt. The two lions clutching upward on a coat of arms—Doss had always wondered about the image's origins—featured on the cigarette pack.

Kingfishers clucked as they darted across the broad rim canal that surrounded the lake, while a few red-winged blackbirds 'ker-lonk-aleed' from nearby palmetto bushes where myrtle warblers scurried and an eastern phoebe gently swayed in the evening's light breeze. Birds rose, lifted, and passed overhead, the blue fan of heron and white of egrets, wings rustling as they searched for a meal at twilight. Ray's face showed clear happiness as he watched the winged creatures, for he loved anything nature, and especially the beauty of nature, and particularly the gorgeous, colorfully-plumed flying creatures. Even more than his prize-winning orchids, Ray loved birds.

Doss noticed that Ray reached for a *Pell Mell*, pulling the pack out of his front pocket, gently rattling the silver coins, pulling a particular one from the pack halfway, then tamping it back down into the soft pack and replacing the pack into his pocket.

"Why did you put it back?" Doss asked, noticing every movement of the man, down to the most minute detail, especially when a cigarette was about to be lit with a flip-top brushed steel Zippo lighter sporting the Eagle, Globe, and Anchor insignia of the United States

Marine Corps. Doss was intrigued by cigarettes and aspired to smoke them one day.

"Just changed my mind," Ray responded.

"You didn't want it?" Doss continued.

"I need to cut down." That last response satisfied the boy.

Chapter Fifty-five

D oss wished Ray would explain the loops, circles, swirls and deliberate placement of hooks, lines, weights and soap chunks into what Doss later learned was called a racking box for the catfishing line. The square frame of a box prevented entanglement of the trot line, set with hundreds of small fishhooks about to be deployed into the water.

"Some people build these racking boxes out of cardboard box lids, but trouble is, when that gets wet, it's finished. Best to build a wooden box," Ray explained to the curious boy who was still in awe of the bar of soap from which small chunks were being cut to bait the hooks.

"Your box needs to be approximately 14 inches square by 4 inches deep, but those dimensions don't have to be perfect," Ray explained.

"What are those for?" Doss asked, pointing to the cut slots inside the top edge.

"You cut your slots about an inch apart. We commercial fisherman cut 25 notches per side to rack 100 hooks per box," Ray continued to explain.

"How does that catch catfish?"

"What you're doing, son, is making a trot line," the man responded in a husky-throated, cigarette-irritated Georgia drawl. It's a long cord with hundreds of fish hooks dangling from it. That line allows you to cover the width of a channel, like the one here in the Rim Canal, with your hooks. What you do is tie your line to one side of the channel, stretch the line across and tie off to the other side. Any fish that passes through the canal will then come close to one of your multitude of hooks."

"What about over there in the lake?" Doss wondered, pointing to an area about a mile off that opened into the monstrous body of water.

"Lots of people run a line out into the actual lake. What they'll do is tie a brick to the end of the line to weigh it down, and then tie something that floats, a marker, to it. Here in the canal, a lot of fishermen tie to a tree then mark it with a rag or torn piece of cloth," Ray continued, "but that's when you get thieves that steal your catch."

"How does the fisherman know if he gets a nibble?" Doss asked, thinking about how his mother and father fished on their small boat *Sum Fun*, out in the Atlantic Ocean, usually for sheepshead, red snapper, yellow tail, and grouper. Cory and Earlene would anxiously anticipate any twitch of a rod from fish inspecting their bait.

"What's clever 'bout a trot line is that a fisherman doesn't have to sit with it. He puts his line out in the morning, then goes to work or back home, then comes back to check the line later at dusk. Some folks, including me, leave a line tied up to a favorite spot, bring a fresh bar of soap with plenty of lard in it, check for what was caught overnight, then rebait the hooks, leaving the rebaited line in the water."

"Do you catch a lot?" Doss asked.

"Yea, but trouble is you get a lot of turtles and crappie on a trot line too. Crappie's good eatin' but them other two, the mudfish and gar, are no good for any-thing. One time I had an alligator caught on a trot line, and believe you me when you're pulling in a line with that monster reptile, he's madder than a wet hen and got that long string of fish hooks to snag in you. Gotta be really careful with those things," Ray instructed.

"Glad my daddy doesn't fish with trot lines. He's got his rod and reels. I don't think he'd have the patience for all this. He even throws a temper fit when his mono-filament fishing line gets tangled only a little."

"Yea, Cory's got a temper. Always has had. A lot like his granddaddy," Ray added. "Needs to be more like his daddy was. Now there was a good man. Calm, kind, even-tempered. Percy liked rum a little too much, but I loved that man. You never knew him did you, son?"

"No, Grandpa Percy died way before I was born. Only grandparent I ever knew, only one I have is Pa."

"My daddy," Ray responded. "Another good man. God bless him, it's sad to see him a-gettin' so feeble. He wants to live here with me and her, but we can't take care of him. Plus, we got them teenaged boys. Daddy don't want to, but we all gotta pool our money and get him into an old folks' home purdy soon," Ray sadly reported.

As the boy and his uncle got into the little boat with the oil-smeared, grungy, 15-horsepower outboard motor, Ray pulled hard a couple of times on a cord he had wrapped around the starter at the top of the motor. It fired up, and the two rode about a quarter mile to the edge of the Rim Canal where the birds had been seen fif-teen minutes earlier.

"By now, you know I use soap, like this right here," showing the off-white colored bar sliced and cut and reduced to half its size. A lot of catfishermen use grass shrimp, crawdads, grubs. Whatever they're quick enough to catch, what don't get away from them, they'll grab it, then bait their hooks with 'em."

Stopping the boat and shutting down its motor, Ray said "Okay, this is where I like to run my line," Ray motioned with a nod of his head over toward a tree 30 yards distant. "This is my spot, so I'll tie the line to a tree on one side. Ya always gotta make sure no one else is already using the same tree a little lower in the water, 'cause you don't want your lines to tangle with his. Couple of times I picked what I thought was a perfect spot then discovered that someone else liked it too. Another thing to consider, you got fish thieves, so you gotta hide your line so they don't discover it and steal your catch."

"How do you do that?"

"First, be sure the line is low in the water, yet not touching bottom, then cover anything that's visible with grass from the lake so the fish thieves can't easily spot it. Next, you gotta run your line out, making sure to weight it down with a brick at intervals. One person can do that task, but it's a lot easier with two, that's why I need someone like you," Ray said, smiling at Doss.

"I'd like to help ya' Unka Ray." Ray said nothing.

"I'm gonna run the engine slowly, while you watch the box to make sure the line feeds out smoothly from the racking box. If it's coiled like it's s'posed to be, the drop lines will gently pull out of the slots as the line feeds into the canal. Doesn't always work perfectly, sorry to say. Sometimes you'll have a line get caught a lil' tight and you're gonna have to tug at it real easy to help ease it out. Then, we wanna come back after four or five hours to check the line. Fish eat in the early morning or dusk, so it's best to check a little after those hours. And, 'member, 'gators keep a close eye on trot lines, doubly so if they're left in one place for a long time, and you're liable to find empty lines, fish that have been bit in half, or worst of all, some ole 'gator completely tangled in your line, destroying it—ripping it to bits. What's even worse, like I told you before is the ole 'gator still being all tangled up in the line and having a bad attitude."

"I'll bet they could hurt you," Doss responded in a soft, mumbled voice.

"When you go to pull your line in, you gotta drop it loosely into the box while you clean off each hook one-by-one. Then, you gotta' flip the box upside down to start rewinding the line. You don't wanna leave bait on the hooks and throw the box in the car. The smell would later be overwhelming," Ray informed the boy.

"Those fish do stink. I know from my daddy's boat when he goes fishing over at Port Salerno out of the St. Lucie inlet. I can't hardly stand to smell my parents' clothes on the way home, when they pick me up from Marie's or Melrose's, after they been fishing."

"What you don't want to do when you rack your line is to tie a brick on the very end and throw the brick out into the water. It'll fly out and uncoil the line behind it. If your throw is perfect, you can get by, but if not, you'll get multiple hooks in your hand and forearm. Next, you wanna check the line carefully—pull it gently to see whether or not it pulls back. Remember, if you get a strong pull-back, it's better to cut the line and lose it than be pulled screaming, full of fish hooks into the water," Ray patiently instructed the boy.

The two spent another hour laying the trot line, making sure it was well beneath the surface, yet several feet off the bottom. At some points it arched higher below the water line that at others, but it was most important that swimmers or other fishermen not get tangled in the trot line.

Doss remembered that day spent with Ray for the rest of his life, but he never saw the man alive again, because Ray died not long after.

Chapter Fifty-six

A happy-go-lucky man, Loco felt completely fulfilled a year after taking Marie and Hope into his tar paper shack, and providing for them, adoring, even doting, on the curly brown-haired, brown-eyed baby. His job with Cory, which continued for well over a dozen years after Percy had died, promised a higher quality dwelling, and occasional meat on the table, but, if that didn't happen, everything was quite satisfactory to this smiling, happy, loud, talkative man. While highly deficient as a farmer or fisherman, Loco was good at what he did. Cory and Percy had been lucky to find his talents as a labor broker for pole bean farmers. And, since he had married into the family, the Neesh team felt as though he would stay with them permanently. Loco's Irish family had been proud of their potato-famine heritage, having traced their Celtic roots to *County Wexford*, not far from the little village of *New Ross*, where John F. Kennedy's forebears had lived in Ireland. They had loved stew, pot still whiskey, dancing jigs, and singing sea shanties. Those melodic tunes redolent of sea-faring, love-struck young men were often sung in rounds at least once a week when Loco was a child. He and Marie had a son, Padrick within four years of getting married. Padrick's addition to the tiny family in what Cory often kidded him was a "shanty-Irish shack," was a joy to Loco, who not only had progeny of his own at last, but also now a brother for Hope, whom she adored. To Loco's credit, being benevolent beyond measure but with little hint of intellect, much less common sense with tools, his role as a model citizen for the two children was superb.

Since the bald, stocky, blue-eyed, round-headed man of Irish descent recognized his limitations with manual labor and business shrewdness, the role of agent—labor contractor who interceded for the bean farmer—hadn't been a bad choice. He and Marie did not enjoy an idyllic marriage, at least on her side of the equation. Marie, tall, dark-eyed with high cheekbones, was completely in awe of her older sister, Earlene, who had facilitated the union of these two, this marriage of convenience. It was especially propitious in that it supplied a means of survival and a pittance of comfort to the pretty, slender woman with an infant daughter, both of whom were in desperate need.

Marie eventually lost her nostalgia for Georgia and after Mabel's mother Hattie died, any hankering to return to that state, was out of the question. Florida even became a place of hope for Marie. During the Great Depression, few if any went hungry, given the vegetables and produce grown pretty much year 'round.

But, in conversations between Percy and Cory before Percy died and left the business to Cory, Loco's antics with the laborers were chronicled. When labor trucks were slow to fill up with workers, especially those headed to a small one or two-acre farm, a contractor had to use artifice. Tiny farms didn't have the draw of bigger ones. If Loco could get the crowd in a state of levity, there was hope for an obscure farmer over in Lake Harbor, South Bay, Sand Cut, or Port Mayaca whose beans needed picking as much as the fat cat who owned two hundred acres or more. Various skits continued to be contrived to attract prospective pickers, with Loco and his counterparts being ever more creative week after week. One, at which Cory laughed so hard his sides ached, involved having a young man, much too lazy to pick beans, attempt to load a croker sack filled with grapefruit, onto the open-bed, slat-sided truck. After a drink or two, but not fully intoxicated, the actor could perform marvelously. He would try multiple times to heave the burlap sack, the kind typically filled with potatoes, up onto the rear of the empty truck. Failing several times, then climbing a crude homemade ladder, he would amble up and pretend to catch himself before seeming to almost fall, by which time the crowd was roaring with laughter and cracking the air with a cacophony of guffaws. The comedian finally surmounted the obstacles of intoxication, height, gravity and coordination, to land face first, but successfully with his load, onto the bed of the truck.

Simultaneously, a barker whose job it was to convince workers to board his truck for a given farm, would resume the chant "Beans jumpin' in hampers," "Bountiful and no sticker weeds," or "Going up a nickel a hamper, now to 65 cents," to a point that within ten minutes, the truck was replete with still howling, side-clutching workers, drunk themselves from laughing so hard, and now ready to work. Percy had told Cory on more than one occasion before he died, "The laborers should be paying us for those damned stupid skits. Free entertainment."

Women—some slight, even tiny, others buxom and large—wore high-laced boots, typically with flowered dresses and wide-brimmed hats under bandanas tied around their heads. Men's trousers were often worn under their dresses, tied securely near ankles to keep out muck dust which for many field workers caused severe itching. The hats varied from felt to wide straw, the latter tied beneath chins. All were stained with broad swaths of sweat near the brim.

No worker seemed ever to want to be the first to board the labor truck, especially for a farmer who might be a strict taskmaster. Women who were too shiftless to work, loved the feel of a couple of silver half dollars in hand, enough to go into acting mode. There was one who would laugh gaily and push through the crowd, singing, shouting, displaying dramatics, but ultimately climbing aboard, while others soon followed. With her silver safely tucked, this non-worker, really a gifted actress, quickly but quietly sneaked back to the end of the truck, creating some lame excuse for needing to disembark. She oftentimes headed straight over to the jook joint to spend her easy money on a bottle of watermelon wine. Trucks not filled would cause labor brokers to raise the paying price another nickel because farmers in a tight with beans needing to be picked, had to have hands to pick them.

White-headed black patriarchs stared at the ground in silent dignity, or sipped hot coffee and stared towards the sky, but largely ignored the exuberant younger workers, some with striped jackets, prancing and gesturing in pre-work levity. Peanuts in tiny paper sacks were offered for sale by Rufus Pouncy, a one-armed black man who had made a small fortune pushing a grocery cart, yelling, "Gittem while they hot—boiled and parched!" Pouncy was rarely absent in the early morning, pre-light hours of labor round-ups when he knew laborers headed for fields might want a snack to stave off hunger before lunch. Ham or turkey sandwiches on plain white bread were handed out for lunch.

Farmers or their labor contractors enticed workers with "first pickings," "bountiful fruit," "good stand, fifty cents," and other similar promises. One obstacle to be avoided were the loathsome sticker weeds that pushed forth, seemingly overnight in the muck, and another was a mean foreman. Perhaps from slavery days, or those following immediately in its aftermath, when masters-turned-employers were more bitter than ever, black workers in the muckland seemed to sense with amazing prescience, a boss who tended towards cruelty or hostility. Ones with an ounce of compassion were discovered equally as quickly.

There was reluctance even to appear to be in a hurry to climb on a labor truck, notwithstanding the benevolence of the farmer. Even when the barkers would yell "They's a-jumpin' in the hamper!" recalcitrance seemed the norm. The scene would often have a male or female laborer grudgingly drift towards a truck, hoping for another farm representative to yell out, "Tender green, second pickings, good yield, and paying 60 cents." While first pickings were much preferred, given greater abundance of fruit, an added dime in pay attracted many, just never in a hurry. Even when more money was offered, many were loath to switch allegiance and jump to another slatted truck or dilapidated bus, because of the desirability of first pickings and the perceived mutiny many labor bosses might infer from abandonment. So, with 50 pickers jammed into or onto the trucks, oftentimes with young'uns peeking through the slats, the vehicle's gears grunted and a rusty chassis would creak and groan at the vehicle's first movement.

Passengers could be heard still laughing, some cackling, others roaring, a cloud of dust all that remained as the transporting machine lumbered toward black fields of muckland replete with acres of verdant pole beans, sometimes limas, green glistening moist from morning dew.

Filled hampers were hauled to packing houses, but not before trucks oftentimes got stuck or slipped off the soft, rutted muck roads. When wet, they were slick as Georgia clay—or ice. Those treacherous paths had no rocks, much less asphalt. In fact, a field truck may haul only a fractional load to the paved highway, and at that point the beans would be reloaded onto another, larger truck headed for town. Farmers knew a full field truck loaded with hampers was not only were destined to bog down, but at times, necessitate tractors to pull the vehicle out of a rut or merely to move it along. There were times in which even a sled, forget wheels and tires, might have to be used.

Once the black bean pickers returned to town, they jammed the streets. Instead of dissipating to go home, the crowd seemed to form. Hours later, when it did finally disperse, it did so only slowly, despite the collective fatigue. Muck-heavy clothed blacks drifted about, a couple of them passed out on a bench from sheer weariness, usually children. Others headed to the wine store, seemingly indefatigable. Some laughed, others cackled, a few guffawed with tales of irony and levity, while another amorous few hugged, flirted, and a pugnacious one or two squabbled, despite the exhausting day of labor. Zora Neale Hurston was a fixture around Belle Glade during bean picking days of the early 1940's writing her future classic novel, *Their Eyes Were Watching God*. Hurston commented that, "These folks work all day for money and fight all night for love."

Beans picked one day too early or one day too late oftentimes had an effect on price. When the market for the produce was relatively high, fields may be picked five times. Even the 'dogs,' or relatively sorry pickings might bring the biggest cash payout of all.

Fires in trash barrels provided warmth while jook joints and pool halls were packed with dark figures squeezed close to the entrance nursing cheap wine from bottles. Fainter profiles towards the rear played 'skin', a card game for hard-earned nickels and dimes. An antique, upright mustard-yellow piano tinkled off-key, sounding harsh to most ears, but melodic for couples dancing to ragtime music through the night.

Beans became popular only after 1927, which was the year of a big freeze. Prior to that, squash and other vegetables were grown, or attempted, but beans were a dream crop because they could be picked after a rather quick maturity of 55 days. When frost or torrential rains occurred, business came to a halt and store merchants, who sided as creditors, went unpaid on the credit extended, which meant laborers used bamboo poles to fish for their nightly rations. And, they were good with bamboo poles. Forget boats and outboard motors. Alongside a riverbank or canal slope, many black men and women—a few white folks, too—caught a mess of fish in a hour's time, enough to feed themselves and their family, plus have some left over for needy neighbors.

But, when beans were selling, and frost or rain held

off, they were a lucrative crop. Even after the 1928 hurricane, one of the worst ever to hit Florida, 2,700 freight cars brimmed full were shipped to points north. At the peak, in 1946, 4,088 carloads chugged northward to feed a bean-hungry nation. A huge disadvantage of the bean crop was the number of laborers needed to facilitate those shipments. Also, top quality beans had to be picked at that perfect moment, which only skilled farmers could discern with amazing judgment.

White workers didn't often pick beans, but they did mechanical work, and lifted, packed, sorted, graded, hauled, and drove. Most working-class folks lived in migratory government labor camps such as *Osceola Center*, row after row of tar paper houses many called 'the labor camp', or simply 'the camp'. Many residents were women, single women from pre-teenage years to grandmothers. Grading beans, and later radishes and celery from moving conveyor belts made of rubber, occupied most of these working-aged women. The men of the camp moved hampers to refrigerated trucks or railroad cars. No work began before noon, but it went on into the earliest hours of the next morning until the last of the beans arrived and were on board and ready to ship.

∞∞∞

Chapter Fifty-seven

L oco's son Padrick continued to thrive and grow into a strong, hardy lad, even insisting in his early years that he would be a farmer one day. When sugar cane began to be the crop of choice, 35 years after his father had worked so adroitly as a labor broker with Percy and Cory, Padrick turned 28, and decided his niche in farming would be that of sugarcane planter. Fidel Castro had gained power over the dictator Fulgencio Batista, and established a totalitarian government on the island of Cuba. In retaliation, President Kennedy established a strict trade embargo to break the back of the Socialist government which the Cuban people, particularly those of affluence, felt was harshly oppressive and brutal. Many Cubans believed that had Carlos Hernandez, a well-respected senator from Camaguey Province, specifically the little village called *Florida*, become Prime Minister, ousting Batista, Castro never would have succeeded. Hernandez could have thwarted the dictator from establishing what he saw as a socialist paradise on the tropical island with turquoise waters and sugary-white beaches. But, Hernandez had perished in a freak airplane crash that hit some power lines while dropping campaign literature for his upcoming election, allowing Batista to rise to power. Batista's corruption and conflicts of interest lent credence to Castro's strong calls for reform of a 'Yankee-controlled state' that was selling out Cuba's interest with little regard for humanitarian conditions of the masses. It was from that sordid and revolutionary setting that Padrick's future wife, Maribel, emigrated with her family from Cuba during the 1961 'release' by Castro of certain affluent families desiring to leave.

Resources and wealth had to remain in Cuba but the young Communist dictator who had encouraged spying and routine re-education of dissenters, permitted a flight to freedom towards the United States, after jailing thousands of men implicated in the Bays of Pigs uprising. For those with even a modicum of wealth, the opportunity was welcomed, and millions left Cuba forever, most settling in or near Miami. So, with only basic goods, plus the clothes they wore, the erstwhile Cubans of means transformed themselves into refugees of poverty to seek 'liberalis,' that Roman ideal of freedom, many gravitating to the muckland and its sugarcane and sugar mills.

Whatever else the Kennedy embargo accomplished, it promoted the growing of *Saccharum officinarum*-sugarcane-on the muckland, seemingly overnight, beginning in 1961. Cubans who came to Miami initially made their way to the Lake, around which sugarcane grew splendidly in the rich soil. As a tropical crop, the perennial grass of the *Poaceae* family cannot withstand temperatures much below freezing. It requires some measure of cold weather to infuse sugar content into its stalks, but not too much. Sugarcane stalks reach 10 to 24 feet, and feature long, sword-shaped leaves. Each stalk has several segments, each with a joint. The joint features a bud from which new growth emerges. That was the part Padrick was especially interested in as a planter. He didn't care about acquiring grinding rights at a mill, or the processing or marketing aspects of sugar production. As a planter, it was those segments, joints and buds that he focused on. The crop didn't have to be planted each year, but roughly every four years.

Treacle or black treacle, more commonly known as molasses, is a syrup that remains once the sugar is crystallized out of the cane. It's separated from sugar crystals by centrifuge, a separation that occurs repeatedly once manufacturing begins. Sugar crystals are what ends up on dining tables for sweetening, either in raw form or more refined white sugar.

Molasses was popular prior to the 20th century in the United States as a common sweetener. First boilings of sugarcane juice produce what is known as 'first syrup', which has the highest sugar content and Southerners typically refer to this as cane syrup, rather than molasses. A second boiling extracts a less sweet molasses that's used in cooking, and a third leads to blackstrap molasses, robust, heavy, viscous, dark and bitter, since most sucrose has long since crystallized and is now absent. There is but a small amount of sugar remaining, along with an abundance of minerals such as calcium, magnesium, iron and potassium. That's why blackstrap molasses is ideal for cattle feed. It's also used in baking or producing ethanol. Another use is fertilizer. For most tates, blackstrap molasses would not be a suitable sweetener.

Vast acreage of sugarcane was already grown in Clewiston, *America's Sweetest Town*. It had been for decades one of the largest areas of sugar production in the United States, along with Louisiana, Texas and Hawaii.

Belle Glade, South Bay and Pahokee were just some of the villages many Cuban refugees intermingled with back-woodsy vegetable growers from Alabama, Mississippi, Georgia, and South Carolina, most of whom had heard nary a word of the Spanish tongue. Turns out, the muckland grew cane even better than the sandy loom of Clewiston. There was muck in Clewiston, but it was mixed largely with sand and not nearly as rich as land east and south of the Lake. Eventually, seven cane grinding mills would be established between 1962 and 1987. The one in Clewiston had been established in 1947, well before Castro's dictatorship.

Castro's rise to power was a double boon for Padrick: It not only provided him the opportunity to plant sugarcane, and thus realize his dream of becoming a farmer, but it also provided him with Maribel, his future wife. She was a beautiful raven-haired, black-eyed child of a well-off, if not wealthy, young engineer from Guines and his vivacious wife from Santa Clara, near Varadero Beach. The girl displayed excitement and appreciation of Americana—events centered around her new world. Her exceptional intellect gravitated towards books and reading, especially Revolutionary and Civil War histories, places and architecture of her new land, notably, Monticello, Mount Vernon, the Capitol in Washington, D.C., and Williamsburg. Inspired by a history teacher, the girl's burgeoning fascination was driven to new heights. This child of Cuban refugees thought deeply, yet melded her brainy singularity into an affable camaraderie and discourse with others, that Padrick, who lacked her academic flair, found irresistible. Many of the young Cuban refugees had a strong predilection for the honor roll. So abundant were Cuban surnames on each six-week's list of high-achieving students, that Anglo-American names paled in comparison. Many Americans who were less talented than Maribel, nevertheless found her fun—a social equal—and sought her out as a companion. Her beauty was matched by an intellect and personality equally as aesthetically pleasing. Any slight flaws of physicality distracted not at all from her enthusiasm and ready gaiety. As so many of the other Cuban girls, Maribel was, in her overall presentation, a true goddess of the Iberian peninsula, whose great-grandparents had braved the wild yet seductive lure of a tropical Caribbean island. Much as had American revolutionaries, Spanish pioneering spirit was laudable.

Attempts to create a more propitious existence in a Cuba later given the sobriquet *Pearl of the Antilles*, met with resistance. It had a brutal, untamed remoteness for these colonists. After all, they had come from a sophisticated world populated for millennia by Moors, Goths, Sephardim, and Iberians. The ancestors of those colonists had established cultural centers in Madrid, Lisbon, and Barcelona and had a great deal of savvy. Cuba's settlers had succeeded.

Padrick and Maribel, produced two beautiful, talented children, a boy and a girl, both of whom had the intellectual prowess of Maribel, and the good-natured, affable personality which Padrick had acquired from Loco. The daughter, Frances Christina, had eyes just as black as her hair, and the son, Sean Ryan, was popular with his classmates, male and female, for his outgoing love of talking, and it didn't matter much the subject, as long as someone was nearby for whom he could perform. Frances Christina was an intellectual as her mother had been in high school and college, yet could easily relate to those less gifted than she—which included most everyone. She was blessed with an infusion of childlike enthusiasm that idealized the world with its sadness and suffering as one still worth enjoying to the fullest. Maribel told her and Sean Ryan about the brutal totalitarian dictatorship where many Cuban capitalists saw possessions expropriated by the Castro government. The young woman was not unmindful of ugly facets of reality, yet suppressed those to believe that the United States of America, and particularly, the fertile mucklands of Lake Okeechobee was a veritable land of opportunity. Her quick wit and good sense refused to see the "land of the free and home of the brave" as meaningless platitudes to be discounted as nationalistic chest-beating. Thanks to a healthy dose of Iberian idealism, tinged with Irish common sense, the girl kept distinct the realities of a life under a dictator with few checks on his power. She was proud her ancestors had jumped at the chance to trade it for one which offered freedom.

Doss himself had first seen the strange-sounding youths, out on the edge of his residential neighborhood street, with a bicycle lying on its side. Two boys spoke not a word he understood, trying to fix a flat tire and increasing the volume of their voice when Doss shrugged his shoulders to indicate that he didn't understand what they said. He had even asked Earlene, "Who were those boys fixing their bikes out on the road, the ones who are dark-haired and dark-eyed and spoke words I never heard?" Earlene tried as best she could to explain the political realities that President Kennedy was even then grappling with.

Comic books in that same foreign tongue, but featuring Disney characters like Donald Duck, appeared on the shelves of the *Latin Grocery*. Kids coming to school had tri-colored red, yellow and green Cuban suckers, Christmas-tree shaped, routinely poking out of their mouths. Both Cuban refugee students and American kids alike. After word got around that the suckers, made in Connecticut, ironically, could be acquired only at the Latin Grocery, many American school-age students began to patronize that tiny store to purchase them.

Then, there was the malt beverage called *Malta Hatuey*—thick, black, molasses-like, with hops, along the lines of beer, but with no alcohol. There was *Iron-beer*, a carbonated soft drink that despite its name also contained no alcohol. *The Sweet Shop, Your Food Store* and *Case-Rate,* even *Kwik-Chek* had stiff competition thanks to new Cuban immigrants.

Cuban sandwiches became a popular afternoon snack with students after school's final bell rang. Even American adults began to shop at the Latin Grocery. Many bought ham croquettes. Others purchased media noches—midnights—a favorite sandwich snack of Cubans with ham, spiced pork, swiss cheese, mustard, and pickles between pan dulce-two sweetish hoagie buns. Black beans and rice were a favorite for others, along with cassava or yuca, much like a potato but grilled typically in butter and garlic. Cuban food became incorporated into the diet of Americans who began to appreciate the basic produce which had taken on such lively flavors thanks to the liberal use of *mojo criollo* and garlic, not to mention bitter orange juice with which formerly tough beefsteak had been made tenderer through marination. Platanos could be yellow or green--even black. The yellow plantains were sweeter than the green, but the black was even sweeter still.

Known as maduros, owing to the overripe black color, they contrasted with the tostones, which are green and taste more like a vegetable. The cooking banana is larger than bananas grown for domestic consumption, though they have similar geneses.

Vinyl records, one red and transparent, were played for American students during recess in third grade, where a portable record player would repeat the popular phrases "¿Coma esta usted?" "¿Donde va Flora?" and "Vamos, Juan." And, Doss noticed, the interrogative sentences such as ¿Coma esta usted? had an upside down question mark at the beginning of the sentence, as well as the normal one at the end, a feature of Spanish, yet strange to readers of English text.

———

Hope had grown up to be an attractive and vivacious, if not quite beautiful, auburn-haired girl, popular in high school with four or five close girlfriends. She was well mannered, even-tempered, and had found true love her junior year of high school. Upon graduating, Hope married Bobby Barwick, whose mother had died while he was but a teenager, suddenly and sadly, leaving him to raise his younger siblings. Bobby's family had hailed from Georgia, just as Earlene's had, in the 20s. His father, Poop Barwick, experimenting, tried diligently to find a substitute for lard during World War II. He had discovered the utility of peanut oil. It had worked wonderfully, and his company, the *Berlin Farm*, called the substitute lard *Kreme-Krisp*. But, Germany, the USA's enemy in that war had a virtual monopoly on peanut oil. The United States would have to come up with its own. Barwick was placed in charge of 71,000 acres in South Florida. Peanuts grew superbly in the muck, and *Kreme-Krisp* proved to be a thriving product which housewives and cooks loved because of its granular form—it would neither deteriorate nor become rancid. No refrigeration was required as with lard, and the product was clean to work with. But, after the war, lard was again plentiful and *Kreme-Krisp* was relatively expensive. The Berlin Farm had to discontinue marketing the product because it was no longer competitive. After that, Bobby joined his father in growing celery on the Berlin Farm, west of Belle Glade. Their celery was treated before harvest which bleached it white. Ironically, the bleaching also improved the flavor. Not only did it taste good, one could smell it growing in the fields a mile away. Ole Poop was proud of his tasty celery, which he bragged, "Was so much better than the Pascal celery that is pretty and green, but tasteless as a piece of straw, compared to mine." Bobby and Hope produced a pair of daughters, both smart and successful. One became a business owner, the other a teacher. They both adored Loco especially, whom they called Papa, until he died in 1991.

Cory lived until 1995 and Earlene died in 1997. Marie would live until 2013 and Melrose died one year later.

∞ ∞ ∞

Chapter Fifty-eight

There had been a scuba trip to Key Largo last September, during which the Neesh boys had photographed various sea creatures, but the one particularly sought was a *cephalopod,* an octopus, whose ability to hide itself defies imagination. More than ejecting an ink-like substance to lose would-be predators, this variety can morph into its surrounding environment in such a way that detection is all but impossible. Whether taking the shape of a boat's rudder, an edge of a coral reef, or the very sand into which it is partially dug, the animal's ability is nothing short of incredible. Two varieties of camouflage are especially common: *crypsis* and *mimesis.* Mimesis involves a disguise that is a built-in part of the creature's anatomy, causing an insect or animal to look like something else, such as a caterpillar on a twig, or an insect that resembles a leaf. Crypsis, in contrast, is strange and complex. It involves disruptive coloration, transparency, silvering, counter-shading and the elimination of shadows, much as a desert lizard become almost impossible to detect when it flattens out. Included as a form of crypsis is coloration change. With the octopus the Neeshes wanted to capture, there are chromatophores, mirror-like cells made of protein which permit skin patterns and color to change to resemble its background. A squid, chameleon, and peacock flounder have similar capabilities to escape detection.

Doss had not been part of this trip because he had died a month earlier from a heart attack in his sleep. The family mourned his loss, but not in any official way, because he hadn't desired any formal mourning or service. He knew, as Heidegger had written, that life must be fully embraced in its ephemerality and that death must be constantly in the mind of the living so that tasks one aspires to are acted upon in a death-conscious authenticity. Instead of hiding and escaping reality with distractions and prosaic trivialities, pretending to have an eternity of time, a realization sets in and causes one to be ever conscious of the finitude of life. Because of that, one's aspirations are acted upon instead of merely dreamt of. The authentic person reminds himself the end is coming—and soon. And, so it had for Doss, who had just finished a key project he had feverishly worked on for decades.

This trip was bittersweet in that it served for the family as a kind of memorial to Doss, who would have had to be dead to miss a scuba trip, especially one in which a camera was being used to capture the moment. In conjunction with the dive in September was a trip to Miami that lasted a couple of hours. It was a visit to a lawyer's office, and not just any lawyer, but an A-rated expert in estate planning and probate. This portion of the journey proved heart-warming and joy-filled for the surviving Neeshes. Turns out, the tribal elders of Sewauwee, the little settlement on the spit of land at Lake Okeechobee, had set in motion a trust 90 years earlier, that these surviving scion of Peter, Percy, Cory, and Doss, were learning about for the first time. Aaron,

David, Daisy and Todd sat and listened in amazement at what had transpired over the entirety of their lives:

A lawyer which Billy Tyger and Red Osceola's father had hired in the early 1930's, had drawn up a trust. After the flood control division of the state had voted to raise the level of Lake Okeechobee to accommodate a burgeoning population, particularly near Miami, the Natives would have to relocate, and they needed someone local to look after the land, and prevent trespass and squatters.

There had been an occasion in which water had been too scarce to fulfill the needs of Miami Beach citizens. Already, there was a wealthy population beginning to congregate in Miami-Dade County that, while in no way as affluent as the super-rich at Palm Beach, still had a great deal of money that had been brought down from an industrial North and invested heavily in real estate. Politicians, as they so often tend to do, pay attention when big money speaks. Pressure had been placed upon state officials, who ordered the inauguration of a flood control bureau, which would be officially anointed after FDR became President, and in fact, fit in nicely with his Works Progress Administration, which employed out-of-work young men.

The idea was to manipulate water levels to provide an ideal flow into Miami. The awful downside was that the little village out in Lake Okeechobee where the Seminoles and Miccosukees had raised families and crops, and buried their dead for generations, would cease to exist and its inhabitants would be forced to leave.

The chiefs of the tribal group, as fate would have it, had so appreciated the Neesh's act of kindness years earlier towards Red's daughter and the procurement of medicine to ameliorate her infection, that they devised this trust mechanism in which the Captain and Percy, if events turned out as designed, would play an integral role. Chief Tyger had learned of the state's machinations regarding the water level, and his anger was beyond measure, and the indignity that frequently arose in him was palpable. Tyger remembered the little bottle of salve that Peter, and really Percy, had secured from Dr. Tabb across the lake for the child. While the balm may not have been the cause of the child's cure, the act of charity had resonated strongly among the entire group. So, it wasn't the efficacy or lack thereof inherent in that ointment, it was Percy's rare act of benevolence toward a Native child that impressed Tyger and Osceola and Bowlegs. That fueled aspirations of a legal device which would remunerate *Corona's* operators and perhaps salvage Sewauwee. While the Natives did not feel themselves pariahs among residents of Chosen, Pahokee, and Belle Glade, most had never been treated with civility on this order by a white man, and especially by Peter, a former segregationist whose father had been a Ku Klux Klan leader in Georgia, and who himself was known for having little civility towards anyone, especially those with origins and cultures different from his own. To Billy's thinking, Peter had risen to the occasion when he reacted to Tyger's anxious countenance those many years ago, and acted in a way that demonstrated a deep show of humane propensity. That act had been magnified by ten in importance in the Chief's mind over any impression it had made on Peter or Percy.

It was actually Tommy Bowlegs, a scion of the famed Billy, who while not an official leader of the tribe but, rather, one of its elders, had suggested that a deed to Sewauwee be placed in the name of the Neeshes, as trustees of tribal interests. That occurred three years after Percy had brought Dr. Tabb's medicine for Red's daughter. Neither Peter nor Percy was aware of the legal instrument at the time, nor would they become aware, or agree to its terms for almost two years thereafter. According to trust terms, the rights to land rents or increases in value would be husbanded by a trustee, and if the Lake's water level were ever normalized so that the land again became inhabitable, there was a fiduciary responsibility that the land be returned to the Sewauwee branch of Natives if a majority of elders voted for that eventuality. During the 30-year time period when the two-mile stretch of land could not be lived on or farmed, owing to the raised water, the trustee's responsibility lay in ensuring that no structures or accretions could have an untoward impact on the little island. Chief Eddie Bowlegs, of the Everglades group 70 miles south, upon recognizing that the Sewawee tribe would be forced to relocate and assimilate into his tribe, acquiesced in the Sewauwee plan after a few days of heated dissension about the wisdom of trusting yet another white man. By late 1931, just a week after the attempted assassination of Franklin D. Roosevelt in Miami, both Peter and Percy had been apprised of the full import and terms of the trust, after being summoned to a lawyer's office in Miami, very near Bayfront Park, where the assassination attempt left a bullet in the body of Cermak, the Chicago mayor. Peter demurred, but Percy seemed ready to take on its mandates.

Two years earlier, leaders from the Native group

hoped, as was promised by flood control managers, that maybe, just maybe, a return to Sewauwee might one day come to pass. It was at that time Bowlegs proposed Peter as a prospective trustee. The flood control planners had assured the tribe's leaders that at some point, a more sophisticated system of levees, dikes, locks and canals might bring about a stabilization of Lake Okeechobee's water level and, if that happened, the group would indeed be able to return. It wasn't long after that assessment that with a great deal of doubtfulness about any system of levees, or possible return, plans were grudgingly drawn up. A trust it would be. Now, they asked, "Whom to trust?" After the Natives looked to Peter, but more seriously towards Percy, and apprised him and his father of the plan, having explained the niceties of trust management and fiduciary responsibilities which would be placed squarely upon them, Percy, and then after much exhortation, Peter, had agreed.

Within twenty years, water tables were indeed brought to a relatively stable level, that is, within a foot or two from one year to the next. Plenty of leeway for the land to be farmed, yet not for a return of any residents yet. It would be another ten years before natives could safely live in Sewauwee. When that milestone was finally reached, not one native ever returned. Not one Indian ever set foot again on the island they'd been compelled to vacate years earlier. Members integrated into the Seminole community of the south Everglades. Young folks fell in love and married, older members died, and those in the middle acculturated themselves to the larger concretion of Natives, enjoying the colorful ritual and lively affairs of daily life. Since no return to Sewauwee ever occurred, despite dreams by many toward that end, the successor trustee, Percy, had leased the land to local farmers, within a month after learning the land could be farmed. He was given power to do that through the terms of the trust. Peter had done little as trustee, mostly because he had only lived for eighteen months after agreeing to its terms.

Percy, in contrast, had been a genius as the successor trustee. Just as it was he who transported the medicine to Sewauwee, it was he who worked hard and took his fiduciary responsibilities with great sobriety. This student of history, philosophy, and cultural studies, this man sidetracked by good rum, had done what Peter most likely never could—or would—have done. Through diligent fiduciary management of the legal arrangement, working countless hours studying law and especially trust law, Percy rose above his predilection for torpor and reading history and philosophy, and in general, a life of ease. Completely out of character, in some respects, he trekked to Miami at least twice a year, with no fewer than two tire blowouts on each seventy-three mile sojourn on a lonely, one-lane sand road. He had sought out, conferred with and planned the future both with tribal elders and a lawyer. An estate planning specialist had taken a humanitarian interest in the fate of the Sewauwee natives. Among this motley group of individuals, Percy administered the trust, leasing the land to vegetable farmers, later to sugar cane growers, many of whom had moved from Ohio. One such group of Ohio Germans, the Gerlachs, had read in agricultural journals about the potential of two crops a year. Plus, they wanted out of the cold North. Within five years, four brothers, all excellent agriculturalists, were producing some of the most beautiful celery, leaf lettuce, radishes, corn, bell peppers, and beans that had ever been produced around the Lake. They eventually farmed sugarcane as well. All over Locha Hatchee, right up to Sewauwee, crops were grown and lease rents paid that enriched the trust and maximized its assets, just as the trustee was charged with, according to its powers clause.

In later years, after President Kennedy imposed a strict trade embargo on goods coming from or going to Cuba, that "imprisoned island," sugarcane become probably the second most prevalent crop for Florida after citrus. The financial yields for the trust exceeded by several times those associated in earlier years from vegetables.

When Percy died in the late 1940s, Cory picked right up where his father had left off. Cory continued to husband the island's resources for the enrichment of the trust. He kept a close eye on proper crop rotation and other agricultural and land management niceties. In total, lease payments over a thirty-three year period exceeded three million dollars, and that measured in 1960s inflation index dollars. Later, as Doss got involved after completing law school, even before Cory died, the trust continued to prosper. Over three times that much in value had been added to the trust by the time Doss died.

Those sums had financed, the Neeshes were currently learning, a progressive school system with highly skilled teachers for Seminoles and other natives. Communal activity centers were established, and at the most basic level, a 2,000 unit housing complex for former tribal members. Units could be rented or acquired on a lease-to-own arrangement. A dwelling had a relatively low down payment at a low interest rate. For the first time in tribal existence, many members owned a solid roof over their heads. Despite being small, each unit was comfortable, complete with cooking and bathing facilities, and was owned in perpetuity by them and their issue, as the law called it. The Natives were empowered to send their children to school that was both well-equipped and staffed by educators aided by paraprofessionals. Teachers focused on infusing students with deep, sturdy and practical learning. Salaries for these teachers were 10% higher than those earned by large high schools in the state, whether public or private, thanks to Sewauwee trust assets.

On this visit to the Keys after Doss's death, the surviving members of the Neesh family learned something that would cause any family member's heart to swell with pride: Their most immediate family member had, just two months before he died, engaged a contractor to build a school.

Upon Cory's death, Doss had become the successor trustee. For five years, Doss had done little to further the trust's ambitious vision, busy with his own law practice and teaching responsibilities. Eventually, he began traveling to Florida, but that never seemed odd to his wife and family, given the scuba diving, and his enjoyment of eating at a kosher delicatessen in Miami Beach, and taking the boys to visit relatives in Belle Glade. None of his family was aware of the key import of his quick trips. On three occasions within a year of his death, Doss's visits were inspired by his mission to build a school on the vacant lot where his elementary school had stood. Following his discovery of its having been razed and the empty field with the sole banyan tree, Doss worked in double-time with trust lawyers. With funds still being generated on a healthy scale, that project was set into motion. And, the school would match the one that had enjoyed so much success for Native Americans in the south Everglades near the Tamiami Trail. It would serve whoever wanted to attend, and would group students based upon ability into various programs. The school would repay those who had devoted so much of their lives to building the muckland's wealth all those many years, for so little remuneration.

Plus, this school would serve as a magnet institution that would attract the more affluent and intellectually gifted. It would feature programs and equipment to which students would gravitate. Some students aspired to attend college, while others sought to serve in trades and occupations. So, comprehensive technical training would be offered. The school would be stocked with the most practical programs that would equip students to learn and apply skills to solve problems such as climate change and environmental poisoning that threatened to destroy Earth's ecosystem. They would be taught not only history, math, science, philosophy and literature, but also mechanics, plumbing, air-conditioning, environmental sciences and cleanup, and agricultural and electricity maintenance. There would be medical assistants and paralegals and hairstylists who would graduate ready to work.

The four Neeshes were most proud of the huge housing project that they learned had been planned as a low-rent, lease-to-own alternative to the Osceola 'camp'. That had been a superb benefit for migrant farmers. Franklin Roosevelt's Works Progress Administration had put millions to work building infrastructure back in the 30s. But with the new project, as was true of Seminole housing south of the Everglades, countless numbers of Native Americans would pay low-interest lease payments that would encourage hopeful unit owners to put forth a tad more money each month than a mere lease payment required, but an amount that that would translate into deeds of ownership in ten to fifteen years. No more leaseholds for those aspirants—fee simple ownership, as the lawyers called it.

For Peter, but even more significantly, Percy, then Cory and Doss, countless hours had been worked feverishly, yet with a laconic unwillingness to aggrandize self. There was a genuine desire to improve the lot of the most oppressed peoples on the North American continent—its Natives, especially those few Creek and Cherokee natives, formerly from Georgia who had dared flee advancing troops ordered by President Jackson, and led by Zachary Taylor, and had become known as Seminoles. They had boldly receded far into the darkest corners of the Everglades with its swampy wetness and relentless mosquitoes and alligators, to avoid a trip on the *Trail of Tears* to Oklahoma, to forced segregation, and for some, forced reservation life, with little if any incentive to work or feel pride.

While the family regretted that Doss never won the photo prize he had aspired to for so long, Aaron had placed second in *The Fin* for his photo just six months before Doss died. It had secretly thrilled Doss that the accolade and a $10,000 prize went to Aaron, rather than himself. The capture had been of a golden-yellow and blue-striped Angelfish swimming in the midst of a pink sea anemone, a sliver of action whose nuances came together in that millisecond of a shutter click featuring a backdrop of bluish-grey coral that contrasted color so vividly in turquoise, pinks, and yellows. It would have been luckier still if they both could have won in their many years of striving for a prize, but that wasn't to be. Luck, Doss felt, was as important as skill towards success. But without hard work, neither luck nor skill would be enough.

Even to imagine any sort of comfortable life in a world of such erstwhile inhospitable alienation and brutality, Natives and Colonists alike had had to dream big. Indian hunters, desperate to snag a Seminole, had even said 'No' to chasing 'savages' that far into the desolate sawgrass and wetland, despite the big dollars. The Neeshes and especially the Thompsons, had had similar misgivings about the Lake and its feral untamed nature. Most members of each group, among the multiple generations, were replete with benignity, a few, more malevolently inclined. Most felt empathy for the underdog, the poor, the disaffected. Anyone sick, oppressed, handicapped, whether by mental or physical limitations, were to be aided. After all, weren't we all "handicapped in some way?" Doss used to ask. "We're all flawed: mentally, physically, and spiritually." Borne no doubt as a blessing, that deep-seated charitable tendency, and the resultant favorable outcomes to so many, meant even a tide that 'waits for no man,' had at least to slow down for.

THE END

Addendum

Printed in full below is the *Our Story* word definitions that Doss created for his sons so that they could learn vocabulary words. Chapter *fifty-one* refers to *Our Story*. For those of you interested in reading it, I've included it as it was originally written, along with a huge 'thank you' for reading the book. I truly hope you enjoyed it and learned some new details about the great state of Florida and its pioneers in the early part of the twentieth century.

Carl T. Cone

N ear a pond in Bulloch County, next to a cotton field and not far from some storage bins of peanuts that were weighed and later sold for transformation into peanut butter, three boys who are amply blessed, first by their natural or as is said, God-given abilities, but even more by their having a glorious a mother who is talented and industrious, possessed of inexhaustible work habits and an indefatigable energy level, and withal an intrepid provider, possessing of lofty integrity, and, in a word, a woman who inevitably exhibits a nurturing disposition towards her family, reside.

That the father was blessed by God while still in the womb, none would, I daresay, disagree. His is a scholarly intellect, and one not **inconsequential**—laden with talent of disparate and multitudinous facets, yet whose exhibition of those gifts did not occur without a great deal of **prodding** and **cajoling** by his own loving, caring mother, and an **officious** and **meddlesome** wife whose entreaties for the man to succeed, played no small measure in unfurling his gems.

The eldest boy David, an **amiable**, yet serious young man with an **austere countenance** much of the time, but with a ready smile, is a football and baseball **aficionado**. He loves to play and observe as a spectator, those two sports. Basketball, he adores, and, to speak plainly, he exhibits a not small number of African traits in him, viz., love of that particular game, tall stature, ability to leap off the ground rather highly, or as is popularly said among participants in that sport, 'has great 'ups.' There is little Negroid resemblance in his physiognomy, being dark blonde in hair color and a blue tint to his iris, yet he is singularly aroused by that music with its characteristic beat—drums pounding, the torso-vibrating bass, words referring rather vulgarly to 'motherly affection,' music, if one dare call it such, all wrapped in a *Boom, Boom, Boom dee daa Boom*, blaring, nay, pulsating from loud speakers. His body can be seen swaying to and fro with the measures, head bobbing to drums that may have sounded at one time for a tribal gathering in the deepest part of the jungle of the most remote of the African continent. The lyrics, that is to say, those few words that can be deciphered, put the listener in mind of themes of injustice, police brutality, love gone sour, and that excessive maternal affection referred to above, and, very curious indeed, bears a particular fondness for the loathsome, distasteful, and not at all flattering epithet "nigga," a **moniker** despised by most, but routinely and curiously spoken with regularity from the African-American tongue when referring to each other of that culture in sometimes a playful, and others a **wounding, nettlesome** way, intending to arouse **ire** in the listener or object of the **epithet**.

David's younger brother Aaron, a **benevolent**, yet **aloof** lad, at least towards those who are not a part of his inner circle of friends and family, has a **sinewy** aspect about him, that is he is lean, yet muscular. In addition, the teenager is fast in running, and appears, and is indeed, quite athletic. Aaron's is the kindness and most empathetic disposition, replete with kindness. The youngest of the three boys is Todd, an unusual young man, obsessed as he is with **flatulence** and **eructations**. In fact, when he burps or passes gas, he is insistent that all in his presence be aware of the din created, assuming the **malodor** associated with the **expulsion** would not otherwise inform. One of his recent acquisitions included a device with the crude and somewhat uncooth appelation of *Fart Machine* with which the lad is able to place an electronic speaker device near where the individual is seated, and then with a gentle touch of the button placed on the operating remote control of a cheap plastic mechanism, activate a "blaaaaaaaat" sound that both surprises and embarrasses. Todd is, otherwise not at all unpleasant to be around, and, in a word, is quite intelligent, affable, and gregarious. Although thankfully not **narcissistic** about it, Todd is handsome, homologous to his two brothers, according to the **plethora** of girls that call the boys' house **incessantly**. In fact, it is probably **inevitable** that he will marry someday, owing to their imposing and arresting good looks.

As **matriarch** of the boys, the mother, Daisy, is a **fastidious** worker, **impassioned** in and by her work, but more towards the **impassive** side when it comes to romance, caressing, holding hands, and other shows of affection, and surprisingly too, for she is not an unhandsome woman by any means, and, in fact, has physical qualities that quite commend her to the opposite sex.

Doss, is **erudite**, that is to say, educated beyond **saturation**, **adept** in matters that interest him and skillful, nay, masterful with words, especially the oral presentation of a law lecture or the construction of grammatical syntax. He is **effervescent, vivacious and animated** in his personality, and is a gentleman in every sense that word could be supposed to be used in, and is, to say it plainly, the pride of the family, with his generous and high-minded **magnanimity, solicitude and charity** towards others—both family and friend, as well as stranger, of which he often brags 'he's never met one of.' He has safely secured for himself a special place in the hearts of the above mentioned, and indeed of humankind in general who have the propitious and felicitous fortune to become acquainted with the **sublime**, delightful gentleman.

David has an outstanding **discernment**, both as to people, and to baseballs-- whether strikes or balls. He can distinguish a **rogue** from a **mensch**. He is not only athletic, he is an **astute** pupil in school, usually earning A's on his grade card. In playing football, he is judicious about throwing the ball into tight coverage by the defense, and, as a result, rarely throws interceptions because of that **acumen**. And, despite his minority, that is, merely an adolescent, David is shrewd in business matters, knowing when a **reprobate** or garrulous **opportunist** is trying to take advantage of him with **voluble**, fast-talking nonsense or when a

charlatan is trying to persuade him into a deceptive scheme or scam. On the other hand, when an honest, upright person of **amicable and benign** intentions desires **to facilitate** or promote noble interests through **magnanimous** gestures of genuine goodwill, David perceives that as well.

Aaron has both **timidity** and **temerity**. On one hand, he exhibits a bit of the **timorous** nature and is highly self-conscious of his presence, but his reckless athleticism on the football and baseball field would convince an observer that he doesn't care much for his safety. Despite the rigor of a **dogmatic**, **resolute** coach, who **upbraids** him routinely, this, the middle son, appears detached from the criticism and maintains a focus toward his tasks. As a young boy, he was on occasions full of life and **ebullience**, but as an adolescent, Aaron became more **taciturn** and **circumspect**, with tendencies to be a loner, not at all **loquacious**, in fact, just the opposite-- very **reticent**. He refrains from engaging in meaningless prattle when **coalesced** into a crowd, that is to say, by nature not given to social or collective endeavors, somewhat reclusive, yet by no means a **pariah** or social outcast. In fact, he has been almost venerated by many of the students at his school who have, at many basketball games, **extolled** him, almost as **sycophants**. These young fans in a **convivial** way, often praise his athletic **prowess** by displaying a sign that reads, "**GO WHITE BOY!**"

Todd. What can I say? What can be said that is in keeping with words to be spoken, as is said, in polite company? Todd at his birth was three weeks premature. Not that there was anything wrong with that. Nor have any signs of his being a premature neonate exhibited themselves, neither as a **bane** nor a **boon**. He is an exuberant little fellow, nay, the lad has no **sedentary** inclinations nor **torpid** moments; in a word, he never sits still, but fidgets with this contraption or that contrivance and with restless heebie-jeebies, moves incessantly— his body and his jawbone. He has neither egotistical self-absorptions, nor **narcissistic** notions of vanity, but rather possesses an affable air, a **gregarious** personality, a **peripatetic**, never stand still energy level, whose concentration is **ephemeral**, that is to say, short lived, and in a word, quite fleeting. In sports, Todd is **peerless**, with an **intrepid** courage to stand at the baseball home plate and face a 90-mph fastball without flinching, wincing, or **quivering**. And his **prodigious** skill at quarterback is the talk of the town. Though the boy has a tendency to mock his elders, even to the point of **contentiousness**, some would say **impertinence** or **insolence**. He refutes any claim that he acts with a **cheeky** or cocky demeanor, brazen and **audacious** as it is bold and **impudent**, but whichever is the true case, after a thorough **reproving** by his teacher, or a solid **rebuke** by his mother or a scolding reprimand from his **stentorian**, **austere** and authoritarian father, the boy's mocking or **captious** ways can be stifled-- well, at least **mitigated** or **exacerbated** to a level that can be tolerated by most—in minutely small doses.

Todd's nature, though not **pugnacious**, for he little likes to fight, is oftentimes vocally **belligerent**, much like his mother, who, when **disgruntled**, shuffles the pots and pans in a **clamorous** manner, causing a ruckus that ends in a **cacophonous** tirade that **reverberates** throughout the house-- I say, Todd and his mother are much alike, she with her **belligerence** and the **rancorous din** she stirs up in the late evening after a long day suffering the completion of **mundane** tasks at her work and the rebukes and scolding from an **odious tyrant** for a boss, who fails to hide great **indifference,** and demonstrates outright **disdain** towards the woman and her talents. The boss has a **supercilious** air that is **replete** with **haughtiness** towards subordinates, not to mention a stentorian attitude towards those minions, whom the boss pretends to shower with a smile that is hoped will exhibit munificence and an **amiable benevolence**. With her **mellifluous** voice and hints of **camaraderie** in front of her own superiors, the boss conveniently rids herself of a true rancorous, spiteful, and acrimonious aspect, spiced with **imperious, overbearing** commands to do this or that 'right now,' and **supplants** it with an obviously forced, but constant smile and bobbing head that seem to suggest **acquiescence, collegiality**, and, even charm, though kindly note the key phrase 'seem to suggest.'

Despite her benevolent **mien** and quick willingness to back down in the presence of the alpha-boss at work, Daisy M. F. Neesh is a predator in her own right, but not like a *Tyranasaurus Rex*. To those she views as incompetent, or not doing a fair share, or competent share of a given chore, she can **literally** and **figuratively** devour, much as she is devoured further up the food chain by her boss. She refuses to be or accept second best in her vocational pursuits. At her work, whether teaching or in administration, Daisy will not acquiesce in doing her job in a half-fast way. Nor will she be fooled by **spurious** people, who with their **euphony** or **mellifluous** talk, or **specious** persuasions, might bait one less **chary and circumspect** than she. Daisy is **frugal** with her hard-earned money, yet not **parsimonious** to the point of stinginess. She can be miserly in a positive sort of way, yet extravagant when there is a 50% off sale at the local department store, especially if there's an extra 30% to be subtracted from that total. And, the woman's **prowess** in the kitchen would please the most **gluttonous epicurean.** Her **adroit** cooking skills are in high demand around the house, having three boys residing under its roof, all of whom are anything but **sedentary**, having **voracious** appetites that consume her delectable meals sometimes right out of pot or pan. As a result, they simply can't eat bland food. They do eat junk food, but only that which is **savory and piquant with** multifarious and diverse spices—namely garlic, turmeric, curry and cumin, not to mention cinnamon, nutmeg, dill, tarragon, cayenne pepper, bay leaf, and rosemary.

In her teenage years, Daisy appeared **emaciated** from a continual diet and an **obstinate** refusal to partake of proper nutrition. She was especially **obdurate** in refusing to consume the most important meal of the day, that is to say, the king of meals—breakfast. Nevertheless, she has blossomed in later years with fuller figure, that is to say, somewhat **buxom, though by no means voluptuous,** yet **curvaceous** and pleasing. And, all of that is owing to her willingness to indulge a bit in **alimentary** delights and quit her **abstemious** ways, by which I mean fasting.

With an **unwavering, persevering resolve**, Daisy completed a doctorate degree as a young maiden. Her **fervent** studies and

impassioned research yielded a dissertation not a little impressive, one that exhibited a **zealous** devotion to her an area featuring the practicalities of attire and beauty of garb—clothing and textiles. Fighting sleep deprivation from the **soporific** effects of allergy medicine, she remained **animated** enough, and with a **stolid** determination that exhibited an **indifference** to her health, finished the studied **treatise** just in time for the deadline, which, as **recompense** for her **servile** manner and **sycophantic** deeds of goodwill, such as baking cookies or brownies for her major professor, was extended just a few days.

A classic **opportunist**, she seizes a boon as she discerns one, and maximizes it to utmost profit. Having said that, let the reader note that she is an adversary of even mild cupidity or benign rapacity. The giving woman cultivates an altruistic bent to her innate benevolence and nurtures a self-denying posture that is **anachronistic** in a world **of self-aggrandizement** and **egocentric self-absorption**. In a word, the creature is **magnanimous** and **munificent** to the extreme.

As for her husband, Doss Neesh, the **patriarch** of the clan, what can I say? What can I NOT say? He is at once the most affectionate, **ungrudging, bounteous**, warm, and gentile, nurturing man, nay, human being that ever walked on the face of the Earth, that is to say at least from his little **hamlet** of Belle Glade, I mean, at least as to the northernmost end of a neighborhood of that hamlet, viz., 543 Southeast First Street.

Dossy, as he was called by his relatives, D. N. by some collateral relatives, namely cousins, has a deep **veneration** for that which is good— as well as great **reverence** for the word of God, whether that word come through the vehicle of Buddhism, Judaism, Hinduism, Zoratorism, Christianity, Jainism, or Islam. When not working, he can seem **indolent**, but far from being **slothful** and **shiftless**, the blessed creature exhibits much **enterprise** and **zeal** and loses any **sedentary** aspect when his **incisive** intellect is **galvanized** by some **privation** that demands fulfillment or some hurt that demands to be **assuaged**. In the words of his south Georgia kinfolk, the man is smart—he can and will work. His shrewd, yet **judicious** manner is evident in the measured **decorum** and kind **civility** with which he deals with his childrens' misconceptions, **foibles** and **misapprehensions**. His decisions are **astute**, his judgment **sagacious**, yet his **egalitarianism unwavering** as the sons come to him for **counsel** and **enlightenment**. His **sage** inner core is **melded** with a **prudent saavy** that only Providence could give one whose judgments and decisions are so seemingly

ethereal to the point of **sublimity**. Yet, he would never tell you that about himself. His understated, humble reserve is fueled by a passion that lifts others up, never **impugns** them, nor, in a **pernicious** way, **derides** them or **berates** them. On the contrary, his **accolades** are heaped upon a young man or woman he is coaching or teaching, whenever they achieve a noteworthy goal. Rarely will he be heard to **chastise** or **reprove** a child for anything but the most **insolent** behavior.

David Neesh, despite his successes on and off the diamond, field or court, is not egotistical. In fact, despite an occasional **ostentatious** show of dunking the basketball, one would be loath to detect a **pretentious** bone in his towering anatomy, nor does he exhibit any **contemptuous** traits towards those less athletically **adept**, such as a lesser person might with a **swagger** in his walk and talk, I say, one will not discern a hint of **disdainful scorn** in his **countenance**. The reason is David's **diffidence** and humility to the extreme, nary an **imperious** or **supercilious mien**, grateful to Providence for the **attributes** he possesses. **Altruistic** in his caring for others and their concerns and problems, David realizes that each of us is gifted in a **singular, unique** way. While he is **austere** in worldly possessions, and that owing to a **mean** income earned by his father, he shows no

animosity or **antagonism** towards those of **pecuniary**, that is to say, monetary, means. While David has had a **modicum** of success in academic achievements, that is to say, borders on **mediocrity** as a student, his intellect probably equals that of his father's, at least the kind father permits such indulgences of fancy on the son's part, though his involvement in sports and social activities leaves little time for academic pursuits. He is by no means **apathetic** or **complacent** when it comes to academic quests-- in fact, quite the opposite from being **nonchalant** towards his studies, he can be quite the **zealot** when studying for a test or making up tardy homework assignments, the latter of which are far too frequent.

The Double A, as he is lovingly called, is, like the Energizer bunny, unstoppable and **indefatigable**. Aaron, in the morning, especially, seems **lethargic** bordering on **languid**, but he comes to life, as it were, by midday. In an **obsequious**, compliant way, he erases the chalkboard and performs unremarkable tasks for teachers when asked. Somewhat submissive, Aaron likes to please, but not in a **servile, sycophantic** way, and never as a **toady**. He jumps in with **alacrity** to solve an **enigma** or **conundrum**, especially as it relates to the **labyrinthine esoterica** of electronic or mechanical systems, whose **cryptic** fuses, transistors, resistors, capacitators, semiconductors diodes, and integrated circuits tend to **intimidate** and **inundate** the average person. Some think the lad **aspires** to be a **renowned** engineer one day, but his talents probably lie more liberally in his mechanical **prowess.**

Aaron is not **mercenary** in nature, and is **frugal**, with few, if any, **avaricious aspirations**, as some cretins have. Those fools whom cupidity has overtaken, nay consumed, obsess about acquiring wealth with a passion that might show Ebenezer Scrooge a pinchpenny miser by comparison. Nor is he **devious** in acquiring the paucity of money he possesses. Neither **cunning** nor **wily** in tricking others out of their chattels, the boy would use neither **stratagem** nor **artifice** to acquire. He believes in a good hard day's work and, in **recompense**, a just, if only **middling** salary. But far above **pecuniary** cares, Aaron's intellect soars to heights of **astute** understanding, **disdaining** as it does routine cares of **temporal** pursuits, and embraces a **profound** understanding of Providence and spiritual matters, whose **profundity,** he is sure, is greater than material possessions.

Despite his feelings of **ambivalence** towards his younger sibling Todd, Aaron, in his **candor**, would grudgingly admit that he loves his little brother greatly, yet without an **amplitude** of patience for the younger brother's **levity, ranting**, and **prattling**—not to mention his **doltish** trivialities, such as the *Fart Machine*. On **myriad** occasions, Aaron has been spied helping Todd with this problem or that, or resolving some **perplexing** dilemma facing the younger. Todd, it almost need not be said, can typically be observed with words **emanating** from his mouth--in **incessant profusion**. Whether from a motivation to **enkindle** mirth in his listeners, or a **loquacious** endeavor to impress others nearby, for the most part, the ludicrous nature of his **fatuous** mumblings and mutters, simply **diffuse** into mere thin air with no apparent effect on those quite accustomed to paying little heed to the **prattling inanity**. Despite Todd's **verbosity**, Aaron patiently **perseveres** in assisting the silly lad on the rare occasion he can be said to engage in a consequential endeavor.

While focused on Todd, it might be added that he has an **implacable** curiosity, at work first on this scheme, and then on that one. His **insatiable** appetite to acquire pleasure from life's **multifarious** treats is **laudable**. Not quite as praiseworthy, however, are his efforts at schoolwork. In a word, he is **phlegmatic**, nay, lazy in his studies at school. The **verbiage** with which he expresses himself is impressive--never **hackneyed** nor **vapid**, but alive and creative with ideas and questions that never cease to impress his family. Although a

lackluster, uninspired, and vapid student, he is a **prodigious** scholar in words and their meaning, and the **milieu** around his home is never **insipid** as long as his **prolixity** entertains. From the **inception** of his education, it was clear he was destined to be a wordsmith, and perhaps an author. If not as **fastidious** with his studies as might be desired by the boy's teachers and parents, at least he is **scrupulous** in his **reverence** for God and commercial intercourse with his fellow man.

Aaron can work through the most tedious task with a sustained resolution to get the job done. Far from being tempted with the **allurements** of the world, he prides himself on being thorough, and having a **turbulence** in his soul that will not rest until the work is complete, and skillfully so. There is no greater **ignominy** in his mind than a lackluster, **pedestrian** performance that **deteriorates** from what could have been a great success to a **debacle** or risible failure. Great indignation on his countenance can be perceived when viewing the **mediocrity** or **apathy** of others, and someone even witnessed him **castigating** others owing to their **nonchalance** towards a task that demanded zeal and inspiration instead of **lethargic ennui**. And so it is with Aaron, or indeed anyone who desires to succeed; he or she must be vigilant, ready to toil with gusto and avidity—all while showing a **stringent**, **exacting focus** in his planning of an aim to be realized.

Todd can bring about a **conflagration** more quickly than anyone you have observed, yet with an **innocuous** demeanor, nay, even a charming one that a person could not help but have **approbation** for, if not downright **endearment**. His canny, perspicacious way of provoking his brother Aaron is **artful**, if not downright **nefarious**, yet because of the **surreptitious** manner in which he accomplishes that task, one would think him a mere innocent, deserving of no **rebuke** or **chastisement** at all. Todd's culinary skills, though not as refined as Aaron's, are nonetheless **prodigious**, so much so that at one time he gained the moniker *Chef Todd*, an appellation quickly **imputed** him on the strength of bread pudding he **fabricated** from mere scratch. Anyone far short of **a gourmond** would readily consume the savory dessert, even to the point of **surfeit,** could he but smell it cooking on Chef Todd's stove. An **epicure** whose **connoisseur** tastes are **keen**, would have been in a **rapturous ecstasy** at a mere taste of the **sweetmeat** so lovingly crafted by the lad.   Even a nibbler, with little **acuity** for what is pleasing or not to the palate, would become **ravenous** upon witnessing the pouring of the whiskey-flavored, buttery sauce upon the **culinary** creation.

Although Todd could indeed be **clandestine** and duplicitous, he was at other times **conciliatory** and **amiable**, if not downright cordial, readily willing to **assuage** hurt feelings or **mediate** when his parents argued. His **mollifying, placating** influence oftentimes had a **mitigating** effect on the atmosphere that was adulterated by **dissension** and **animosity.**

David Neesh has such confidence in his own abilities that he will **placate** the coach's **trepidation** when asked whether this play or that might be viable. He, calmly and in a very placid, and some would say **equable** manner, explains: "If I run the plan, Coach, it will work." Coach Pomarico is then **mollified** and fully anticipates with **alacrity** to witness the results David promised. Nor is it likely that the quarterback's confident **prognostication** will be **debunked.** More times than not, the play does demonstrate a **utility** that advances the ball and permits conquest. In a true **complementary** way, his receiver, Grady, **facilitates** David's **prowess** as he wrests the ball from an opponent in a **picturesque** reception. David's **adroit** passing enhances Grady's flair for receiving the thrown ball. In fact, the **aggregate** of not **mediocre** athletes at his high school have made David's career successful and earned all of them high **kudos** and lavish **commendation**. While not monsters of the midway, the participants demonstrate **pluck** in their **indefatigable** energy, not to mention their **lithe**, nimble movements in play.

A **misanthropic** person Daisy is not, yet after several months of working with her "temporary" supervisor, she has become **embittered**, and, in a word, **scornful** of **spurious** displays of **superficiality. The petty frivolity of chicanery has made the woman circumspect and chary** of an **ersatz** boss whose presence has generated only **peripheral** benefit to the institution, yet in whose own mind, lofty accomplishments have **transpired.** That **delusion,** along with trifling **exhortations** and shoddy supervision over school concerns negate any constructive input she might otherwise have tendered. To put it plain, the **discordant** lack of harmony among her employees, who evince a **disgruntled**, almost **surly countenance** towards her **machinations**, nay, her virulent presence, I say, that disharmony is palpable, even to one without sight. Subordinates, whose **vigilance** and **fervent** attention to the **minutiae** of the job are **ineluctable**, facilitate more than the **paltry** accomplishments that would otherwise **transpire**. Although lacking an **ebullient, vivacious** manner, Daisy possesses a **rectitude** of dignity, that **culminates** in an indifference to obstacles that might cause **trepidation** in a lesser **minion**, and, in a word, the woman is **obdurate.** That is, not stubborn per se, except with the venerable man she is privileged to call husband, but in possession of a **tenacious**, steadfast determination in the face of **acrid** allusions regarding her ineptitude by the cruel taskmaster of a boss dictating that the endeavor get done--and expeditiously. She has no **delusions** of **grandeu**r, nor **illusions** that she is **indispensable**, yet her talents, though **unobtrusive**, are at the same time unprecedented and fecund. In a word, her skill yields results.

The talents of Doss Neesh are **multitudinous**. No creature has ever been favored as with such **superfluity** of God-given ability. In fact, he is forever in a **quandary** about whether to pursue this objective or that aim, so **replete** the blessings Providence saw fit to bestow upon one so unfit. In addition to a **persona** that enlightens others whose presence he fills, there is that profound intellect, and, to put it plain, the blessings create, not infrequently, a great deal of **turmoil** and **vexation** over whether to traverse this path or trod over that— or, whether to pursue this goal or that, such that, I say, the seemingly endless possibilities preclude his **tranquility.** Never one to involve himself in **trifling** affairs or trivial relationships, and **shunning** as he does a **hedonistic** lifestyle, the man's **oratory** in the classroom and **prodigious** writing skills outside of it, are surpassed by few of his contemporaries, and, though not puffed up because of them, he cannot help, given his **perspicacity**, to be aware of the **judicious** perception and **sagacious** scholarship given from above. Beyond that, his **incisive** wit and keen intellect allow him to laugh at himself and life, realizing that both are but **evanescent**, leading down a road of absurdity toward a place called **obscurity**—what Heidegger called **Das Nicht.**

Not that the honored and humble servant of goodwill should be exalted for his talents, nor **extolled** for his virtue—those are but the net effect of an **unwavering** quest for knowledge and truth and a **dogmatic** belief that through reading and studying, humankind can change and, in a word, become better. While a student in high school, the man was **recalcitrant** towards studying. He simply would not crack a book. His **intractable** determination not to learn combined with a **hidebound hedonistic** bent, whose **glutton** for worldly pleasures obscured the **efficacy** of hard work and study, eventuated in an intellectual starvation that reached the point of an **emaciated** mind. That he is now a **voracious** reader and student of law is a **paradox** given his earlier proclivities to "just have fun."

"If there were one word to describe Doss,"

according to Daisy," it would be his **circumspection**;" in other words, he is **conscientious** about things and situations." He really thinks things through." At times, it could even be said, he goes too far in his imaginative rambles, almost to the point of **paranoia**. He thinks of all angles, or at least tries to, so that, in the end, it cannot be said that he' left any stones unturned.' "Contemplate all contingencies" he often says. The line between **paranoia** and **vigilance** is but a thin one, after all.

In choice of food, Doss is a true **eclectic**. It cannot be said that he prefers lo mein to pizza or chimichangas to turkey and dressing, nor chitterlings to raspberry mousse. In fact, except for obviously **exotic** foods such as pigs feet or alligator tail or rattlesnake meat, there is very little in the way of food that the wordly **epicurean** will not **partake** of, including picadillo, gyros, tacos, cheerios, spaghetti-o's, tostidos, and burritos—and those are just the foods that end in "o." In fact, when a traditional Spanish restaurant in the Tampa area was to be **razed** and a new shopping mall raised on the site it stood on, Doss insisted on making a trek to his once beloved Florida for a meal of arroz con pollo, or in English, chicken and yellow rice.

Aaron visited New York one year when he was in the intermediate grades of school.

Like David two years earlier, Aaron was **ebullient** as he and his mother landed in the Big Apple, and the **allure** of the big city **lingered** in his mind for quite a time, because he often mentioned he wished he could take up domicile there. After explaining that it was not **pragmatic** for him to reside in a big city like that without a job that paid a high salary, due to the **exorbitant** prices and costs, he was finally **dissuaded** from an otherwise **stolid** determination to make the gargantuan city his home. After cogitating more seriously, he concluded that such an environment, though exciting and **scintillating** for a time, could be but **deleterious** to his interest in the long run with so many people running hither, thither, and yon, with but little solicitude or empathy for others—quite simply, a rat race. He also surmised that one could **squander** an amplitude of pecuniary resources in a short period of time with the multitude of sites to visit, stores to patronize and museums and theatres to divert oneself. The **munificence** of most people in small towns and the **discrepancy** between them and our brothers and sisters in the big cities, with the **insouciance** and **apathetic indifference** to the plight of others, also **permeated** his thoughts, crashing in upon him in a moment of **reverie**.

So, while for a long time a **devotee** of New York culture, refinement, and sophistication, he soon concluded that the more **palatable** way of life lay in the Deep South, and that it was to that region of the country he would pledge his allegiance. But, despite remaining in Dixie, the lad never lost his **wanderlust** to revisit, nor did **nostalgia** for the good memories and agreeable **furlough** from the prison of school, disappear. The experience left more than an **evanescent** mark on Aaron.

Aaron talked of the **epicurean** delights of New York City for several years, including the knishes, pizza, corned beef sandwiches, tortes, tarts, blintzes, souffle, and cheesecake, not to mention frappes, lattes, iced tea, hot tea, Thai tea, coffee, iced coffee, cafe au lait, reubens, mufalattos, falafals, hamantashan, rigatoni, fettucini, ravioli, lasagna, Peking duck, Cornish hens, spetichio, dolmades, lox, gefeltafish, moo goo gai pan, foo young, dim sun, Asian dumplings and Vietnam eggrolls and Pho, and even sidewalk hot dogs, nay--they're called frankfurters, in Central Park.

Even a nibbler on the opposite end of the continuum from a glutton, would return from such food choices **engorged** to the last degree, and, in a word, if **emaciated** before, would afterwards be bloated to the point of **turgidity**. **Savory** aromas blended into themselves and **wafted** around corners and down the boulevards across broad avenues, into Times Square and over Rockefeller Plaza, down the canyons and walls of financial and corporate **megaliths** on Wall Street, even to the edges of the brownstones encircling Central Park. The aromas **accosted** one at every intersection, and he fought vigilantly, while waiting for the "WALK" sign, not to cave in to his stomach's rumbling **entreaties**, but to continue walking, **intrepidly** and **ascetically**, denying himself the **culinary** pleasure he knew awaited him in every little dive and nook off the sidewalk.

Aaron came to realize that while **aesthetically** pleasing, that is to say with all the old buildings, statues, artwork and pretty girls, not to mention the beauty of Central Park, there was a great deal of something lacking in the big city. There was a feeling of loneliness and emptiness—a feeling of angst and estrangement not a little **paradoxical** in a city with so many millions of fellow human beings practically crawling over one another. While there were a lot of churches and cathedrals, and they too **aesthetically** delightful, for the architecture was **ingenious** and the stained glass magnificent, there seemed to be a **paucity** of spiritual values that even the allure of the metropolis could not **obscure**. Not a small group of **atheists** proudly coalesced into a group at Lexington Avenue and 52 Street, **audaciously** proclaiming freedom from religion   Not that Aaron was offended by that, in fact, he would be first to inform that every person, as to religion is agnostic, given the Greek etymology of that word, meaning quite simply, 'don't know.' No one can know, he would say. Believing strongly is not knowing. Undoubtedly, the boy received that wisdom **vicariously** from a **sagacious** father, who repeated it on occasion

And while Aaron appreciated the **expansive** nature of the huge **megalopolis** of the tri-state area, in that there were so many ideas and cultures and cuisines to pick and choose from within a relatively **proximal** radius, he admitted at one point that a more **homogenous**, less **heterogeneous** group with a more uniform lifestyle was much more to his liking, that is to say, one as he enjoys near Savannah, Georgia. Most people there adhere to kindred ideas and beliefs, with only mild **disparity** and a few impassioned non-conformists. There is truly a **uniformity** of opinion and thought in that Southern environment with little **discrepancy** from this group or that one, at least on basic, core beliefs. His jaunt to NYC debunked him of any romantic illusions that it was a kind of **utopia** where people lived in harmony in a state of **nirvana**, that perfect peace that Buddha yearned for. Nonetheless, the allure of big city life lingered many years in his thoughts, that is, until he caught a whiff of urine-soaked bums over near the Bowery.

Upon her return, Daisy's supervisor intimated that the woman had taken time off to go to New York she was not entitled to. As the young assistant became more **indignant**, she told the woman "I don't mean to appear **obtuse**, but unless I am truly stupid, or seriously wrong in my **discernment**, I would say you are accusing me of wrongdoing."

In response, the obnoxious woman appeared **disgruntled**, almost to the point of **exasperation**.

"Why, I most certainly am not," she retorted, "but pray tell what you were doing on a school trip to New York," the intimidating shrew demanded **belligerently**.

"I accompanied my son on a trip to New York, and had time for sick leave acquired to do so," the **lackey placidly** explained, with an **eloquence** and composure that **belied** the **bellicose** tyrant she could be at home with her husband and children when they crossed her.

"Well," the boss continued, "get to work on the budget--that must be started at once," **digressing** onto a whole different topic, squealing in her rambling way some **claptrap** about how **dilatory** "we seem to be lately" in getting work done "around here."

Daisy found herself in a **quagmire** regarding which way to go in the conversation. Should she defend her integrity by telling the boss how and why she was entitled to the time off to be in New York, or should she in a **subservient** way or endeavor to complete the budget task she had been **cryptically** reminded of, all while remaining calmly indifferent to the **denigrating** rant of this mad **despot**? Always the pragmatist, the young woman **magnanimously** overlooked the perceived **slight** from the wench, decided to **mollify** the situation by returning to her desk until the **conflagration** could be brought under control, that is to say, by mere passage of time, into a more **placid** state.

Meanwhile, David, ever the **nomadic** type, never content to remain at home, **peripatetic** in his excursions, was happy to have his sports coupe drivable again. A few weeks earlier, in a moment of harmonious **confluence**, by which I mean he and the boom-boom-boom-did-a boom bass became one, it pounding through 60-inch speakers in his trunk, blaring out a clamor. While cacophonous, the din was skillfully constructed, especially as to the laughable rhyming lyrics of preposterous and improbable events--rap sounds, for I dare not call it music, caused such swaying and bopping that the driver maintained a careless **indifference** to the road in front of him, such that he quite collided with the rear end of another vehicle.

He later repeated to his parents the **hackneyed disclaimer** "it wasn't my fault." Culpable or not, his parents **doled** out a **copious** sum of money to the object of the collision, I dare not call him victim, as will be seen, for a radiator malfunction **allegedly** caused by the misadventure and to the body repair shop personnel for a paint job, that **embellished** the vehicle to such a degree that it might be said to have been more attractive after the mishap than it was before. For that, the beneficiary of the wreck, received an unjust enrichment to his bank account. The repair job was discharged with such **dexterity** that an inspector could not **palpate** any irregular area over the surface where the indentation had previously been. Poor fellow, he felt so contrite, I mean my David, that one could easily imagine his heart **palpitating** at the happening of the thing, that is to say, the wreck, and his **countenance** being so **forlorn** and dejected after it that a person of even a hint of ruth or goodwill could not bring himself to reprove the foolish lad for the incident, though he was not altogether **irreprovable** in the matter.

When thoroughly interrogated about exactly what **bellowing rumble** was issuing from the speakers while driving, he admitted it was his favorite, by the artist *4 Bad Ass Dog to da Bone*. That the song was one of his very favorites, and proceeded along the lines of "My name is Jamood, I stay in the **hood,** I talk to the wall when my girl I can't ball. She stay in North Bibb while I lie in my **crib**; I should get a job, but my freedom I can't rob--I need my time so I can sit here and rhyme--I'll stay on the **dole** in this here rathole, etc., etc., with other witless gibberish to that end.

Well, against his parents' entreaties, nay, ultimatums, the speakers remained in the **refurbished** vehicle, but the volume was set to a minimum of 20 decibels, enough to deprive the listener of his hearing in three years, instead of the usual two, which it usually took to divest one of that splendid sense given by Providence.

Not that the oldest of the three boys is **maladroit** when it comes to driving an automobile. He possesses a great deal of shrewdness and physical coordination, especially as it relates to his hand reacting as his eye dictates, that is to say with alacrity. In fact, when playing Nintendo a few years ago, before he became an adolescent, he beat his father in a game by the unusual name of Dr. Mario, where capsules of varying colors and combinations are lowered onto others of like color so as to dissipate them all. Any color remaining is a bane, while removing the same is, at least toward the object of the game, a boon. When an aggregate of three or more have descended, and that purpose carried out more swiftly than one's opponent, the participant whose time was quicker would be **proclaimed** the victor. At the moment the boy proved his proficiency at the little game, the father conceded with ungrudging zeal that the boy had the requisite skill to be successful in most activities where such coordination was **prerequisite.**

In fact, when the boy was but a **pre-pubescent** youngster, he asked his father to permit him to drive the car down a dirt road that was lightly traveled. Doss **acquiesced** and David found himself behind the wheel at five years of age, maneuvering the machine over deserted terrain, raising a cloud of dust which, with its **inevitable evanescence** settled back onto the roadway before they came back again over that same terrain. A certain gadget in the car, a toggle switch, whose purpose had never been known, if ever it had one, could be flipped up or down while the road was traversed, giving the appearance that the said switch was the cause of the smoke, for such was what the father told the boys it was, all to the delight of these children, innocent as to its true purpose, which might well have passed from mere **desuetude.**

Todd. Todd Neesh. Christopher Todd Neesh. The name Christopher means literally "bringer of Christ," a name, I daresay does not fit the child. One would find himself in a quagmire bringing to remembrance examples in which the boy represents the doctrine of that wise teacher. Perhaps it was **presumptuous** to **nominate** the baby with that sacred **appellation** as could be said to set him apart from the meaner and less **sanctimonious of** mankind. But, while **loquacious**, he is at once reverent, at least in those few moments that he is not **disputatious**, and comical. He recites verses of poetry and Shakespeare, the Koran and Torah and has accomplished that in his few years—to an extent greater than most people can be said to have done in their whole lives. While **listless** in his studies and **impassive**, nay, **irreverent** in the classroom, he is **pertinacious** in studying. In summary, maybe his name is **apropos**, given the association with a man who preached love and peace.

Even as a little child, the boy was **sagacious** and **inquisitive**, asking about God, rainbows, sunsets, mortality, and other **ponderable** topics that his parents were intimidated at having to answer, so that in a **stealthy**, sly way, they pretended not to hear the question put to them. But the child's little intellect was too incisive to be ignored, and, in a word, demanded an explanation, placing them in the **precarious** position of either **prevaricating** through some contrived, made-up deception, or telling the truth quite plainly, that is by admitting "we don't know."

To prevent that debacle, for so it would be in the eyes of an innocent having as he did complete faith in the sagacity of his parents, Daisy resolved to avoid a tempting, though **mendacious** story that would be but a mere tale, but instead opted to tell the truth, and that being life is a true **enigma**, that God alone knows the answers, by whatever name that one great being is called, and in a word, those notions were not for us to ponder, but to put our faith in the Almighty's **omniscience** and **omnipotence** and not to lean on the **ephemeral** and fleeting ideas of mankind, that today hold to this, but tomorrow cling to another thing altogether.

A dear friend of the family, Bobby Taylor Langdale, a unique, though deeply intellectual, man with several degrees from a **myriad** of scholarly institutions, the last one received just a few years ago as the man approached the age of seventy, I say, this Langdale friend even believes Todd may one day be a rabbi. The learned man holds fast to the notion of a true **ecclesia**, that is, a gathering of believers in a body of **asceticism,** denying themselves **superflous** pleasures of the world that the **hedonist** lusts after continually, and instead serving God, and **flouting** calls for excess consumption, while **flaunting** intellectual and spiritual achievement. Langale deems the one group more important than the other comprised of so many **superficial, sanctimonious**, yet **ersatz** believers. Their **iniquitou**s ways are clear in the indifference shown toward spiritual matters, **pretentiousness** in social interaction and complete lack of **empathy** for the **plight** of the less fortunate and, most importantly, their **ostentatious** shows of material **acquisition**. "You shall know them by their fruit," Langdale pronounced, and the luxuries they fetter themselves with belie their true god, that is to say, **mammon**. These pretenders, while **ostensibly** believers, are, in truth, heathen to the last degree, bound for the wide gate.

"What do the believers believe," I have often heard Bobby ask, to which he would reply: "in the buying power of the dollar bill?" Or do they fancy themselves a part of God's inner circle because of their success in **garnering** wealth?" he would continue to **rant rhetorically**, not truly seeking an answer, but rather making a point about the **hypocrisy rampant** in Christianity. "Straight is the gate and narrow the way that leadeth unto life," the diminutive figure would proclaim in a **tirade** of **cryptic** references to the shibboleths of the Bible, those too having been learned in the classroom at the fifth of the eight institutions of higher learning from which his degrees were **conferred**. "God is real: Jesus bears no resemblance to these so-called Christians," the preacher would harangue anyone who would stand within shouting distance long enough for him to sermonize.

The man had a rich, **mellifluous** voice, and when singing could quite cause tears to leap into one's eyes as the **melodious** chorus was repeated several times and the **euphonious** organ hummed in the background its harmonious chords. The listener could feel a **proximity** to God when the baritone voice sounded the notes that spoke of God's **largess,** challenging humans to rise above the **prosaic** affairs of the world and be **transmuted** by the **redemptive** grace and unearned love, both qualities offered for no charge. "No **pecuniary** amount could purchase those gifts," Langdale would proclaim in his **soliloquies,** or as he called them, sermons.

Although **paradoxical**, considering the level of his education, or, should I say the acquisition of his many degrees, his misuse of English grammar oftentimes made a **cogent** point. Take for instance the words "ain't a whole lot of us gonna make it through them there pearly gates," by which he meant that too many ostensible believers and worshippers were **hypocrites,** who truly did not believe what they seemingly professed.

In a **cryptic** reference to one job he re-
tained for a couple of months back in 1987
as a temporary night watchman, and one
that I may add he performed in the most
diligent and heedful manner possible, that
is to say did absolutely nothing but sit
and watch for prospective miscreants who
might burglarize, I say, Bobby made the observation that "you learn things when you
toil in the real world." Unfortunately, his
foray into that world did not last long,
as he soon found himself back in an institution of higher learning, **relegated** to
pupil status, sitting, as it were, in a desk,
taking orders subserviently from some **cur-
mudgeonly docent** who **tyrannically** demanded **didactic** results, or "I'll fail you."
In his **sniveling** way, the **perpetual** student
obsequiously acquiesced in the **despot's
stentorian** demands, tucking tail and **saun-
tering** off, licking his wounds as it were,
to complete the assigned endeavor, **pon-
derous** as he walked, contemplating what
the real world might have been had he remained there instead of a classroom.

Let the reader note that I am not proud
to pronounce the following judgment of another, but it must be said: Brother Langdale
is not **savvy** in worldly matters--to turn
right or left, or chew his food or swallow it
requires **copious cogitation** and **glacial** in-

decision. Whether to scratch his back or comb his hair, the indecisiveness lingers, much like molasses in cold weather being poured onto pancakes. Not that the good reverend is slow in mental faculties, but rather excessively **fastidious** in a surplus of concern over **trite** matters of **negligible** moment to the vast preponderance of individuals.

In fact, permit me to **eulogize** him now that I have seemingly **denigrated** him and **castigated** his habits. The man is tremendously sage in scholarly views, and has a **piety** for scripture and a deep **veneration** for the words the Talmud.

But, alas, it seems he cannot endure the **mandates** from a superior in a position of authority relative to himself, that is to say, a boss. He simply refuses to **grovel** when commanded, when oftentimes a show of subservience would advance him. No matter how pressing the matter facing the business concern of which he is servant, the man has a complete and **unwavering resolve** never to bow **slavishly** or **obsequiously** to any **taskmaster** whom he deems inferior or **peripheral** to his capabilities. He undoubtedly perceives himself to be, and in fact, quite possibly is, on a level tantamount to, nay, far above that of many of those superiors. If not for that, he claims, he would acquiesce to their directives and edicts.

Far from **obeisance** and **deference**, his attitude towards these masters, whom he sees as minions, is one of **derision** and disdain. He is **contemptuous** due to their perceived inferiority of intellect, all the while he refuses to admit that in the affairs to which they have adapted themselves, and to which little chores they've been ordered to perform, they are more **adroit** than he, though the tasks they have mastered be of mere trifling compared to the universal **dogmas** and **dictums** he has focused on and studied so **meticulously.**

Daisy M.F. Neesh adamantly declared one day that "one rancorous, **devious** bitch is not going to push me around any longer." She resolved to leave the **tenuous** position and put behind her the volatile, never predictable superior, and instead ply her trade in the another office. Forget those dreams to be the head honcho, she finally realized. After all, there's merit in the lowest, meanest tasks to be performed, she thought. Furthermore, she reasoned, "where would we be without the janitors."

One concern she had was that she would be perceived as **nomadic**, wandering first to this job, and then to that one; however, her head superior **assuaged** any unease by assuring the delicate woman she would remain with position office for many years, or at least for as long as he was privileged to remain himself, which as the reader will observe, was not to be long at all. That there would be a more permanent, less **itinerant** future to her job checked her despondent impulses and **buoyed** her spirits.

Among her new tasks was one that required her to contact potential donors to the university. Philanthropists oftentimes give money for this cause or that, and it was the professor's obligation to persuade them to send a check to the university, as opposed to some other **charitable** purpose they might have in mind. These people are not so much driven by **philos** towards humankind as **philos** towards their money. It shouldn't matter whether their donation goes to this charitable cause or that. And, many of these supposed **philanthropists** very well could be **misanthropes** in reality, not at all caring for their fellow man, but protecting, as it were, their pecuniary acquisition. True **philanthropy** would seek avenues to **subsidize** the tax roll instead of running away from it. That way, the public could benefit from the **largess,** as the money would go towards some need, and that dictated by our government leaders, instead of a few select students at her school, most of whom are destined for a good job anyway, given their **inevitable** graduation and degree.

Speaking of **misanthropes**, Doss comes to my mind, not that he is in fact **mis-**

anthropic, but he is socially timid, nay, **maladroit** to the extreme in the face of societal demands. His **aversion** for large crowds and his **aloofness** when placed in one, are not the least bit unknown by his close friends and family. He claims to "save up" his affection for those most in need, (I would say 'deserving of love,' but I won't, for who could truly fit in that category)? Perhaps because of some **benevolence** another possesses, or a special act of kindness shown, he shares love and himself, but it has been argued to him that "there is enough to go around." And, as alluded to, those in greatest need of affection are often the least deserving of it. Remember, "the well person has no need of a physician, only they that are sick," the 'good book' reminds us.

That being said, Doss looks upon humans, and indeed most all in the animal kingdom as continually and woefully in need of endearment and tenderness, not to mention, nurturing. Many are undeserving due to this flaw or another that stifles a right or good nature in them. Not that he is anyone who should be judging, exhibiting as he does **roguish** traits on occasion, not to mention possessing an incendiary temper now and then when **hindrances** in life rise up to frustrate him. A hose that gets tangled or a button that won't fasten can be the fount of fulminating rantings and puerile seething that would make a Navy member's face color red as beet juice.

There is a genuine love about the man that is seen in few other people, though he himself does not **relish** but brief moments of hugging, caressing, fondling, and the like. There is yet another quality to his character that is **laudatory**, nay, **adulatory**, and that is his willingness to be honest with himself, even to the point of laughing at his shortcomings. That feature, it may be said, is rare and deserving of **approbation** indeed.

With his students, he is a lecturer **extraordinaire**, a true **virtuoso** on topics related to law. His **proteges,** that is to say the students under his **tutelage** would call him a **taskmaster**, and so he is, in the sense that he assigns **copious** amounts of **grueling** work and expects it to be done in a timely fashion and correctly, that is to say, with few or no errors, and with great **eloquence**, I say, that considered, this expert in the law and its origins is a **mentor** who is exacting on himself as well. Even during convalescence from surgery, he resolved to be in class because "only he knew what material he wanted covered, and how he wanted it to be so." **Complacency**, or lack of interest have no place in his classroom, and the surest way to acquire a low grade is to approach one's work in a **torpid**, unenthusiastic manner.

In fact, without a great deal of **zeal** and **verve**, one should not attempt to study law in the first place, he believes, as it is demanding, exacting, **tedious**, and, at times, confounding. In addition, the study of law is **replete** with words and word meanings, and phrases, both in old English and in Latin, which, in a word, is much akin to learning a whole new language. In fact, some students are **hampered** because of their unwillingness to **dispense** with informal speech and **verbiage**, and become **indignant** towards this blessed and talented teacher when instructed they must do so.

There is a friend of Daisy's by the name of Vern Vick, who, to put it simply, was her **mentor** in that he hired the professor to perform an administrative function within the university that she later came to have an **aversion** for. It is he who preceded the wench that currently occupies that office and dictates hourly functions to those seen as mere lackeys and, to say it quite plainly, it was the **benevolent** gentleman whose sagacity placed the gifted creature in a role in which it is her **bane** to endure the daily scorn and incessant **derision** from a **malevolent martinet** whose **antipathy** is as great as her incompetence. Not that Vern had any **prescience** that such would be Daisy's lot. No one could have **augured** that the current occupant of that job would in fact occupy it, but thanks to an **officious** benefactor that was in a high position, and that none other than the president of the school itself, took it upon himself painstakingly to place the winch securely in place when Vern left for a more **propitious** working environment, viz., one in which he is the very chancellor of the entire institution.

After several weeks of **circumspect cogitation** on whom best to occupy an open position in his office, Dr. Vick remembered Daisy and the **resourceful** job she was carrying out as department chair, and how **shrewdly** and **judiciously** she had handled a **rancorous** episode between two of her colleagues. In a word, the man resolved to name Lily as a possible replacement for the previous occupant of that position, and called one day to **apprise** her of his **meditations**. With **alacrity**, she assured the man that she could think of no greater honor that could be conferred, nor any higher trust that could be **reposed** in her than to be nominated for that position.

After an **interregnum** of several months with no assistant in that office, he assured Daisy that her name would be suggested **posthaste** to the administrators in whose **discretion** the decision about the opening resided. Although the **hiatus** with the position unfilled had been a lengthy one— there was work that had piled up and needed to be done—the benevolent man did not with **temerity** rush to name just anyone, but on the contrary, **meticulously perused** his list several times, eliminating this prospective candidate, and then that one, until he had **painstakingly** gone over it fourteen times.

The man was, it seems, the most **beneficent, conscientious** individual an employee could hope to have for a boss. He was never **acrid** or **churlish** in his demeanor, and while **astute** in the details of his job, never **officious** as are some, watching one's every move, micro-managing over their shoulders, to **allay** skepticism that a worker might be shirking responsibilities. Nor was the man **pedantic,** or a show-off with his knowledge, which, given the degree he held, viz., PhD, and that in the difficult subject area of chemistry, he might be supposed to be. Beyond that, he was **jocular**, that is to say with an **animated** laugh at this funny incident or that, and always armed with a little joke, whose telling would bring about an atmosphere of **levity** in an otherwise **humdrum** workplace. That a man of such learning and high education could be so knowledgeable and yet so **droll**, was **commendable**, and suggested a **lofty**, yet **self-effacing** character.

Patricia Dolt is an acquaintance of the family's that I know not how to describe, nor to say how she came to be acquainted with our family. She is at once the most half-witted, **babbling boob** that ever one met with in this life. To judge her as such is harsh, nay, sinful to the last degree, and **opprobrium**, even guilt, accompanies the writer's description, you may be sure, in stating so plainly what a simpleton the **pitiable** woman is. But to ignore the reality of her **buffoonery**, and the **addleheaded** simplicity of her fancies, for I dare not call them thoughts, and the **grandeur** of her **chimerical** delusions, I say, to deny these as insanity, which are outrageously **fatuous** and **ludicrous**, or as may be said quite plainly, preposterously foolish, would be to ignore what is **veritable**.

Her imagination is as great as the Atlantic Ocean, for one would not label her crazy, owing to the mental **prowess** those of that nature are usually imbued with. In fact few, if any, of those who can justifiably be called crazy typify such moronic behavior, but the ones who truly share that sad malady of mental illness are usually of the very intelligent variety. A person twisted owing to the presence of an illness of the mind, but for that setback would be sound producers in society, nay, even vanguard thinkers to the last degree, as some noted scientists, writers, inventors, poets and playrights have been.

But, as to my story, Pat has a great imagination, almost to the point of being hopelessly delusionary. On several occasions she has telephoned the Doss Neesh residence to inquire about the well-being of a friend by the name of Mike, who, by the by, shares the surname with the Neesh family, but of only distant kinship, if any at all. Despite that, and ignoring the fact that Mike, who once resided with the Neesh family, following an altercation with his brother, an overbearing and **swinish buffoon** in his own right, not unlike Patricia Dolt, except for his male sex, which while truly he is, does not serve him to any delight in the sexual pleasures, for he never mentions desiring companionship of any kind, has long since moved on, I say, despite that fact, the woman is **unpersuaded.**

That Mike has departed the Neesh residence means nothing to Pat, who, believing he is still present in that abode following a two-year period of time during which he has been altogether absent, inquires of his activities and his whereabouts in such detail and with such curiosity, nay with a strong conviction of his continued residence there, that one makes as much a fool of himself trying to explain his absence and his having been but a temporary guest whose departure after a couple of weeks was inevitable, as she does in her harebrained inquiry. Being unconvinced of the credulity of the speaker at the residence, Patricia proceeds with moaning, crying, muttering and whining to an extent that anyone with a **modicum** of empathy could not help pitying the poor creature, whose carrying on would sadden a dog, if listened to long enough. Nor do her delusions end with speculation about his presence at that residence. On other occasions, she **fancies** that he has crept in from a little wood in back of her mobile home wherein he supposedly maintains some semblance of existence, and crawls into bed with her to the purpose of sexual relations, even going so far as to claim on one occasion that Mike had impregnated her while she was sleeping, and at the age of 57, was proud to announce she was great with the absent man's child. He had impregnated her.

Pat has no teeth. Her "f's" sound like "p's" so that if she is trying to say, for instance, that she "feels good," it sounds to the listener as though she had said that such and such "peels good." Once, when deriding her former husband, whose abuse she allegedly withstood for a great while, she denounced him as a "pucking idiot," which while not certain, I thought clearly described her feeling of **enmity** towards him. Not that her lack of teeth distort her words only. Her lips, quite possibly once of sufficient size, lie tucked in over her gum so that little, if any, line of lip appears, and while overly large lips are not necessarily an end in themselves, I cannot say that her lack of some semblance of those oral features is at-tractive.

Acknowledgement

I would like to thank Lawrence Will and his superb books about Lake Okeechobee and its people. Mr. Will was a true scholar and student. He wrote seven books, and if you get a chance to read any or all of them, please do. I would like to thank Cornelius Taft Cone, Ellis O'Neal Murphy, Joseph Murphy, Tom Gaskins, Georgia Frances Armstrong, Earlene Thompson Cone, as well as Harvey Poole, Annie Mae Jenkins and her family for countless interviews and info sessions about the muckland. To the many readers and proofreaders of this manuscript, thank you sincerely.

About The Author

Carl T. Cone

Carl T. Cone was raised in Belle Glade, Florida between 1953 and 1973. He learned many facets about the muckland firsthand, and from stories told by friends, relatives and acquaintances. Cone later studied law and practiced  as an attorney for 30 years. He served a stint as a prosecutor in North Carolina, and taught law. He is a pilot, writer, photographer and scuba diver. He is married to Diana and the couple have three sons, David, Aaron, and Todd.

Made in United States
Orlando, FL
21 April 2022

17073162R00245